C000027167

THE
COMING
STORM

GREG MOSSE

MOONFLOWER

Published by Moonflower Publishing Ltd.
www.MoonflowerBooks.co.uk

1st Edition

1 2 3 4 5 6 7 8 9 10

Copyright © Mosse Futures Ltd 2024

ISBN: 978-1916678002

Cover design by Jasmine Aurora

Printed and bound in Great Britain by Clays Ltd, Elcograf S.p.A.
Suffolk, UK

Moonflower Publishing Registered Office: 303 The Pillbox,
115 Coventry Road, London E2 6GG, United Kingdom

MOONFLOWER

For Moose, Martha and Felix

PROLOGUE

There were seven people present in Montparnasse cemetery, including Alexandre Lamarque. In theory, none of them would ever speak again of what they saw that night. The private interment was intended as a kind of full stop, the final punctuation on a life lived in service to the ideals of the French Revolution and nation: freedom, equality and community.

A life sacrificed to those ideals, in a sense.

The Internal Security agent with flame-red hair, Emmeline Cantor, had been given responsibility for the eulogy, despite her modest rank. It turned out she had worked very closely with him – much more closely than Alex had ever known.

The time was just after one o'clock in the morning, half an hour after curfew, so that the event should pass off unobserved. The sky was an uninterrupted dome of inky blue. A pleasant temperature, Alex estimated, no warmer than twenty-two or twenty-three degrees. Not bad for early autumn, if such a season could be said still to exist.

The coffin was already in the tomb – a small stone building about the size of a garden shed. The lintel above the open iron door was inscribed with his family name. They had all already been inside. By the light of two LEDs, powered by a battery charged from a photoelectric panel on the sloping roof, they had inspected his shadowed face, composed in eternal sleep.

Why had they done that?

It had been, Emmeline Cantor told them, one of his last requests. Alex supposed it was so that, should the question ever arise, there would be enough people to confirm that he was truly gone.

Once they had filed back out, they sat on folding outdoor chairs – rusty metal frames and narrow slatted seats – and Cantor spoke from the entrance to the tomb, a halo around her head from the lights behind her, her face hard to read, her voice unsteady.

'He asked me to tell you that time is precious and should never be wasted. That he was sorry to die when so much was left still to do. That he trusted you and believed that your future triumphs would at least equal your past defeats.'

She paused and turned her head towards each of the six pairs of eyes focused on her. Alex was wishing he was anywhere but here, trapped between the cypress trees and the excessive monuments to the dead. Then Cantor bowed her head for a moment. When she looked up, she sounded more composed.

'This is what he said: "The conspiracy must still be out there, even now preparing new attacks. Without the traitor at the heart of our defences to mastermind them, they will be less grandiose, perhaps, smaller, more local. But that means they will also be more devious, more insidious. And harder to prevent. Obvious in hindsight, but invisible until they are in train, at which point it will always be too late. It falls to you to stop them. You each gave me your word that you would do so. Now that I am dead, it would be an insult to my memory, don't you all think, if you failed in your promise?" Er…' Cantor paused. 'Perhaps I should add that he asked me to tell you that was a kind of joke. He was worried it wouldn't come across.'

'We understand,' deadpanned Amaury Barra, Alex's friend and colleague. 'We're all laughing.'

'Stop it, Amaury,' chided Mariam Jordane, the woman Alex loved.

With a slight frown, Cantor went on: 'He wanted you to hear a

8

definitive statement concerning his illness. Doctor Labeur has prepared a summary.'

Cantor returned to her seat. The light from the doorway struck the side of her face and Alex could see her cheek was damp from tears.

The man to his right stood up. Dr Labeur had been instrumental in saving many lives – just not quite enough lives. He pulled up the right sleeve of his sand-coloured linen jacket and popped out a holo from his comm-watch, raising it in front of his chest, so that Alex was obliged to watch his mouth move through the scrolling teleprompt.

'We believed his infection to be in remission. His prognosis was good and his test results trended towards eradication. His relapse was unexpected. Madame Lamarque …' Labeur's eyes flicked away from the scrolling words to Alex's mother, Gloria Lamarque, a handkerchief scrunched tight in her right hand, but her face calm, her eyes dry. 'Madame Lamarque,' the doctor repeated, 'a victim of the same infection, will continue to be monitored closely. But we believe her case to be quite different. His rapid decline was the result, we fear, of an unpredicted – indeed, unpredictable – mutation in the new virus brought about by exposure to a persistent older virus, which had already developed resistance to the available prophylactic. The virulence of the final attack was rapid and did not respond to any treatments, pharmacological or physiotherapeutic. There are, of course, no other documented cases.' He tapped his comm-watch and the scrolling holo disappeared, as if sucked back inside. 'He was, and remains, Patient Zero.'

Labeur sat down and Alex surprised himself by feeling the need to speak. He got awkwardly to his feet, encumbered by the plastalloy brace on his injured leg. All six pairs of eyes turned towards him. He wanted to say that it was shocking that this interment should take place in private, away from popular recognition, without pomp or ceremony, but he cleared his throat and told them: 'This day is a disaster. I can imagine no blow more severe, no deeper wound to our safety and security, than this death. I want to reconfirm my promise, that I will do everything in my power to find and destroy the remnants of the Coming Darkness conspiracy.'

He sat down. There was a pause, no more than two or three heartbeats, and then Amaury stood. He said something similar, though Alex didn't register the precise words. His mind was already drifting away from the tombs and trees.

Damien Gerest, head of the Directorate General for External Security, followed – a few brief formal phrases – then Mariam took his place. She spoke very quietly, catching Alex's attention and drawing him out of his reverie.

'Without him, I don't know what I would have done. My sisters and I owe him everything. For twelve years he supported us. It is a tragedy for us and for so many others that he is gone.'

Gloria, Alex's mother, stood, looking fit and spry in her black linen trouser suit.

'The friends we lose remain in our hearts,' she said, speaking clearly and precisely. 'We will not forget.'

Alex was struck by how each person seemed to offer words that he might have written for them: Gerest officious and dry, Mariam driven by emotion and loss, his mother in the voice of a professional historian. He wished he had paid attention to Amaury. Perhaps his friend's words might have surprised him.

Cantor and Gerest stood to seal the tomb. Gerest reached a pudgy hand inside and flicked a switch, extinguishing the two dim LEDs. They closed the door – a slab of iron decorated with a pattern of metal leaves – with a dull clang. Gerest locked it with a heavy iron key, then turned back to the gathering.

'I have a few words for Captain Lamarque, Mademoiselle Jordane and Monsieur Barra. Would the rest of you please leave us?'

Gloria Lamarque, Doctor Labeur and Emmeline Cantor followed a path of pale gravel through the dark cemetery, towards the gate and

10

the ministry cars that waited there, armed with their dispensation from curfew. Once they were out of earshot, Gerest said: 'Madame Poiret wishes you to accept once more the nation's gratitude for your efforts and sacrifices.'

Now the Professor was gone, Claudine Poiret – a senior civil servant in the French government – would be Alex's most powerful ally.

'However?' he asked.

'However,' said Gerest, nodding, 'the defeat of the conspiracy has generated so much panic and distress that Madame Poiret would be grateful for you all to accept three weeks' leave and isolation, to allow things to calm down.'

'I can't leave Paris,' Mariam objected.

Gerest glanced at her. 'Your sisters will continue to be monitored, Mademoiselle Jordane. Have no fear.'

'Where do we go?' Amaury demanded.

'That is up to you,' said Gerest, 'so long as you are out of reach of the news streams.'

'We could all go together,' Alex suggested. 'Maybe a closed resort?'

He glanced at Mariam and, to his relief, she didn't immediately argue.

'Also, Monsieur Barra,' said Gerest, 'I have two selected journalists who would like to speak to you before you leave.'

'Why me?' demanded Amaury.

'Because Captain Lamarque and Mademoiselle Jordane have declined and I need someone in front of the cameras.'

'Fine,' sighed Amaury and strode away.

'What about us?' asked Alex, watching him go.

'A closed resort would be a good idea,' Gerest told him. 'There is a suitable location near Biarritz. I can give you details.'

'I need to see my sisters first,' said Mariam.

Gerest inclined his head. 'Of course, mademoiselle. Take one of the cars. Captain Lamarque will meet you at their facility.'

Mariam followed Amaury, her shoes crunching on the gravel. Alex didn't move.

'Give me a moment,' he told Director Gerest.

'I will wait for you by the gate, captain.'

Soon, there was quiet. Alex contemplated the sealed tomb. In the moonlight, the family name on the lintel stood out quite clearly, lines of black-carved shadow on pale stone. Stepping closer, he reached up to trace the grooves with a finger. He heard some nocturnal animal rustling the early-autumn leaves, shed self-protectively by centennial lime trees that lived, in the year 2037, in perpetual drought.

'Goodbye, Professor Fayard,' he said quietly.

Then he, too, left the old man alone, to eternal sleep.

1

Three weeks later, Alex sat on a hotel veranda overlooking the Atlantic Ocean. He and Mariam had followed instructions and disappeared. Amaury had too, although Alex didn't know where he'd gone.

A waiter in a traditional long black apron appeared alongside his table. Alex ordered coffee. Not far away, the children of two government employees were laughing and arguing, building sand castles, chasing one another down to the water's edge, and running back to their parents as the power of the tide confronted them.

The waves rolled in, two- and three-metre breakers, grey-green, topped with curls of white foam. He could hear the crash of each collapse, the scour of the shingle like a desperate indrawn breath.

A kind of movie played in his mind – the final twenty seconds of his flight into Al-Jaghar in Cyrenia, his comm-watch vibrating on his wrist, knowing it was Mariam who was calling, wanting to speak to him in the last few moments before he died.

He hadn't been able to answer and he hadn't died. Instead, his desperate gamble had paid off. But he had almost left it too late to eject from the doomed aircraft, ending up with severe bruising all along the left-hand side of his body and persistent pain below his left knee. After the private medal ceremony at the Ministry in Paris, it had been diagnosed as a severe strain to the medial collateral ligament and hairline fractures in his tibia and fibula.

As well as escaping the public eye, convalescence for his broken leg was another good reason for this escape to the Atlantic coast, beautiful but also bleak, remorselessly pounded by the ocean.

The coffee came with a dish of fine chocolates.

'*Avec nos compliments, capitaine.*'

Obviously, he had been recognised. This small consideration was a gesture of respect, of thanks.

The wicker chair creaked as Alex shifted his weight. The waiter skipped away to fetch him a cushion to put beneath his damaged leg, lifting the plastalloy brace gently onto a rattan foot stool.

'Thank you.'

'*Je vous en prie, monsieur.*'

He drank the small black coffee, bitter with over-roasting of the beans, and pushed the saucer of chocolates aside. He stood up, using his crutch for leverage, and crossed the veranda to the rail, looking down on the beach. The kids were both clad in bright yellow 'fishskins' – lightweight quick-drying beach gear designed to protect them from the sun, caps on their heads, squares of cloth draped over the backs of their necks. They were building a sequence of dams, fetching water from the surf in buckets, pouring it into the soft enclosures and watching it run away.

Then, all at once, at some command he did not hear, they dropped what they were doing and headed for a patch of desperate sea-grass where an early supper was laid out on a rustic table beneath a sun-shade roof made of bleached rushes. The parents were there, opening a bottle of wine, pouring it into paper cups, looking happy and fulfilled.

Is that the secret? Alex wondered. *To have children and look after them, to be promoted and win access to government perks like this old-fashioned hotel on the Atlantic coast?*

Alex raised a hand to shade his eyes, looking west towards the bright ocean. There were eight or nine surfers, including Mariam, all competing for a wave. He felt an urge to join them, to feel the challenge

14

of the water shifting beneath his feet, adjusting his weight and balance to compensate, riding the energy. He wondered if he could remove his brace and …

No, that was stupid. As the orthopaedic consultant had told him: 'You're not about to grow another leg. Look after this one.'

He made his way down a set of shallow timber steps onto the beach. Soon, the wooden pathway disappeared, submerged by the sand. His crutch became more of a hindrance than a help, but he pressed on, feeling an ache in his bones.

I'm not ready even for this, he thought.

The tide had turned and there was a strip of firmer sand and gravel closer to the water's edge. He made for it and found that he could stand squarely, without pain. Again, he raised his hand to shade his eyes, picking out Mariam maybe two hundred metres away, just pulling herself up onto her longboard, poised and symmetrical against the grey-green wall of water. Just three weeks and her natural athleticism had made her an expert. He watched her find the sweet spot inside the curl, riding it until she was out of sight, five hundred metres up the beach, dangerously close to the rocks. Then he saw the tiny electric launch buzzing over to join her, towing her back out through the surf, ready for another skilful negotiation between her own newly acquired skills and a vast and indiscriminate power.

Had she been in the water too long? They had eaten a late lunch together, discussing their return north. Then she had been quiet, studying the forecasts for weather and surf. Finally, wordlessly, she had left him, returning fifteen minutes later in her wetsuit.

'I wish I could come with you,' he had told her.

'You hate the water.' Then she had smiled and walked away, calling over her shoulder: 'The forecast is good.'

'Good' meaning that the waves were dangerously big and building.

Left alone, Alex had taken some time to read a collection of confidential briefings passed on by his ultimate boss, the senior civil servant Claudine Poiret. It detailed additional actions taken by the French security services to extirpate the final remnants of the Coming Darkness conspiracy. In the fragmented diplomatic world of 2037, Paris had been obliged to act mostly alone.

Did the other nations, traditionally sympathetic to French diplomacy, truly understand how close they had come? He wasn't sure they did. Were there new allies out there, capable of helping in the fight? Perhaps.

Then he had watched several online videos comprised almost exclusively of threats of revenge: on him, on Mariam, on Amaury, on the world. Two particularly sickening ones both claimed credit for Fayard's death, though Doctor Labeur had been very clear. It had been caused by an unpredictable natural mutation in the novel pathogen introduced into his system by the traitor – and partly Alex's fault.

That was the thing that haunted him most – how slowly he had pieced together the conspiracy, even though he had known from the very first that what they should all fear was Darkness.

One of the traitor's final triumphs – achieved posthumously – had been the destruction of the databases and algorithmic intelligence of the Directorate General for Internal Security. The traitor had installed a kind of 'dead man's lever', like the control on a train that the driver has to hold in order for the motors to drive. Once let go, a failsafe operates, bringing the train to a safe halt. In the case of the DGIS systems, it was a sensor bio-coded to the traitor's thumbprint that had to be touched every twenty-four hours in order to postpone a complete meltdown of everything that the Internal Security services had ever known, suspected or achieved.

Because the traitor had also gained access to many public databases – social security, tax and employment records, marriages, births and deaths, voter registration, land registry – those records were gone as well. Alex read a report at the highest level of confidentiality, documenting the efforts being made to reconstruct those essential databases without their absence becoming public knowledge. It reminded him of the moment in Albert Camus' *La Peste* when one of the characters comments on the difference between the haphazard medieval response to plague and the twentieth-century with its accurate bureaucratic records of every failed treatment protocol and every unprevented death. With bitter sarcasm, he remarks: 'The progress is undeniable.'

Could they have worked to undo the software bombs secreted throughout the security network, had they known of their existence? Or kept the traitor's hand permanently available, perhaps on ice or embalmed, in order to be able to apply the pad of flesh to the sensor in a kind of daily ceremony? Or would the sensor have required living tissue in order to keep the destructive programs at bay? Since the meltdown, no one knew.

The only investigative resource that had entirely escaped the posthumous attack belonged to Camera Control, an independent service, siloed and out of reach. Alex learnt that its image-matching algorithms had tracked down the locations where each of the threatening videos was filmed but nothing had come of the ensuing investigations – both abandoned shops at the foot of suburban apartment buildings on the periphery of greater Paris. And the speakers had slipped away through camera shadows into anonymity once more.

How many believers were still out there? No one knew for sure. The traitor had acted cleverly and in secret, creating cells with no shared channels of communication. One arrest wouldn't necessarily lead to another. And, in a cult of destruction and death, it was rare for one of them to be taken alive.

Finally, Alex had put aside his doc-reader to order his coffee and now he was down at the water's edge.

Standing on the compacted shingle and sand, he saw the launch dragging Mariam out, well beyond the breakers, glimpsing her intermittently, disappearing into the troughs, riding up onto the crests. Then the launch turned and came humming quickly back in, alone.

17

How long had Mariam been in the water? How much strength could she have left?

The sun was falling down into the ocean and all the other surfers had wiped out on their way into shore. Only Mariam was left, far out, determined to ride the last wave alone. Alex tried to keep his eyes on her, like a sailor determined not to lose sight of a body in the water, but she winked out of view. Then, for less than a second, he saw her, just a speck, much further out than he had anticipated, looking frail and insignificant against the churn of the waves – vast now, rising to ten or twelve metres, some combination of tide and wind and the seabed driving them to new peaks, greater forces, heavier impacts – more powerful, surely, than one frail human could withstand.

He had a momentary vision of Mariam's body, flayed by the shingle, the wetsuit hanging in tatters from her limbs. The sea was not a human environment. Balancing on a longboard was nothing more than a way of delaying disaster, a means of maintaining precious equilibrium in air that could be breathed, not being pounded beneath the waves, rolled over and over in the scouring undertow, lungs filling with water and sand.

Then a hooter sounded, a definitive signal from the lifeguards to clear the water as they changed the colour of their flags, indicating that the day's sport was over.

And Mariam was upright.

Of course, he thought. *That's what she was waiting for – the transgression, picking a forbidden wave, beyond the rules that others lived by.*

The wave drove her fast, parallel to the sand. Alex walked as quickly as he could along the beach, but failed to keep pace. She was coming closer to land, but further and further away from him. The wall of water was behind her, folding its awesome weight over her head in a flourish of foam. And she, tiny and implausible against its might, kept her balance until she was only fifty metres out and …

18

She had travelled too far inside the curl. The breaker was collapsing chaotically as it began to run onto rocks beneath the water. In a sudden movement that looked urgent and conflicted he saw her flex her knees and bend to detach the safety strap that attached her board to her ankle, then she was gone.

Alex threw away his crutch and ran, swinging his stiff left leg. He felt ludicrous, like a clown. All the while, time was ticking by in his mind – twenty seconds, thirty. How long could a person survive in the undertow, their breath forced from their body by the weight of the water?

When he was just forty metres distant, he saw the longboard, riding in and out on the surf, trailing the line that had attached it to Mariam's ankle. Then he noticed a smudge on the sand, something dark and flat. Breathlessly, he staggered on, came close and knelt down awkwardly, stretching his left leg out straight.

Mariam was lying on her back. Her wetsuit was intact and she was breathing heavily, her chest expanding and contracting. She had a hand over her eyes to shield them from the dying sun. The water ran in and out around them. His clothes became sodden. He heard her speak.

'Best wave ever.'

He felt a flood of relief, like stepping out of a blizzard into a warm room. She put the palm of her spare hand against his cheek and he felt time pause, a still point at the centre of remorseless motion.

'I don't want to lose you,' he told her.

'I know,' she replied.

2

Three days later, Alex and Mariam were on their way home to Paris, sleeping overnight in a tourist enclave just outside Bordeaux. He was trying – and failing – to sleep.

He got out of bed and limped quietly to the window, easing it quietly open, feeling the damp air on his bare skin. The streets were so quiet he could hear the nearby tributary-stream running fast through a pinch point in its course towards the estuary of the mighty Garonne River and the ocean.

He changed position, trying to put a little weight on his left leg. Not bad. The ache was still there, but running down the beach didn't seem to have set back his recovery.

He pulled on the soft travel clothes he had been wearing the previous evening and strapped the plastalloy brace over the top. He found his crutch leaning against the frame of the door and went down to the hall.

The hotel was little more than a guest house, a few modest rooms in a home that had grown too big for its owners – or whose lives had shrunk too small. He lifted the lid of an upright piano, the yellowed keys dusty, untouched in years. Beside it, there were board games and physical books trapped behind glass in a locked display cabinet. Interested to turn the pages, he had asked for the key.

'That hasn't been opened since I've been here,' the manager had replied, a drab man in a crumpled pale-grey suit.

'How long is that?'

'Five years, nearly six.'

Alex made his way to the kitchen, wondering what had woken him. A cloudburst?

He found a set of crockery in the steriliser, still warm from the cleaning cycle. He poured water from a bottle in the fridge and drank, gazing at the dark window glass, wishing he was outside somewhere, in woods or snow, a place that was green or white, with clean air, where he and Mariam would meet no one, speak to no one. Beyond the glass, the moon was close to full until the grey clouds closed over its brightness like curtains.

He heard a new sound. Was it rain, hissing as it struck the leaves of the trees? No, there came no distinctive perfume of dampened soil or tarmac.

There it was again, a low sound he could identify. An electric motor, a vehicle, the sound coming closer, increasing in volume, then receding. Doing what?

Exploring the neighbourhood, looking for someone.

For Mariam and for him.

Suspicion bloomed in his imagination. He felt a connection forming with the waiter at the hotel, who had recognised him, given him chocolates. Over three weeks hiding from the news streams, the waiter had asked a sequence of apparently innocent questions, one at a time, carefully, so as not to seem to be pumping them for information. And Alex had responded because he was in the habit of doing so. Everyone wanted to ask him questions – from his many official debriefs to the selected journalists who had been chosen to promote the official version of the story, 'the first draft of history' – until he had lost patience and refused to meet any more.

How bad might it have been?

How did you know what the target was?

Was it true, our weapon could have wiped out whole cities?

21

What would have happened if all the satellites had gone dark?

The waiter had hesitated on the last morning, serving breakfast, just as Alex and Mariam had been discussing their return to Paris from Bordeaux on the high-speed train.

'Are there more people like that?' the waiter had wanted to know, his voice timid. 'Still out there?'

For a moment, Alex remembered wondering if this man – small and inoffensive in his long black apron – might be one of them. Had all his patient enquiries been building towards this one strategic question?

'There's no need to worry. Everything's going to be fine,' Alex had replied.

'Thank you,' the man had said, and held out his hand to shake, a sure sign of depth of emotion in a world of closely-regulated human contact.

After a pause, Alex had accepted the gesture, then they had both used the hand san, the waiter with a rueful look, as if he regretted cleansing his skin of the touch of 'the man who saved the world'.

Now, Alex thought he knew. The waiter had eavesdropped and sold the information to a journalist.

He went to the front door and pulled back two bolts, making more noise than he meant. He hesitated, his right palm on the wooden panels, recognising a sensation he had learned to trust, a kind of hyper-awareness of the probable next moment and the next, a chain of cause and effect, marching inexorably into a misty future where permutations and possibilities multiplied swiftly into …

Into what?

Alex eased the front door open and stepped outside onto a brick path, catching the fragrance of dampened soil. There was a bench nestled in deep shadow between two dense camellia bushes. Alex sat down, stretching out his left leg, his eyes open but unfocused, listening.

At first, he heard no human sounds, just the turbulent stream and an occasional bird call. But he was sure someone would come. He could see in memory – as he hadn't at the time – the glimpse of calculation and greed in the waiter's eyes. Alex wondered if he should report the indiscretion, meaning the man would lose his job, maybe the start of a downward spiral that would end with him marginalised, a Blank.

A breath of wind split the curtain of cloud. The moon appeared over the top of the building opposite, making the wet tarmac of the roadway glisten. Alex heard a scratch of gravel and saw a human shape on the far side of the street, the moonlight reflecting off a dark and shiny object held in their hands.

Alex sighed. Should he stay quiet and still in the shadows, hoping they would go away? No, there was no chance of that. They would keep patrolling the enclave until daybreak, until he and Mariam emerged, then bombard them with the same questions.

How did you feel knowing the fate of the world was in your hands?

How did you feel knowing you might die?

How did you feel thinking Captain Lamarque was dead?

Over and over, as if it were possible, in ordinary speech, to share the language of thought and emotion.

Captain Lamarque, how does it feel to be you?

Alex understood. People wanted to experience a kind of vicarious catharsis in order to allay their fears with his triumph.

But did they not realise the threat was still present? Did they really think it was just a handful of deranged terrorists when in reality it was an idea: a potent, enduring idea that everything that is wrong with your life, with the world, is the fault of structures that, if only they were torn down, reduced to rubble, would release their malign hold, and …

Alex took a deeper breath, remembering Professor Fayard's words, quoted outside his tomb by Emmeline Cantor: *Obvious in hindsight.*

From his viewpoint on the bench between the camellias, Alex could see the news-hunter quite clearly now, a woman in a black peaked cap, a carry-case on a diagonal strap across her body, using a camera on a gimbal to film each shabby bijou guest house in turn, not knowing which one was theirs, creating B-roll footage for cutaways and edits. At any moment, she would turn and see him. The camera was bound to be capable of some kind of night vision. What would he do then?

Maybe talk to her, give her something – some fragment of truth that she could sell on for money – then ask her to leave him alone, to leave Mariam alone?

The question became immaterial. The front door of the hotel swung open and Mariam appeared in light cotton nightclothes.

'Alex, are you there?'

Before he could reply, the journalist took four long paces towards them, holding the camera out in front of her on its gimbal.

'*Mademoiselle Jordane, s'il vous plait!*'

Mistake, thought Alex.

Mariam sprang forward, putting a hand on the gate post and vaulting into the street. The journalist understood her error and ran. Alex heard her pounding footsteps and Mariam's lighter tread behind.

Alex got up from the bench, leant carefully on his crutch and followed them. He found them at the end of the street, fifty metres away, where a pedestrian bridge crossed the fast-flowing water. The journalist was face down on the ground and Mariam had all her weight on her back, her knee on her neck. The journalist was trying to speak, but no intelligible sound came from her compressed windpipe.

Alex watched Mariam pull the camera from the journalist's hand, smashing it three times against the tarmac, flinging the pieces into the river. Then Mariam stood and lifted the journalist bodily off the ground, slamming her back against the rail of the bridge, pushing her shoulders over the handrail as if she was about to throw the woman in after her equipment.

'*Ça suffit, Mariam,*' he said quietly, but sufficiently loudly to be heard.

That's enough.

It was more than enough.

3

The next day, as a consequence of being tracked down by the journalist, their plans changed. It was no longer possible to take the train like ordinary citizens.

Yes, the camera and its internal data storage had been destroyed, but the brief footage had been wirelessly streaming from the camera to a base unit in the journalist's car, then on to a reseller. And it was great footage. First, Mariam, in her nightclothes, surprised and then angry, vaulting the gate post. Second, the camera bouncing away as the journalist ran, calling out that she meant no harm. Third, turning and the desperate appeal: 'If I could just ask you one or two questions?' Finally, the camera was on the ground but, clear and distinct, a close-up of Mariam's taut features just before she smashed it three times against the tarmac and the signal failed.

Yes, thought Alex. *More than enough.*

At the airport, soon after 6h30 in the morning, Mariam boarded an electro-hydrogen flight for Paris, and Alex, following new orders, took the autodrive into the centre of Bordeaux. The journey was swift because the hour was early and didn't coincide with the crossover from the dark shift to the day shift, but it was a depressing meander through tired, semi-depopulated neighbourhoods, ugly houses with sparse, scorched gardens.

And, all the while, he felt increasingly certain that Amaury being separated from them had been a mistake. And now Mariam was gone, too.

The suburban streets broadened into avenues – places people went rather than just passed through – and Bordeaux revealed itself in all its 18th century glory with golden and biscuit-coloured façades, public squares and formal gardens, the mighty Garonne River cutting it in two as the Seine bisected Paris.

The autodrive came to a halt at a designated parking space on Place Gambetta, named for the Frenchman who fled the Siege of Paris in 1870 in a hot-air balloon to raise an army in the countryside. Alex got out and breathed the morning air – 'green' smells from the river and from the automatic watering of the flowers and shrubs and trees designed to mitigate the 'heat sink' effect of concrete and stone. He followed a pin on the map program on his comm-watch and soon met a forensics tech in white coveralls who had been tracking his arrival. Walking towards him, she seemed an odd apparition amongst the early commuters, like a cheerful ghost.

'It is an honour to meet you, captain,' she told him, inevitably.

She led him swiftly through a zigzag of pedestrianised streets that opened onto a plaza in front of the magnificent Grand Théâtre de Bordeaux of 1870, all symmetrical columns and witty architectural detail. Opposite, on a wide island of tarmac, was a *manège*, a carousel, with spinning teacups and bounding carved horses, a donkey, a swan and a giraffe. Around the roof were paintings with curlicued edges, depicting views in and around Bordeaux, and a name in flowing letters, perhaps the owner, perhaps the man who, back in the day, had built the 157-year-old relic: 'Monsieur Caramel.'

Alex remembered the three children of the agroindustry couple in their bright yellow 'fishskins', and thought of how much they would love it.

Two gendarmes were busy erecting a perimeter of crime-scene tape where half a dozen rubberneckers had already gathered. The forensics tech led Alex within the enclosure and introduced him to the officer-in-charge, a harassed-looking man with an untidy black moustache. His shirt had come untucked from his regulation trousers, cinched in tight below his gut. He pushed the tails back in and saluted.

'It is an honour to meet you, captain.'

'Thank you,' said Alex, politely. 'Show me.'

The man wiped a hand across his glistening forehead and led him to the upper deck of the roundabout. Alex knew what he was about to see, but it was shocking all the same: two children, thin and undernourished, perhaps ten years old, perhaps younger, beneath the feet of the carved animals. He squatted down to get a view of their faces, both in shadow. Their lips were drawn back from their teeth, their staring eyes bloodshot, their complexions mottled.

'*Empoisonnés, capitaine.*'

Poisoned.

Alex looked more closely. The children's positions were unnatural, their skin marked and contused.

'Some kind of spasms?'

'No, we think it was …' The officer-in-charge made a gesture of pounding. 'The horses, perhaps …'

Alex saw what he meant. The hooves of the carved horse had trampled them as it surged up and down with the action of the roundabout.

'Where's the other body?' Alex stood up.

'This way.'

They went back down the stairs and round to the far side of the roundabout. The forensics tech in the white coveralls was crouched over the third corpse, an adult with the deep-brown complexion of southern Europeans who work outdoors in sun and wind and rain.

Alex noticed that the man's hands were calloused with an unusual patch of hard dry skin in the vee between his thumb and forefinger on both hands, and the backs of his digits were tattooed, five letters repeated left and right – U J S P C – a kind of affiliation or a declaration of allegiance.

Alex had seen the tattoo before, in three languages. The first time in French, then in Portuguese. Finally, he had followed a hunch to Calais and a mortuary slab and the severed limb of an English offender who had killed himself by jumping in front of a cross-channel train. It was a clue that Alex felt he had been slow to decipher. When, finally, he had worked out its meaning, it had led him to other truths – betrayal, contempt for life, a race against time.

'There's a standing algorithm that reports child murders,' said the officer-in-charge.

'I know,' said Alex.

'Then we were notified that you were, by coincidence, in Bordeaux and –'

'There's no such thing as coincidence,' said Alex.

Laid out alongside the adult corpse, on a stainless-steel tray, were the contents of the dead man's pockets: no identity card, no electronic money, just a few coins and plasti-notes, a bag of sweets, soft chews with some kind of liquid centre, and a paper receipt. Alex had very good eyesight and he could see that the receipt was for that morning's date. And there was something in the man's half-closed fist.

The forensics tech was cutting open one of the sweets, squeezing the liquid centre into a specimen tube. The eyes behind her clear protectors were intelligent.

'The poison,' she suggested. 'Don't you think?'

'I'll be guided by you,' said Alex.

'There's a syringe in his hand,' she told him.

Alex had already worked that out, even though the tiny syringe was partially concealed, the forefinger curled over the pump.

'In my opinion, he held the syringe in his fist,' said the officer-in-charge, as if only he had made the obvious deduction. 'He used his forefinger to drive the needle into the heel of his hand and injected himself with whatever he gave the children in the poisoned sweets.'

Alex had the sun in his eyes. His broken night had left him with a headache.

'Let's find some shade.'

They walked a few steps to the doorway of a 24-hour convenience store, escaping from the sun. The officer-in-charge was tucking his shirt back into his trousers again, dark patches of sweat under his arms. Next door to the grocery was a pharmacy with a green illuminated clock: 7h50.

'The roundabout was put in motion very early in the morning?' Alex asked. 'Someone called it in as a disturbance?'

'That's right.'

For a few seconds, Alex visualised the scene: the dead man encouraging the children onto the carousel to choose their rides; giving them the poisoned sweets but telling them not to eat them until the roundabout was moving, playing its jaunty mechanical song, waking the neighbourhood.

So that their deaths became a kind of grotesque theatre.

'Extend the perimeter.'

'It's too late,' said the officer-in-charge, pulling on his moustache. 'There's already a crowd.'

'Don't let anyone else enter the 24-hour grocery. Find out what's been bought in the last two hours.'

'I don't understand—'

'Do it now.'

The officer-in-charge flushed, his puffy face taking on a childishly petulant expression.

'*Capitaine.*'

He moved huffily away to do as he was told.

'What have you seen?' asked the forensics officer. 'There's something we've missed, isn't there?' Alex didn't reply. 'I've read all about you,' she told him. 'Your special skill.'

'I have no special skill,' said Alex. 'I just pay attention.'

'That's not what the reports say. You have ...' The forensics tech stopped. 'I'm sorry, you must get this all the time. It must be annoying.'

'It doesn't matter.'

Alex watched the two gendarmes extending the taped enclosure to a row of bollards on the far side of the square.

'I assume you're local?' he asked.

'Yes, captain.'

'Are there any more food shops in this row, apart from the grocer?'

The forensics tech looked round. Alex could see that she was only confirming what she already knew.

'No, captain.'

She gazed at him with a question in her eyes behind the clear protectors, then her expression changed and Alex saw her making the relevant connection in her own mind – how the poison might have been administered – glancing back at the corpse and the few bits and pieces on the ground.

'Oh, I see,' she said, quietly. 'I was too close. I didn't see the bigger picture.'

The officer-in-charge escorted three customers out of the 24-hour grocery store.

'I told you. I just pay attention,' Alex repeated.

4

Two hours later, Alex was at Bordeaux's main police station. The three corpses were in an ambulance outside, the adult male on the right-hand gurney, the two children top-and-tailing on the other. He had just listened to a voice note from the forensics tech and was writing out his own observations by hand, concluding:

The presumed assailant carried a syringe small enough for close concealment. No other container was found, so the syringe must have contained sufficient poison for both victims and for his own subsequent suicide. The receipt found alongside the plastic packet of sweets indicated a purchase, just after six o'clock, from the grocery store nearby. Concerned at the possibility of contamination of foodstuffs on the shelves inside, I therefore directed the shop to be sealed and investigated by the forensics team that was already at the scene. Puncture evidence was found on three packets of chilled meats. The packages have been sent for analysis. No sales of chilled meats were made between 6h00 and 7h50 when I took action to remove all customers from the premises.

The officer-in-charge re-entered the air-conditioned interview room, looking much more comfortable having changed his sweat-stained shirt. Alex pushed the pad of paper across the desk, putting the lid back on the pen. The officer read it, nodded and asked: 'Do you always write by hand?'

'Not always. You should input what I've written into your networked systems and make the deductions official.'

'Of course. Do you mind waiting? I will find someone—'

'I don't need to wait,' Alex told him. 'And you need to contact the local Blanks. The children were probably enticed from not far away.'

'You will have to sign your report once it's in the system.' He pulled on his moustache. 'It won't take long—'

'I've written it by hand so that you can input and sign it. You can claim the solve. It was your crime scene, not mine. I want nothing to do with it.'

The officer finally grasped what Alex was suggesting, that he should take the credit. His face brightened, then he tried to conceal his delight.

'That's very generous, captain. Thank you very much. I won't forget this.'

'And the man was probably an *éboueur*.'

'A street cleaner?'

Alex explained: 'The callouses in the vees between thumb and forefinger, from the action of sweeping.'

'Of course. I should have seen that.'

'So, once you know his round, you'll almost certainly find the right shanty where he found the children on his route.'

'That makes complete sense. Thank you again.'

The officer-in-charge went on, detailing his profound admiration for Alex's insights and his gratitude for Alex's generosity in letting him make them his own, sliding ham-fistedly into a panegyric of praise for the achievement of saving the world from Darkness.

Alex let him talk, allowing the words to flow out until there were none left.

'Can you give me a car to take me back to the airport?'

'Yes, captain.'

'Then we're done.'

Bordeaux-Mérignac airport accommodated both a civilian transport hub and the military *base aérienne 106*. Alex knew it because it was home to a paratroop regiment where he had spent six weeks training in 2033, partly working with a specialist unit devoted to creating improvised airfields in combat zones, including manoeuvres on the Caribbean island of Haiti. The airport also housed a secure building whose technicians, computers, AIs and algorithms ran a substantial majority of French military logistics.

It was – if anywhere was – a target, so it was incredibly well protected.

The journey west out of the city centre was fine. The police driver used lights but no siren to cut a path through the mid-morning traffic. They accessed the airport proper via a slip road, then forked left into a caged section of tarmac where their vehicle was inspected by robot cameras. It should have taken less than a minute but it turned out one of the car's official tags was faulty or missing. The driver had to go through an exhaustive manual rigmarole proving who he was.

'You know who I am,' said Alex to the remote supervisor through a speaker-cam on the gatepost. 'Can't I leave the car and just walk in?'

'No, captain. That wouldn't be protocol.'

It was gone twelve o'clock by the time Alex reached his plane, driven close to the perimeter in an automated electric buggy. It was a BWB, a 'blended-wing body' aircraft with an array of turbofan engines powered by liquid hydrogen. He swung out his stiff left leg and saw, just beyond the fence, an embankment where sheep grazed, apparently contentedly, on the steep grass. Then, as a motorised flight of steps was driven into place, Alex saw the sheep scatter before three people carrying equipment crestid the embankment.

He had a moment of concern. What were they carrying? Weapons of some kind? Then he recognised cameras and tripods, a long lens on a much smaller camera body, a digicam in a steady-rig. The third person was a woman in a black peaked cap, speaking over her shoulder as she moved, too far away for Alex to hear, but not so far away that he couldn't recognise the journalist that Mariam had almost thrown into a tributary of the Garonne.

A mechanic finished securing the motorised staircase.

'*Vous pouvez monter, monsieur.*'

You can go up.

Alex nodded thanks and limped up the motorised stair to a narrow door into the bulbous fuselage of the BWB, swinging his braced leg awkwardly onto each step. He thought he was just in time. The cameraman with the long lens – that could probably pick out the colour of someone's eyes at 100 metres – had only just planted his equipment. Alex ducked his head and stepped inside.

There were only a dozen seats, six down either side. He was greeted by the pilot, a small man with a handsome face and roguish expression – someone who enjoyed life, Alex thought.

'Forty-five minutes to Paris,' he said. 'I'll be back in Bordeaux for teatime.'

'Why are we so close to the fence?'

'Good question, captain, but I just fly the plane. Where it's parked …' He smiled slyly and made an impotent gesture. 'Not in my control.'

Alex studied the man for a moment.

'You're implying someone within airport personnel arranged for the BWB to be close to the perimeter so that the journalists could get a shot of me boarding. You're saying that there's some kind of collusion.'

'No, I'm not saying that. You are, and who am I to argue?' He laughed, showing his fillings. 'But what a target you would be if someone wanted to make a splash – "the man who saved the world". Here you are, though, safe and sound, no harm done.' His face became serious. 'My guess would be someone in the control tower gave a paid tip-off, a juicy fragment of original content for rolling news. Or maybe air force command, Bordeaux-Mérignac admin, who think it's pretty cool that Captain Alexandre Lamarque is passing through and they want your face, your presence, showing your faith in their facility, on the streams?'

'You have no opinion which it might be?'

'Just making conversation.' The pilot laughed again. 'I really don't know. But you're a hero, Captain Lamarque, and I, for one, respect that.'

The pilot saluted and knocked on the door of the cockpit, showing his face to a fish-eye lens. The door opened and before he disappeared, Alex caught a glimpse of a co-pilot, going through pre-flight checks.

Alex took a seat on the starboard side, hoping for a good aerial view of the French coastline from a flight path over the ocean. Eight minutes later, they were in the air, gaining altitude into a strong south-easterly wind, then banking over the city, the confluence of the Garonne and the Dordogne, the wide brown estuary, millions of litres of valuable fresh water flowing out pointlessly into the undrinkable Atlantic.

Alex thought about thirst and drought, the wars being waged over natural resources, surreptitiously or overtly, in several dozen corners of the globe. He thought about hunger and transgenic disease, about the growing populations of Blanks, the non-persons living outside full citizenship. He thought about over-population and under-population – too many people in total, too few young people to service the swelling numbers of the aged.

The BWB levelled out and he focused his eyes on the clouds that covered thirty per cent of the sky, calming his mind by naming them: cirrocumulus, altocumulus, cumulus, stratocumulus, altostratus.

A nice day in fact, not a severe scorching dome of blue.

He turned his attention to the tasks awaiting him on his return to Paris. At Fayard's tomb, he had reiterated his promise to continue working, to try and complete what was referred to euphemistically as 'mopping up' – arresting or otherwise terminating the remnants of the conspiracy. That was what he had just witnessed in Bordeaux – the fag-end of a fragmented network of deranged individuals whose actions seemed only loosely co-ordinated.

Was there a chance, though, that it might not be over, that there was more than just 'mopping up' to do? Could the new web-videos promising a 'Coming Storm' indicate that some kind of controlling intelligence persisted, more potent even than the dead traitor, capable of new acts of nihilistic desperation?

The murders and the suicide at Monsieur Caramel's carousel looked much more like a freelance operation by someone wedded to the philosophy of chaos who, on the supposed big day at the beginning of August, had missed their opportunity. A few weeks later, the anonymous street cleaner had acted – and had perhaps, in certain circles, achieved a kind of posthumous glory.

The BWB flew on, eating up the distance. Out of the starboard window, Alex recognised the islands off La Rochelle. It was a lovely landscape but under threat, of course, from rising sea-levels and ocean storms.

He saw another plane two thousand metres to the west, glinting in the sun, above the ceiling of the clouds. It was heading south, maybe to Spain or North Africa – not big enough to complete the long haul to Cape Town or even Lagos. He imagined himself aboard that plane, flying away to a place where no one knew who he was or what he had done.

But that was ridiculous. He was 'the man who saved the world'. There was nowhere he could go where he wasn't known.

He tried to calculate how much of his life had leaked into the public domain. He and Mariam had made a serious mistake in making an enemy of the Bordeaux journalist. It would be a good idea to change his appearance. Was it common knowledge where he lived, where his mother lived, where Mariam lived? And what of Amaury, who had chosen to disappear entirely following a round of news interviews?

Eventually, the BWB began its descent into Paris-Orly. Out of the window he saw the vast reservoir that had been created by damming the Seine just south of the airport, drowning the suburbs of Vigneux and Draveil, displacing 200,000 people. The project was, according to official documentation, a huge success. To Alex, it looked like a threat.

But he didn't yet know why.

5

Back in Paris, Mariam went to visit her sisters in their long-term medical facility and received the awful but inevitable news – that there would soon be more death. Of the twins, Ablah was the weaker and had very little time left.

Distressed by her three-week absence, Mariam returned home to share the news with her family. As she walked to her apartment near the Panthéon, she saw long lines of people outside the public offices, trying to renew their identity documents, their rights of residence, their access to state benefits. The digital signatures on their phones and comm-watches had all been erased by what people were calling a 'freak data meltdown'.

She put down her bag on the sofa, opened a window and flinched back from movement above her head. A large dragonfly made a single bustling circuit of the room, then perched on one of the exposed beams.

Mariam used her tablet to photograph the insect, then an image search to identify it – an adult male 'blue dasher'; an immigrant from the southern United States. Apparently it was endangered, like so many creatures, not just in France where it was recently arrived, but also in its home territories. It was the usual ugly cocktail of habitat loss, predation and climate change, but with a twist. The ornamental black patterns on the male blue dasher's wings, crucial to its ability to find a mate and perpetuate the species, made it susceptible to overheating. The pigmentation was capable of raising the dragonflies' body temperature by two degrees.

Two degrees of average global temperature rise had been the 'manageable' target the world had signed up to when Mariam was a child. It had turned out that two degrees was an uncomfortable difference – for the world and, apparently, for the blue dasher.

It was depressing, always having to take in bad news – weak human interventions and inexorable loss – but she read on and, in this case, it didn't all seem negative. The blue dasher had undergone a kind of accelerated evolution, changes appearing in just a few generations – less pigmentation meaning less overheating. On the other hand, a less impressive display meant less successful mating, the females beginning no longer to recognise their own kind. The article concluded with a quote from an entomologist who suggested there was hope in what he called 'rapid beneficial adaptation'. Mariam wondered if this was a rogue voice, the classic media trope of promoting the dissenter, as if their argument carried equal weight to the consensus.

In the corner of her tablet screen was an urgent news alert about a breaking story of wind-and-flood devastation in Haiti in the Caribbean. Huge resources would apparently be required to prevent massive loss of life. She remembered that Alex and Amaury had both completed a training mission there, but she had declined to take part, the dates corresponding to Ablah's first serious relapse.

She powered off the tablet and went to take a shower, to remove the dust of travel from her skin and hair. When she returned to the living room, the blue dasher was gone.

She went through to the kitchen and sat down at the rustic kitchen table that had been her mother's before she died, finding she had a couple of minutes before her scheduled call to her Aunt Sara, her mother's sister, who lived in the Saint-Médard valley in the Pyrenees, far from the hustle of modern society. There were no modern comms on the family farm. In order to take the call, Sara would have made her way down the steep and broken road alongside the mountain stream, to the nearest café, bouncing along on her electric quadbike.

Eventually, it was time. Mariam spoke a voice command and a translucent vee of pale blue light pulsed from her comm-watch then resolved into a static image of the café logo – a chair with orange cushions and a shady umbrella.

'Hello?' she asked. 'Do you have vision?'

'How are you, Mariam?' Sara replied.

'Is there no camera?'

'No, there's a problem – as usual. But I can see you. What's happened?'

'I'm sorry about that. Can you fix it? I wish …' Mariam stopped. It felt dreadful to share the news with Sara's disembodied presence. 'I have to tell you that the doctors say Ablah will not live much longer.'

'Oh,' said her aunt, after a pause for the time-lag on transmission. 'Well, we knew it was coming. We should prepare. And Janaan, too?'

'She's stronger.' Mariam waited. When Sara did not reply, she added: 'A little stronger.'

'Janaan may follow her sister,' Sara said. 'You'll bring Ablah here, won't you?'

Mariam sighed. 'Yes, of course.'

'How long exactly?'

'Probably a day or two.'

'We will be ready. I'll tell Benjamin. I'll tell the neighbours. Bring her home.'

Mariam's sister Ablah had never seen the family's native valley, so the idea was a sentimental fiction, but Mariam was too sad to argue.

'I will. Thank you.'

'I keep hearing on the radio about what you did. You're a hero.'

'No, I just happened to be there. How is everyone?'

Sara told Mariam about her livestock and her crops, about the weather and the changing pattern of the seasons, about her cousin

Benjamin's life, how he seemed to have no prospect of bringing home a wife. Mariam told Sara about the blue dasher.

'Dragonflies are beneficial,' said her aunt. 'Pollinators.'

'I know.'

There was another pause. Mariam let it stretch out, wishing she could see her aunt's weather-worn face, not just the bland café logo.

'You look tired,' said Sara, unexpectedly.

'I've been travelling.' She sighed. 'I should never have gone away for so long.'

'You should rest.'

'Yes.'

'Keep well,' said her aunt.

'You, too.'

The static image of the café logo disappeared as if sucked back inside the comm-watch. Mariam undid the buckle from her wrist and left the device on the kitchen table, wandering back through to the living room to look out of the open window at the wide roadway that circled the massive bulk of the Panthéon, the vast domed sepulchre that housed the remains of France's most distinguished citizens. Near one of the buttresses, she recognised one of the rotating team of security officers delegated to watch over her, his gaze constantly moving, seeking anomalous behaviour – someone wearing a coat in summer or carrying a package that might conceal a weapon or a long-range camera.

She left the window and sat on the sofa with her tablet, summoning live satellite images of the Saint-Médard valley from French interior ministry surveillance. It took a few moments to load and required a biometric log-in – her thumbprint touched to the screen – because access was restricted.

The sky was clear and the shadows deep. The valley had been carved into the limestone over hundreds of millennia by mountain streams, then filled up over the same time frame with organic matter to provide deep fertile fields of loam. At the top of the valley, the vast sheen of the reservoir was like a sheet of dark glass, an organic shape with crinkled edges, extending out into inlets cut by tributaries from snowmelt on the peaks, much larger than she remembered it. The satellite imagery was embedded with data points, both historical information and contemporary news. Mariam touched one of them. It told her a story of glaciation and melt. She touched another that sold an alternative fable – that the mountains had been thrown up in anger and despair by the mighty Heracles, hearing of the death of his lover, the princess Pyrene. Another gave details of a particular mountain pass used by herders and their flocks – sheep and goats – and by refugees from persecution or war. Another pinpointed the underground river, cut by water through the limestone.

One data point was pulsing, indicating it was current news. It popped out a holo of a reporter, telling the story of a 'tragic accident' and the 'death of a peaceful campaigner' at the small mountain airport near the hydro station on the dam. There was a written report available, so she swiped the holo away and read eight hundred words on what had occurred, wishing she hadn't begun, hating herself for not simply looking away.

There was already too much death.

6

On a small plateau in the Atlas Mountains in Algeria, North Africa, beneath a stark sun, a stocky man with hard eyes was building a wall. His materials – irregularly-shaped stones from the mountains themselves – were lying around him on the ground, grass growing between them, fallen from some previous construction destroyed by time, perhaps a shelter for goats or even for a goatherd and their family.

Amaury Barra had discovered, to his frustration, that he wasn't very good at building walls. He balanced the stones awkwardly, often changing his mind. He used excessive quantities of mortar from a steel wheelbarrow, wasting a lot of it by letting it ooze out and fall on the ground. Now and then he bent down with his trowel and scooped it back up, slapping it untidily into a crevice. Every so often he drank from the neck of a dark-brown glass bottle. At other times he dipped his left hand in a bucket of water to rinse it imperfectly clean and then picked at a dish of reconstituted couscous, protected from the many black flies by a cloche of gauze.

Eventually, there were no more rocks close at hand and the wall seemed capable of remaining upright – at least long enough for the mortar to go off and become rigid. He looked at the wheelbarrow. There was barely a trowel of wet mortar left. He scraped it out and slapped it into the face of the stones.

The muscles in his neck and shoulders were stiff from the repetitive labour. And what was the point of it? Nothing. It was just a way to make the time pass while he was following orders, lying low, 'taking some heat out of the news cycle'.

He picked up the bucket and took it into his low dwelling, pushing aside the curtain of chains that hung in the opening. It was a rudimentary bungalow, divided into two rooms, both with beaten-earth floors. In the first, a panelled door on a couple of trestles served as a table. Against the left-hand wall was an old-fashioned two-over-three chest of drawers with a clock and a dirty mirror on top. On the wall opposite, a noisy converter was processing the energy being captured by the photovoltaics on the roof. It sent alternating current to the cooker and water heater; meanwhile, direct current went to the sleek wall panel that contained the storage batteries. Beside these were a UV insect zapper and a small fridge. Amaury crouched down and looked inside, tipping the box containing his last few dehydrated meals towards him, counting how many were left.

Enough to keep him healthy and nourished for a couple of days. Time was almost up.

He shut the fridge door. The dehydrated meals didn't need to be kept cool, but it was the only place guaranteed to be free of insects.

He went through into the second room, pushing aside another curtain of chains. His mattress lay on two fork-lift truck pallets to raise it off the dusty ground, a mosquito net suspended from a hook in the ceiling. Against the far wall was another incongruous item of bourgeois furniture – a mid-twentieth century dressing table with three mirrors, the centre one fixed, the two either side swivelled in so he could see himself from several angles at once.

Amaury sat down heavily on a hard chair. His face, reflected three times, was tired and unhappy. His beard was growing untidily, like dark weeds across his chin. His eyes were red – perhaps from the dust, perhaps from the stark sun, perhaps from illness, perhaps from unhappiness. He dropped his gaze, his hands idly lining up four boxes

44

of drugs in tablet form, two exhausted tubes of antiseptic cream, some steridressings.

Moving very deliberately, he used his left hand to undo the Velcro straps that secured the sophisticated prosthetic to his right stump, releasing sensors from probes embedded in his flesh where they fed information to and from his nervous system. His stump was raw in three places, rubbed and scratched by the fine sand that got everywhere. No, not fine. Sharp, prickly and irritating.

He returned to the living area for his bucket of water, but there was a scum of particles on the surface – dust and sand and caustic cement powder. No good.

He picked up the bucket and went outside, his eyes narrowing against the glare.

It took a while to operate the pump mechanism of the well with only one hand and the bucket seemed determined to tip over on the uneven ground. When he had finally managed to fill it with clean water, he dipped his angry stump into the cool liquid and moved it gently back and forth, not wanting to scrub at the irritated areas but needing to rinse away the grime. As he did so, he sighed, his eyes on the jagged horizon.

Why had he chosen this place? He could have gone to Biarritz with Alex and Mariam. But no, he had decided to hide from the world in an abandoned hamlet high in the Atlas Mountains, far from the helpful technician at the Rothschild Institute who took such good care of him, who would be 'personally and professionally disappointed' to see the mess that Amaury was making of his wounded arm.

Amaury wandered away to the area he thought of as his patio, almost enclosed by his amateurish low wall. He sat down in a steamer chair made of some red wood, perhaps teak or a less-endangered, cheaper substitute. It was dry and dusty, like everything else, and would probably last only another couple of winters before it fell apart. For the time being, though, Amaury could lie back, his legs stretched out on the foot rest, his stump across his chest, drying in the sun, the ultraviolet radiation disinfecting the raw areas of flesh.

What next? That was the question. He had come here, to the place where his ancestors had lived, or near enough, to this abandoned, windowless two-room building with its rudimentary latrine, a pile of sand alongside to cover the human waste and hygienic paper …

That was a point. He was down to his last toilet roll. Soon he would have to improvise. What else could he use? Medical dressings? Dry grass? A wet kitchen sponge? Socks?

Amaury almost dozed, but biting insects soon sought him out, leaving him with two puncture wounds on his left hand and another on his right cheekbone. He went back inside and sat on the dusty mattress beneath the mosquito netting. He lay back, seeing the dark creeping dots of more biting insects on the far side of the gauze. They knew he was there, lying quietly out of reach with his huge reservoir of warm nourishing blood.

Amaury rolled over onto his left-hand side, putting his stump on the pillow, his eyes focused on nothing, wondering why he had chosen this punishing interlude, living like a squalid hermit. Was it in search of meaning and connection to a heritage he had never known, a people he had never met, three and four generations back in his undistinguished family tree?

He sat up, pulling aside his pillows, revealing a small black case, rigid and tightly closed with a zip around its waist. He opened it. Inside, protected in a bed of plush cotton, was his comm-watch. He tapped the screen and pressed the reset button but, of course, three weeks on the rocky mountainside had drained it of all charge.

He found the cable under the plush lining, climbed off the mattress and exited the mosquito net, making his way to the battery panel in the outer room and flipping on the ultraviolet insect zapper. Within seconds, he heard the fizz and pop as the mosquitos were lured away to their deaths.

He leaned to one side to move his shadow and allow the last of the grey light to illuminate a set of charging sockets. He identified the correct one and plugged the comm-watch in.

He waited.

After five seconds, the device came to life, displaying the icon of the French External Security service – an outline of mainland France at the epicentre of a network of interconnected lines. Experience had taught him that it wouldn't be available for a few minutes, until after it had rebooted its operating system.

Who would he call, once the device was ready?

Alex, obviously.

When it came to it, Amaury changed his mind. He was back on his bed. Through the doorway and its curtain of chains, he could see his comm-watch dangling on its charge cable, the square screen softly pulsing with unread messages, unlistened voice notes, unacknowledged orders.

He rolled over, his stump on the pillow in front of his face.

No, it could wait. Tomorrow, or maybe the next day, he would leave this place but, for now, for one more night at least, he would eat a last meal and watch the sunset before falling asleep – far from the hyperconnected world, in a rudimentary shelter on a sloping plateau of a dusty mountain range, safely unseen.

7

The offices of the French Directorate General for Internal Security were located in a nondescript six-storey building on a nondescript street in Levallois-Perret, a suburb on the western edge of the Paris conurbation, outside the capital's orbital motorway.

Alex exited the lift, pushed open the doors and stepped through into the huge conference room. He crossed to the west-facing windows where a nest of uncomfortable swivel chairs stood grouped around an ugly rug with a geometric pattern in orange and brown. Looking out over the suburbs, he could make out the gap in the buildings a few blocks away where a shanty town had been built by or for the Blanks – ragged tents and shacks, a plastic bowser of tainted water as a bare minimum of human charity, stewing in the sun.

'Good afternoon, captain,' came a voice.

Alex turned. It was Director Damien Gerest. He rumbled over, his suspiciously black hair looking in need of a trim.

'Let's not sit in those awful swivel chairs. What on earth was Fayard thinking?'

'I always thought he chose them because he didn't want his meetings to last any longer than they had to,' said Alex.

'Perhaps. How is the convalescence?' Gerest asked.

'It's annoying.'

'You would rather be active?'

'Yes.'

Gerest went and took a seat at the centre of the conference table, facing into the room so that Alex would have to sit opposite, dazzled by the bright windows behind him. Alex sat down – his braced left leg stuck out straight – and picked up the remote control to darken the glass.

'Now, I was thinking,' said Gerest, in the tone of someone telling a funny story, 'what a pleasure it would be to see you in the flesh, rather than on the news streams. Tell me, when did you and Mademoiselle Jordane decide it would be a good idea to attack Emilie Olsen, a member of the free press, and threaten to throw her in the river?'

Alex ignored the sarcasm.

'The waiter at the hotel must have overheard us talking and put two and two together. An early flight from Bordeaux and, therefore, somewhere to stay the night before. It was bound to be one of the tourist enclaves. There were probably more journalists elsewhere, looking for us in other likely locations.'

'So it was nobody's fault,' Gerest concluded, with a thin smile.

'Are we interested in the future or the past?' asked Alex.

'Perhaps you should answer that question. The future is your speciality, is it not?'

Alex sighed.

'I'm sorry about the incident with the journalist. It was a mistake, but an innocent one.'

'Even so, Mademoiselle Jordane didn't have to—'

'We could have requested security, created a perimeter in the enclave, but we judged that would bring too much attention.'

There was nothing to hold his attention in the room so Alex allowed his gaze to drift past Gerest to the darkened window glass, through which the sun was a cold white eye on the horizon.

'Am I boring you?' snapped Gerest. 'We are all on the same side, are we not?'

Alex turned back, composing his features.

'For us to be on the same side, there would have to be a plan, but there is no plan.'

'The loss of data and algorithmic intelligence has had a crippling impact, but that will soon be at an end. The rebuilding process is underway.'

'How so?'

'Fragments of information from non-networked silos. I have put André Chambon in charge of recompiling and correlating.' Alex knew who Gerest meant – a determined analyst with External Security, trusted by Claudine Poiret. 'And the command structure has been updated in your absence,' Gerest concluded.

'Is that why we are here at Internal Security rather than in your own headquarters?'

'I have been given responsibility for both services,' said Gerest, complacently. 'For the protection of the nation from external threats, and from those originating closer to home. Under Chambon, I have established a working party to understand what happened, because it is the past that shapes our precarious present and our uncertain future. But what do you intend, captain? To return to active service?'

'Yes. I can walk. I carry the crutch because I don't want to slip or trip or stress the healing process. There is nothing to stop me from resuming my duties.'

'Your enthusiasm is noted. What has changed since you tendered your resignation?'

Alex wasn't sure whether Gerest knew that Claudine Poiret had blackmailed him into returning to work with a promise of preferential medical treatment for his sick mother.

'Circumstances changed. I made a vow to myself and to Professor Fayard to complete the job.'

'You believe there is another controlling intelligence or just randoms looking for validation in terror and destruction?'

'What difference does it make? If enough of them exist, it isn't necessary that they should be coordinated.'

No reply came. Alex watched Gerest carefully. There was something the fat man was not saying.

'Thank you for your candour,' said the director. 'Your medical support says your injuries require another week of inactivity, then a graduated return.'

'And meanwhile?'

'Read the briefing I've sent you, complete your physio and your post-trauma counselling. Mademoiselle Jordane's security detail remains in place. I could do the same for you?'

'No, thank you. Is that all?'

'For the time being,' said Gerest.

'Good.' Alex stood up, swinging his braced leg out from under the enormous conference table. 'I'll go and do all that.'

In the lift down, Alex saw his own expression in the mirror – sullen, closed off. He shook his head. What was the point of antagonising Gerest? For the time being, he would have to work with him. And he was a capable leader, albeit a highly political one, as were all those who achieved high rank.

Emerging on the ground floor, he requested an unmarked autodrive taxi with darkened windows to cross the city. He would have liked to walk, but it was too far and might set back his convalescence – and it would make him too visible. On the way, he messaged his mother at her bourgeois apartment on the fourth floor of a six-storey building on Boulevard Henri IV, near the Bastille. Her typed reply told him she was in the nearby library housed in the Napoleonic ammunition store, the Arsenal, reading about the emperor's scientific and military expedition to Egypt in 1801.

Why?

Because it interests me.

Alex went to join her and spent a pleasant half-hour looking over the documents she had spread across her study table, enjoying the feel of the ancient paper and leather beneath his fingers while she searched the digitised records. Then it was time for her to take a break and they crossed the road to a café in welcome shade, close to the river, where they discussed the trip to the surf hotel and Alex's return to service.

'But how are you?' he asked.

Gloria indicated the chunky med-watch on her left wrist.

'I'm being monitored night and day. That man Chambon has been to see me.'

'Good.'

'You, though,' she told him, 'look very different, unshaven, with your untidy hair. I had to look twice to recognise you.'

'I know. It feels weird.'

'How is Mariam?'

'She's with her sisters. It was hard for her, being away for three weeks.'

'Poor thing. But for me, it worked,' said Gloria, smiling. 'When I left my building this morning, I wasn't followed. I think the news hounds have grown tired of my scent.'

'I'm glad. But tell me really, this Napoléon in Egypt thing, why now?'

'It's the tension between conquest and learning. Napoléon took more scientists than soldiers. Co-operation was at least as possible as war.'

'Until the British came and took the Rosetta Stone off their hands.'

Gloria shook her head.

'I'm not talking about the race to decipher hieroglyphics. It's the expedition's intentions that I'm talking about.'

Alex smiled.

'Are you becoming an idealist, *maman*?'

'If I am, it's because I have you as my devoted and hard-working example.'

Leaving Gloria, Alex considered finding a discreet vantage point from which to scope out his boat on the canal basin – to judge whether it was under observation from journalists or bad guys. He thought it probably would be. But he was hungry so he got back into the autodrive.

'New destination,' he voice-commanded. 'Café des Phares.'

8

Alex got out on the shaded western side of the Place de la Bastille, moving quickly to conceal himself in the dim interior of the Café des Phares. He ordered a risotto with a lot of vegetable protein, leaning back against the mirrored wall beneath a cooling air-con vent, his eyes on the street.

The Place de la Bastille was dominated by its enormous commemorative column, erected in memory of the 13th century prison that had once formed part of the Paris city fortifications. On the 14th of July 1789, before it was torn down by anti-monarchist revolutionaries, the prison would have been easily the largest building on the skyline, but it didn't exist anymore. It was one of his mother's favourite stories. As a historian, she loved the unexpected patterns of cause and effect.

No longer required to defend the east of Paris from siege, the Bastille had for centuries been used as a jail. Its inmates were allowed to keep pets and welcome visitors, and received a stipend for the purchase of alcohol and tobacco. Voltaire, the writer, philosopher and social critic, spent nearly a year in one of its windowless cells. The Marquis de Sade was transferred out just ten days before it fell.

The Bastille's symbolic importance for the anti-monarchist revolutionaries came from the fact that it housed prisoners condemned by King Louis XVI. Under attack, the prison governor ordered his garrison of former soldiers – invalids exempt from regular service –

to defend the bastion to the death. More than a hundred lives were pointlessly lost in order to liberate only seven prisoners, including two lunatics and a nobleman convicted of a sex crime. The governor's head was carried away on a pike through the streets of the city.

We don't do that sort of thing any more, thought Alex. *We parade our heroes and villains in the media, feeding the 24-hour news cycle.*

His risotto arrived and he ate it, viewing a comment piece popped out from his comm-watch. The speaker was talking about a 'military-industrial complex', something Alex considered an intellectual trap – a raft of coincidences, common objectives mediated by money and power with consequences that only looked as though they had been planned.

He shut it off, musing on the idea of 'common objectives'. Where international politics used to be a competition between ideals or systems, now there was only power and a set of fixed defensive positions, like the city states of classical antiquity or the mighty medieval chateaux. Although the future depended on co-operation, not isolation, this was the past to which 2037 seemed to be regressing.

What we have, we hold.

Alex finished his meal and put an ice cube in his espresso coffee so he wouldn't have to wait for it to cool down. He paid using the bank details on his comm-watch, then hesitated, just inside the door, looking out. At the base of the commemorative column, a group of tourists emerged from the exhausting spiral staircase, looking for a break in the traffic to cross the intersection. As they did so, a lightweight electric truck pulled up and a worker in a hi-vis vest got out and placed a plastic barrier across the door. Apart from that, nothing unusual seemed to be happening – no obvious surveillance, no inexplicable figures lurking endlessly around a Métro entrance.

Alex took a circuitous route back to the canal basin via the narrow side-streets. He passed the dusty shopfront that used to serve as the headquarters of Tabula Rasa, one of the rallying points of the Coming Darkness conspiracy. It was being gutted by builders, like history being erased.

On Boulevard Bourdon, which ran south from the Bastille memorial column, he waited for a guy in an electric disinfectant truck to complete his spraying before crossing and acknowledging the civilian canal basin security guard on duty at the top of the stairs that led down to the water. The eighteen worn stone steps were shallow and fairly easy to navigate with his braced leg and crutch. His boat's AI recognised the presence of his comm-watch and he turned sideways to hobble inside, then waited in silence as the hatch closed behind him, sealing him into his own private space, steady on its twin hulls.

He dropped the crutch on the floor and opened the built-in fridge, looking for one of his green drinks, specially concocted by a consultant dietician to provide his unique metabolism with the nutrients it most needed. Of course, there were none. He had been away too long. He opened a bottle of filtered water, then booted up his information systems with a word: 'Wake.'

He sat down, not quite enjoying the taste of the water – somewhere between stale and metallic.

'Messages.'

A rectangular holo-screen popped up above the surface of the desk, showing him who wanted his attention: Chambon, obviously, who had been charged with rebuilding the databases; a junior from Claudine Poiret's office, announcing her sideways promotion to serving the president; the text of Fayard's posthumous farewell message from Emmeline Cantor. All of that was the past. At the top of his inbox was the promised briefing from Gerest.

'Open most recent message.'

His holo had a new interface, the set-up on his boat having been upgraded by a grateful nation. It enlarged into two virtual screens, one for the message window and the other for any attachments – in this case, a slideshow of captioned images. In response to Alex's circular hand gesture, the captioned slideshow enlarged, wrapping around him, as if he was present in the landscape.

He drained his glass, surrounded by fragments of the bad-news story, suspended around him like translucent dreams. It was a mining complex – brutally martyred soil and rock, vast diggers scouring the land, a huge water-retention bund.

Inevitably, this was where he would next look on death. Because he was an agent of justice. Or, if not justice, then law, at least – a set of principles devised in common for people to live by, so that something was certain in the shifting relativism of a world that had almost ended.

He pulled himself together, launching text-to-speech with a wave of his hand, so he could listen, not read, and get on with removing his leg brace and changing into lighter clothes. The synthetic voice had a sing-song quality.

Another report told him about a campaigning organisation called Lenca with strong ideas for a brighter tomorrow, reminding him of what Gloria had said. He found it heart-warming, in a way, that ordinary people still thought they could influence the web of self-interests that governed the planet.

Another report described the actions of several extremely wealthy families who, through a combination of luck, intelligence, manipulation and judgement, had amassed vast fortunes. Each was looking to create a stronghold – one of them had actually named their project 'Stronghold' – retreating from complication and compromise behind walls and fences, in valleys in the mountains, on tracts of land bordered by a bend in a river or other natural frontiers—

'Pause.'

The trouble was, Alex could see their point. The hyperconnected world had almost been wiped away. The 'common objectives' that brutally exploited working people and the natural world had almost been reset. He, Alexandre Lamarque, had prevented that catastrophe.

But should he have? Was there a chance that, had he failed, the future could have become … well, better? More brutal in the short term –

meaning a generation or two of starvation and devastated populations – but he understood the urge to begin again. A kind of cull, back to what some people called 'manageable' numbers.

'Manageable', in this context, meant several billion deaths.

That was the thing about numbers. The bigger they got, the less impressive they became.

9

After ninety minutes, a soft chime from his comm-watch informed Alex that he had been still for too long. He shut the holo with a word, stood up and stretched, replacing the plastalloy brace over his loose-fitting trousers. Awkwardly, he climbed the steps out of the boat onto the gangplank that connected his floating home to the cobbles of the walkway, feeling increased humidity in the air.

Later, he thought, there would be a storm. Rain might fall. The city might be cleansed.

He squinted towards the top of the steps. Profiled by the sun, the civilian security guard was talking to the man who drove the lightweight electric disinfectant truck. He recognised neither of them. Was it likely both had been replaced?

He swung his stiff left leg over the gunwhale. A seagull flew up and Alex swayed back. In the same moment, a shot rang out and Alex's subconscious and conscious mind began making calculations, stretching time, separating three sounds. The first was a whine, like a mosquito, but a mosquito moving at several hundred metres per second. The second was a clang as the projectile struck the superstructure of the boat, perhaps the rail that Alex's hand had just left, or maybe the grille of the walkway connecting the boat to the shore. Then a third sound, from further away and out of sync – the detonation inside the weapon whose soundwaves had taken X amount of time to reach him.

In the end, it didn't matter. The order was immaterial. They were so close together, the three distinct noises, that only someone with extensive experience of firearms would recognise them for what they were – which was why Alex was already lying flat on the cobbles, in the narrow band of shadow cast by his boat, edging closer to the slimy gap of water between the hull and the stonework of the bank, calculating trajectories and likely vantage points and probable enemies.

No, that question was irrelevant. It didn't matter who. Not at this point.

A second shot and another set of three distinct noises, striking stone not metal, and from a different angle. Different enough to indicate a second shooter or the same person having moved?

Alex edged closer to the water, improving his cover, feeling the gritty cobbles under the heels of his hands.

The two shots had come from close together but from above. High above. He was only uninjured because the seagull flying up had made him sway back, arching his back, taking him out of the line of fire. Wherever the shooter was, they needed not to attract attention. They couldn't release a volley of six or twenty projectiles.

Where, then?

The platform at the top of the Bastille Tower? That was possible and would also provide enough angle, from one side to the other of the circular platform, for the difference between the two shots. And it was a location that it would be possible to seal off, temporarily at least. In fact, hadn't he seen that happen, the worker in his hi-vis vest with his plastic barrier?

From the shadow between the hull and the bank, half his body hanging down towards the water, Alex tried to send a back-up request from his comm-watch.

Nothing.

That was ridiculous. He was close to the data hub inside his boat. Even if that were disabled, he was in the city centre, surrounded by a dense mesh of wifi signals. If his comm-watch was off grid, it was because someone was jamming his signal, maybe broadcasting white noise. But where from?

Maybe the electric disinfectant sprayer? That was big enough to house the necessary equipment. And, if there was someone close enough to jam his comms, they were also close enough to provide a second line of attack.

No sooner had he worked that out, than the second line of attack began with another shot – the same whine, the same detonation, but another impact of projectile on stone rather than metal, close to where he lay half-concealed, safe-ish but not safe enough.

Alex let himself slip down into the gap between the hull and the bank, holding tight to a rusty metal mooring ring, allowing his body to slide into the sludge-green basin water, which was oddly viscous – or was that a psychosomatic thing because it felt unclean, semi-stagnant, inhabited by all kinds of scavengers of organic waste? He let himself sink further, joining that ugly soup, taking a deep breath, the water closing over his head. He pushed down beneath the hull, scraping his knuckles on the shells of the molluscs that clung to it despite the anti-foul paint, finally finding himself in the cavity between its twin chambers, a design that gave the craft stability, but provided another advantage, too – an air pocket between the hulls.

He came up with his chin just above the surface, treading water with his one good leg, concealed from view, in a gap big enough to keep him safe for …

How long?

Twenty minutes, perhaps, before the carbon dioxide exhaled by his lungs began to poison him with each new breath.

The boat lurched above his head. Someone had climbed on board, someone looking for him, obviously. Maybe the man from the electric disinfectant truck? Maybe the unknown security guard? How hard would either of them be to impersonate? Violence wouldn't necessarily be required. It would be enough to give the real guard a food voucher for a restaurant in the restricted zone or a travel permit for somewhere special – plus instructions not to come in to work today.

And by the way, I will need to borrow your uniform.

Alex felt his good right leg beginning to ache with the effort of keeping his chin above water in the narrow gap. Then the boat rocked a second time.

Alex could visualise the intruder, stepping from one side of the hull to the other, looking for a tell-tale splash in the water – ripples or bubbles indicating where he was, maybe a disturbance as he kicked away, holding his breath, swimming underwater to the cover of the narrowboats moored on the opposite bank.

Worried the beating of his right leg might give him away, Alex manoeuvred himself closer to the stern, finding a handhold in one of the openings for the water-jets that the boat used for forward propulsion. Clinging to it, he was able to relax, frustrated that he couldn't activate the high-voltage defences, making the rails and handholds live, but to do that he would need to connect to the boat's …

He realised his comm-watch was glowing in the pitch-dark space. He had a faint connection. How was that happening?

Yes, of course. Concealed in the pocket of air between the twin metal hulls, he was in a kind of protective steel pod, out of reach of the jammer but only a metre or so away from the data hub on board.

With the watch boosted by the boat's systems, Alex used the enhanced remote capabilities of his comm-watch – another upgrade from 'a grateful nation' – to search for adjacent devices in the surrounding miasma of electromagnetic radiation, finding the jammer integrated into the disinfectant truck, as he'd guessed. With a word of command, he told his comm-watch to piggyback the signal and power the truck down. Once that was done, it took only seconds to restore maximum connectivity.

He spoke a command: 'Defence.'

A set of three options appeared on the large square face of his comm-watch. A couple of months ago, he might have said: 'Dissuasive.' Or, if he felt the danger was significant enough, he might have said: 'Severe.' Not now, though. Not since he had faced a conspiracy determined to create devastation through famine and war, those evil old twin Gods.

'Lethal,' he said.

The comm-watch asked him to confirm.

Yes / No.

Of course, for the lethal electric charge to take effect, the intruder would have to have a hand on a rail or a window frame or some other metallic element of the boat's superstructure – an element capable of carrying a fatal combination of current and voltage, enough to stop someone's heart.

But he already knew that must be the case from the way the boat's hulls were slightly slewed to one side. His attacker was leaning out, balancing their weight above the oily surface of the water by grasping the length of tube steel that ran the length of the deck. Whereas Alex himself, holding onto the fibre-glass hull, was safe.

He gave his confirmation.

Yes.

The reaction was instant. Alex felt the hull bob as something heavy fell from it, then a small disturbance in the sludgy water that surrounded him.

He let out a breath, deliberately driving buoyancy from his lungs, and allowed himself to sink, dragged down by his sodden clothes and the dense plastalloy of his leg brace. He put his two hands above his head, walking them along the roughness of the hull, feeling the colonies of crustaceans that made it their home. As he reached the edge furthest from the bank, light began penetrating the water.

A dark shape was drifting alongside, no more than a couple of metres away – the shape of a human, its arms and legs hanging vertically from a torso that semi-floated, head down, arse up, just breaking the surface.

Still holding his breath, Alex contemplated his victim, wondering what might be learnt from this corpse. It would depend on whether they were known to Internal Security's database, a surveillance tool that probably went further than even the most dedicated privacy campaigners feared—

No, he reminded himself. *No longer. That tool self-destructed with the traitor's death.*

Maybe there was nothing to learn anyway. It was possible to wipe a person from the records, to create a Blank out of a citizen. Hadn't he seen it done, more than once?

He felt his lungs demanding more oxygen so he pushed himself back between the twin hulls and kicked gently up into the air cavity. He took an unwilling breath, unhappy at the staleness of it. Moving his face close to his comm-watch, he spoke another command – a standard call for assistance from an agent under attack, a three-word identity code followed by a status number and then its translation in ordinary vernacular language.

'*Secours immédiat.*'

Immediate assistance.

10

The help Alex requested came within minutes, before the accumulating CO_2 began to poison him but long past the point where the stuffiness had become oppressive. He received a message giving him the all-clear – another three-word code, one of a sequence of thirty-two different trilog combinations, each with a different meaning, unique and only pertinent to Alexandre Lamarque.

He pushed himself out from beneath the hull, kicking to maintain depth, looking again for the victim of his electric-shock deterrent. The corpse was four metres away so he kicked towards it and broke the surface just as a lifebelt hit the water, attached to a buoyant plastic rope. He pushed his arms through it, took hold of the heavy cotton shirt on the shoulders of the corpse and allowed himself to be dragged towards the bank. Two pairs of strong hands – Paris police officers – helped him onto the cobbles, then hauled the body out of the water alongside. It was the unknown civilian security guard.

Alex stood up and allowed his comm-watch to communicate his Internal Security details to the two police officers. They stood back and saluted.

'Don't say it,' Alex ordered them.

'I'm sorry, captain, but you have no idea the honour –'

'That's enough,' he barked. 'You see that hose over there?' There was a tap on the far side of the cobbles, under the stone staircase. 'Pull that over here and rinse this crap off me.'

'Yes, captain. My pleasure, sir.'

It took two minutes of jet-washing for Alex to feel he had been cleansed of the microbes and other tiny predators from the semi-stagnant basin, taking his clothes off bit by bit until he stood in his underwear under the grey dome of the storm-heavy sky, looking for all the world like someone being punished with a cold-water torture.

'Okay, that will do.'

He stood for a couple of minutes, allowing himself to dry, flicking the water from his chest and limbs. He began recording a report on what had happened – he had already communicated the probable vantage point at the top of the Bastille Column and the officers confirmed that the shooter had fled. Not an easy shot, on reflection, even on a still day. He included the fact that it had been the seagull flying up that saved him, not the incompetence of the assassin or his own reactions. The fake security guard was dead but the others had escaped to try and kill him another way, another day.

He logged his report and took a moment.

How long will this go on? he wondered. *How long will I remain a celebrity and a target?*

There were two answers. He would remain a target for as long as it took for someone who still believed in Darkness to kill him, but he would be famous forever. His celebrity – preserved in the ones and zeroes of digital media – would endure beyond the grave.

Alex was taken to the Rothschild Institute for observation and a laborious and time-consuming sequence of tests. Apart from a skin rash on his hands from rubbing against the colony of crustaceans on the hull, he was declared healthy and – assuming nothing untoward showed up during overnight observation – he would be allowed to return home the next morning with a course of prophylactic antibiotics.

He received a message from André Chambon telling him nothing had been learnt from the corpse of the attempted assassin – no tattoos, no chip. Neither was the corpse's biometric data flagged by any surviving database. That didn't mean he hadn't once existed in the bureaucratic realm – his birth, his vax history, his educational qualifications. But concealing identities was something the conspiracy was very good at.

Alex slept badly in his private hospital bed, the air overcooled and the negative pressure of the hygiene-con creating a constant draft. And he was hungry, having missed the evening meal service while his tests were being carried out. The next morning, just after six o'clock, he was grateful to speak to a clinician on early rounds who signed him out.

He took an autodrive with darkened windows, pausing twice, the first time for coffee and pastries and the second to buy fresh food to prepare an early lunch. When he reached the canal basin, he found a police officer on duty who told him that the civilian security company had no idea how their man had been replaced. They had received no message from him for more than forty-eight hours.

'Someone else will look into it,' he replied.

Alex found his still-wet clothes tied up in a bundle to the rail of the boat. He left them where they were, intending to send them with his regular laundry for deep cleaning. Inside the boat, everything was as he had left it. The array of holos had gone into sleep mode but came back to life as the hatch closed behind him, growing in intensity and clarity.

He put his food shopping in the fridge and, overcaffeinated and full of carbs, remembered he had forgotten to order a new batch of medically mandated green drinks. He took another unsatisfying glass of chilled water and sat down at his desk, waving a hand to surround himself with the curve of state-of-the-art holos, feeling oddly as though the attack on his life had happened in a dream. The meta-data on Gerest's briefing had updated, informing him it was now 'time-sensitive' – meaning 'urgent'. It comprised more than ten thousand words, plus footnotes, plus video.

No thanks, he thought.

He shut the message software. What else had Gerest told him to do?

Post-mission counselling. More tiresome screen time.

Still, if he wanted to return to service in the field, it was a necessary step.

He requested a connection to the therapy AI in audio mode, without the ludicrous animatronic human avatar to try to persuade him it was real. He had committed to forty hours and had accumulated only seventeen – no, sixteen hours and forty-eight minutes.

'Good morning, Captain Lamarque,' said the voice. 'Shall we resume where we left off?'

'Sure,' said Alex. 'Where was that?'

'On your return from Norway, you told your mother that you saw something coming – a void, an emptiness.'

'That's right. I did,' said Alex. 'And I was right.'

Alex finally closed the program after three hours of repetitive probing.

And how did that make you feel?

What do you feel about that now?

You seem resistant to this process. Is there somewhere else you would like to be?

Then Mariam arrived, tapping a fingernail on the lens of one of the boat's external cameras.

He let her in. They lost themselves in one another, passionately, urgently, revealing the only possible answer to the final question.

Here. This is where I want to be.

Later, they lay in one another's arms in the velvet dark, cradled by the faint vibrations of the boat's stabilisers and climate control. He told her his news – Gerest's anger at the debacle in Bordeaux, the attack on his life – but eventually he realised that she was listening in silence because she had something more important to share.

'Ablah died,' she said quietly.

'Oh no,' he told her. 'I'm so sorry.'

He stopped, reluctant to probe. There had always been a gap between them – a shadow from Mariam's past.

'I think I want to tell you how it happened,' said Mariam. 'It's stupid. I don't know why I needed to keep it all secret.'

'Because our relationship was against regulations,' he told her. 'We might both have been demoted or fired.'

'I know,' she said quietly, almost a sigh.

Alex was intensely aware of Mariam's body against his, her strong limbs and taut skin. He wondered if she was drifting into sleep. Then she began again, telling him the whole story from the start.

11

Mariam's story began twelve years earlier, in 2025. She was enrolled on the same cadet training program at the École Militaire as Alex and Amaury. In time, only the highest-performing candidates would be retained. Like Alex and Amaury, Mariam was on track to make the final cut. Circumstances meant they had not yet met.

The École Militaire was built for the purpose of training future officers, like Britain's Sandhurst and America's West Point. It was located at the head of the formal rectangle of Parisian parkland known as the Field of Mars, the god of war, beneath the Eiffel Tower.

That day, Mariam's afternoon training session had been cancelled at the last minute due to an instructor going into isolation. She left the École Militaire by a secure exit on the south side, passing through a hygiene station, standing patiently for twenty seconds, breathing cool, oxygen-enriched air. Then the outer doors slid sideways into a cavity in the wall and she stepped outside, keeping to the back streets, out of the sun.

Paris felt alive. People were enjoying a period of relative freedom. Most cafés and restaurants had spread their outdoor chairs and tables onto streets that had been recently pedestrianised. Bicycles were chained to every railing, many of them old and rusty and damaged, but that didn't matter. Aside from horses, they were the most energy-efficient means of transport there was. Any effort made grinding uphill was repaid by freewheeling down the other side.

Mariam walked through the sixth arrondissement, with its plethora of boutiques serving the wealthy, whose clothes must apparently be replaced every season. Other shops served the faithful, whose desire for religious paraphernalia, it seemed, could never be entirely satisfied. Then she crossed the Latin quarter, the intellectual heart of medieval Paris, uphill past the Sorbonne to where the streets narrowed, feeling the uneven cobbles through the soles of her shoes.

Enjoying the unaccustomed freedom of an empty afternoon, she stopped in Place de la Contrescarpe for a cool drink in the shade of a sun-bleached umbrella. Children were playing in the fountain – poor children in their underclothes, with brown outdoor skin, prominent bones, home-cut hair. Mariam wondered whether the water was safe, or whether it was recycled from a cistern beneath the fountain, going round and round, picking up and incubating bacteria as it went.

Later, she pieced together what must have happened.

Mariam's mother, Aliyah Jordane, went into labour, alone in her untidy apartment, the contraction doubling her over as she opened the door to her freezer, taking out an ice-cube tray of chicken stock to add to a pan of soup simmering on the stove. The pain was crippling – not like she remembered from when Mariam had been born – telling her that something was wrong. She sank to her knees, dropping the ice-cube tray.

After a few seconds, she felt able to crawl away, leaving behind a smear of blood through the hand-dyed fabric of her kaftan. In a living room crowded with mismatched furniture and hand-embroidered textiles – the windows closed and the curtains drawn against the heat of the sun – she failed to pull herself upright using the coffee table.

The smear became a puddle, a pool. Due to a vertiginous rise and then a precipitous fall in blood pressure, she lost consciousness. Her right wrist was lodged in the soft gap between two seat-cushions of the dusty-brown sofa, reaching up for a cheap mobile phone, balanced precariously on the arm, connected to power.

Fully charged. Good signal. But out of reach.

Her eyelids fluttered. Her unborn twins became deprived of oxygen and nutrients. No help came.

On Place de la Contrescarpe, Mariam finished her drink and stood up. Her shoulders were stiff from the combat sessions she had completed that morning. She walked a few hundred metres downhill, towards the sun, then left into an alleyway with a few cramped in-fill buildings, just two storeys tall. The ground floor of the first building was a defunct sandwich shop. Beside the dark shopfront was a separate door giving access to the apartment she shared with her pregnant mother.

Mariam opened the street door with an old-fashioned key – the electronic lock had been smashed in an attempted robbery and she and her mother had not yet been able to afford the cost of replacing it. Mariam had confronted the robber and ended up throwing him down the stairs. There was still a brown mark on the wooden treads where his nose had profusely bled.

She stepped inside, closed the front door behind her and called out.
'*Ça va?*'

All right?

No answer came. She relocked the door on the inside, hung her backpack on a hook on the wall and climbed the narrow stairs. At the top, a shaft of sunlight came dazzling in through a gap in the living room curtains. Mariam raised a hand to shield her eyes and felt a moment of stillness, of reassessment.

What was it she could see? Her mother lying down, but awkwardly, with one hand trapped in the soft gap between the cushions of the dusty brown sofa.

Mariam acted quickly. She moved her mother into the recovery position, noticing at once the blood-soaked kaftan, the puddle on the floor. Her analytical mind began calculating possible quantities of loss. How much was survivable, for her mother and for the twins?

She snatched up the phone, drawing a kite shape on the numerical pad to wake it from sleep – 2, 6, 8, 4. The public med-centre was at the top of the recent call list. She dialled and found herself on hold. She hung up and called emergency. A mechanical voice answered, asking her which service she required, her name and address. She had to confirm who she was using the call-sign alphabet: *Juliette, Oscar, Roméo, Delta, Alpha, Novembre, Echo.* The mechanical voice told her assistance would arrive in seven minutes.

Seven minutes, thought Mariam. *But how much deadly time has already gone by?*

An alarm came from somewhere, beeping insistently, every fourth tone long and shrill. She followed the noise to the kitchen and shut the freezer door. On the stove, a saucepan had nearly boiled dry. She turned off the induction hotplate. A tray of frozen stock cubes had melted on the vinyl floor.

What does that all mean? Ten minutes? Maybe fifteen?

She opened the fridge, finding a bottle of filtered water in the door. She took it to her mother and tipped it carefully against her lips, encouraging her to drink.

'*C'est moi, maman. Bois. Ça te fera du bien.*'

It's me, Mum. Drink. It will do you good.

Would it, though? Would anything, ever again, do her mother any good?

The emergency services' chatbot was as good as its computer-generated word. Assistance arrived exactly on seven minutes. Mariam's mother was intubated and lines attached to major blood vessels in her arms. She was strapped to a gurney and carried down the narrow stairs, out into the bright sunlight.

Mariam rode in the rear of the ambulance to Hôpital Cochin. From triage in the emergency room, they were quickly moved to a maternity suite on the first floor. Mariam waited outside on a stiff chair in a stuffy corridor.

Guiltily, she saw herself, in memory, sitting down to a cool drink on Place de la Contrescarpe, worrying about the poor kids and the quality of the water in the fountain. And meanwhile, her mother …

After forty-seven minutes, a doctor emerged, a tall woman with a narrow face and uneven teeth. Mariam stood up too quickly, able only to hear the rush of blood in her own ears. Then the doctor's mouth stopped moving and Mariam asked her to repeat herself.

'We did all that we could. We employed all of our capabilities but we were unable to save your mother's life.'

'She's dead?'

'She is dead. I'm very sorry.'

Mariam looked away, receiving the news like an unwanted gift. She glanced at the signage on the walls, directions to different departments, places where people survived, where the medical teams' capabilities were not exhausted in failure.

'And the babies?'

'There were complications.'

Mariam realised she had spent the whole wait-time listening for a particular kind of noise from beyond the door of the delivery room.

'I haven't heard them cry.'

'They're alive,' said the narrow-faced doctor. 'Would you like to see them?'

'Can I see my mother first?'

'Not yet. She is still being attended to.'

'But you said she was dead?'

'There are protocols,' said the doctor, as if that explained everything. 'I will send you a nurse to take you to your sisters. There is no father?' The doctor had a tablet screen in her hand. 'Your mother's notes make no mention.'

'No,' said Mariam. 'No father.'

'I will speak to you again before you leave.'

The doctor went back into the delivery room. As the door began to swing closed, Mariam followed. The doctor turned and held out a hand to prevent her from entering, but too late. Four other surgically masked faces turned in her direction.

Mariam's mother was on the table, almost naked, draped here and there with hygienic paper, her belly exposed, cut open with a long incision to enable the emergency caesarean section. There was blood on the floor – less than Mariam expected.

'What's happening?' she asked.

'We are collecting evidence,' said the narrow-faced doctor.

A little later, Mariam found herself in a small room crowded with equipment, looking down on two small babies, their tiny, frail chests moving rhythmically in the heated incubators. They appeared to be breathing but it was, of course, an illusion. Machines were pushing oxygen-enriched air in and out of their inadequately-formed lungs.

'You should not expect them to live normal lives,' the doctor told her.

Mariam contemplated the poor little things in their austere plastic wombs.

'No,' she said. 'I won't expect that.'

The doctor held up a handful of printed A4 sheets.

'These are the crucial pages of your mother's medical records. Our network has just crashed so I had to get you hard copies. Perhaps you are aware that she was prescribed a prophylactic to prevent infection crossing the placenta?' The doctor raised an eyebrow, uncertain what Mariam might understand. 'Drugs cross the placenta as they do any other biological membrane, depending on molecular mass, solubility, degree of ionization. Opiates, for example. Benzodiazepines are noted to produce significant foetal effects.'

'My mother was an addict. She suffered chronic pain from a road accident. It changed her behaviour. She became reckless, hence no father.'

'I see. Well, that is no longer important,' said the doctor brutally. 'But the drug she was prescribed to protect her unborn children has been recalled. Her primary care physician must have informed her.'

'The drug from the damn med-centre caused this?' Mariam realised she had spoken more bitterly than she meant. It wasn't this doctor's fault. It was the world and the mess people had made of it. 'Forgive me. Please continue.'

'From a respiratory standpoint, new-borns are highly sensitive to maternal morphine. Then, of course, there was the pre-eclamptic shock and the blood loss. But that, too, might be attributed to the prophylactic. There is a class action in progress. I can give you the details.'

'You are suggesting I try to make money from my mother's death?'

'Yes,' said the doctor, meaningfully. 'I recommend it very strongly.'

Mariam looked at her sisters. A possible chain of future events was unfurling in her imagination. Would she be able to complete her training? It was her escape route. Without it, she would probably end up back in the Saint-Médard valley, working on the farm. Beautiful, doubtless, but narrow and isolated.

'You are suggesting I should join the class action,' she said, 'because my sisters will never be independent; they will always need care.'

'If they survive the next forty-eight hours,' the doctor warned. 'You should go to the sub-basement and speak to legal liaison.'

Mariam looked from one compromised new life to the other.

'Should I name them?'

'It will make things easier than referring to them as "Twin One" and "Twin Two",' the doctor told her, pragmatically. 'Did your mother leave any instructions?'

'Why would she? She didn't know she was going to die.'

A little later again, Mariam was sitting on another stiff polypropylene chair in another corridor – this time in the sub-basement, waiting for legal liaison to admit her. She was thinking about her fragile mother's childhood on a farm in the arcadian Saint-Médard valley, raised by Mariam's observant Muslim grandmother alongside her robust and well-adjusted sister, Mariam's Aunt Sara. She realised what she ought to do.

Mariam sat up straighter, using her comm-watch to search for names. She didn't want to choose badly.

In deference to her grandmother's heritage, she scrolled some lists and found 'Janaan', a name derived from Persian, meaning 'beloved' or 'beloved because good'. She thought it would do well for the older twin, the one who had first been lifted out of their mother's brutalised womb.

At the top of another list, she found 'Ablah', another acceptable though non-Quranic name, this time with Urdu origins. She chose it out of a kind of defiance because it meant 'perfectly formed'.

An elderly man emerged from the office, another relative she supposed, touching a handkerchief to his eye, walking quickly away, hiding his distress from strangers.

Telling Alex her story, lying in his arms in the velvet dark, cradled by the faint vibrations of the boat's stabilisers and climate control, had made Mariam feel empty, not better. She had accepted his sympathy and kindness, but she had spent so long keeping her secrets, hiding the details of her pain, that sharing still seemed like betrayal.

A few days later, she found herself alone at the street entrance of a classic Parisian townhouse, not far from the Observatory, with an expensive glazed lobby. She stepped through the neg-pressure airlock, smelling the distinctive fragrance of the purified and scented air, and placed her ID in the slot. An array of sensors read her medical history, took her temperature, checked her lung function and blood-oxygenation

77

levels – and probably also did some other tests she knew nothing about.

A musical chime indicated that she was cleared to enter. She took the elevator to her sisters' floor and met the nurse, a chunky man in his forties called Xavier. She didn't know his family name. They both stood over Janaan – a small shape beneath a pristine blanket, pale skin, dark hair, dark lashes. The bed alongside was already painfully empty. After a pause, Xavier told her: 'There is a problem with your payments, mademoiselle. Will you check your bank transfers?'

'I will. It may be a bureaucratic error,' she prevaricated.

'Yes, there are so many of them these days. People's records have simply vanished. It's like everything is falling apart.'

'I'll look into it,' said Mariam, knowing that the money awarded by the court for her mother's mismanaged pregnancy had been exhausted and she had had to borrow to continue to afford the luxurious facility from which she couldn't bear to move her sisters.

She brushed a strand of Janaan's thin hair back from her eyes. Remarkably, for the first time in she couldn't remember how long, Janaan's eyes fluttered open. She leaned in. Might there even be a kind of focus, a fragment of personality, for so long hidden by her physical frailties?

'She is saying goodbye,' Xavier told her. 'This surge of energy will not last long. Do you want me to go?'

'Does this "surge" often happen?' asked Mariam.

'Working in end-of-life care, decline is mostly inexorable, like a light receding remorselessly into the distance – sometimes slower, sometimes faster, but never stopping until it is so far away that it becomes impossible to see. Now and then, though, I have seen a final brief flare of brilliance.'

Sunlight from the west-facing window was creeping across the medical equipment beside the bed, closer to the edge of Janaan's pillow. Xavier went and drew the translucent blind. With the tip of her finger, Mariam traced the Arabic word for 'love' in Janaan's palm – حب . Her

78

sister's fingers closed over her own, immensely gently, with no more force than a butterfly's wings coming together after flight.

'Oh,' said Mariam.

'Yes,' said Xavier. 'She is giving you her blessing.'

Time passed slowly. Eventually, as they watched, Janaan closed her eyes. Her breathing slowed, became shallower, then ceased. Xavier put a hand on Mariam's shoulder as she wept.

Mariam watched the ambulance leave, taking away her sister's corpse. In the end, there had only been seventy-two hours between Ablah's and Janaan's deaths. She felt disconnected and resentful, but also felt a sense of release from the frustration of two lives narrowed each to a wordless hospital bed, expiring in pointless antiseptic luxury.

She walked away from the converted townhouse, thinking about how she would probably never again buy pastries from that particular patisserie on the corner, no longer eat them herself because Ablah and Janaan couldn't manage solid food, never again give them to Xavier, pretending that she had bought them for him all along.

A message to her comm-watch broke in. She found a corner of shadow, away from the harsh sunlight, where she could pop out a holo of a man with short-cropped ginger hair, a desk lamp reflecting off a large *chevalière* ring on his middle finger.

'I am very sorry for your loss,' said André Chambon. 'Please forgive the intrusion. I have Director Gerest on line.'

Despite her emotional turmoil, Mariam instantly deduced that Chambon's rebuild of the surveillance databases already included the most intimate details of her own life.

'Go ahead.'

The image changed to a wide desk bearing several executive toys. The man sitting behind it seemed so distant that she pinched the image out to see him more clearly.

'You must feel a very difficult combination of emotions,' Gerest began, his eyes down. 'My condolences, mademoiselle.'

Was he reading a prepared script?

'Thank you.'

'With the death of your second sister, the care package agreed in compensation for your mother's mismanaged pregnancy comes to an end. You have, in any case, exceeded the limits awarded by the court.' Briefly, he looked up at the lens. 'Your debts are substantial.'

'I will sell my apartment.'

'That is for you to decide,' said Gerest. 'I did, however, ask Chambon to get in touch with the pharma company. It was not hard for him to persuade them to cover what you owe as a gesture of goodwill.'

Mariam was taken aback.

'That's extraordinary. What do they want in return?'

'You would phrase it better by asking what they want to avoid, Mademoiselle Jordane.'

Mariam worked it out.

'They don't want the public relations damage that would result from bankrupting a national hero in her bereavement.'

'Once again,' said Gerest drily, 'your celebrity is in play.'

'Will they want me to make a public recognition of their largesse?'

'They will, but Chambon has put them off.' Gerest swiped at another screen beyond the perimeter of the pinched-out close-up. 'For now. This is good news, is it not?'

'Yes, thank you.'

Mariam waited. Clearly, he had something else he wanted to say. His eyes came up once he had found the information he was looking for.

'You will take your sisters to your family farm for burial, rather than cremation?'

'Yes.'

'Your leave is extended, of course, but there is the coincidence of the facility at the head of the valley.' Momentarily, Mariam pictured the black expanse of the reservoir on the sat-image. 'You will receive a briefing.'

Mariam realised she was standing very straight, almost to attention, and tried to relax.

'Understood.'

'Your travel documents will be with you within the hour. I will be in touch.'

The holo snapped out of existence. She called Alex and found him frustrated and bored, confined and wearied by convalescence and his post-mission counselling. She told him what had happened, that she would soon make the journey south to the Saint-Médard valley where, in a modest cemetery beneath the imposing limestone mountains, she would inter the remains of her 'beloved' and 'perfectly-formed' sisters beneath a stone that would simply read:

Janaan et Ablah
2025-2037

12

Alone in the cabin of his boat, Alex was feeling much more confident in his recovery. Soon, he thought, he would be able to engage in more strenuous physical activity – so long as it didn't include any kind of impacts on his damaged left leg.

He had been unexpectedly busy because it turned out that his own ringfenced archives on the boat were useful to Chambon in the rebuild of the Internal Security database, the urgency of that process trumping Gerest's 'time-sensitive' briefing. Finally, though, he had returned to it, prompted by a terse reminder from the director.

'These are some of the first results of a working party I have established to trawl our archives and the media, looking for connections, balancing our artificial intelligence algorithms – which so conspicuously failed in identifying the traitor – with your own intuition. I will not sign off your return to service without a full report.'

Alex knew many of his colleagues believed that he had a special intuitive gift and wanted to know how he did it. The answer was simple: a combination of experience and focus. As he had told the forensics tech in Bordeaux: *I just pay attention*. What was unnerving for him was that his hunches often led to legal or quasi-legal direct action, sometimes resulting in judicial murders justified by 'hot pursuit' or 'necessary to prevent collateral damage or injury or death'. That challenging responsibility was one of the reasons he had been moved to resign.

On his boat, Alex was surrounded by the wrap-around holos – a mountain panorama of forest and trapped water with a pop-out description of a tragic death and some sparse details of a pending legal case targeting the head of the dam company. His name was Davide Castile.

With a couple of hand gestures, Alex found a biographical note that told him that Davide Castile was forty-seven years old and had left the army with a raft of medals and a substantial pension from twenty-one years of service. That pension, however, was dwarfed by coming into, as sole heir, the wealth and influence of his family's energy company, including mining, solar, tidal, clean-burn waste disposal, massive intangible assets – and a dam at the head of a Pyrenean valley whose hydro-turbines spent every minute of every day spinning gold out of gravity, turning the weight and pressure of water into money, power and influence.

How much power and influence?

A lot.

How much money?

An incalculable and ever-growing pile.

Alex knew there were people whose job it was to count and manage such unimaginable wealth, to make it work in its turn, money making more money, but the size of the numbers defeated him.

He read on. Castile's family company had a record of conflict. Eighteen months before, a flash point had been the seeding of clouds, a geo-engineering practice that required a special governmental permit that Castile Energie had failed to obtain in advance, though it had been granted in retrospect by a pliant bureaucrat.

Gravity was always an issue with the storage of water. There was always the worry that the precious resource would flow away, taking the path of least resistance, ending up uselessly merged with the undrinkable vastness of the oceans. Snowpack was a reservoir in its own right, holding the water in solid form, so it didn't simply run away down the slopes.

Castile Energie had allocated what it called 'modest resources' to generating winter precipitation of snow, sleet and gritty rain to renew the snowpack on the Pyrenean peaks. A demonstrators' encampment had been established, just below the dam, close to the perimeter of the small airstrip. The protestors had tried to prevent the refuelling of the cloud-seeding aircraft. Davide Castile had arrived by helicopter – one of the super-fast X^3 models – at the controls himself, touching down and immediately going to speak to them.

What did he imagine? Alex wondered. *That his charm or his sense of purpose or the force of his personality could change their minds? That he might persuade them that to disrupt the natural pattern of snow and rainfall in order to serve his financial ambitions was logical and wise? That their concerns for local communities, struggling for self-sufficiency in the arcadian valleys of the Pyrenean mountains, were misplaced? That big business and big power were wisdom?*

Anyway, whatever he said, no one believed him, so he got back in his X^3 and …

Well, at that point, the narratives began to differ.

The protestors claimed that he buzzed them. His own deposition claimed that his flight-path was intruded on, that the ground crews had cleared the area around the H-pad but the protesters – the 'trespassers' – had returned, putting themselves into danger. And that the weather conditions were tricky, the X^3 potentially faulty.

Alex scanned the court papers, stretching them out to fill the cabin so his eye could chase through the dense legal phraseology, extracting the gist. One of the helicopter's landing skids struck a woman holding a baby against her chest. The shock of the impact shattered the woman's skull and she dropped like a skittle, spinning round and then lying still, the baby pinned beneath her.

On balance, he judged it possible that Castile had done it on purpose. He was beginning to get a sense of the man – someone that luck and life had taught that he was invulnerable. And Castile had three experts – one on his payroll and two apparently independent – who confirmed from black-box analysis that the chopper had simply been leaving with no intention of trying to frighten the protestors, no point to prove beyond the 'amicable discussion already described', no assertion of dominance. It was an accident caused by …

Alex stopped reading. He wasn't interested in what the 'three experts' had been paid to say.

He followed another link to a biography of the deceased protestor. She went by the nickname Berta and was a recipient of the Goldman Prize for environmental defenders. She came from Honduras, part of the twisted leg of land that connected Colombia to Mexico – what one historian called 'the sweet waist of America'. As a child, she had been part of a caravan of refugees, walking north to the United States. She and her parents had eventually obtained US citizenship and she graduated in hydro-engineering from the University of Houston, marrying a French doctoral student studying there. When the opportunity arose, the couple came to live and work in Bordeaux on the construction of wave-power facilities on the tidal estuary of the Garonne and the Dordogne – a plant owned by Castile's family. Two years later, she abandoned her career to become a full-time activist, promoting environmental consciousness in business, founding the campaigning organisation 'Lenca'. Her French husband left her and their son without a backwards glance.

With a gesture, Alex froze the text-scroll, a memory on the edge of consciousness – a connection between Honduras and the unusual name. He made some parallel searches in a newspaper archive and soon found the reference. On 2 March 2016, a Honduran activist called Berta Caceres had been killed on the banks of the Gualcarque River in the Rio Blanco region of the country after years of threats linked to her opposition to the 22-megawatt Agua Zarca dam.

Alex thought that the woman killed by Davide Castile had probably been named for Berta Caceres at the height of her early fame. And this second 'Berta' had named her campaigning group 'Lenca' because that was the name of the indigenous people Berta Caceres had represented.

And now this other Berta was dead, too.

Alex wondered if she had embraced death. After all, she was dislocated from her heritage and culture. The haven her family had struggled to find – the holy grail of immigration into the United States – had nurtured but not held her. She had moved to France and sought new causes to espouse, new powers to oppose.

No trial or inquiry date had been set for Davide Castile. Interestingly, the Lenca campaigners from the dead woman's group recognised this as an opportunity and were trying to turn the delay to their advantage, to leverage it into a public scandal by staging a fake trial of their own, presenting evidence with considerable attention to detail both in fact and in law. The footage was included in Alex's briefing, so he played it, finding that the actor chosen to play Davide Castile resembled the man so closely that he had been given a T-shirt to wear on which was printed: *NOT Davide Castile*.

Alex paused and checked the log of views. They ran into millions. All the same, it was hard to tell if the fake trial was making any headway in spreading the word. Comments were disabled and, in any case, it was the sort of thing that people would probably only want to talk about incognito, using channels with end-to-end encryption. And, of course, the view-count might be a fiction itself, a marketing ploy, racking up an impressive log of streams, all of which were actually generated by bots.

In the end, though, it didn't matter whether or not the fake trial was widely viewed. It wasn't essential that Alex agreed that the dam had drowned what Lenca called 'sacred land'. Alex didn't believe in sacredness. He believed in justice, but he worried that laws designed to protect the weak were often abused for their own advantage by the powerful.

He ran the video and was interested to discover that Castile had employed an ex-military junior officer called Arnaud Sy to infiltrate

Berta's group. That, thought Alex, was the most promising lead for anyone who wanted to pursue Castile in law because it could be construed as evidence of conspiracy. Even if Berta's death were judged an accident, Castile might still be guilty of culpable intent.

The film ran on into some closing remarks from the 'judge', played by Berta's eldest son, a man of about twenty, very thin in the face but quite heavily built around the shoulders and arms. He was the only 'character' to break the fourth wall and address the audience down the lens of the camera.

'You can decide for yourselves. We wanted to be even-handed. We wanted to provide the facts and explain the law, but we found that was impossible. You can't give the benefit of the doubt when there is no doubt. You can't take the high road when your opposition offers only lies. People who haven't lost their mothers, who aren't bereaved and grieving, tell you: "Stay classy." But what is a "classy" response to death by helicopter? And don't forget, this is simply one more atrocity in a never-ending undeclared war that ...'

The closing remarks seemed to be accelerating into a tirade. Alex shut the stream and launched the final fragment of Gerest's briefing, the section that addressed the question of whether the blow to Berta's head from the skids of the X^3 was deliberate or accidental. It was non-committal, though Alex discovered that the baby had survived.

He sat back, realising that he was making a character judgement on Davide Castile – that he wasn't the sort of man to kill by accident. It made him wish he could request an AI interrogation of all data connected to Lenca, to Berta, to her unnamed son, to Davide Castile's military record and business dealings. But he couldn't, because that comprehensive interrogatable database was gone.

'Sleep.'

The holos collapsed into themselves and Alex went outside. The civilian guard was there with two builders, measuring up for some kind of screen to protect access to the canal side. Alex climbed the steps to the boulevard and the bicycle garage, a domed metal security cage. He released his bike, swung his stiff leg over and carefully checked left and right. The artificial white noise from electric vehicles formed a kind of background blur, not necessarily useful for avoiding collisions.

Loosening the knee joint on his leg brace, he waited for a gap then pedalled away to the embankments of the Seine, long since closed to motorised vehicles. He followed the water, past the encampments of Blanks in the shade of the bridges, across the islands to the Left Bank and – gently, gently – up the hill towards the Panthéon and Mariam's apartment. As long as he didn't push too hard, he thought the no-impact exercise would do him good rather than harm.

Outside the great domed mausoleum, he met the leader of Mariam's security detail, Sébastien Ménard, who told him she had just left for the Pyrenees – 'not five minutes ago' – and that he would have gone with her but he was detained in Paris for a long-planned training assignment.

'It's okay. She told me she would be leaving soon,' Alex told him.

'She was very sad, captain.'

'Will you continue to protect her? Nothing is more important.'

'She refused, as you did yourself. But I will send a team all the same.'

'Thank you.'

Taking the narrow side-streets, grateful for the soft, adaptive suspension in his bike forks, Alex let gravity pull him back down to the river. Then he pushed on, using the flat embankment as a test track for his injured limb.

It held up.

Back at his boat – sweaty, dusty and pleasantly tired – he found a messenger waiting with a printed order, signed at the foot in Gerest's aggressive handwriting: 'Finish your counselling and physical assessment then come straight to see me. You may need to re-enter active service sooner than planned.'

'Your reply?' asked the messenger.

'This is an order,' he told her. 'It doesn't need a reply.'

'What shall I tell the director?'

'That I am capable of following orders.'

The hatch opened and he climbed down inside, feeling no discomfort from flexing his left knee. Inside, the heat exchangers had been doing their job, keeping the atmosphere cool, the solar interface powering the dehumidifiers. He took a shower, added his dirty clothes to his growing laundry pile, then relaunched the therapy AI.

13

While everyone knew that Alexandre Lamarque was 'the man who saved the world', only a small number of important protagonists were aware of the crucial role played by a small, grey man, an important politician from the North-African republic of Cyrenia, Faroukh Al-Medawi, member of the presidential council, Mayor of Tobruk. He was at a meeting at the headquarters of the North African Defence League in Algiers. The plush room was too big, really. As each of the four delegates spoke, they automatically raised their voices as if they were addressing a much larger meeting.

After an hour, there was a pause as mint tea was served in small glasses decorated with intricate patterns in gold foil. Al-Medawi had said nothing for some time, pondering a question of his own.

In a world awash with information, what is the purpose of the spy? To confer a tiny but discernible competitive advantage? But why, when co-operation is always more productive?

The habit, it seemed, was hard to shake.

'So, I can confirm,' the Malian delegate resumed, 'that a senior officer in the engineering corps, a man close to our honourable President Manouche, is under investigation for "delivering information to a foreign power", specifically one of the Russian factions. Our investigative AI has pinpointed his actions as warranting further inquiry, but the circumstances are rendered opaque by the fact that he has, in the past, been ordered to communicate with the Russians quite legitimately, regarding investments in Malian lithium.'

'No human has cause to suspect him?' asked the Egyptian dubiously, a man with childhood chicken pox scars on his brow. 'Do you trust your all-seeing AI?'

'Egypt has observer status in this meeting,' reminded the Malian. 'You have no skin in this game, unless there has been a change in approach from the government in Cairo? Should we be preparing ourselves for a renewal of diplomatic relations?'

'The Egyptian government will maintain its policy of isolation and self-determination,' came the reply. 'But is this a local issue or do you believe that this engineer was connected to the Coming Darkness conspiracy?'

'No, there is no reason to think that,' said the Malian. 'Though the remnants are still active, are they not?'

All eyes turned to Al-Medawi as the man best placed to respond. He replied with another question.

'Why do you use the word "remnants"? Who is to say that the conspiracy was the end point?'

'But it would have been apocalyptic, with billions of deaths,' said the Algerian delegate, shocked into speech.

'It might have been,' said Al-Medawi, 'if every element had succeeded. But what if that moment of potential catastrophe was simply an opportunity that presented itself? Might there be a greater purpose, with a controlling intelligence still in play?'

'I have an idea,' said the Egyptian. 'What if I contact this military engineer – what's his name?'

'Major Chaka Kassam,' said the Malian.

'What if I contact him and draw him out? I could give him a rare opportunity to travel to Egypt. That might tempt him. Or could he be named Mali's political representative for the upcoming ceremony at Aswan, for example?'

There was general agreement.

'I will make that happen,' said the Malian.

'Good,' said the Egyptian. 'And I will report back.'

Only a few people had read every word of the exhaustive testimony collected from Alexandre Lamarque's lengthy debriefing sessions with Claudine Poiret's civil servants. Faroukh Al-Medawi was one of them. Another was an old man who sat hidden in a basement beneath a nondescript townhouse, wondering if the transcripts might not contain further clues, ideas that had been missed, connections that hadn't been made. At that precise moment, he was re-reading a conversation about islands and their importance in the international communications sector.

Networks are more secure when they have multiple flows, shorter routes that can back one another up. Islands shorten the spans across the oceans. More than half the world's connectors come ashore on islands. Whoever controls the islands controls the flow of data.

It made the old man think about the simultaneous attacks on different international methods of communication and how no one had ever quite got to the bottom of what their purpose was, in particular the severing of undersea cables.

It made him think, also, about an image that had recurred frequently in Alexandre Lamarque's descriptions of his investigation, until it had all become completely clear in its brutal potential for destruction.

He had spoken of spiders in their webs.

Though the traitor who had acted closest to home was dead – the old man had seen him die and made sure that his body had been disposed of without ceremony or memorial – surely there had to be another 'spider', still out there?

Unfortunately, even if that insight did turn out to be true, the old man, trapped in his Parisian basement, knew himself unable to do anything about it.

Leaving the headquarters of the North African Defence League, just as the street lamps were lit, Faroukh Al-Medawi felt inclined to shake off the stiffness and formality of cagey diplomacy. He dismissed his official car and made his way into the popular heart of the city, through restaurants and shops that opened onto the pavements, filling the air with the noise and smells and sights of teeming human life. Twice he stopped, feeling someone's gaze upon him.

Was it his own security, though he had ordered them to stand down? Or was it someone else, taking an interest in a stranger in fine grey linen, walking among the rough robes of the locals?

Four thousand kilometres to the south, in the Saharan Republic of Mali, a French citizen named Drissa Sidibé with relatives in the capital, Bamako, was enjoying a late snack in a popular restaurant, not far from the central square. He was eating a rich *bouille*, a classic Malian dessert with a sugary biscuit-like crust and a custard filling. From a rake-thin waiter, he ordered a glass of *djablani*, a drink made from ginger, lemon and mint, to cut through the stickiness.

As he drained his glass, a young woman approached wearing a bogolan dress with a loud pattern.

'Where have you been, Drissa?' she asked.

'I have been travelling.'

'Where did you go?'

'Just to the south, Aminata. It isn't important. I am here now.'

The young woman pursed her lips.

'Drissa, you won't do anything bad, will you? When will Kadidia come home? Do you have money, now?'

'I have sold everything I brought with me,' he lied. 'Perhaps I will come back again.'

'I have passed all my exams. I am top of my class,' said Aminata. 'I have good references from my work. We could be happy in France.'

'I know. You told me.' He picked at a piece of crust from his *bouille*.

A man in the long blue robe of a Dogon priest approached the table.

'Now leave me,' Drissa said. 'This is private.'

Aminata's frown deepened.

'Did you do something to … make me worry?'

'I did what has to be done. Now, go.'

'Isn't it over?' she asked quietly. 'Narissa is dead and—'

'It will never be over,' he snapped.

Aminata slipped away, choosing to believe – at least for a short time – that all might still be well and, soon, she would be working alongside her brother in the pharmaceutical factory in Marseille, the city where their older sister had died.

After a while, Al-Medawi began to find the cars and scooters and mobikes annoying, so he took a left turn into an area where vehicles were not allowed. A butcher in a bloodstained apron stood by a pile of cages – live chickens and rabbits – sharpening the long blade of his slaughtering knife on a whetstone.

Al-Medawi walked on, still with that prickly feeling of being observed. A man in traditional dress – a long white gandoura covered by a hooded brown burnous – brushed past him and turned, holding out a small rectangle of card. Al-Medawi thought at first that it was an advertisement, perhaps from a fortune-teller or marabout. Then the man took hold of his forearm and hissed: 'It is coming.'

Al-Medawi watched the man slip away along a side-street lined with shisha bars. Was he meant to follow? Was it a trick or a trap of some kind?

He turned the card over in his fingers. It seemed at first to be blank, then he felt the embossed print on the smooth surface and angled it so as to catch the light from a weak orange streetlamp, actually quite clear once you knew the image was there.

A distant sunrise through cloud.

Al-Medawi knew what that meant. It was a symbol he had seen many times in reports on the Coming Darkness conspiracy, usually in the form of screengrabs from the dark web – but he didn't know why it had been given to him.

A threat, perhaps? A promise?

He set off in the same direction, through clouds of sweet-smelling shisha smoke, men and women drawing on long tubes attached to ornate bubble-towers, each topped with a grate of tin-foil in which their flavoured tobaccos smouldered on pieces of glowing charcoal. He saw the man look back to ensure that he was following, standing beside a dozen or so mobikes, parked in a disorganised crowd, leaning against one another in a dusty triangle of undeveloped land. The man was talking to a boy, a scrawny fourteen-year-old with close-cropped brown hair who gave him a starter-fob.

The man didn't immediately climb onto his rented mobike. He had to push it thirty metres, out of the pedestrianised zone to a junction where the narrow side street opened onto a wide boulevard with an orchard of date palms running down the centre. Al-Medawi saw him hitch up his robes to perch on the upholstered seat, one sandalled foot on the ground for balance, the other on the pedals. He raised a hand.

At first, Al-Medawi thought it was a gesture of farewell. He was on the point of responding in kind when he realised it was intended for someone standing beside him. He half-turned, in time to see the knife – but not quick enough to parry it or step away from its thrust.

It was the boy from the dusty mobike park – actually older than Al-Medawi had first thought, his hand emerging three times from his sleeve as he stabbed a trio of quick thrusts at Al-Medawi's chest, then jumped back, a confused frown on his unlined brow.

Al-Medawi was unharmed. He wore a protective Kevlar vest beneath the fine grey burnous. He drew a sonic immobiliser from a hidden pocket.

The boy took another step back – but not to flee. He raised his knife and plunged it into his own throat, carving it from side to side, choking and falling forward onto his face on the uneven paving slabs, an awful gargling sound plainly audible from his blood-drowned trachea.

At that same moment, in a different time zone, another man – not quite as old as the one voluntarily trapped in his Parisian basement, but physically infirm – was enjoying almost limitless reach. Despite his remote geographical isolation, he was connected to a network of international energy and communications cables that criss-crossed the oceans and seas, many of them coming ashore on islands that served as nodes in the web.

He was watching a documentary about sea defences in the Samoan archipelago. In 2025, when a worldwide conference had revised an acceptable global temperature rise upwards from $1.5°$ to $2°$ centigrade, Niulakita's highest point had been less than five metres above sea level and Rose Atoll less than four. Yes, they were only micro-islands but today, twelve years later, they were gone. The land masses of the more substantial volcanic outcrops of Vanuatu and Nu'ulopaat had halved.

None of this was news, just evidence that he knew well of human beings' inability to face the truth of their own suicidal natures.

He turned to another strand of information. Major Chaka Kassam of the Malian engineering corps had been in touch with him through covert means in order to apologise for becoming a 'person of interest'.

Was that a problem, the old man wondered? Might it not in reality become an opportunity, a way of intensifying the imminent smokescreen of terrorism in southern Mali? Kassam could admit to his old friend, President Manouche, that he had shared information about the potential of the newest lithium deposits at Yanfolila, but by accident, not design. Associating the chaotic Russian factions with the attacks would make it more certain that Alexandre Lamarque himself would take an interest.

In any case, Kassam was dispensable.

The man drove his electric wheelchair outside onto the terrace that ran round all four sides of his home, built like a citadel on a hilltop. His pale eyes narrowed as he looked out across the rugged land towards the bright and apparently limitless ocean, a white sunrise through cloud.

Was it a problem to be so far from the epicentre of the action?

No, not if the one in whom he had placed his greatest trust proved worthy.

In Algiers, a crowd had gathered, close but not too close. Al-Medawi stayed still, his son-imm in his hand, non-lethal but a serious deterrent. He now knew that he had been given the embossed white card as a trap, to entice him towards his assassin.

Two police officers arrived, nosing their electric patrol car in from the boulevard, climbing out with their own rudimentary projectile weapons already drawn, demanding Al-Medawi place his son-imm on the ground.

Of course he complied, informing them that it had not been discharged, as could be seen from its on-board computer. He presented his diplomatic credentials via his comm-watch. It took a few moments for the officers' handheld to find a secure connection. Meanwhile, he stood with his hands raised at the level of his shoulders, thinking about the wish for death, the wish for darkness – how alien it was, how inexplicable, when the alternative was life in all its pointless but teeming glory.

Finally allowed to leave the scene by the two police officers, he summoned his official car to meet him at the junction of the precinct and the boulevard. He sat in the front passenger seat. Through the dusty window-glass, he saw the man in the brown burnous on the far side of the wide road, beyond the central reservation with its orchard of date palms, almost invisible in the early-evening shadows.

What was the expression on his face? Disappointment.

From the vehicle, Al-Medawi made a report to the security detail at the Cyrenian embassy, knowing any response would be too late. Al-

Medawi's driver pulled away but it was impossible to instruct him to give chase. They were facing the opposite direction on the wrong side and, though the car was the smallest available from the embassy pool, it was still hard to navigate the busy arterial traffic.

Al-Medawi thought back to the North African Defence League meeting in the over-large meeting room. Before he reached the embassy, he had time to dictate a second brief message for the attention of Captain Alexandre Lamarque of the French security services, concluding:

'Given this attack on my own person, have you taken sufficient steps for your own, for Mademoiselle Jordane's and for Monsieur Barra's protection?'

14

Alex completed a significant chunk of his mandated AI therapy, then left the canal basin at dusk, using his high-level accreditations to take a closed autodrive through the quiet streets of the restricted zone in the heart of the city. At each intersection, misting devices sprayed extravagant and refreshing sterile water on the wealthy pedestrians. Despite – or because of – going out on his bike, the deep ache in his leg had diminished almost to nothing.

Unencumbered by steering, he sent an encrypted message to Claudine Poiret, asking about the reorganisation of the two security services into one administration, headed by Director Gerest. To his surprise, he received a prompt reply.

Why do you ask?

Because I don't like him.

After a pause, Poiret sent back: *Keep me informed.*

Alex told his autodrive to stop at a brasserie beneath the dome of the Saint-Augustin Basilica, sitting at a pavement table under an awning. His unshaven face and untidy hair were beginning, he thought, successfully to disguise his appearance.

As he was finishing his cold drink, a tiny visual alert popped out of his comm-watch, indicating that Amaury was calling him. He stood up and signalled to the waiter, paid his bill and climbed back into the autodrive, setting it for 'return'. Then, in the privacy of motion, he replied to Amaury's call, casting his friend's image to the heads-up display on the windscreen.

'How are you?'

'I'm in a car hire office in Tangier,' replied Amaury, ignoring the question. 'I'm trying to get a vehicle to drive back to Paris. There's a whole fleet of electric vehicles available with ranges of four-hundred kilometres and more and …'

Amaury's voice became broken and inaudible as Alex passed an imposing building belonging to one of the ministries.

'I didn't hear that,' he said, raising his voice, as if volume would help penetrate the accidental comms shadow.

'I said there's a whole fleet,' Amaury replied. 'But they're all bricked for an automatic software upgrade.'

'Don't they roll those out one vehicle at a time?'

'That would make more sense. Hang on. I think we have progress.'

Alex waited, watching the people on the pavements – wealthy people, advantaged people, living secure, cushioned lives, protected by money and privilege.

'Yeah,' said Amaury. 'This is happening.'

There was another pause and Alex thought about the fragility of the networked world. A routine upgrade could take an entire fleet of cars out of circulation.

'Okay,' said Amaury, 'Tangier to Tarifa where I will take the world's longest shower, then Madrid by lunchtime tomorrow. North to Bilbao and across the border to you in Biarritz.'

'No, I'm in Paris.'

'Okay, not Biarritz.'

Amaury sounded upbeat but brittle. In a few words, Alex told him about the attempt on his life.

'So, good news,' Amaury replied. 'You killed another one of them.'

That's one way of looking at it, thought Alex.

'My point is, Amaury, you must also be a target.'

100

'Yeah.'

'So, I'm asking you, I'm asking myself, is this road trip a good idea?'

'Only you know what I'm doing. I have all tracking apps disabled.'

'When did you become a surveillance expert?'

'When did you start to worry so much?'

'When I was almost too late. When we were all almost too late.'

There was a pause.

'Okay,' said Amaury briskly. 'I've got the key-fob. I'll see you in a couple of days.'

'Log your route somewhere, just in case,' Alex suggested.

'If I do that, there'll be someone who knows where I am, won't there? *Hasta luego*.'

Amaury cut the connection and his image disappeared from the heads-up display. Alex realised he had lost all sense of where he was, the autodrive moving smoothly and quietly through the depopulated streets. Then, all at once, there was the Bastille column, the vantage point for the attempt on his life.

The autodrive avoided the major intersection, weaving its way through side-streets. He got out and the vehicle trundled away to find a recharging point. A civilian security guard accompanied by a uniformed police officer checked his credentials.

'You know I'm the person you're here to protect?' he asked them.

'Protocol,' said the guard.

The police officer looked starstruck and Alex knew what was coming before she spoke.

'It's an honour, captain,' she told him with a kind of childish breathlessness.

'Thanks.'

Back on board, he removed his leg brace and did a few stretches, as defined in his physio program. Flexibility was about 95%. There was a little heaviness from the persistent haematoma on his hip and thigh, but that too had lessened, slowly being reabsorbed into his body.

'Wake.'

The encircling holos filled the cabin and he walked through them to his desk. He waved a hand to swipe back through the information on Davide Castile, finding a log of military achievements, but also reprimands: 'deviating from agreed tactics'; 'insubordination'; 'putting at risk, with recklessness, the success of an action'. Alex knew that a soldier from a less privileged background would never have achieved promotion with that charge list, whereas Castile's rank had risen five times in a relatively short period. Then, in a biosphere experiment, he had hit a ceiling after 'disobeying lawful authority in order to subvert discipline'.

Appended to the biographical information was a link to 'associates', including Arnaud Sy, the man Castile had sent to infiltrate Lenca. He had a vehicle maintenance business not too far from the canal basin – after a good night's sleep, within walking distance.

The next morning, soon after dawn, the time when most people employed in day shift manual trades began work, Alex made his way to a mixed neighbourhood not far from the train lines running southeast out of Paris from the Gare de Lyon. He had already introduced himself and was now sitting on a bench under a dusty hoheria tree, opposite Arnaud Sy's vehicle repair shop.

Sy was a tall man with heavy hands, swollen with hard manual labour and, perhaps, the chemicals that his work brought him into contact with – hydrocarbon fuels, lubricants, brake fluids and so on. Their conversation had been interrupted by the arrival of a customer to whom Sy was now explaining the work he had done on a twenty-five-year-old hybrid vehicle. The customer was elderly and intended never to buy another car.

In the same way, thought Alex, *that he must be on his last dog, if he has a dog.*

'Your vehicle is basically illegal,' Sy was saying. 'I mean, it isn't, but that's because of the dispensations due to its age. Nothing like this has been allowed to be manufactured for personal use since 2030.'

'But if we continue to maintain it,' said the elderly customer, a man with thin wisps of white hair across his sunburnt scalp, 'as we have maintained it all this time, we are doing more for the environment than someone who buys a new vehicle.'

'You don't have to tell me,' said Sy, impatiently. 'But anyway, it's done. I was telling you; it's done.'

'You've fixed it?'

'Sweet as a nut.'

'Oh, I am pleased.'

Alex watched as the transaction was completed, updating the digital paperwork on the vehicle's on-board computer, then carrying out a peer-to-peer transfer of funds. The old man drove away, looking very happy at the wheel, accelerating prudently so as not to kick into operation the anti-social petrol-driven element of his engine.

Sy went inside the repair shop, into deep shade, and re-emerged carrying an open bottle of beer, despite the early hour. He crossed the road and sat next to Alex on the bench beneath the hoheria tree.

'This is my last one,' he said, by way of apology.

'Maybe too early for me, anyway,' said Alex. 'So, you were saying …?'

'Davide Castile was fine,' Sy resumed, without preamble. 'A normal officer, right? The sort you feel you can trust to make a decision, whether or not that decision turns out to be the right one.' He drank from the neck of his bottle. 'You know what I mean?'

'You mean someone you can rely on to take a view, rather than hesitate?'

'You're a military man. You want that, right?'

'It depends.'

'Obviously, it depends, but you want that.'

'Sometimes you want someone who quickly decides to do nothing.'

'Fine, you don't want to hear. I don't need to tell you all this.'

Sy made to stand up, but Alex needed him to stay.

'I'm not arguing with you. I need to understand him. You worked for him after you left the army and infiltrated the Lenca protest group?'

Sy nodded.

'Early on at the dam and before, when they were disrupting a fracking site. I was with them till they clocked me, yeah? They're not stupid. But I didn't want that life anymore anyway, and Castile had changed. I just wanted evenings and weekends, you know, and this job …' He waved a hand towards the garage. 'It's quiet but it's meaningful.'

'Tell me, how and why did Castile change?'

Sy half-laughed.

'Isolation in the experiment.'

This was one of the things Alex had read about on Castile's list of reprimands.

'The biosphere?'

'Eight months sealed in for a meaningless volunteer trial that was never going anywhere, never going to teach anybody anything they didn't already know. It was like they were chosen for conflict, not harmony, you know? They weren't being challenged to survive. They were being observed like rats in a lab to see how they behaved.'

'That sounds entirely plausible, but wasn't there a genuine survivalist element?' Alex summarised the data in Gerest's briefing. 'The biosphere was supposed to teach the administration about how their subjects would cope with very limited options, sealed into a dome with nothing but their own training and ingenuity to guide them.'

Sy shook his head.

'They weren't supposed to need ingenuity. It ought to have run like clockwork, just following orders.' He drank again from the neck of the bottle. 'And it did, for five months, maybe six. Day after day, just doing what they were told. In the end, though, how do you think that was ever going to turn out?'

'They were supposed to become self-sufficient?'

'Yeah, but after six months they were starving. The hydroponics and the atmospheric scrubbers were failing. Turned out they didn't know how to fix them.'

'How come?'

'Castile lied about his qualifications. He claimed to have completed the relevant training when he was first apprenticed into his family's company. You know he started out on the bottom rung like any other grunt? But the docs were forged or lies, or given to him because the minions in his organisation were always going to do anything the heir asked for.'

'He put them all at risk by falsifying his credentials. Then someone died.'

'Salim tried to escape. He breached the dome and fell from the fence – caught on the wire, gashing his thigh. He bled out from his femoral artery.'

'People don't often bleed out, especially if they get medical attention.'

'At that point, the medic was sick. I mean actually sick, with vomit and delirium – no use to anybody. Had to be woken up from their cot and …' Sy drank. 'Too late.'

Alex sat back.

'And Castile?'

'He behaved as he'd been trained to behave and … Look, it doesn't matter. You asked me to tell you about it and that's what I'm doing but I really don't care either way.'

'Tell me about the animals,' said Alex.

'The biosphere was big enough for a separate dome for livestock. They were supposed to look after them so they might breed with the livestock brought by the replacement crews that were meant to come after. The idea was to mimic the colonisation of Mars or interstellar travel, as if that's possible in any way.'

'They were "supposed to"?'

'They ate them – every damn one. Oh, and you know they had coffee bushes as well as the hydroponics under the biosphere, crops ready to pick and roast and grind? Castile told them he'd seen this thing about some author percolating his coffee then putting his coffee back through another load of beans.'

'Balzac famously did that,' said Alex, 'writing a cycle of novels about all kinds of people called *La Comédie Humaine*.'

'Right. Anyway, Castile said it would make this crazy-strong caffeinated power-blaster to help them get through more work.'

'What work?'

'Cutting trees, stripping bark, weaving branches, building a new encampment.'

'But why? They had a perfectly serviceable biosphere. I mean, that was the name of the project. They weren't supposed to go outside it.'

'Yeah, but they had to, didn't they, with the atmosphere scrubbers failing. Once Salim breached the dome, Castile told them they were going to bust out and start at zero, take the outer fence as the new perimeter.'

'And the external supervisors of the experiment?'

'That's what I'm telling you. They didn't care about the biosphere habitat. They just wanted to study the human beings under pressure.'

'So they didn't intervene when, a couple of months later, the biosphere was burnt down?'

Sy laughed. 'They destroyed it in a coffee-craze. Maybe there were other drugs involved – painkillers or tranx. I wish I'd been there. I mean, what an adventure. Survival of the fittest, right?'

'The word "fittest" refers to being well suited, not the strongest. Castile was creating circumstances that no one was suited to.'

Sy looked at the ground.

'How do you know so much about it?' Alex probed.

'I applied to be one of them, but my buddy Salim got in ahead of me.

Better on the written tests, probably. But there were two of us held in reserve, in case of sickness, who could go in and make up the numbers, because there was still this fiction that there was a balance of skills and experience in the team, blah-blah-blah …'

'Like a substitute in a football match?'

'Yeah.'

'But you never got called onto the pitch?'

'No, but we watched what was going on, me and the other sub.'

'And your friend Salim was the one who bled out on the wire.'

'What does it matter, man? People die. You don't join the army to live a long life, do you?'

Not like that, thought Alex.

'And Castile?' he asked. 'Do you know why he volunteered?'

'He said it was practice for what was to come.'

'Meaning?'

'It was a thing he used to say – that there would be darkness, that a storm was coming. I don't know – some kind of prepper crap.'

Sure, thought Alex. *That sounds right.*

Another customer arrived, a neighbour, a youngish woman wanting help with an air source heat pump. Sy asked Alex if that was all and Alex told him it was more than enough. The mechanic locked up his workshop and followed the woman to a four-storey building at the end of the street, carrying a heavy bag of tools and a diagnostic computer, the woman talking at him as if they were old friends.

And why shouldn't they have been? Perhaps they were having an affair, the fault on the pump just a pretext? As Sy had suggested, life was short.

Alex waited a while in the shade of the hoheria tree. He thought about Davide Castile. Was the man unbalanced? It looked like he had been back then. Anyone might become a little strange under the pressure of an experiment like the biosphere. But then, when he left the army, did he carry that trauma through into a life of extraordinary

107

power and influence? And was it just a coincidence of terminology – 'darkness', 'storm' – or was he connected to the cult of destruction? The Coming Darkness conspiracy had been years in preparation. Or was he an innocent prepper, certain that the 'end times' were on the horizon, looking after Number One, thinking about his 'stronghold'?

Alex considered why he'd never come across Davide Castile before – in his work or in the news. Probably because Castile had people dedicated to keeping him out of the public eye. But that anonymity had been spoiled by the eighteen-month protest at the Pyrenean dam – the one Arnaud Sy had spied on until he chose a 'quiet' and 'meaningful' life with 'evenings and weekends' instead.

And, to Alex's concern, Mariam was there, at her aunt's farm lower down the valley.

He asked his comm-watch for a swift data search of the location, finding the place was known as the Saint-Médard valley. He followed an etymological trail, discovering that Saint-Médard was a bishop of the early French church.

And he was the patron saint of storms.

15

Nobody pays attention to you if you adopt the right attitudes, the correct demeanour. There was a skill to it – almost an art – a way of blending into the background and seeming insignificant, because one has chosen to be insignificant.

It was a skill that Amaury had never mastered.

He was in a service station just outside Madrid, waiting for his electric hire car to recharge. He had drained the battery to the dregs, driving fast, accelerating sharply, braking hard, all the time with the windows open and the air-con running. He was looking at snacks to buy for the road – a Serrano ham sandwich in a paper wrapper, a glass bottle of yoghurt drink, a pack of three protein bars. When he reached the checkout, the camera system had already calculated his purchases and he paid by touching the 'tick' symbol on his comm-watch.

He went outside, feeling eyes on him, curious eyes, wondering why he, Amaury, moved like he was about to start a fight or had just come from a fight. He shut his eyes in the partial shade of the brise-soleil. It was quite an old building and had been built with a southern aspect, to face the light, not cower from it. He did a thing he knew Alex was in the habit of doing – counting his breaths, steadying his pulse, emptying his mind.

Yeah – the first thing and the second thing, the pulse and the breaths, I can do them. The third thing, not so much.

What normal person can empty their mind? The moment you try, you just think about all the things you're trying not to think about, adding a layer of extra thinking to some already desperate thoughts.

He drained his glass bottle and returned to the yoghurt dispenser to refill it, checking out a second time. He paused at the map on the wall, showing the principal road routes towards the Atlantic Ocean and the semi-autonomous Basque Country. Driving north was a blessing on a hot day. Once he had a full charge, another five hours would get him to Bilbao. It would only remain to find somewhere to stay – a motel of some kind in the nowhere territories beyond the suburbs, away from the lives of normal people.

Separate and isolated, where he belonged.

When Amaury left the service station, one of the people who had noticed him – a man with sly eyes and a leather waistcoat – spoke briefly into his cheap phone, sharing what he had seen: the hero Amaury Barra buying snacks and tracing a finger along a line on a map, heading north.

Four hours later, Amaury was listening to a radio station that specialised in historical documentaries, discussing the impact of rising sea levels on the eastern seaboard of the United States of America: drowning marginal coastlines; habitat loss; pressure on the great seafront cities of New Orleans, Tampa, Miami, Charleston, Boston, even New York itself. He found it restful. The past was done with, unalterable. For the moment, the present was under control. Only the future could still cause pain.

He only silenced the audio when he had gone far enough to almost smell the Atlantic Ocean, thinking that it was a shame that Alex and Mariam were no longer in Biarritz, just over the frontier into France – another couple of hours, maybe three, depending on border and hygiene controls. On another day, he might have found a charge point and driven on, joining them on their hotel terrace late at night, watching the bright foam of the breakers in the silver moonshine.

He was bored with the asphalt endlessly unfurling in front of him, the dry grass of the verges, the billboards that became somehow more contemptible the more you saw them, the same images repeated, the same advertising catchphrases, until finally they switched and became welcome breaks in the monotony, almost old friends.

The motel he chose was a low, boxy building on a roundabout, with car parking spaces in front. He checked in at an automated reception, the scorching day conducted back up through the soles of his shoes from the superheated pavement.

Three weeks of washing in a bucket had not endeared him to 'the simple life'. He felt dirty again. The 'world's longest shower' in Tarifa hadn't been enough. He paid an additional fee for extra water and a narrow slot spat out a slip of printed paper with a six-digit code and a room number.

The motel was two-storey and wasn't doing great business. All the rooms faced west – too hot, too bright. But the sun was about to go down and Amaury was used to living without climate control, stifled beneath his mosquito net. And he was feeling the need to economise. Whatever job a hero and a cripple could hope for from External Security, he suspected it might not be rewarded at the same level as his previous full-agent status.

His room was on the ground floor, the last in the row. He moved his vehicle to the space in front, got out and inputted the six-digit code, then pushed open the door into an unwelcoming antiseptic space: vinyl flooring; plastic panelled walls; a faint dampness and an odour of disinfectant, as if something unpleasant or shameful had occurred that someone had worked hard to efface.

Not true. Just the hygiene protocol.

He went back outside to connect his vehicle to the electricity supply for an overnight trickle recharge, then looked round, wondering who would come and when. There was bound to be someone. He had seen the sharpening of interest in the eyes of the man in the leather waistcoat, back at the service station outside Madrid.

He stretched his arms behind his back and rolled his neck. The parking spaces in front of the six hotel units were separated by metre-high fences smothered with rosemary and lavender. If someone wanted to approach him, it would have to be through the only door and he had a useful device that would make that an awkward proposition.

In the asymmetrical cathedral in the heart of Bilbao, built in a mish-mash of styles from the fourteenth century onwards – when the town was little more than a fishing village – a service was ending. Many local people liked to attend, but the ceremony was really designed for the pilgrims who used Bilbao and its Roman Catholic temple as a waypoint on their pilgrimage all along the northern hills of the Iberian Peninsula to Compostela. In that city, the pilgrims would take part in another identical service in another medieval cathedral, also dedicated to Santiago, Saint James the Great, perhaps the brother of Jesus Christ.

The service was quite long, especially the consumption of the symbolic bread and wine, although it had been several years since traditional methods had been abandoned for reasons of community hygiene. Now, the faithful brought their own bread to serve as the 'host', their own wine as metaphorical 'blood' for the priest to bless and transubstantiate. When, finally, it was over, the assistant verger, a young man with wide eyes named Jaime Moreno, began tidying away the thurible and the crucifix and the acolytes' candles in a corner of the robing room in the south transept. He took off his own drab cassock and hung it on a peg. From the locker beneath, he retrieved his keys and a cheap phone that blinked at him, indicating a pending message.

He flipped the phone open and pressed two buttons to read it.

His eyes opened even wider.

Amaury stepped into the shower, setting the temperature to tepid, feeling his skin and muscles contract at the impact. Once he was wet, he stopped the flow and soaped himself with gel from the dispenser on the wall.

Yes, someone would come. It was part of his training to be aware of everyone around him, for his brain to analyse what strangers were doing with their day – hurried or relaxed, focused or vague, attentive or lost inside their own thoughts. Standing outside the service station, drinking from his glass bottle, he had seen the face of the watcher with the sly eyes, reflected in the windscreen of a car parked just outside the door. He hadn't wanted a second drink, but he had gone to buy one so that he could study him in peripheral vision. Then he had looked at the map and traced his direction north to Bilbao, apparently unaware that he was giving away his route, but actually doing it on purpose.

What had he told Alex when he heard of the attempt on his life?

So, good news. You killed another one of them.

And he had meant it. If they come for you, you can kill them, no questions asked, no procedure to go through, no warrants to draw up and deliver, just self-defence and hot pursuit and all the rest of it.

Amaury turned the water back on. He knew he was a target, too.

The assistant verger from Bilbao cathedral had a biddable cousin – a civilian unconnected to the Coming Storm – who worked with the police department and had access to street cameras. Number plate recognition at the hotel complex found their target, via a private surveillance system integrated into the city feeds.

'Is that him?' asked the cousin.

'Yes,' said Jaime Moreno.

'Is he part of the church?' asked the cousin, innocently.

'That's right. I've been asked to give a welcome,' he lied. 'That's the reason. I'm supposed to look after him, but I lost his contact details.'

In reality, the assistant verger was worried. Barra looked tough. He would have to get someone else's support – someone with more muscle.

113

Amaury finished his shower, draining his water allowance completely dry, and stepped out onto the non-slip textured vinyl of the bathroom floor. He dried himself patiently with a beige non-bleached towel, taking care not to rub, avoiding heat from friction, just dabbing away the excess cold water, leaving himself damp so that the latent heat of evaporation could continue its work, cooling his body. Then he lay on the soft bed and dozed.

'I want to do it,' said Jaime, six hours later. 'I want to be the one who kills him.'

His companion – a big man with huge arms and a jowly face – was, simultaneously, a stranger and an ally. Jaime thought he was local, working at the docks or on the boats, because he carried a faint odour of salt and fish and was the owner of a slim filleting knife, long and thin with a highly-sharpened edge. Jaime had contacted him via the conspiracy's end-to-end encrypted dark-web comms, and met him before dawn near the motel, showing him a rectangle of white card with a faintly-embossed image of sunrise through clouds.

'Stab him half a dozen times quickly in the area of the heart,' the big man told him. 'I will prevent him from fighting back. One of the blows will kill him.'

Jaime nodded.

'I can do that.'

'He's the one with the robot hand, isn't he? We'll have to be careful of that.'

'Maybe he takes it off to sleep?'

'Probably. Do you have the code?'

'I can get it from the check-in bot. If he's driving a long way, he'll probably wait for the sun so as not to drain his batteries with headlights, but we should still go soon.' There was a pause, then he asked: 'What would you have done if the Coming Darkness had succeeded?'

'I have a safe place in the mountains,' the big man told him. 'Everything was ready. A new life was waiting for me.'

'You have a stronghold,' said Jaime, nodding. 'What will you do now?'

'I will wait for the Coming Storm.'

In another 'stronghold', on the far side of the Atlantic Ocean, the man in the electric wheelchair was once more watching the waves from the high terrace that completely encircled his impressive home. He too was waiting for the Coming Storm and thinking about the future population of his island home.

How many humans would be enough to serve his needs?

Back in prehistory, tectonic forces had thrust the peak of Haré about 120 meters above sea level, easily enough to cope with the rises predicted for his lifetime and for his son's. The island was the same length as a marathon race and between 15 and 30 kilometres wide, honeycombed with crevices, caves and pits. It had a tropical climate, with annual rainfall of around 1.7 metres. The terrace he was slowly circumnavigating was designed to harvest that precipitation into enormous underground cisterns, making his home immune from drought.

A stronghold can only survive in places where raindrops reliably fall.

The population of Haré had reached a peak of around seven thousand in 2024, but subsequent waves of pathogenic infection had reduced it by twenty per cent. The islanders – of whom he was not one – were almost exclusively of indigenous descent and spoke a language akin to the Nengone of the Indian Ocean, evidence of that people's extraordinary ancestral spirit of exploration. He looked down on them from his high citadel with a mixture of condescension and contempt. He distrusted their fervent Christianity but admired the fact that their communities – *chefferies* – were closed to outsiders. He approved the determined spirit of independence that meant that the grave of one of the leaders of the island's independence movement – assassinated forty-eight years before – was, to this day, regularly garlanded with flowers.

He manoeuvred his wheelchair to a halt beside a table laid with a starched white cloth and fine silverware. At the same moment, a servant brought his supper, even though time by human clocks had little meaning for him. It comprised air-dried ham from his own pigs, flatbread made with grain from his own fields. He could survive here – wait out the Coming Storm – though the same could not be said for every one of the remaining five-and-a-half thousand Haréans.

How many was enough, though?

That was a question to which, thus far, he had not found a definitive answer.

For the old man in the Parisian basement, it was the middle of the night and he could not sleep, contemplating the prison inside which he had voluntarily concealed himself.

Had there been any point? Had he been able to achieve anything of importance?

No.

He was like a chess piece that everyone believed had been removed from the board and returned to the box. Yes, he was safe from harm but he was also impotent, futile.

Would the time come when it would be useful to re-emerge? He hoped so.

He got out of his chair and, awkwardly, his elderly limbs complaining, lay down on the floor, preparing to engage in some stretching exercises designed to encourage his circulation. He felt vibrations through the floor and assumed it was a Métro train going past, carrying normal people doing normal things, people who had no idea that – contrary to the message promoted by government and the streams – the threat of Darkness would soon give way to the threat of the Coming Storm.

Back on Haré, the servant cleared the table. The man in the electric wheelchair had barely touched his meal. He was perturbed – not by difficulties, but by a coincidence that seemed too propitious, too harmonious with his aims.

He knew, as everyone with a connection to the streams did, that 'the man who saved the world', Alexandre Lamarque, was romantically involved with Mariam Jordane. Unlike most people, the old man knew her tragic family history, too. And he was aware that she was now in the Saint-Médard valley, a location he had targeted – because of the coincidence of its name and because of the Castile Energie dam – for the Coming Storm.

Problem or opportunity?

That was another question to which he had so far found no definitive answer.

16

In the end, Amaury slept until almost dawn. When their presence finally woke him, he didn't, at that point, know who 'they' were.

He had positioned a proximity and motion sensor on the bonnet of his car. It was parked just three metres from where he lay on a soft bed behind a well-insulated wall, in a current of forced air that fell from a chiller vent in the ceiling. The sensor woke him by sending a signal to his comm-watch, making it vibrate on the night-stand like an angry electronic insect. He was still tired and wasn't instantly fully alert, his muscles stiff and his skeleton misaligned from the long day of driving.

And the chilled air, for God's sake, falling like a painful draught, when the temperature outside was no worse than twenty-three or twenty-four degrees, completely liveable, definitely sleepable.

And the noise the air-con made, a security risk in itself, potentially covering up more important sounds.

Amaury popped out a 3D live schematic of his surroundings with two dots indicating two human beings approaching his door, their presence tracked by the sensor's lidar. As they approached, he refitted his prosthetic, inserting the probes, tightening the velcros, feeling the mechanical right hand displace the phantom of his obliterated human one.

Why hadn't he called for back-up?

Because he was on foreign soil and it would have taken forever.

Because he wanted the opportunity to kill them himself.

He arranged his pillows and quilt to look like there was still someone in the bed and went into the bathroom. Its window was designed not to open but, before going to sleep, he had used his pocket knife to ease out the beads that held the triple-glazed panel in place, protecting himself with another sensor-alarm. Soon, it was just a square space in the wall. He positioned two damp beige towels over the bottom edge of the frame in order to cover the sharp edges and used the edge of the toilet seat to climb up and out, allowing his body to slip down the outside wall, landing on his hands in a gravel courtyard designed to allow quick drainage of storm rains. The sharp stones hurt the heel of his left hand so he let his prosthetic take most of his weight, then dropped into a forward roll.

He waited, listening. Might there be someone else on the far side of the hotel? No, it was just him in a soakaway-garden planted with drought-tolerant trees and shrubs.

He crept along to the end of the block, past another five bathroom windows, making more noise than he wanted, but the hum of ventilator fans masked the crunching gravel. He skirted the end of the building, a hot air-con exhaust on the back of his neck, peering through the gap between the concrete blockwork and a rain downpipe. Above the fence and the rosemary and the lavender, he could see two of them standing by the door to his room. One looked young, a slim man or maybe a woman. The other was taller and heavier.

He bent down, picked up a piece of gravel and flicked it with his thumbnail. It struck the windscreen of a car ten or twelve metres away with a sharp 'plick'. The two figures turned and he was able to see the shapes of their faces, an abstract arrangement of shadows. Their heads went close together and he knew they were talking about him and about the sound of the gravel on the windscreen and wondering what to do next.

Who were they? Not professionals. Not trained assassins. They were too hesitant. They had come without a plan. They were only now debating the best way to kill him. And he caught a glimpse of a blade, passed from hand to hand. That was the futile weapon they had chosen.

Then, suddenly, they didn't look so foolish. The slim assailant inputted a six-digit code and Amaury heard the door unlock. One of them – or perhaps an unknown accomplice – had hacked the hotel system.

He saw them slip inside and heard scuffling and a sequence of repeated dull blows. He sprinted from his position, hearing their raised voices, no longer taking care not to be overheard. They would straight away discover that they were stabbing his pillows and his quilt. Then he was in the doorway and they turned to look at him, an immature young man and a labourer of some kind with strong arms, low brows and an expression of dull surprise.

The young man snatched up the lamp from the nightstand and tried to throw it at him but it caught on its power cable and fell to the floor between them. The big man grabbed the boy's wrist and took the knife, grasping it downwards in his fist, ready to stab. The boy fled in panic, past the end of the bed, into the bathroom. Amaury imagined him jumping up and slipping away through the unglazed window opening – probably much more easily than he had done it, being slimmer and younger, though not necessarily more agile. The big man held his ground.

'Put the knife down,' said Amaury.

'Or you could leave,' the big man replied in a surprisingly calm voice.

'That's not a choice I'm offering you,' said Amaury.

'Call it a stand-off,' said the big man. 'You leave then I leave.'

Amaury was watching the man's eyes. They were steady. Conflict was something he had faced before – and he had the wisdom not to fight if fighting could be avoided.

But it couldn't, not on this occasion.

Amaury took a step closer and, as he had expected, the man retreated, his calves against the bed frame. Now the big man was at a serous disadvantage, trapped and easy to overbalance.

'Why don't you sit down?' Amaury asked.

Before he had finished his apparently innocent question, Amaury spun on the ball of his right foot and planted his left heel in the man's throat. The bed prevented the big man from stepping away from the lightning-quick attack and he took the full force of it against his windpipe, dropping his blade, snatching his hands up, not to protect himself from another blow but to grasp his damaged trachea. Amaury retracted his leg then struck him again, sharply, his heel sinking deep into his solar plexus. The big man was forced to sit by his knees buckling against the edge of the divan. Amaury picked up the fallen lamp and crashed its heavy base against the side of his head.

Outside, Jaime, the assistant verger, was running.

'Hail, Mary, full of grace, the Lord is with thee. Blessed art thou amongst women and blessed is the fruit of thy womb,' he panted.

Like Amaury, he skirted the end of the block but then ran away through the car park to a quiet roundabout and the access road to the main route into the city. The unaccustomed exercise and panic left him breathless. He stumbled and almost fell, crouching on the verge. A truck went past, its lights dazzling, then there was quiet.

He listened. No, he was not being pursued – at least not yet. Then he had another thought. Had he been recognised? No, of course not; he was nobody. But what about the cameras, the same cameras he himself had used to track Amaury Barra?

What had he been thinking? He hadn't been thinking. He had simply acted, carried away by an adolescent fantasy of … Of what? Of decisive violence, of significance.

'You've been a fool,' he told himself.

He would go back to camera control and speak to his biddable cousin, find a way to persuade him to erase the recordings.

And then, no more. Never again.

Amaury was sitting on the bed, the filleting knife in his human hand. Up close, he realised his would-be assailant smelt of fish. The man was struggling to breathe, his hands clasped around his throat, supporting the damaged structure of his trachea to ensure the passage of air into his lungs.

Amaury pulled one of the man's hands away and saw the panic in his eyes. The man was strong, despite his physical distress, and resisted, but Amaury closed his prosthetic fist like a vice, the bones grinding together under the pressure. The big man tried to protest, but his voice was husky and inaudible.

'I know, said Amaury, 'that you people don't know much. That's the nature of your organisation.' He squeezed a little harder and the desperate man's eyes widened. 'You have a cellular structure. If caught, each of you can only give one thing away.' He squeezed some more and heard a crack – felt it, in fact, through the mechanical musculature of his prosthetic – and the man gasped and whimpered. 'Tell me that one thing you know that could make me want to inform the police that you are useful.'

The man's eyes were wet, as if he was crying, but Amaury knew it was just a stress response to the pain.

'Nothing,' he whispered. 'I know nothing.'

Outside, Jaime had reached the main road. He had his thumb out, trying to get someone to pull over and give him a lift. It was something he had seen people do in films but had never tried in real life. It seemed unlikely that anyone would stop, but someone did – a van that was part of a charitable meal-service with a distant connection to the cathedral.

'I've, er, been tending to the sick,' Jaime told the driver, the lie forming hesitantly on his lips. 'And I couldn't get back, so ...'

'You seem upset,' said the driver. 'Was it a very unhappy home?'

'And someone stole my mobike, some Blank,' Jaime embroidered in reply, the words tumbling over one another.

'Oh,' said the driver. 'I'm sorry. But their need was almost certainly greater—'

'It was a present from my mother,' Jaime interrupted, the story seeming to grow of its own accord. 'Before she died.'

Then he burst into tears.

'There, there,' said the meal-service driver.

Jaime could see that he was wondering what he had let himself in for.

Amaury didn't believe in 'nothing'. But it seemed to be true. Despite the pain, despite the man's desperate need of medical assistance, the only information he thought to share was the location of his 'stronghold', somewhere in the hills above Zaragoza.

'You're sure?' Amaury asked, his prosthetic still clamped round the man's carpal joint.

Almost imperceptibly, he nodded his head.

Amaury still had the filleting knife in his weaker human hand. He liked the feel of it, the way the finely-sharpened edge had been worn almost concave by the application of a steel. The sun was just up, too, shining in through the empty frame of the bathroom window, through the open doorway, painting the knife and the big man's strained features yellow-orange.

Official interrogation was the obvious next step, but …

Amaury stood up and let go of the damaged wrist, allowing the man to tip onto his side, ending up half off the bed. Then gravity took over and he slumped heavily to the floor.

Amaury pondered putting him in the recovery position, but found he no longer cared. His would-be assailant had become something abstract and separate from real life, an object without purpose or meaning.

He went outside, closing the door behind him, seeing the lavender and rosemary borders edged with smooth round stones, each about the size of a honeydew melon. He chose one and used it to smash the digital lock on his bedroom door, setting off an alarm. Then he carefully replaced the stone in the dirt, disconnected his vehicle from trickle-charge, climbed in and put the cheap phone and the filleting knife in the compartment between the two front seats.

He drove away. Once he had found the motorway, he would drive till he found a service station for coffee and a stack of vegetable protein – preferably beyond the border in France – and maybe then he would dictate a statement and tell André Chambon's data recovery team what had happened.

Or maybe he would leave it all behind and never think about any of it ever again.

17

Mariam's journey south had been uneventful. Despite her refusal of a security detail, Sébastien had sent a two-team with her on the train, discreetly seated in an adjacent carriage. The swiftness of her departure meant that she had not, in any case, been followed by the press. On arrival, Mariam had given in, sharing a vehicle from the nearest mainline railway station. Then they had learnt from the owner of the café whence Sara was in the habit of placing her video calls that the place had twice been visited by journalists.

'It's fine,' Mariam had told the two agents. 'I can look after myself.'

'No, Mademoiselle Jordane. We will take rooms here and be on hand should you need us – even if it's just to ensure your privacy…'

Mariam had lugged her bag all the way uphill to the farm, finding her aunt on her knees in the large vegetable patch outside the farmhouse. Sara had greeted her with a gesture that meant: 'I must finish this before I speak to you properly.'

Mariam had gone inside and found the place unchanged since her last visit, a week spent helping Sara and her cousin Benjamin – a wiry innocent-faced man who had lived his entire life in the mountains – to rebuild a dry-stone wall that had collapsed, undermined by unseasonally heavy rain. She'd made herself coffee in an old metal jug, pouring the liquid through a strainer. After drinking it, she had taken the grounds outside to mulch the marigolds, planted here and there to deter insect-pests. Then she had knelt down alongside her aunt, mirroring her actions, twitching the weeds from beneath the valuable food-plants. They had worked in silence until sunset, shuffling along the rows, then eaten a sober meal, speaking only of what was in front of them.

The next day had passed in the same vein – and the next. By the third morning, for Mariam, the peace and quiet and her aunt's reticence had become a balm. Her long-held sense of guilt – that she had not gone straight home and saved not just her mother but her sisters, too – had been transformed into no more than an uncomfortable burden on her heart, rather than a wound.

That same morning, Alex made another circuit of the pedestrianised embankments on his bike, invigorated by returning fitness and vanishing pain. On his return, he avoided the congestion of the street market on Boulevard Richard Lenoir, clinging on by its fingernails to its traditional intersection of rural and urban ways of life. At the street door of his mother's building, he buzzed her fourth-floor apartment, without reply.

Probably out shopping, he thought. *I'll leave her to it.*

He was right and he was wrong.

It was easy to tell people: 'Yes, I feel well' or 'Really, I feel fine'. Easier than the alternative which was: 'I don't feel right.'

What did that mean? That one was ill, still? Or just convalescing? Or tired, perhaps, with the aftermath of illness, drug therapies, the mechanical ventilation, isolation, inactivity, loss of focus and drive? All those were real things. But none of them solved the problem of feeling 'not right', not oneself, diminished.

Gloria Lamarque was just one hundred metres from her own front door, unaware that Alex had just called, watching a team of primary-age children harvesting the apples from the orchard that ran down the middle of the boulevard. How old were they? Nine or ten, perhaps?

They were accompanied by two teachers and she imagined they might use the apples in their home economics classes. It was a good system – a circular system – learning about the life cycle of the fruit trees, seeing the care required if they were to produce food, to benefit humanity.

That's good, she thought. *Life goes on.*

But not for Professor Fayard. He was dead.

She had dismissed her security team, remotely managed by André Chambon, picked up her shopping basket and made her way to Boulevard Richard Lenoir, then sat gratefully on a handy bench. How far had she walked? No more than three hundred metres.

You are a poor old thing, she told herself.

The market was 'a poor old thing', too. The way of life it represented – plenty, choice, the tactile experience of shopping – was dying. There used to be half a dozen butchers selling meat from their own animals – or from farmers they had known all their lives. The same number of olive stalls. And three or four weathered growers selling purple garlic and almost nothing else, maybe a few onions and leeks. Others with hardware and cleaning products or fashionable and utilitarian clothing, though who would buy clothing on the street without being able to try it on she never could understand. Poor people, she supposed. But everyone was poor, these days, in comparison to the 'golden age' of a generation before.

Yes, that was the nature of the new economy. The middle classes occupied properties that were worth less than the debts they had signed up to, the money they had borrowed to pay for them. Meanwhile the poor scraped by, living hand to mouth, and the Blanks hid themselves and subsisted like insects in the cracks.

What is the point of it all, if tomorrow has no chance of being any better than today?

Gloria stood up from the bench. She knew depression was a hangover from her illness. She knew that tiredness and muscular weakness would persist until she became active enough to counteract them. Unfortunately, her body had become used to its 'new normal' of convalescence.

Would she ever have the energy and drive to fight back? Of course she would. She was only middle-aged – late-ish middle aged. She wasn't on the downslope into frailty and loss of independence.

Well, she was, of course. Everyone was. But not the steep downslope where everything accelerates. Just a gentle incline for the time being.

Someone carrying a pile of empty vegetable crates nudged her on their way past, unable to see clearly beyond their burden, apologising indistinctly. Gloria sat down again.

Yes, poorly; properly poorly.

She checked her med-watch. It was new and unfriendly, not a cheerful analogue dial with hands that circled a mechanical axle. It had a dark digital screen too big for her thin wrist and a chunky square face she was obliged to wear tight to her skin in order to provide permanent diagnostic surveillance. She tapped the dark screen. The time was just after ten. Late, really.

Gloria had spent thirty years of her life rising at six-thirty, then heading straight to her desk to squeeze in a little independent study before the demands of the day. Now, she was doing well if she was dressed and out of doors before the dark shift went home.

The digital clock faded to reveal a warning icon that she didn't entirely understand, like the enigmatic 'check engine' lights on the petrol vehicles of the first half of her life. She knew it meant that she should seek medical advice, but she wasn't sure why. That was the trouble with icons and symbols – they could be interpreted in different ways.

There was a scuffle nearby as a couple of Blanks tried to make off with an armful each of the vegetable crates, and their owner – a man who sold green beans and asparagus and brassicas – saw what they were up to. But it ended in the classic standoff – the grocer telling them to leave his crates alone and the Blanks edging away, warily, fearful of the stick he held in his gnarled farmer's hand, but knowing he wouldn't want to touch them, to let them breathe on him.

Gloria decided she would go to the supermarket instead, a place with temp-control and neg-pressure ventilation and fewer unpredictable human interactions, with produce sealed under bio-film to keep it safe from touch.

Just this once.

The supermarket was close at hand. As she travelled dreamily down an escalator to the food department in the basement, Gloria felt a vibration at her wrist. She glanced at the screen – the same incomprehensible icon, plus another one.

She supposed two icons meant an increase in intensity, a doubling of the warning, whatever it was, or perhaps two things, two deregulations of her metabolism, her physiology. She looked round for a chair.

There was nowhere to sit, just the rows of chilled produce, pristine and blameless.

She put a hand on the edge of the nearest refrigerator, wondering if the machine was really necessary. The stuff at the street market wasn't refrigerated, was it? It didn't go bad overnight.

She crumpled downwards onto the tiled floor. She felt the delicious cool of the tiles against the side of her face, aware of a high-pitched chirruping from her med-watch, calling for assistance.

Yes, this was what she needed – to rest, to sleep. It had been a mistake to get up and go out when there were services that delivered to one's door. There was no need any more to leave the safety of one's home. One could live like a troglodyte hermit in a Parisian apartment.

Her sight became cloudy. She was aware of people near her, close but not too close.

Don't worry, she wanted to say. *They will come for me. The watch will bring them. The watch is in charge, now. All will be well, as far as anything anymore ever can be well.*

*

On a good road in southwest France, Amaury was half-an-hour outside Bordeaux. He had phoned in the events in the motel in Bilbao once he had crossed the border into France.

In his boat on the canal basin, Alex was listlessly responding to the therapy AI's final remorseless questions.

When the emergency response team arrived, they found Gloria's breathing slow and shallow. Their devices were able to translate the messages the med-watch had been trying to communicate – low pulse-oximetry and a dangerous dip in blood pressure. It told them she was a priority patient. Then one of the paramedics recognised her name.

'She's Gloria Lamarque. She's the mother.'

'Which mother?'

'Of Alexandre Lamarque.'

'You're kidding?'

'I'm not.'

They carried her out and put her in their lightweight electric ambulance and drove her southeast to the Rothschild Institute where, the med-watch told them, she had been treated a couple of months before because she was somebody, a woman with connections. They communicated the same important news to the receiving nurse. The information filtered quickly up to the clinician responsible for the care of the mother of the hero, Doctor Labeur, a man in a bright white lab coat with close-cropped grey hair who sat behind an untidy mahogany desk in a sleek office overlooking a shaded courtyard. Before even seeing his patient, he contacted a genetics research lab in Norway. Director Genmis picked up straight away because, in the defeat of the Coming Darkness conspiracy, the two men had formed a bond.

They discussed the way the virus might have concealed itself in 'reservoirs' where synthetic drugs or the body's own immune system found it hard to track down, the testicles in men or the ovaries in women. The eyeballs, too. They were interrupted by a summons from the Intensive Treatment Unit.

'I will go and see her in person,' said Doctor Labeur.

'Please keep me informed,' Genmis replied. 'I feel a sense of responsibility, still.'

In the Saint-Médard valley, Mariam was working at the roots of some persistent weeds that spread rhizomatically underground while vigorously winding their fast-growing green shoots around the raspberry canes. Her aunt brought her an earthenware cup containing sweet mint tea, made the previous day and allowed to cool overnight on a windward windowsill. She drank it, refreshing her determination, but knowing that she could never hope to find every fragment of the fleshy white rhizomes. Later this year or the following spring, the combat would have to begin again.

Because Gloria Lamarque was a person of interest to Damien Gerest, he was notified of her condition before anyone else – even her next of kin. He wondered if it would be wise to inform Claudine Poiret and decided that, for the time being, it wasn't necessary. There was political capital to be made from appearing to solve this new problem alone.

18

By the following morning, Alex had finally completed his mandated hours of therapy, speaking to the algorithm, hearing his own words played back to him, questioning, probing, suggesting, evaluating.

Had it done him any good?

Actually, yes.

Was he surprised by that?

No. Many thousands of hours of genuine human interaction between traumatised patients and well-qualified and experienced practitioners had been processed and systematised to create the AI therapist. Why shouldn't it work?

And, of course, allowing oneself to learn from the past – the lessons that life wants to teach – was always valuable.

What lessons?

That fulfilment is more important than happiness. That the ability to accept inconvenience and discomfort is a kind of superpower. That the advice you most resent is the advice you most need. That the future is out of your control. That human beings have tactics but not strategies and everyone you meet is responding on the fly to circumstances of which they can only ever be victims. That self-sacrifice should never be an end in itself. That sometimes it is important to leave people and situations behind, whatever the short-term cost.

In reality, these were not the recommendations the algorithm came up with. He wasn't privy to those. He supposed they would be communicated up to Damien Gerest who would use them to exert influence upon him, to keep him in line.

Whatever. That was number four again.

The future is out of your control.

His next step was Physical Assessment at the headquarters of the Directorate General for External Security, known as the Piscine in memory of the sports centre absorbed and demolished by its expansion. He hoped for a sign-off there. It was just a question of the strength of the natural mend to the hairline fractures in his leg.

That was what it was all about. Being mended and the strength of the mends.

Alex went outside onto the deck of his boat. It was a humid day, unpleasantly sticky, water vapour rising visibly from the sunken canal basin, thickening the air. On the far bank, on the parapet, maybe sixty metres away, a mob of journalists sprang into action, needing images to fill the 24-hour streams – and he was still news, for what he had done, for his 'hero' status and for the recent attempt on his life. He wondered if Emilie Olsen from the confrontation in the Bordeaux enclave was there.

He left the boat and climbed the stone stairs up to Boulevard Bourdon. The builders had installed a perimeter on the near side that meant he could climb into his autodrive without shouted questions and intrusive lenses. At the Bastille roundabout he saw several journalists on mobikes, armed with cameras with specially-mounted lights designed to penetrate the privacy glass, maybe capture his expression, the nobility of his brow, the sadness or the triumph in his eyes. They followed him northeast, right up to the gate to the underground car park at the Piscine, where he lost them.

Parked at a charging point, he got out, walked between the rows of vehicles then passed through a hygiene station into a basement reception area, where he was provided with a temporary badge that would simultaneously grant him access and track his every movement.

Physical Assessment was another AI therapy on sub-basement level two. The door swung open as he approached, triggered by the RFID component in his badge. He went in, glancing round at the exercise equipment, the plasma displays on the walls, the hemispherical pod of the VR module, the 'soft area' with Pilates stretching devices, rollers and gym-balls. Every aspect of his physical condition would be prodded and probed. Detailed records would be taken, analysed and kept.

Why?

Because that was the nature of civilisation. Whatever terrible things society allowed to happen, bureaucracy preserved it all in a kind of non-judgemental stasis, as if that was a good in itself. He thought again about the bureaucratisation of death in Albert Camus' visionary novel *La Peste*.

'Good morning, Alexandre,' came a synthetic voice from one of the plasmas, the words simultaneously displayed on the screen. 'Your assessment will require between forty-five and fifty minutes. Please read through the sequence displayed on the second monitor.'

Alex ran his eye down the list of activities, frowning because some of them had arcane names from the science of physical training that he couldn't visualise.

'Each activity,' reassured the voice, 'will be accompanied by on-screen illustrations.'

The AI had interpreted his confused expression, of course. The process had been developed and refined by thousands of uses. Alex had no reason to believe, whatever the world might think, that he was special.

Just then, in the Saint-Médard valley, Mariam was drawing water from a well in the time-honoured tradition, tossing down a bucket on a rope – but the rope was made of ultra-modern synthetic paracord and the bucket was carbon fibre.

In an isolation room at the Rothschild Institute, a nurse was cross-checking the output of seven monitors, all of them attached to different parts of Gloria Lamarque's body. The AI had already completed the same task – was completing it every second, in fact – but it had been shown that even unconscious patients benefitted from the shadow-play of human attention.

At his untidy desk two floors above, Doctor Labeur was reading the same data on a large-format tablet, noting that the AI considered that, taken together, Madame Lamarque's symptoms had not breached the next threshold of concern.

Yet.

After forty-eight minutes of vigorous physical activity, Alex was invited to use a bathroom to wash and change back into his street clothes. When he re-emerged into the climate-controlled atmosphere of the physical exam suite, there was a message on the plasma: 'Captain Lamarque to level seven, room one.'

He passed through a hot-desk area with a score of workstations, all occupied. What were the operatives doing? Trying to stop bad things from happening. But the bad things were like a tide, like the sea rolling in, always and forever, wave after wave.

In the elevator, he experienced the unpleasant sensation of it beginning its ascent without him having to speak a command or press a button, simply from the presence of his badge and the fact that the building knew where he should be – a queasy abandonment of autonomy. The elevator came to a halt and the doors opened onto a lounge area with two sofas, a water-and-beverage station and a view east to the tower blocks outside the orbital motorway, beyond the protected perimeter of the historic city.

'Captain Lamarque.' It was the intense André Chambon. He stood up from one of the sofas, pressing his forearm diagonally across his chest, his fingers closed in a fist, by way of greeting. 'I understand you had a close shave.'

'I did, yes.'

Suddenly, another door opened and Damien Gerest was there, fleshy and wide and oddly impressive in his finely-cut suit with his sleek over-black hair.

'*Entrez, messieurs.*'

Chambon was only required for ten minutes or so, providing a report on the follow-up to the attack on Alex's life. He confirmed the shooter locations that Alex had already deduced under fire, cowering in the slimy canal water beneath his boat. He itemised the steps that had been taken to preserve Alex from future attack.

Alex allowed his mind to drift, his eyes on the row of executive toys on the edge of Gerest's desk: a Newton's cradle; a glass bird that periodically dipped its beak into a tiny glass jar as if drinking; a malleable sculpture of tiny, magnetised metal shapes, squeezed into a pinnacle, presumably by Gerest's fleshy fingers. Also on the desk were two paper reports, one focused on lithium mining and the other on hydro-electricity.

'But the environment cannot be made completely secure,' concluded the ginger-haired analyst. 'All the while Captain Lamarque has been recovering from his injuries and pursuing his post-mission therapies, we have been worried that—'

'Have I passed?' Alex interrupted.

Chambon looked at Gerest, uncertain whether it was his place to say.

'Flying colours,' said the director. 'Both psychological and physical.'

'So, I can get back to normal life?' Alex asked, the words echoing ironically in his own head. What would that entail, after all, a normal life? 'Straight away?' he insisted.

'Leave us, Chambon,' said Gerest. The analyst got up without a word. Neither Alex nor Gerest watched him go. 'It's not as simple as that. Your celebrity is simply too much trouble,' the director continued. 'You can work, but you mustn't be too visible.'

Alex took a beat, then nodded in agreement. 'Okay.'

Gerest went on: 'You are aware of the burden Mademoiselle Jordane has been carrying? I have arranged for her debts to be written off, in recognition of her service and yours. You know that Monsieur Barra was reinstated, albeit at a lesser grade, and will benefit from an enhanced pension.'

'If he lives that long,' said Alex. 'If any of us do. Anyway, what are you suggesting? I assume it's to do with David Castile?'

There was a pause as Gerest weighed something up.

'Before we get to that, I am sorry to inform you that your mother has relapsed.'

'When?'

'She has re-entered the Rothschild Institute.'

'She hasn't. I would know.'

'It was deemed better that you didn't.'

'Messages have been kept from me?' Alex asked, his temper rising. 'Deemed better by whom?'

'By your counselling algorithm, pending completion of assessment.'

'By the damn robot?'

Alex stood up and swept all the executive toys from the edge of Gerest's desk onto the floor. The neck of the glass bird snapped in half.

'I want to see her,' he said in a tight voice.

'You will,' said Gerest, shrinking into his leather office chair. 'There will be time before your flight.'

'What flight? No, never mind that. When was she taken in?'

'Yesterday morning.'

'Yesterday morning?' Alex repeated.

He took a step to the right, picked up the side of Gerest's desk and

137

flipped it, sending it end over end, crashing into a sideboard, knocking a tray of decanters and crystal glasses to the floor. He stepped in close.

'Who gave you the right?'

'It is my job to make such judgements,' said Gerest, uneasily, leaning back like a child recoiling from a wasp. 'There is much at stake.'

Behind him, Alex heard the door open and two sets of footsteps. He spoke quietly to Gerest.

'This is my life, you understand.'

Alex felt a hand on his shoulder. He grabbed it in both of his and bent double, flinging the man over his shoulder into Gerest's lap. The leather office chair toppled over, the director and his security officer tumbled in a tangle of heavy limbs on the floor. Alex spun round, ready to disable whoever the second set of footsteps belonged to.

'I enjoyed that,' said Amaury.

'Of course you did,' Alex replied.

Ten minutes had passed. The security officer had disentangled himself from his boss and slunk away. Gerest had had a few cold words to say about continuing the briefing on another occasion, then Alex had followed Amaury – the owner of the second set of footsteps – to the refectory.

It was a quiet time. There were only a dozen tables out of fifty or so in use. Amaury was drinking sweet mint tea and Alex a green smoothie – not his usual protein and vitamin concoction, but in the same ballpark. He had spoken to Doctor Labeur who had reassured him and had given him an ITU appointment for later that day.

'We're under observation right now,' said Amaury, glancing round the room, counting the cameras on his fingers. 'One, two, three, four.'

Alex replied to him in Arabic.

'How are the lip-reading apps?'

'It's a shame you don't speak Berber. I'm sure that would be beyond them.'

138

Alex switched back to French.

'I might have hurt you. You shouldn't have been so close behind me.'

'I retreated when you went ballistic.' Amaury nodded. 'Gloria is strong. Her recovery was fast. She'll bounce back again.'

Alex shook his head. 'You don't know that. Look what happened to the professor. What about you?'

Amaury made a wryly comic tale out of his own experiences, concluding: 'I filed a report. The big one may have choked but the little one will be followed up and interrogated. They're nothing, though – the remnants, the dribs and drabs. If they succeed, it will be by accident, not by design.'

'Sure,' said Alex.

But he wasn't sure at all.

Alex made his way from the headquarters of External Security to the Rothschild Institute, a beautiful late nineteenth-century stone building with a profusion of more modern extensions that sprouted like tumours in coarse concrete and cheap red brick. He asked for Doctor Labeur and was told he would soon be available. His assistant, meanwhile, could help him to observe Gloria by a camera link. Just like the last time he had come to this place, she looked tiny under regulation blankets in the wide hospital bed, a mask over her face, a tube connecting her to a ventilator, encouraging oxygen into her lungs.

'What is her prognosis?'

'It's too early to say.'

'Is it the same pathogen?'

'You will have to wait for Doctor Labeur's judgement.'

'Have you been in touch with Genmis in Norway?'

'I have no information on that.'

Alex sighed.

'What is Labeur doing?'

'Rounds. I'll take you to his office.'

'I know the way.'

Alex navigated himself to a sleek office overlooking a shaded courtyard. Twenty minutes later, Doctor Labeur, in his bright white doctor's coat, took a seat behind his untidy mahogany desk.

'Her condition is mysterious. The speed with which her malaise took hold – whether it is a new pathogen or not has yet to be established – is baffling. All our test results are being communicated to Professor Genmis, of course. In the meantime, she seems stable. It may simply be a chronic sequel to the previous infection.' He rubbed a hand over his close-cropped grey hair, saying: 'I will not tell you not to worry, but you shouldn't.'

'Because you are optimistic?'

'No. Because worrying doesn't help.'

'Is she sedated?'

'Sedation of critically ill patients, including those requiring mechanical ventilation, is a complex health-care intervention. It is difficult to achieve the correct level.' He broke off at a ping from his tablet and read a message. 'That is good news,' he said, looking genuinely relieved. 'Her stats are trending upwards.'

He turned the tablet to face Alex who scanned the numbers, recognising some of the labels, though he didn't know what 'good' or 'bad' readings might be.

'You overestimate my knowledge, Doctor Labeur.'

'Go about your business. She could not have better care. By the way,' he added with a frown, 'I was against Director Gerest's instruction to keep you out of the loop.'

'Thank you.'

Alex went out into the street, pausing for a few minutes to absorb the warmth of the sun as an antidote to the air-con chill and austerity of the clinic.

19

Amaury was right. The big man who smelt of fish had choked, but a broad investigation into his known contacts was underway. The assistant verger from Bilbao cathedral, Jaime Moreno, had been traced by Spanish camera control, arrested during a choir rehearsal and delivered to the frontier. French military investigators took him to their closed compound within the perimeter of Bordeaux-Mérignac airport, where he was subjected to an automated interrogation system that analysed his cerebral reactions to visual and auditory stimuli, uncovering concealed patterns of thought.

The interrogation took place in an austere cell, one of whose walls was a screen onto which was projected a series of enormous images. Jaime was strapped in a seat uncomfortably reminiscent of an executioner's electric chair, with a thick velcro strap holding his head in position within the arc of a metal headrest. His eyelids were held open by devices resembling eyelash-curlers so he was unable to look away.

A helmet placed over Jaime's shaven skull analysed the electrical impulses inside his brain. Whether he had a strong reaction to an image or not was visible to the AI – not perhaps significant in itself, but reinforced and cross-correlated with thousands of other images, it became a kind of mind-reading.

By the time an hour had gone by, remorseless and draining, Jaime was sweating through his clothes. The second hour pushed him into a kind of trance, all will to resist long since departed, allowing the robot intelligence to do its work, probing what he knew and what he didn't, what he recognised and what not, following its own pathways, cross-referencing crime scenes with the faces of known aggressors, of the traitor, of places where bad things had occurred, where bad things had been prevented. His shirt gaped open, revealing the tattooed letters on his collarbone: UDSMC.

By the end of the third hour, Jaime thought perhaps he had soiled himself, but couldn't be sure. His eyes felt as though they must be bleeding, or perhaps it was only tears.

In southern Mali, on a road not far from the almost-exhausted Goulamina lithium mine, two police officers were out on patrol in a converted Kantanka pick-up truck. The road was quiet and the day hot. They were talking about what they would do if they had lots of money – maybe emigrate to somewhere it still reliably rained, build a house with a big roof terrace for catchment, plant vegetables and fruit in a courtyard, stay up late every night in the cool and the dark, playing cards and watching football from all around the world with half an eye, drinking beer and chatting to one another about anything and nothing.

Further down that lonely road, they were flagged down by a woman who appeared to be distressed, perhaps dehydrated in the 40° heat. And she seemed to be carrying a small child wrapped in mud-cloth, a rough cotton textile typical of the area.

The two police officers brought their vehicle to a halt. As was regulation, they both put on their caps before they got out, straightening their light-beige uniforms because she was young and slim and had an attractive innocent face. She wore gloves, but that was not suspicious in a world where touch could be fatal.

'What has happened? Where is your vehicle?'

She let fall the mud-cloth wrap, revealing an automatic weapon – a stubby automatic with a magazine full of shells that she used to shoot them multiple times, tearing into their flesh, splintering their bones, causing great blooms of blood to fan out across the pale fabric of their nicely ironed shirts.

Close to the mine workings at Goulamina – close in Saharan terms, meaning within a couple of hours' drive – was a much newer site. Extraction work was tough and management had agreed with the workers' representatives that they should labour for a cycle of four days on, sleeping on site, then return to accommodation in the nearby town of Yanfolila for four days off. To make sure the work remained continuous, two teams crossed over every ninety-six hours.

It was changeover day. Two minibuses had just arrived with the replacement teams. The drivers knew that they would have to wait an hour for recharge of their vehicles, so they sat on the steps leading up to the veranda, in the shade outside the management office, chatting to the security team, made up of two pairs of police officers, because the mine workings were a partnership between MaliLith and state control.

'How are things?' one of the drivers asked.

'Quiet.'

They would not remain that way for long.

The woman with the stubby automatic weapon stood listening, watching the blood from the police officers' wounds seep noiselessly into the dirt. Her name was Kadidia Sidibé. The place she had chosen was lonely, a cutting carved into the soft hillside. Either side the land rose abruptly with sheer edges still showing the marks of the teeth of the digger. The rattle of her automatic weapon would have been deflected upwards. Probably, no one had heard the shots and no one was coming.

But it was important that, eventually, they should.

Kadidia picked up the mud-cloth wrap in her gloved hands and used it to conceal the stubby automatic weapon once more, leaving it on the bonnet of the Kantanka pick-up truck. She sat in the driver's seat, still

143

warm from the police officer's body heat. In the cup-holders were two steel bottles of water she would take with her.

She could hear a voice, a scratchy distant sound, coming from the radio. She found the volume button and turned it up.

Nothing much: routine check-ins, no emergencies.

Kadidia picked up the microphone and pressed a button on the side, cutting out the broadcast.

'Hello, hello,' she said, acting uncertain, though her eyes revealed that she knew precisely what she was doing. 'Can anyone help me?'

She released the talk-button and waited.

'Come in Echo-six-two?' came the officious reply.

'Something's happened,' she said desperately. 'They're outside in the dirt.'

'Who is this?'

'You must send help. They've been shot. I think they're badly injured.'

'Who's injured? What's your name?'

By this time, she knew, they would have located her from the transponder on board the vehicle.

'My child is with me.'

'Who is this?'

Kadidia banged the microphone on the dashboard, wrapped its flex around her hand for purchase and pulled its wiring out of the console. She could still hear the despatcher through the speakers in the dashboard.

'I repeat, who is this? Who is injured?'

At the police station in Yanfolila, the despatcher referred the panicked message to a superior officer. A drone was urgently despatched to overfly the scene. It would take about twenty minutes to arrive, eventually relaying video back to base using the satellite comms network.

In the Malian capital city of Bamako, a hundred-and-sixty kilometres

144

to the north, Chief of Police Konaré was on the roof of the Hôtel Étoile, concealed behind a parapet, peering with binoculars through a gap in the concrete mouldings. He had requested a bedside rug from one of the hotel rooms to lie on, but the gravelled bitumen was sharp all the same.

A stage had been set up on Place de la Liberté, alongside the Monument to the Heroes of the Black Army, a statue cast in dark green bronze on a tall brick plinth. The monument depicted five black soldiers, led by a white officer, in the uniforms of French World War I infantry. Konaré knew there was a sister statue in the Champagne region of north-eastern France, cast from the same mould, inscribed with the same words: 'In recognition and gratitude for the adopted children of France who died fighting for freedom and civilisation.'

Chief of Police Konaré was not one of those who wanted to wipe away all vestiges of the colonial past. He liked to ask: 'Were the statue removed, what would end up in its place? A few scrubby flowers and a billboard? No, better to keep the imperialist representation of "Heroes of the Black Army" and stay alert to what it means.'

A new speaker climbed up onto the stage, a woman from the displaced persons camp outside the city. She wore an off-white jellabiya that reached right down to the floor. The crowd greeted her with polite applause. Konaré could hear her voice, broadcast by a powerful public address system. She started her speech in Bambara, the most widely-used Malian language – expressing her yearning for a better world, bewilderment that things should be as they were, disappointment and incredulity that her words might go unheeded.

After a pause, she switched from Bambara to Dyula. Her gesture of inclusivity brought another round of applause from the sparse crowd. Konaré picked out a man in a heavy blue sweatshirt who joined in the clapping and shuffled his feet. His hood was up and his face remained elusive.

The police drone arrived at the cutting in the soft hillside. The remote despatcher scanned the area, sweeping left and right in a methodical pattern before hovering over two bodies, one face down and one face up. She turned to her manager.

'The vehicle is missing.'

'Bring the drone in closer.'

The despatcher did so, revealing multiple wounds in the body of the officer who lay face up, his blood a feast for flies.

'Move to the right,' said the manager. 'Hold steady.'

The image on the screen showed a few coloured wires trailing from an electronic device that had been ripped from its housing.

'Is that the transponder?' asked the despatcher.

The manager ignored her question.

'Get the call out. Priority one. All vehicles within range to proceed to the scene.'

At the Yanfolila mine, the two pairs of police officers, lounging with the minibus drivers on the veranda, heard the simultaneous instructions from the radios in their Kantanka pick-ups.

'Both of us?' one of them said.

'I'll go,' said another.

He strolled away from the shade of the management building and opened the door, leaning in for the microphone.

'Echo-four-nine. Go ahead?'

Once the officer had digested the message – a murderous attack on their own colleagues – he called out: 'We have to go, both cars. Someone's hijacked Echo-six-two. They're dead.'

Within thirty seconds, the two police vehicles had set off, furious and vengeful, abandoning the Yanfolila mine, lured away by the brutal distraction.

Kadidia Sidibé hadn't enjoyed fishing about for the ignition-fob against the heaviness of the driver's inert and lifeless thigh. Three hundred metres further along the metalled road, she turned off onto a rugged cross-country track. It didn't matter if she damaged the Kantanka's suspension. She just needed not to ground it and get stuck.

The track was a wadi, a dry river bed. It was the most direct route to the second ambush site, meeting the minibuses transporting the workers coming off duty, travelling east on the RN8, a good road maintained by central government and improved by investment from MaliLith. Once she got there, she and a fellow believer would rain down death.

20

In Bamako, Chief of Police Konaré watched the woman in the off-white jellabiya bring her speech to a climax and leave the stage. She was replaced by three musicians, one of them a griot, a guardian of the oral tradition, a musical storyteller and praise singer with roots in the pre-colonial Malian empire founded on slavery and gold. He sang his wavering song accompanied by a middle-aged woman playing a twenty-one-string kora and a very old man seated at a balafon, a kind of xylophone with gourd resonators beneath each béné-wood key. The acoustic performance was amplified by the public address system and filled the open space with gorgeous sound.

The man in the heavy blue sweatshirt was still there. Through his binoculars, Chief Konaré saw the man's face clearly for the first time.

'It's him. Fire.'

Konaré watched the sudden impacts as the man flinched twice, as if struck by two hard swift blows, then he began to fall. Before he hit the ground, Konaré heard the shots, the sound separated from the image by the time it took for the noise to catch up with the light.

'*Mission accomplie*,' said Konaré. '*On dégage.*'

Mission accomplished. Clear the scene.

Konaré hauled himself to his feet and lumbered stiffly across the roof to the access door that led into the stairwell, ponderously making his way down to the hotel lobby. It was already packed with members of the fleeing crowd, looking for shelter. He pushed his way to the glass doors where a security guard was trying to prevent anyone going back outside. Distracted, the guard put a hand on Konaré's chest and told him, in Bambara, to stop: '*I jɔ*!' Konaré waited for the man to recognise him and apologise: 'I'm sorry, sir. Forgive me.'

Konaré stepped out into the harsh light, crossing the tarmac, then the scrubby parched grass to the dais beneath the statue. The man was lying alone where he had fallen. The entrance wound was covered by his hands, clasped across his chest, his blood darkly soaking into his sweatshirt.

Konaré gave an order and a uniformed police officer leaned in and gently moved the hands aside. Both bullets had entered the man's chest in more or less the same place, punching a hole about the size of a child's fist, converting his heart muscle into soup.

'Search him.'

The officer found a small wallet with two plastic cards, a foreign ID and some local currency. Round his waist, beneath his sweatshirt, he wore a waxed-cotton bag containing half a dozen 24-dose packets of a French-made antiviral medication.

The uniformed officer looked at the drugs greedily. They were as good as money – better, in some ways.

Kadidia bounced the Kantanka along the wadi, risking an accident in order not to be late. The drive had taken longer than anticipated, giving her time to wonder if Drissa, her brother, would be on his way to the airport. He had done his job, bringing from France the drugs that financed the purchase of weapons. She hoped to see him again but the future, as always, was uncertain.

Kadidia was aiming for a location just outside Kéméré. Her colleague, Hamady Dara, would probably be wearing his habitual disguise as a Dogon priest. They had scouted an elevated position alongside the road.

She gunned the police pick-up, climbing out of the wadi, barrelling in behind Hamady in a cloud of dust, close enough to hear his automatic weapon. Hamady swung round, his blue robes flapping, spraying bullets over her vehicle, hopped up on adrenaline and holding the power of life and death in his hot hands. She threw herself out of the pick-up and hid behind the front wheel and the engine block, the only part likely to give any real protection.

'Hamady, it's me, Kadidia.'

Then the shooting stopped because his magazine was empty and the loudest noise was the wailing and lamentation of the wounded and dying – civilian drivers and mine workers, trapped in a classic ambush, a few rocks pushed down off the slopes of the cutting to block the road, the steepish sides making escape impossible.

Kadidia retrieved her stubby weapon from the passenger seat and went to meet Hamady, sharing a brief embrace. He apologised for his moment of panic.

'We must be quick,' she told him, gesturing towards the cutting. 'Some are left alive.'

Three men were dragging themselves from the shot-up wrecks, the near side panelling ripped and torn, the insides splattered with blood and bone. Hamady slotted a replacement magazine into his automatic weapon and they skidded together down the cutting, sliding on their backsides, Kadidia's dress rucking up round her thighs.

At the foot of the slope, they advanced on the carnage, firing selective bursts from their assorted calibre weapons. One of Hamady's impacts sent a spray of blood in a wide arc that spattered across Kadidia's face. She swore and dropped her weapon, spitting on the ground. She wrenched open the door of the front minibus and rummaged in the glove compartment, finding anti-viral wipes in a cheap dispenser. They were dried out but there was a bottle of water on the seat and she used it – she hoped – to revive them, wiping her features carefully, even going so far as to put one of the moistened wipes in her mouth and chew.

Then there was a different sound, much higher in pitch, just two barks from a hand-held weapon, and Hamady – her colleague and friend – was on the ground, the right side of his face blown away.

Kadidia snatched up her stubby weapon and sprayed bullets for cover, watching them ricochet under the chassis of the nearer minibus. She took three decisive strides forward, just in time to see the light go out in the eyes of the man who had fought back – an older worker who had made the mistake of bringing a handgun to a machine-gun fight.

But, of course, he hadn't known there was going to be a machine-gun fight.

Simultaneously, several hundred kilometres south in Côte d'Ivoire, another wisp of the distracting smokescreen of terrorism was being woven. A man who spoke French with a Malian accent was loitering outside a rest stop in the town of Samatiguila. He was waiting for the driver of a heavily loaded forty-tonne lithium truck to leave the stinking concrete latrine. As the driver emerged, the man struck him from behind with a lump of rock and left him dazed at the side of the road. Then he drank from a half bottle of scotch, draining it completely and smashing it against the wall.

The Malian climbed into the cab and set off, grinding the gears, gunning the accelerator.

At the ambush site, Kadidia was the only person left alive. She felt queasy. Was it because Hamady was dead or was it because she had swallowed a stranger's blood?

No matter. She had the next part of her plan to accomplish. Back in August, the Coming Darkness conspiracy had failed. Even before that, she had lost a sister in Marseille in the failed attack on the Bunker Martha data centre. But the war on the hyperconnected world wasn't over. Her losses meant she felt a greater determination to show the world what 'darkness' really meant.

To increase the level of distraction, she used a cigarette lighter to set the upholstery in one of the minibuses on fire. As the black smoke rose into the parched air, she climbed out of the cutting, got back in her stolen Kantanka and drove along the wadi to a cairn of rocks where she retrieved an improvised explosive device with a remote trigger. On the radio, news of the hijacking of one of the mine trucks was beginning to contribute to the general panic.

The massive lithium truck was barrelling down the road towards San Pedro on Côte d'Ivoire's Atlantic coast. Its drunken driver was looking out for vehicles like his own, returning empty from the port.

He twitched the steering wheel to strike his first victim on the right-hand side, level with the diesel tank, as the two vehicles passed one another on a bend in the road. The impact drove the unladen truck off the tarmac and into the hard wide bole of an iroko tree. The sudden stop propelled the driver through the windscreen, visible to the hijacker in his large side mirror, a crumpled doll on the dry grass.

He drove on, meeting his second victim about thirty kilometres later, catching sight of it parked outside a café with a large sign advertising *kedjenou*, a kind of Ivorian chicken stew. The empty truck was parked at right angles to the road. The hijacker slammed into the side of its cab, spinning the much lighter, unladen vehicle around, leaving its rear axle in the ditch.

His third victims were simply a hit-and-run accident – two children playing by the side of the road, waving and smiling as they did to every heavy truck that passed, giving structure and rhythm to their days. Inside the cab of the forty-tonne behemoth, the hijacker barely noticed the impact or the two small bodies, crushed beneath his wheels.

By this time, reports of an out-of-control driver had been communicated to the Ivorian police force – two glancing collisions and two collateral deaths. They, in turn, had been in contact with Police Central in Bamako and the mines at Goulamina and Yanfolila. The Yanfolila comms office had shared the news with the entire fleet, warning all vehicles on the San Pedro Road of what was happening.

'Pull over. Get right off the highway. It's carnage, absolute carnage.'

Arriving at high speed from the Yanfolila mine workings, the police officer with the wide-set eyes and sharp cheekbones was the first to see the smoke. It rose in a black-grey column from a cutting, maybe a kilometre ahead. Had it been safe to accelerate further, he would have done so.

When he got there, he slewed his vehicle to a halt, opening the driver's door, slipping out and crouching low beside the vehicle. His partner did the same thing on the other side. The second police pick-up skidded sideways on the dusty tarmac, coming to an awkward halt behind them.

For a moment, there was quiet, then the flapping of the wings of half a dozen carrion birds, returning to their feast.

The officer with the sharp cheekbones wasn't a fool. It began to dawn on him that they had made a mistake. If they were here, where all was quiet and still, the real action must be taking place somewhere else.

Kadidia arrived at the Yanfolila site, crashing through the barrier, splintering the fragile timber and bringing the unarmed gate attendant running out of his hut, clutching his cap, trying to jam it onto his bald head while galumphing after her.

She drove past the truck stop where three huge vehicles were being maintained and loaded, one of them getting refuelled by a motorised diesel bowser. She bounced past two huge mounds of spoil, along a dirt track that led to a bland wall of soil and rock and concrete. It towered over her, at least twenty-five metres high. In her rear-view mirror she saw the bald gate attendant with his hands on his knees, getting smaller, giving up the chase.

Kadidia had only ever seen the site in satellite images. In reality, the different elements all seemed much larger and further apart – and she didn't have much time. Someone else at the site might be armed, like the old guy from the minibus.

She reached a sloping retaining wall. A sign in huge letters was stencilled on a large sheet of plywood: *SUPERNAT*.

Driving on, she found what she was looking for – a huge metal sluice resembling the gates on a canal lock. She skidded all four tyres to a halt and leapt out, the IED in her hands, a sharp metal corner piercing her glove. She powered up the receiver and transmitter, making them operational, then placed the device at the base of the sluice.

In the cab of the hijacked truck, the steering had become heavy. One or other of the collisions must have damaged the power assist. Plus the windscreen was crazed with cracks and the hijacker wished he had something more to drink.

He heard a radio warning message from Yanfolila, broadcast to 'all vehicles', and wondered about snatching up the microphone and responding, perhaps with a slogan or two, or some well-considered words about exploitation of the people and the land.

The hijacker didn't know it but the driver of the next northbound truck, making his way back to the mine, was laden with twenty-five tonnes of steel pipework for the industrial-scale plumbing. He, too, was thinking about replying to the warning to get off the highway. Not with slogans, but with a request for more information because it all seemed so far-fetched.

But he didn't, because he had a sandwich in his spare hand and didn't want to steer with his knees round the upcoming bend.

In that moment of partial inattention and indecision – the hijacker wishing he had more whisky, the other driver eating his sandwich –

both swung round a blind corner. All at once, they saw one another, their eyes meeting through one dirty and one crazed windscreen as a head-on collision became inevitable. In less time than it would have taken to pronounce the words, both realised that this impact would mean their deaths.

Forty tonnes of lithium ore hit twenty-five tonnes of pipework head on, each mass moving at around fifty kilometres per hour, somewhere between fifteen and twenty metres per second. The impact for each was as if they had driven into a granite cliff, too sudden for the drivers to stamp on the pedals, for the energy of motion to be absorbed into the brake system. Instead, it was suddenly and cataclysmically dissipated by crushing, tearing and twisting the chassis and bodywork of the two massive vehicles and the destruction of the much more fragile skeletons and flesh of the two drivers – one innocent and surprised, one drunk and bent on 'purposeful destruction'.

At the Yanfolila site, by the drainage sluice of the enormous supernat tank, Kadidia heard the sound of a diesel engine and saw the motorised fuel bowser come creeping round the corner of the heaps of spoil, like a wary animal nosing into view, wondering what was going on.

She removed the transmitter from its housing on top of the receiver, got back in her stolen pick-up and pulled away, making for another path back to the main gate – less used, less well made. As she drove, she held the transmitter over her shoulder and pressed the button.

There was, as always in life, a gap between expectation and reality, in this case made up of the infinitesimal length of time it took for the radio signal to travel from the transmitter to the receiver, then the reaction time of the detonator. Once the explosion had taken place, there was the time it took for the muffled sound and the shockwave to reach the Kantanka, driven by a wild woman, half laughing and half frightened, bouncing from one side of the rough track to the other, then drifting all four tyres as she swung hard left out of the secondary gate and away.

Back in Bamako, Chief of Police Konaré had been summoned straight from Place de la Liberté to the Malian foreign office to explain himself to a senior civil servant who spoke, so he said, 'with the authority of the minister'.

'This could create a diplomatic incident. This man, Drissa Sidibé, had a French passport.'

'But you agree,' Konaré prompted, 'that in these dangerous times it is necessary to show that we are in control.'

'He was a petty smuggler, yet you had him shot in the public square, during the Festival of Independence.'

'It is important to remind them that they must remain insignificant if they want to survive.'

'They?'

'Criminals of all kinds.'

Konaré looked round the room. It was pleasant – very pleasant – with a wooden fan with enormous blades turning lazily, high in the generous ceiling. He was keen to make the side-step into politics himself.

'The man was a French citizen with relatives in Mali,' insisted the official. 'His travel permit was legitimate.'

'But it did not include Yanfolila and the south. Why should he be travelling there if his family are here in Bamako?' Konaré sat up straight, showing the civil servant that he was about to leave but first had some words of wisdom to impart. 'It no longer matters, does it, now he is dead? Police work is like cleaning. It is not necessary to analyse the specific type of dirt you are dealing with. It is only important to sweep it away.'

Konaré left the ministerial offices – for the time being unaware of the events unfolding at the mine and on the roads of Côte d'Ivoire – thinking about whether the sun had passed the zenith, where he would have lunch and whether, on this successful day, a midday cocktail might legitimately be drunk.

Not far away, in the presidential palace on the outskirts of Bamako, Major Chaka Kassam had just finished presenting his apologies to President Manouche for the leak to the Russian faction. He and the president had grown up together. Gracious forgiveness had been forthcoming.

'You are not a smart man, Chaka,' President Manouche had told him, condescendingly.

'No, your excellency.'

'And in any case, old friend, I don't care what beans you spilt. I don't mind the Russians thinking we are about to do business with them. Let's see if they come to you again and we can play a double game.'

'Yes, your excellency.'

On his way out of the palace, Kassam had been approached by a diplomat he didn't recognise.

'Major, a word, if you please?'

The man introduced himself as the Malian delegate to the North African Defence League. The discreet location for this private 'word' was a diplomatic car, making the return journey into the city centre, plush and cool.

'There is to be a celebration of the defeat of the Coming Darkness conspiracy at Aswan, important because it might constitute a significant step forward in the normalisation of relations with isolationist Egypt, but it would not be appropriate to send a senior politician at this stage.'

'You wish me to attend?'

'As a military man of middle rank, you would not be out of place.'

'That makes good sense.'

The Malian diplomat took Kassam's comment as acquiescence.

'You will travel by air to Al-Jaghar, then overland. My Egyptian counterpart at the North African Defence League will be in touch.'

There was more – diplomatic niceties, what to say and what not to say, how to develop President Manouche's idea of playing 'a double game' – but Kassam made only a pretence at listening. Instead, he was brewing a plan in the back of his mind, one potentially capable of making himself the fiercest blast of the Coming Storm.

21

Next morning, the news from the Rothschild was good. Gloria's stats were still trending upwards. Alex managed to get hold of Director Genmis on a vision call at the Norwegian laboratory.

'Your mother has resumed her normal activities too soon. That would be my first guess. She should recalibrate herself to "convalescent mode", yes?' Genmis made a serious face. 'For as long as it takes.'

'Thank you. I appreciate your concern.'

Before setting off to meet Gerest and perhaps apologise, Alex scanned the streams. The news of terrorist attacks in southern Mali held his attention because of a remote connection to Cyrenia and the Coming Darkness conspiracy. It was followed by a weather report including an 'extreme heat' advisory – very matter-of-fact, almost as if there was nothing really to worry about, but warning of 'excess deaths' among 'vulnerable populations', as if that was a specific and slightly shameful subset of society that couldn't be helped, whose fate was somehow their own fault for being 'vulnerable' in the first place.

As well as heat, there would be downpours. The heat advisory was amber, meaning the weather would also have an impact on resource management – power and water supplies. Each a finite commodity, the two utilities worked on the same pattern. When demand skyrocketed, flows of each were reduced to a trickle.

Alex recognised the language as something he had become used to hearing at quite a young age. How young? Certainly childhood. Maybe 2015 when he was 10 and first noticed people living on the streets and had asked his mother why they had no homes. She had told him: 'Because we choose not to help them.'

'Do you mean us?' he remembered asking her, innocently.

'No, Alexandre. We as a society.'

Alex knew that 'extreme weather' was a euphemism. It sounded innocent but what did it mean? Scorching temperatures, of course, but also flash floods and overtopped drains, sewage on the pavements, wildlife desperate to escape …

Alex had seen such a nightmare just once with his own eyes, in Haiti, in a parched lowland shanty town whose name now escaped him, towards the end of a training stint with Amaury. The rain had come cascading down on the rocks and hard ground, waterfalling off the hillsides in great cataracts, drowning all the hidden habitats. Within minutes, a horrific moving carpet of brown was coming towards them – thousands, perhaps millions of spiders and crickets and beetles and worms, looking for higher ground, climbing doorsteps, sliding under doors into the improvised homes. From all around, they had heard shouts of disgust and horror and fear.

Quickly, the two of them had climbed into their open-topped jeep, switching on the wipers to keep the windscreen clear, smearing bugs on the glass. And he remembered seeing what he thought was a vine on a eucalyptus tree, some kind of ivy that was inexplicably in motion, winding itself in real time round the trunk. But it was a handful of snakes, different species, six or seven of them, also fleeing drowning. Then he had seen a mouse, scrabbling up the bark, picking its way round the snakes, but not quickly enough as a set of reptilian jaws grasped it on the way past.

They'd driven away at top speed on a road that led to a pass between the hills and stopped there for half an hour, watching the sudden flood abate, most of the improvised dwellings under at least fifty centimetres of water. Then they'd driven away, leaving the drowned shanty town to its gradual recovery.

Back in the austere break room at the military training centre, a scientist – probably an entomologist – had come on TV asking people to show empathy to the creatures whose homes had been inundated, 'even if they sicken you'. It wasn't clear if he meant the bugs or the shanty-dwellers.

Alex climbed up from the canal basin to the boulevard, screened from journalists on the far canal bank by newly erected hoardings. He was greeted by the police officer and the civilian security guard, working there in tandem. He felt a crackle of electricity in the air from the dark clouds sliding past one another in the heavens.

Gerest had been given access to Claudine Poiret's office at the Interior Ministry offices on the esplanade of Les Invalides while she was away with the disaster relief team. Alex wished he could walk there, keeping to the shady side of the streets. The clock-time was half-past ten, but that was only half-past eight by the sun, once you took into account the two hours of daylight saving. He couldn't, though. He would have to take an autodrive because he was still too easily recognised, despite his uncut hair and growing beard.

His designated vehicle pulled alongside and he climbed in, secure behind the darkened windows. Two paparazzi mobikes followed him all the way to the controlled zone, where they were obliged to abandon their chase while he queued with six or seven other cars at a checkpoint just south of Concorde to gain access to the political quarter, still thinking about the heat advisory.

In the northern European latitudes, in his youth, each year could still recognisably be divided into four seasons: spring, summer, autumn and winter. Today, it seemed, there were just dry months and wet months. Would Paris end up like cities in the tropics or the monsoon regions, with occasional droughts in the wet season and unpredictable downpours in the dry? And when had the tipping point come, when people had stopped smiling and telling one another 'It's summer at last' and 'What a glorious day', instead referring to July and August as 'hard work'? Quite recently, he decided, probably from around 2025. Basically, all of his adult life.

Alex wondered how much of what he was thinking made scientific sense and how much was informed by scaremongering and fear. He was no longer sure. It was a long time since he had made it his business to keep on top of environmental science.

He made an effort to come out of his own head, out of his own dark thoughts, just as the queue moved forward, the credentials on his comm-watch relayed by the vehicle to an automated ID reader set in a fake-stone pillar designed to blend in with the older materials of the bridge. A uniformed officer in an air-conditioned kiosk recognised his name, peering out at his obscured windows.

What did she see?

A blank exterior designed to maintain privacy.

What did he see?

Curiosity – deeply felt but fleeting.

He moved on, his vehicle's machine-intelligence provided by a combination of pre-programmed knowledge, twenty-four cameras and eight lidar sensors that told the autodrive where it was in space, adn reached the esplanade ten minutes early. He got out and stood opposite the main entrance, looking up at the heavy sky, seeing it darkening from greyish-purple to purplish-black. Heavy raindrops began to fall, laying in the dust on the parched grass.

He had to wait for two official cars to disappear into the underground parking garage, following his autodrive to a charging station, before crossing the road. At the canopied entrance, a hard-faced army security officer gave him a lanyard embedded with another traceable RFID, using electromagnetic fields to automatically track his location, without the need for line of sight, just from the miasma of EM radiation that surrounded contemporary humans at all times.

'Don't take it off and don't put it down,' said the security officer. 'Where it is, you are.'

'I understand.'

The guard stepped aside and Alex followed the canopied walkway, the plastic roof already under tension from the weight of water collecting in bulges between its stanchions. At the far end, there was a gap between the waterproof fabric and the building. He paused for a moment, looking out at the rain, wishing it could wash all the paraphernalia of surveillance clean out of the sullied air.

Alex knew his way through the many corridors of the Interior Ministry, but wasn't allowed to walk alone past the offices of state. Another guard preceded him to the stairs, up to the first floor and along a magnificent passageway lined with oil paintings, depicting famous battles from French military history. Eventually, he was offered a seat – a generous upright chair in gilded carved wood and red velvet, next to a water dispenser.

He drank three paper cones of chilled water, thinking what a luxury that would be for the majority of the population of the planet. He wasn't even sure he was thirsty. It had simply become a habit, always to keep hydrated – mostly with the green drinks provided by his medical consultant, but also with clean H_2O.

He scrunched up the third paper cone and dropped it into a bin, realising he could have used the same one three times.

How easy it is, he thought, *to destroy without thinking*.

The last time he had been in this building he had been awarded twin medals of honour from France and Cyrenia. Would today be an official reprimand for flipping Gerest's desk – or would the director allow him that outburst as a fair response to being withheld information about his mother's relapse?

On the wall opposite was a painting that didn't depict soldiers or fighting ships. It was a rendering in oils of the death of several dozen horses, driven from a burning forest in north-western Russia into the supercooled waters of Ladoga Lake, well below zero degrees centigrade yet still liquid, until the terrified animals, fleeing the flames, plunged in, provoking instant freezing solidification, and were trapped in ice.

Alex knew the story. 'The Horses of Ladoga Lake' was often used as an allegory for the difficulty of plotting a middle course between two extremes. The panicked horses were doomed by their inability to hold a steady path.

A door opened. Damien Gerest appeared, looking very solid and round in a dark suit, white shirt and narrow blue tie.

'Come in,' he said, without a smile. 'And try not to damage any furniture.'

Alex followed him inside, shutting the door behind him. He sat down and waited on another carved wooden chair upholstered in red velvet. Gerest landed heavily in his own uncomfortable-looking tubular chrome seat behind Claudine Poiret's genuine antique desk.

'First on my agenda, the news of your mother is good – a relapse not a new infection. There is no need for an alpha-fold study.' Gerest was referring to a technique that mapped the three-dimensional structure of pathogenic proteins to determine novel ways to combat them. 'Second, I had you in mind to lead a training exercise for a select group of your fellow operatives and analysts, but you won't have time.'

'Will they be told the identity of the traitor?'

'No, that remains classified.'

'Some of them will already have a good idea who it was,' he said quietly, 'if they're worth anything.' Alex frowned. 'When will Madame Poiret return?'

Gerest failed to hide a sneer before he answered and Alex surmised it was because he resented the fact that Claudine Poiret was his superior.

'Following her promotion, she now works exclusively under the authority of the president. She is no doubt very busy with the disaster

164

relief operation in Haiti.' Gerest tapped his stylus on the glass desk. 'Third item on my agenda, having clocked all your mandated hours of therapy, what is your opinion of the process? Perhaps you should continue, as a kind of maintenance? Although you have been given a clean bill of mental health, would you say your behaviour in my office was normal?'

'Normal is shaped by circumstances.'

'Perhaps,' said Gerest. He waved a hand, indicating a return to his previous thought. 'So, you take my point about sharing your process with your colleagues – how you acted when no one but you perceived the danger.'

'I would have told them to beware letting things slide, hoping the worst won't happen when, in reality, it almost certainly will. But, of course, I had Professor Fayard's support.'

'Yes,' said Gerest, nodding. 'Anyway, Monsieur Barra will lead the training exercise with Sébastien Ménard.'

'But Mariam's security detail—'

'Is still in place. Have no fear. Fourth item. I have received a high-level civilian request from an extremely important—'

'One moment,' Alex interrupted. As Gerest had been speaking, a combination of thoughts had coalesced in Alex's mind. 'There were reports on your desk yesterday – lithium mining and hydro-electricity. How are they linked?'

'Why don't you tell me?'

'Davide Castile.' Alex told Gerest what he had learned from Arnaud Sy. 'There's more to it, I'm sure.'

'You were not empowered to go and question that man.'

'I know. Anyway, Castile. What's your interest?'

'As Arnaud Sy's evidence suggests, he may be unstable,' Gerest admitted. 'But Castile is an entrepreneur in energy and communications at an internationally strategic level, most of which he takes a managerial interest in, and he has requested our assistance – your assistance.'

165

'To do what?'

'To accompany him to a mine in southern Mali, standing next to him, keeping eyes open and senses alert. Also, meeting with the president in Bamako.'

'A political meeting, then?'

'Yes.'

'He requested me by name?'

'Yes.'

'Because people know who I am, something of what I've done?'

'Precisely.'

'I see ...' Alex dropped his gaze, frowning, talking to the polished floorboards. 'But there's another connection, isn't there?'

Gerest sighed.

'Why don't you tell me what you think it is? That way, you won't need to interrupt me when you work it out.'

Alex took a moment to visualise a few possibilities. Gerest was agreeing that there was a stronger connection than the desire of a wealthy man to be accompanied by the most famous security officer his money and influence could buy.

'Southern Mali is fundamental in lithium-ion energy storage for intermittent renewable energy sources.' Gerest nodded so Alex went on. 'The explosion that destroyed the port in Cyrene City back in July was deliberately triggered by the Coming Darkness conspirators, but most of the devastation came from the fact that it ignited mining explosives ready for overland transit. So, Castile is connected to Cyrenia and ...' Alex raised his eyes. Outside, heavy rain was still falling but the sky beyond was blue. 'Genmis talked to me about "viral reservoirs", still potentially active, ready to do more harm. He meant pathogens, but you and I mean cells of conspirators.'

'Yes.'

'You want me to accompany Castile because of the attacks I heard about on the news this morning. Castile isn't the focus.' Gerest shifted in his chair. 'No,' Alex corrected himself. 'He isn't the only focus.'

'Correct.'

'If it came to it,' Alex asked, 'would you want me to keep him alive?'

'Don't you think the world needs a little stability?'

'The sort of stability that murders a woman by helicopter?'

'The X^3 was faulty. Several expert witnesses have –'

'Don't,' said Alex. 'Just don't.'

Gerest scowled.

'Fine. This is the mission. Accompany Castile to Mali. Meet the president. And there's a minor issue, concerned with drug smuggling. It's well below your pay grade but it will keep you out of range of the streams.'

'Legitimate drugs?'

'Medical grade but illegally traded. A French citizen has just been shot by local police.'

'Who will brief me?'

'Chambon.'

'Am I not Internal Security now? Chambon is still at External, unless you've brought him in-house at the Ministry?'

'As I told you, oversight for the two services is mine. There's no difference anymore.'

Alex stopped asking questions. He couldn't work out what was important in all this and what was merely a distraction. Twenty seconds slipped past.

'Captain Lamarque, is there something else you want to ask me?'

'What about Amaury?'

'He is, for the time being, the public face of your triumph, leaving you free to apply yourself to new challenges.'

'Fine.' He stood up. 'When do I start?'

'Chambon will meet you at Base Aérienne 117.'

Alex nodded. That was the military airport closest to Paris.

'Now?'

'Is that a problem?'

'Not at all.'

22

Alex was – unusually – travelling under his own identity, a known operative on a declared mission. The traffic was heavy and he arrived late for the departure window for his flight from Base Aérienne 117 – not a great start if his job was to protect the chief executive of a French corporation with worldwide interests in primary resources and energy. Chambon's briefing was rushed, but just before Alex boarded, to 'give a sense of Monsieur Castile's importance', Chambon had told him that the new open-cut lithium mine in southern Mali would provide an estimated 220 million tonnes of rich ore. Rough roads were even now being built from another open-cut mine in the same region that was more or less worked out.

'Where is he?' Alex had asked.

'Monsieur Castile will travel separately, captain,' Chambon had replied, twisting his *chevalière* ring. 'You are also empowered to investigate the death of the naturalised French citizen, Drissa Sidibé, shot by the Malian police. Also, the director would like a report on the terrorist outrages in the south, including the deaths of multiple police officers, two dozen mine workers, an IED explosion at the Goulamina mine, and the destruction of a handful of huge trucks.'

Thirty minutes later, from his generous leather seat on the plane, Alex glanced out of the window, recognising details in the landscape – the

Loire valley where traditional grape varieties were harder and harder to grow. Soon, the Falcon jet would climb higher and he would lose all sense of the topography of the land. While commercial jets typically cruised at around ten thousand metres, the Falcon enjoyed the rarefied air at fourteen or fifteen thousand.

He was one of only two passengers. Given the choice, he would have preferred to sit quietly, lost in his own thoughts, wondering how to help Mariam, how to persuade Amaury that he was taking too many risks. But he knew he ought to make conversation with Davide Castile's marketing director, a woman who introduced herself as Léa Dujardin. They'd already dispensed with him being 'the man who saved the world'. Alex had appreciated the discretion and politeness of her enquiries.

'Could you give me some more context?' he asked, with a smile.

'Regarding?' replied Dujardin. She was sitting opposite him, in her own overbig beige leather seat. 'I expect you're already very well briefed.'

'How about we start with the mines?'

'Of course,' she smiled in return then, unexpectedly, gave a theatrical sigh of pleasure. 'The private jet – one of the greatest inventions known to humankind.'

Alex didn't want to get into any arguments but he didn't agree. There was no real reason for them to be burning kerosene in a Falcon. The front cabin in a biofuel airliner would surely have been quite good enough but, he supposed, it was a question of status. In any case, he was spared the need to answer by the flight attendant bringing them the menu for their in-flight meals – too many choices from a sumptuous list of three courses that Alex anticipated finding too rich. They each selected the same dishes.

'You ran the other mine, Goulamina?' prompted Alex.

'Our corporation was one of the principal partners.'

'Work began in 2012?'

'That's right.'

'And it was planned to end after twenty-five years, so …?'

'The lifetime has been extended. The market tolerates lower yields today than a generation back. The edge deposits are still viable and there's another small geological intrusion with something to give.'

'When the new site was identified, MaliLith became a publicly quoted company?'

'Yes. That was 2030, attracting many small local investors into the game of ladybirds and aphids,' replied Dujardin, with a cryptic smile.

'Go on?'

'Aphids infest your roses. The population soars. You acquire ladybirds. Each ladybird gorges on aphids, fifty or sixty a day. They thrive and breed, predating more and more aphids until there are far too many predators – ladybirds – relative to the number of prey animals – aphids – so the ladybirds die off and …'

She stopped, inviting Alex to compete the argument.

'The aphids make a comeback.'

'Exactly – supply and demand, back and forth, eventually creating equilibrium.'

'Where the two elements are in balance?'

'The right number of aphids and the right number of ladybirds.'

'Good explanation,' said Alex. 'Are you a keen gardener?'

'We all try to grow something these days, don't we, even a window box?'

Alex thought about the apple trees down the centre of the boulevard beneath his mother's windows.

'Yes, I suppose we do.' He decided to confront some of the more contentious issues. 'The new site will use a lot more water, employing the same 29-kilometre pipeline from the Sélingué Dam that serves the local population?'

'It will.'

'In this dry nation.'

'I know. We can't hide from it. It's an issue. But used water is stored and the supernatant is reused.'

'Supernatant?'

'The clean water at the top of the tank. The impurities fall to the bottom with gravity.'

'Supernatant,' mused Alex. 'From the Latin, meaning "over-swimming".'

'I expect so,' said Dujardin, vaguely. She tugged a nicely-bound presentation from her briefcase. Alex had already seen a copy but had left it behind at BA 117. 'What did you think of the briefing? It was prepared by one of my best juniors.'

'I haven't yet read it. I much prefer to learn first-hand, in conversation. I make more connections when I hear it live.'

She laughed.

'Well, it's talking shop, but that's what I enjoy as well. What else do you want to know?'

'Stay with water. It must be a frailty?'

'The water recycling?'

'No, the pipeline from Lake Sélingué.'

'In terms of criminal damage?'

'Yes. Or political protest.'

She nodded.

'Mining is thirsty work. It doesn't happen without plentiful water.'

'Bore holes?'

She shook her head.

'Marginal availability, marginal impact. In comparison, I mean.'

'Meanwhile, the people are thirsty too.'

'I know.'

Alex moved on.

'The mining explosives used to be brought in overland from Cyrenia. Are they good roads?' he asked.

'Pretty good and well policed by Algeria and Niger, but since the

Cyrene City explosion everything comes and goes south.'

'Through Côte d'Ivoire?'

'The roads are reasonable. That kind of infrastructure attracted a lot of development money in the twenties. But access to ports is a significant pilgrimage. Mali is properly landlocked.'

'How many trucks, how often?'

'They go to the ports at San Pedro or Abidjan, about 900 kilometres. There will be about 180 trucks in the fleet when we reach maximum workflow, taking four or five days for each return trip. For the moment, there are a couple of dozen.'

'Big trucks?'

'Forty-tonne capacity, though we generally cap the loads at thirty-two. Most of them return empty but some haul supplies back up from the coast.'

'Guarded?'

'You mean someone riding shotgun?' She laughed. 'No need. Who's going to steal a forty-tonne truck and what would the robbers do with a mountain of unprocessed lithium ore?'

Alex frowned, interested that the marketing director didn't seem to know everything that had been happening on the ground.

'What about at the mine workings? Do you have your own security?'

'That's a sensitive subject. We do, but there is resistance to the idea that we would train our own "private army".'

Alex nodded, hearing the air quotes in her intonation, as well as seeing her gesture.

'And the public share offer was designed to counter that?' he asked. 'To make the corporation seem more Malian and less a faceless foreign exploitation?'

'Yes, and it made commercial sense,' Dujardin told him. 'But, regarding security, we mostly self-finance patrols from the Malian police. And MaliLith makes a significant financial contribution to their equipment and training.'

'Okay, can you tell me something more about the old site, Goulamina? On the sat-images, it looks like about two thirds of the land is a waste dump.'

'So you did read the report?' smiled Dujardin.

'I skimmed it,' Alex replied. 'And trust me, my memory is terrible.'

'I don't believe that, but yes, it's true there's an environmental cost – you might call it an aesthetic cost. But it's lithium. Without it, there is no modern world.' She tapped a finger on the nicely-bound presentation. 'It's all in my report.'

'I promise I'll look at it again before we land. Do you have any specific worries for this trip?'

'Security worries?'

'I suppose I'm asking you if your company has done enough to be well-received, trusted by the local population, or have you alienated anyone enough to inspire acts of violence?'

'I'd like to say the former, but …' She shook her head. 'It's a reasonable question, I mean, if we're asking you to protect the big boss.'

'To be clear, the French government has sent me to observe. I hope not to be doing any protecting.'

'Okay. Anyway, the short answer is, we've done at least as much as any other primary resources company has ever done and the efforts are ongoing, especially the restitution of the landscape …'

'You sound unsure?'

'Well, there's a problem, but not of our making. The south of Mali is tropical – has always been tropical. You know the area is famed for its mangoes? Well, climate change, desertification, soil erosion – all these are making cultivation more difficult, and there are people out there who seem to believe that MaliLith should be fixing the global climate at the same time as we're creating jobs for engineers, managers, miners, truckers, caterers, cleaners and all the rest.'

The flight attendant brought their cold starters. Dujardin excused herself and got up to use the bathroom. Alex knew from Chambon that there had been an attack on the supernatant water recycling tank. The consequences had been minor – the IED was simply not powerful enough – but he wondered if anyone had claimed responsibility. He supposed he might find out once he was on the ground.

He ate his over-seasoned salad and flicked through the briefing document. However Castile Energie dressed it up, the new mine would devastate a vast tract of sovereign landscape in order to enrich a handful of distant individuals who were already extremely wealthy. At the same time, it would provide a subsistence wage to maybe a thousand local people who would remain resolutely poor. It was the nature of the primary resources business – always had been, perhaps always would be – that the people who lived on the land had no right of ownership of the riches beneath their feet.

Dujardin came back and concentrated on eating. Turning the pages, Alex found a digest of lithium's importance in a dazzling array of fields: in Alzheimer's prevention and in the control of mood swings; reducing the frequency of manic episodes in patients with bipolar disorder; encouraging muscle relaxation in Tourette's patients; promoting bone density; its flammability made it a key component in certain powerful explosives; lithium-7 was a common coolant in nuclear reactors; lithium fluoride had multiple applications in electromagnetic radiation and was used in focal lenses for high energy proton beams; as a crystal oscillator, it enhanced signal precision in mobile phones; and it had the miracle property of being able to extract carbon dioxide from enclosed atmospheres – such as a submarine or a space vehicle – and, like a plant or a tree, it could release oxygen in return.

Above all, though, it was the presence of lithium in rechargeable batteries – in small mobile devices, in electric vehicles and in massive storage arrays – that made it fundamental across vast swathes of mid-21st century technology and had led to it becoming known as 'white oil'.

'Your junior did an excellent job,' said Alex, handing back the presentation.

'Thank you,' said Dujardin, checking the time. 'We'll go forward an hour.'

Alex nodded. His comm-watch would update automatically.

Soon, the flight attendant brought the main course – a North African spiced dish made with plant meat. It was pleasant enough, served with millet as its staple carbohydrate.

'You know,' said Léa Dujardin, 'I enjoy all this …' She waved a hand, indicating travel and luxury and all the rest of it. 'But I sometimes think that the world would get on better if we all just sat still at home.' She laughed. 'Don't tell anyone I said that.'

'I won't,' said Alex.

There was something in what Dujardin said, but the bad guys were always the ones least likely to sit still, so the good guys had to go out looking for them, to make sure that a tiny fragment of the world's population could live in splendour, while the majority just about managed to get by, and the dispossessed rump of jobless and Blanks struggled with the challenges of everyday survival.

23

Because Davide Castile wasn't yet in Bamako, Alex would have to wait to meet him. Fortunately, that gave him time to investigate the death of the naturalised French citizen shot by the police. He got his opportunity the next morning, in the noisy breakfast room of the Hôtel Étoile. He'd been thinking about David Castile's marketing director, Léa Dujardin, deciding that she was nowhere near as unthreatening as she first appeared. Then he glanced out of the open window and saw a team of builders dismantling a small stage by the statue in the square.

'Would you mind if I sit?'

Alex took in a man in uniform – heavily built, wearing a shirt slightly too small for his torso – who held out a large soft hand.

'Chief of Police Konaré?'

'That's me.'

Alex stood briefly and touched knuckles.

'Alexandre Lamarque.'

'Yes, I know who you are. The whole world knows who you are.'

Konaré pulled a chair out from under the table and sat down on its edge, looking very straight-backed and pert despite his heavy frame, glancing round. He caught a waiter's eye, ordered coffee and took up a forced pose. A second uniformed officer took a photograph of Alex and Konaré, nodded and left the dining room.

'For our records,' said the chief of police.

'Could you tell me how Drissa Sidibé, a French citizen, came to be killed?' Alex asked. 'I believe you took personal charge of the operation, sir?'

Alex intended to unsettle Konaré but didn't succeed.

'I did,' the chief of police replied complacently.

The waiter arrived with a coffee cup and a metal jug. He put it down on the table and Konaré waved him away.

'And what was the operation's purpose?'

'To show that we are in control,' Konaré replied, then asked: 'Do you want that tiny croissant?' Alex shook his head. Konaré put it in his mouth and chewed thoughtfully. 'Because we are in control.'

'Control is relative, sir,' said Alex.

'A well-ordered society has rules. Without rules, there is no confidence in the future. Control must be restated, demonstrated over and over again. This is the job of the police – to inspire trust and, perhaps, a frisson of fear.'

Alex poured himself more coffee, adding plant-milk from a silver jug. He recognised the attitude – an almost sadistic enjoyment of power. And yet Konaré, despite his words, seemed sympathetic, almost kindly.

'You had solid intelligence?' Alex insisted.

'Very good, very solid.' The chief of police eyed another tiny pastry. 'Do you want that *pain au chocolat*?'

'Have it,' said Alex. 'Sidibé's travel permit was legitimate.'

'Not for Yanfolila. And why did he go south if his family are here in Bamako?' He waved a vague hand. 'In Solidarity City, an eastern suburb. Yet he went to the mining belt.'

'Do you have camera footage from the airport, from customs, from security, then the buses or trains?'

'Ah,' said the chief of police. 'We have cameras and they are very good cameras – the best cameras. But they function *à la malienne* …' He smiled self-deprecatingly, showing fine white teeth. 'Things that function "Mali-style" don't really function at all.'

178

'No recordings?' asked Alex. 'No facial recognition?'

'None of that, no. A human officer caught him in conversation with a supposed Dogon priest, one Hamady Dara, but that man too is now dead ...' Konaré picked up an unused napkin and wiped the corners of his mouth. 'You are a representative of France, captain. It would be a poor use of your time, but would you please help us by formally identifying his corpse?'

'I have his biometric records. But to be clear, you suspected him of ...'

Konaré sighed, pleased with his snack.

'You are an important man, Captain Lamarque, but the conspiracy did not end with what you achieved, isn't that right? And you want to clear away the last vestiges, the lesser players, hiding in the cracks – or some of them, I don't wonder, in plain sight. Isn't that why you are here, in Bamako? I am on your side. It is better to be safe than sorry, *n'est-ce pas*?'

'Time will tell.'

'You will identify him, please, and we will take things from there. Perhaps you will introduce me to Monsieur Castile. I own shares in his company. I admire him.'

Konaré drained his cup. Alex considered the situation. He was not in charge. In a sense, he was there on sufferance, sent by the French government because the French industrialist, Davide Castile, was vastly important. Beyond that, he had no real powers or defined purpose. He was window-dressing, a stage-managed symbol of the diminished reach and power of a decadent colonial power, clinging by its fingernails to past glories.

'What did you mean, Chief Konaré, by "take things from there"?'

The hot wind raised a puff of Saharan dust from the windowsill and blew it across the breakfast table.

'As you said, captain, "time will tell".'

They travelled out into the suburbs of Bamako in a large electric pick-up with a single bench seat. Konaré sat in the middle with the driver on the left – the same man who had taken the photograph in the dining room – and Alex on the right. As they drove, Alex read a police report on what had happened in the square outside the Hôtel Étoile on a screen on the dashboard. When he had finished, Konaré filled him in with more detail of the carnage on the lonely roads between the old mine at Goulamina and the newer workings at Yanfolila.

'Yes,' Konaré concluded. 'A co-ordinated attack with a diversion and then a real target.'

'The supernat tank,' said Alex.

'Yes. Had it been successful, it would have entailed a long clean-up operation, maybe two months of interruption.'

'And the man you had shot was part of it?'

'Is it not clear from the report? The body of the supposed Dogon priest was found at the ambush site. The drugs Drissa Sidibé smuggled and sold paid for the weapons used in the attacks.'

Alex thought that Konaré had probably guessed correctly, but his evidence was far from prosecutable in law. Were there other reasons for Drissa Sidibé's execution?

The driver turned off the main road, skirted Sotuba Cemetery and nosed in through an automated gate into a closed car park. Before the gate could shut, a young woman in a loud print dress of bogolan fabric squeezed in after them, calling out something Alex couldn't hear. She ran in front of their vehicle and put her hands on the bonnet. Her eyes and cheeks were wet with tears.

The driver jumped out, strode round and took hold of her shoulders, shaking her roughly and pushing her back towards the wall. Alex got out as well, hearing an incomprehensible stream of Bambara.

'What's happening?' he asked in French.

'I want to see my brother,' she shouted.

Alex ordered the driver to stand down. He looked undecided. Konaré lumbered out of the pick-up.

'*Ça suffit, laisse-la.*'

That'll do. Leave her.

The driver let go of the woman and stepped away.

'My brother's body has been brought here?' she asked, wiping her eyes with an embroidered handkerchief.

'Yes,' said Konaré. 'You are …?'

The woman wore a small bag on a long narrow strap across her chest. She opened it and found a plasti-card ID. Konaré took it.

'Mademoiselle Sidibé.'

'Yes,' she confirmed. 'Aminata Sidibé.'

He gave the ID to the driver to verify on the police computer connection in the pick-up.

'And your brother was Drissa,' said Konaré, 'meaning a student of knowledge.' He turned to Alex. 'This is not something you could possibly know; even the best briefings wouldn't have covered that.'

'No,' said Alex, soberly. It seemed to him that Konaré was striking quite the wrong attitude with a bereaved relative. He spoke to the young woman. 'How is it you are here, Mademoiselle Sidibé?'

'I've been here since yesterday. I waited in the bus shelter.' She waved a hand, indicating the road outside the car park, beyond the motorised gate. 'I slept there to be here this morning. I have not been allowed to see him, although he is … was …'

Chief Konaré sighed.

'This is a very sad moment in your life. There will be other sad moments, but this is a bad one. I understand that. But time will heal you. New horizons will open, today or tomorrow.'

'Can I see him?' she asked again.

'Yes, you can.' Konaré turned to the police driver. 'Go and make sure all is ready.'

The driver saluted and went inside the building.

'What was your brother doing in the square?' Alex asked.

'He was listening to the musicians,' said Aminata.

181

'No,' said Konaré. 'That is foolishness. Tell the truth.'

'But that is the truth.'

'It is not the whole truth,' said Konaré loudly. 'Nothing like it.' He took a step towards her. She was still cowering against the wall where the driver had left her. 'What is the point of lying about a dead man? Eh?'

'He was my brother –'

'I know,' shouted Konaré. 'We know.' He made a gesture to take in Alex. 'Even the special agent from Paris knows – the "man who saved the world". Why do you think he is here?'

Aminata looked very small with the bulk of Konaré standing over her. Alex fetched a bottle of water from the pick-up and offered it to her.

'Thank you,' she said, and he wondered if the wary expression in her eyes meant she had recognised him anyway.

Konaré sauntered away to perch on the corner of the bonnet, taking a long thin cigar and a petrol lighter from the breast pocket of his shirt – objects signifying luxury and ostentation.

'Your brother,' said Alex quietly, 'worked in a pharma clinic in Marseille. He gained his right to work in France from studying at the university on a student exchange, achieving top grades. Three years on, he was naturalised. More recently, he was granted a tourist permit to return home when the travel corridor opened. Do you have any family members in the south?'

'No, or yes,' said the young woman in a small voice. 'Perhaps I don't know them.'

'He brought drugs with him, for resale.'

'The drugs were to do people good,' said Aminata. 'That cannot be wrong.'

'He wasn't a licensed trader,' said Alex gently.

'But to do good—'

'Medicines are regulated goods. They can't be bought and sold without supervision. That would be unsafe.'

182

Konaré interrupted again: 'He was a dangerous little man and, with the money he was making, he bought two guns.'

'No, that must be a lie—' began the young woman.

'We have the evidence. He traded his French medicines for weapons.'

'No,' said Aminata. 'He was trading medicines to raise money for me to go back with him to France,' she said weakly, tears on her cheeks once more.

'He was watched,' said Konaré. 'He was seen with a man in the blue robe of a Dogon priest, a dangerous terrorist. We have handheld camera photographs. They are poor, *à la malienne*, but there is no doubt.'

The sun peeped over the buildings. Alex felt the warmth of it on his face.

'Mademoiselle Sidibé, in Bamako, who else did your brother meet or speak to?' he asked.

'I don't know,' said the sister quietly.

'You do, though,' Alex insisted.

'Just that he was with the wrong people,' she told him, her eyes down. 'I knew it because he would not introduce them to me.'

'He was secretive,' said Konaré. 'Of course.'

'Where did he meet these people?' asked Alex.

'I wasn't there.'

Konaré dropped the stub of his cigar and trod on it.

'This is all extremely serious,' he said. 'This is very bad for your family. You know that?'

'What do you mean?' asked Aminata Sidibé.

'A terrorist and a drug smuggler.'

The young woman looked from Konaré to Alex and back again.

'What should I do?'

Konaré nodded slowly.

'I will help you,' he said and held out a hand.

Almost despite herself, it seemed to Alex, Aminata put her small hand in his.

'Thank you,' she told him.

It sounded almost like a question.

24

In the morgue, Alex had a flashback to a similar facility at the international rail terminal in Calais. It was there that he had finally worked out the significance of the tattoos that some of the conspirators had inked on their skin. Drissa Sidibé wasn't marked in that way, either on the backs of his fingers or any other part of his body.

Konaré had asked Alex, as a representative of the French state, to officially identify the dead man. But Aminata, Drissa's sister, took that responsibility, showing great self-possession, laying a hand on his cold forehead without flinching.

They filed back out into an office where Konaré pressed a cup of bitter coffee from a vending machine on both Alex and Aminata and three paper forms had to be signed. While this was happening, Alex was wondering about Konaré's motivation. The chief of police was one of many investors in MaliLith. Could that be a contributing reason for the summary execution of Aminata's brother: to protect his investments? Konaré had been right, after all. The corpse of his associate, the fake Dogon priest, had been retrieved from the ambush site on the Yanfolila road.

In addition, Konaré had asked to meet Castile for a photo opportunity, suggesting political ambitions. And there was the photograph his driver had taken in the dining room at the hotel, perched alongside 'the man who saved the world'. Alex wouldn't be surprised to see that soon broadcast in the Malian media.

'Now, mademoiselle,' said Konaré. 'Go home and wash and change after your night in the bus stop. Then come to police central. You must make a proper statement.'

Aminata acquiesced then tentatively asked: 'Why is he here?'

'Captain Lamarque? Because he knows more than you do.' Konaré laughed. 'Perhaps more even than I. Now go.' Aminata left on foot, moving slowly. 'Her home is not far from here,' Konaré told Alex. 'She will do as I have requested. In any case, I have a man there to watch over her.'

Alex had also been considering Aminata's degree of innocence.

'Why did you lie to her, telling her that you do not know who shot her brother, that it might have been one of his own associates?'

'Because it is useful to preserve a degree of uncertainty before her official interrogation.'

Alex changed tack.

'If the brother sourced the weapons, who is to say that she didn't know?'

'You discern a shadow of guilt?' Konaré weighed the question. 'If there is guilt, it might not necessarily be for something she has done, but for something she knew and took no steps to prevent, a sin of omission rather than a sin of commission?'

'That's possible, yes.'

Alex thought about Aminata Sidibé's performance in the car park at the morgue. Was that what it was – an act?

'When will you interview her?'

'After lunch. The officer at her residence will keep an eye.'

'I would like to be present.'

'Of course,' Konaré replied smoothly. 'I will send a car to fetch you from your hotel for two o'clock. We will expect you.'

They drove back to police central via the Hôtel Étoile. Alex got out feeling a familiar tiresome pressure – the detested bureaucratic follow

186

up. His mission was closing in on the point where he would have to sum it up in writing.

By coincidence, in his room, he found an envelope containing a print-out of the draft police report on the incidents in the south of the country, written in the leaden official style, more or less the same the whole world over. Alex rubbed the first page between thumb and forefinger. He thought he could feel the dust of the Sahara in the fibres of the paper.

Because the satlink for his comm-watch in Bamako was slow and, more annoying still, intermittent, he logged into the hotel network using his own on-board encryption, looking first for unread messages. Among all the routine notifications, there was a 2D video message from Doctor Labeur at the Rothschild Institute. His mother was doing reasonably well. Labeur and the Norwegian specialist, Professor Genmis, were still inclined to the opinion that her relapse had been due to 'an overenthusiastic return to work, weakening her resistance to a recrudescence of the infection'. They did not, however, mention her being released from hospital and they added that the possibility of a second opportunistic infection had not been excluded.

Gloria herself had sent a written communication. Characteristically, she didn't mention being hospitalised but wanted to ask his opinion on the first draft of a paper she had written on the evolution of classical musical styles – and how they were influenced by geopolitical and societal developments. Alex remembered her mentioning the idea before he had travelled to Cyrene City for the armed extraction of the embattled Prime Minister Mourad.

Now that everything – all information, all documents, all artefacts, all evidence – is available to everyone all of the time, it is hard, even for the specialist, to discern the patterns of continuity and change.

Alex smiled. This was the considered voice of the historian. Writing in this way was Gloria's attempt at telling him not to worry, that all would be well. He wondered what the effort had cost her.

The third important message was from André Chambon. Davide Castile was still in Paris or, perhaps, the Pyrenees. Alex was instructed to await his arrival.

Fine. He would be busy enough. And he had an idea it might be a good idea to travel south to the mines.

Next there was a 3D holo from Amaury, recorded that morning,. In it, he was sitting at a table in a bland kitchen, probably the spartan overnight accommodation at the Piscine, the External Security HQ.

Because you were gone, they made me lead the training. You would have enjoyed seeing Paul Sanchez. Chambon was there, of course, and Mademoiselle Cantor with her mess of red hair, Sébastien Ménard, five others. I think they were disappointed it wasn't you, especially Sanchez. He probably wanted to relive his part in your triumph.

In the 3D holo, Amaury moved away from the camera to stir a saucepan. He spoke over his shoulder.

I told them what I was supposed to tell them – that there is always room for personal judgement, within certain operational parameters. Cantor wanted to know how to make that judgement. I told her to wait till you were back, that you would know, that I had no idea. Chambon didn't like that.

Amaury's translucent shape tipped pasta into a colander in the sink to drain, then came back to the table.

Gerest would prefer to have you dancing for him like a puppet, but he likes my optics, too – the 'wounded soldier'. I'm off to Cyrene City this afternoon for the reopening of the parliament building. Have you heard from Mariam? Okay, I'm going to eat.

The pre-recorded holo disappeared. Had he heard from Mariam? That was the next message, short and depressingly factual, sent the previous evening.

Alex, the funeral is tomorrow. I will be in touch afterwards. M

That was it. Stark, unemotional – at least on the surface. He knew that couldn't be true – that she was suffering – but there was nothing he

188

could do about it.

Alex dictated a reply, telling Mariam where he was, that his time was not his own. He opened a personal message from Claudine Poiret – another pre-recorded video. Poiret was on the deck of a ship, dressed in waterproofs to protect her from near-horizontal rain. In the background, he could see a shoreline battered by gales.

Capitaine, when you have time and encrypted connectivity, I want you to look into the use of time-lapse trojans disrupting travel infrastructure. It is an increasing problem. Also, the resumption of normal diplomatic relations with Egypt. You and I need to discuss how best to exploit your celebrity for our desired outcomes of peace and prosperity.

Alex sighed. That wasn't what he wanted.

And probably not while I'm still in Mali, he thought.

He made his way to the gym in the hotel basement. He had a set of fitness goals he tried to keep up with, regardless of his other responsibilities. As a minimum, he aimed to spend three or four hours each week on cardiovascular exercise – running, cycling, swimming, rowing – working at about eighty per cent of his peak heart rate. The thing he found more difficult to keep up with was the strength training. Genetics had given him above average muscle mass, but when he neglected to turn his mind to the tiresome routine of weights machines and barbells, he found himself becoming excessively wiry from the cardio.

The rhythm of his workout cleared his mind and released his imagination. Two ideas bubbled to the surface from the swamp of non-systematic information that his brain had not yet got around to properly cataloguing. The first included a memory of Fayard's posthumous remarks from the tomb in Montparnasse cemetery.

Without the traitor at the heart of our defences to mastermind them, they will be less grandiose, perhaps – smaller, more local. But that means they will also be more devious, more insidious.

That wasn't necessarily the case. There could still be a controlling intelligence – just one that he hadn't yet met.

The second idea was that Aminata Sidibé was not to be trusted and that it was Konaré who was in danger.

25

In the bathroom of her family home, a bungalow in a suburb of Bamako known as Solidarity City, near an important mosque, Aminata Sidibé contemplated several possible futures.

She was aware that men liked to look at her. She had lived with the knowledge – and its consequences – since she was thirteen years old. She did not enjoy their gaze, but she thought she understood that her presence compelled their eyes in a kind of pre-programmed response.

She washed her face and hands, thinking about her brother, shot dead in the shadow of the Monument to the Heroes of the Black Army. She had been there, on the far side of the crowd, coming to join him at lunchtime in a break from her work at the post office, hoping to persuade him to talk again about visas and a new life.

Well, that's all over now.

Looking down at his corpse on the refrigerated stone slab in the morgue, she had challenged the fat police chief.

'You say you don't know who killed him? Was it your men?'

'Why would they have shot him?'

'Then who?'

'Another dealer, perhaps?'

'If he was killed by some gangster, why were the drugs still on his body when he was found? Surely his attacker would have taken them?'

'Because of the speed of my men's response. They were at his side to hear the poor man's last breath.'

Lies, she thought.

Then there was the Frenchman. He had looked at her quite differently – sympathetic but also coolly appraising.

Suspicious?

Aminata went into her bedroom and retied her hair. She had already changed out of her bogolan dress with its dusty marks from sleeping in the bus shelter. She thought about Konaré asking if she had seen the news – a madman who had hijacked a mining truck and gone on a rampage.

Was that also an evolutionary trait, she wondered, for young men to believe in fantasies and commit stupid acts of violence as a consequence? No, not only men. Also, her own sister, Narissa, supposedly dead by her own hand outside the data centre in Marseille. And Kadidia who, she knew, was living in a half-built suburb of Yanfolila. Why? The same reason, surely.

She picked up her clutch bag and checked its contents – her ID, a payment card, some cash, her knife. She checked the time, indicated in red LED letters in the corner of her bedroom mirror: 12h15.

From Solidarity City she could take the urban railway to Police Central and be there on time, as promised, at one-thirty. Then all of Aminata's possible futures, like streams out of the hills in rainy season, would narrow to a single flood. Narissa and Drissa were both gone. She had only Kadidia left.

Chief of Police Bakary Konaré was also thinking about possible futures. In the first possible future, he was magnanimous and kind and Aminata Sidibé rewarded him in a way that his imagination pictured in lurid detail. With an extra frisson of sickly pleasure, the sexual fantasy made him feel ashamed. In the second possible future, he was magnanimous and kind and kept his self-respect.

Konaré's office was on the banks of the Niger River, flowing like a vast artery through the capital city. But he could only see it from his *en suite* bathroom, his heavy arms on the windowsill, the obscured glass flung wide.

This is an opportunity. Through the Frenchman, Lamarque, I will meet Castile. I will be pictured alongside them, as if one with the elite, arms across the shoulders of 'the man who saved the world' and the man whose corporation generates eight percent of Mali's GDP.

That would be the launch-pad for his election to the city council, perhaps even to the mayoralty. Plus he had taken out the terrorist Drissa Sidibé. Wasn't there a slogan in there somewhere?

Bakary Konaré – the man who gets things done.

He pulled the window almost closed. The *en suite* had a shower, a toilet, a washbasin and a small recess with a hanging rail for a change of clothes. He put on a clean shirt and, as he did up the fiddly buttons with his thick fingers, observed his own face in the mirror, wondering if he might have time to shave. His chin was rough to the touch.

Was that important?

He exited the bathroom, glancing round his office: a generously-proportioned room with functioning air-con and a large fan turning lazily in the ceiling; warm waxed floorboards of iroko wood; a large hand-painted map of the Republic of Mali on traditionally-woven cloth on the wall; a capacious chair and an impressive iroko-wood desk; a desk-lamp with a shade made of pastel-coloured glass; a leather blotter; an old-fashioned phone alongside the digital networked device; a shallow cut-glass receptacle for pens and pencils.

He took off his heavy leather belt and holster. His driver – actually his personal assistant, a civilian in uniform who hadn't yet grasped when or where to salute – came in with digital papers regarding a request for reinforcements by the governor of the prison. The building was, in part, Konaré's responsibility, in the sense that he and his men were required to respond when events there exceeded the prison staff's ability to cope – strikes, protests, demonstrations, riots. Originally designed to house four hundred prisoners, it had been extended and, in some respects, improved, but investment had failed to keep up with the growth in the population and the proportional growth in crime. Today, it housed almost three thousand in facilities suitable for no more than fifteen hundred.

Was this where he wanted Aminata Sidibé to spend the next ten years of her life?

No, of course not.

But was there evidence that she knew more about her brother's intentions and connections than she let on?

A suspicion, perhaps – one that the Frenchman clearly shared.

Konaré wanted to get ahead of Lamarque, so he had told him two o'clock. He would have thirty minutes alone with the young woman and much could be accomplished in thirty minutes. Perhaps they might even come to some kind of understanding. She worked at the post office. She must have useful skills. Was there any reason she shouldn't replace his uninspiring assistant? The man could be retrained and redeployed somewhere far away, in the actual police force, and Aminata Sidibé would then be available to him every day, sitting demurely in the lobby outside his door. It would be good for her and for her family – if she had any more family. Perhaps even enough to make up for the stain of the brother's association with crime.

'I am a good man,' he said aloud. 'I can be a good man.'

He checked the time. It was just before half-past one.

Would she be on time? He thought she would.

But if she was guilty, would she run?

If she ran, well, she would lead his men to new evidence, new connections, and he would be the winner once again.

He heard a sound outside, went to the door and opened it. There was Aminata Sidibé, sitting on an uncomfortable bench in the lobby, very upright in a clean dress, her hair retied, holding a clutch bag in her lap. His assistant requested permission to go and pick up the Frenchman.

194

'Be back here at two o'clock. That is what he expects.'

'Yes, sir.'

The assistant gave his slack, pointless salute and left. Konaré nodded with satisfaction. He would have plenty of time alone with his 'witness'.

'Won't you come in?'

She rose and he realised that he had been looking forward to seeing her do so, enjoying the shape of her standing up, moving across the room towards him, her face composed, her eyes on his like a challenge or an invitation. Behind his eyes, the first fantasy – the shameful one with lurid detail – began to recompose.

No, he told himself. *That is not the correct path*.

He stepped back, giving her plenty of space, allowing her to enter the enormous office without obliging her to brush past him. He watched her take up a position in the centre of the room, beneath the fan. There was a slight sheen of sweat on her brow and cheekbones, as if she had been hurrying, so as not to be late.

Gratifying, he thought, closing the door.

'Please take a seat.'

She hesitated and he saw her open the clutch bag.

He was not a fool. He knew at once what her intention was. He could see, as well, that she had read in his eyes that he had guessed. Frightened, he spread his arms, turning the palms of his hands towards her in a gesture of appeasement.

'You do not want to do this,' he told her.

Aminata stood in the dead centre of the enormous office, beneath the lazy fan, allowing her fingers to undo the clasp on her clutch bag. What was his expression? Was he confused, just for a fraction of a second? Her hand closed over the handle of the knife. And was he now afraid? If he was afraid, that meant he was guilty. If he was guilty, she should do the thing she had dreamt of doing – the nightmare thing.

But had he seen it in her eyes? Had she already given herself away?

He spread his arms, turning the palms of his hands towards her in a gesture of appeasement.

'You do not want to do this,' he told her.

But she did want to and she was young and lithe, her reactions quick, while his were slowed by age and obesity and dissipation. She leapt in, quicker than his hands could come round to protect himself, the knife in her dominant right hand, held in her fist, and she drove it backhand into the right-hand side of his neck just as his arms enfolded her in a bear hug.

The air was forced from her lungs and she felt herself crushed against his belly and chest, her bent right arm squeezed against his rough cheek, the top of her head against his heavy chin. She felt the gush of blood from the wound – the very accurate wound that had severed the major blood vessels in his neck – pumping over her left shoulder and down her back, splattering on the floorboards of waxed iroko wood.

The horrible moment stretched out, far beyond what she had imagined, the ghastly embrace dragging on and on. Then, finally, just as she was beginning to find it hard to expand her chest and breathe, his arms weakened, his grip became less tight.

He tried to say something but couldn't. His arms dropped away from her and he staggered back a step, then two more, then the backs of his knees hit the edge of the velvet-covered chaise longue and he sat, involuntarily, the blood still pumping, but much more slowly, with far less force, from the wound in the side of his neck, raising his hand to staunch it as it pulsed weakly through his failing fingers.

He tried to speak again. Aminata Sidibé turned away, looking for something with which to wipe away the blood from her hair, her face, her shoulders, her dress.

And her feet. She was standing in a puddle of blood.

There was a large decorative fabric on the wall – a printed map of the Republic of Mali, a couple of metres across. She pulled it off the wall, sending two drawing pins skittering across the floorboards, and used it as a towel.

It was not enough. The printed fabric was unabsorbent. She was merely smearing the blood more widely across her body.

Her eyes darted round and she tilted her head as she listened. There was traffic outside but no sounds from the outer office, no rattle of a keyboard or voice patiently dictating to speech recognition.

No, of course – Konaré had sent his assistant away. She had time, still.

There was a second door, behind the chaise longue, narrower and more utilitarian. Where did it lead?

She made straight for it and Konaré reached out his hand, his fingers almost grazing her hip, making her pause.

Why aren't you dead yet?

Then he slipped from the velvet seat onto the floor, falling onto his side, folded like a baby in sleep.

She opened the utilitarian door. It led into a bathroom.

Without thinking, she kicked off her trainers and stepped into the shower, turning on the tap, letting the cool water run through her hair, over her shoulders, soaking her dress, running down her calves and away down the drain, swirling with red blood.

She stepped out, snatching a fluffy absorbent towel from a rail, roughly rubbing at her hair, dabbing at her dress.

Could she slip away like this, drenched as if caught out in the rain?

No, not today, with the entire dome of the sky stark blue and utterly without clouds.

Then she noticed the recess with Konaré's changes of clothes – a dress uniform with braid and medals, an everyday jacket and ...

Yes, a beige everyday jellabiya in heavy cotton.

She stripped off her dress, leaving it in a sodden puddle on the tiled floor, and grabbed another soft towel to dry herself more thoroughly. She pulled the jellabiya over her head. It hung around her like a tent, ludicrously large. She rummaged in the recess, finding the trousers of the dress uniform had a broad woven belt. She pulled it from its loops, gathered up the loose fabric of the jellabiya and did up the woven belt around her hips, glancing round for a mirror, the one above the washbasin. For a better view, she stood on the edge of the shower tray. She twitched at the heavy beige fabric, evening it out.

Yes, this would do. Her appearance was unusual, but it would pass.

She rinsed the soles of her trainers and went back out into the office. Almost all of the centre of the iroko-wood floor was covered with sticky blood. She walked round the perimeter, brushing against the shelves of files and books of law, lifting the hem of the jellabiya with the fingers of her left hand. At the door, looking back, she noticed Konaré's gun in the holster on the desk and wished she could go and pick it up, but there was no pathway across the room that would not oblige her to step in the dead man's gore.

His body drew her eye. There he was, a huge fat baby, grotesque, the flesh of his face flaccid and drooping, one hand still on the wound to his neck, the other reaching out, palm up, as if begging for assistance.

This was, she understood, what Drissa had tried to avoid. He – and Kadidia, too – had tried to keep her at arm's length from the violence.

She opened the office door very quietly and peeped outside. The reception room was still empty.

What next?

Travel south to the half-built suburb of Yanfolila and find Kadidia.

How?

She would find a way.

26

Amaury took an early high-speed train from Paris to Toulouse, arriving refreshed and well fed from the on-board catering service. At Matabiau central station, he was met by an air force driver, sweltering in the cab of a weary Renault Trafic, daubed in camouflage paint.

They made good progress, out to the motorway ring road and then south west to Toulouse-Francazal airbase, Base Aérienne 101, about eight kilometres from the centre of the city. At the gate, the duty officers ran face recognition, even though they had addressed the driver by name and knew who Amaury was from the news streams. Finally, they were allowed to proceed.

Amaury was escorted to a holding area in a hangar on the far side of the base, the same facility Alex had used before his extraction mission to Cyrenia – a stack of three portacabin offices inscribed with air force insignia, overseen by a uniformed clerk.

'You have been allocated a seat on a military transport leaving later this afternoon, sir. Would you like to wait in the cafeteria? I can have you driven across.'

'I've eaten.'

She led him up a squeaky external staircase to the top portacabin, opened the door with a plasti-card and stood back.

'Anything you need, sir, I'll be downstairs.'

He sat down on a low sofa with worn-out foam cushions. On the other side of the room was a cheap desk and an old-school computer terminal with a VR headset. The air-con unit above the window was out of order, with a thick strip of gaffer tape over the controls. The temperature, he guessed, was a stuffy twenty-six or twenty-seven degrees.

He stood to look out into the vast hangar. The Renault Trafic was parked so far away that it looked like a toy. A fork-lift was pushing wheeled loading pallets from a secure cage in the corner across the open space towards the enormous doors, placing them carefully alongside one another, ready for embarkation. After the fifth trip, the fork-lift stopped and he heard a much more powerful engine, one that shook the fragile fabric of the portacabin, resonating deep and low.

He opened the door onto the landing, putting his hands over his ears, seeing a military transport plane being manoeuvred back towards the hangar entrance by a vehicle attached with a stiff coupling bar to its nose. Once it was in position, the low throbbing of the idling engines stopped, the rear ramp dropped and two uniformed airmen jumped down.

The transport was a A430M. The two uniforms each had haulage cables in their hands. They attached them to the corners of the first wheeled pallet and called out. Somewhere inside the fuselage, someone else must have actioned a motor as the first pallet was drawn up into the shadowy interior.

The uniformed clerk mounted the stairs, carrying a clothes-protector by the hook of its hanger.

'A dress uniform, sir. Would you like to try it on?'

'Just send it on board.'

'Yes, sir.'

She trotted back down and he watched her hand it over to one of the airmen, who took it up the ramp, probably hanging it on some exposed strut of the plane's skeleton. Transports weren't really built for passengers.

Amaury felt restless and unhappy. Because Alex was out of the PR loop, he was on his way to Cyrene City for a ceremony celebrating the defeat of the Coming Darkness conspiracy, timed to coincide with the reopening of the damaged parliament buildings – the place where he had lost his hand in the fire-fight. Then he would fly on to Aswan in Egypt where a second, more discreet ceremony would take place, part of that nation's tentative diplomatic reopening.

He took the stairs to the ground floor and found the clerk using voice recognition, her words evolving on the old-fashioned screen in front of her.

'I'll go to the cafeteria.'

She took off her headset.

'Yes, sir. I'll call a driver.'

'Is there meat?' Amaury asked.

'Yes, of course,' she said. Then, after a pause: 'Oh, I see what you mean. There's plant meat.'

'Great,' said Amaury.

He didn't mean it.

The assistant verger of Bilbao cathedral, Jaime Moreno, was desperately praying for guidance, on his knees in a cold side chapel after early mass. The security tags on both of his ankles meant that he could not stray more than five hundred metres from his grace-and-favour accommodation in the cloister – little better, if truth be told, than the austere cell in which he had been interrogated.

He had been raised in the church – Sunday school, confirmation classes, acolyte and then thurifer in the local parish church, then the mighty pilgrimage basilica itself, finding employment there just as his faith began to change from belief in the just and forgiving God of the New Testament to the jealous and vengeful deity of the Old Testament, leading him to join the conspiracy.

He felt broken by the trauma of his innermost thoughts being probed

201

by the AI, showing him wicked things, playing him heinous sounds, noting his interest or excitement, channelling him into mazes of carnal and mortal sin.

Somewhere around the fifth hour, he had found the energy to shout out to them that it wasn't fair, that they deserved what was coming – the meaning of the embossed white card he carried – though no one was there to listen, just the remorseless sequence of visual and auditory stimuli chasing his memory and imagination into black holes of self-loathing and hopelessness.

'The Coming Storm just means attacks of all kinds. It isn't about the weather or the wind. And it will never end.'

Faroukh Al-Medawi – Mayor of Tobruk, member of the tripartite presidential council of Cyrenia, trusted ally of Prime Minister Souad Mourad – had a habit of deep reflection. He took his time then acted decisively.

He was in the atrium of the parliament building in the heart of the government compound in Cyrene City. The remedial works were complete, financed by allies overseas who were sympathetic to Cyrenia's self-avowed mission of becoming a safe haven on the Mediterranean's southern shore for victims of environmental degradation and war. Were those allies philosophically in sympathy, or were they simply pleased that someone else was shouldering a burden they didn't care to carry themselves?

Al-Medawi saw the panelled door to Prime Minister Mourad's safe room swing open. Two officers in early middle age emerged. He knew them well – promoted from middling ranks to take the place of the traitor generals who had died in the failed insurrection. As a member of the presidential council, he wasn't surprised when they briefly came to speak to him – out of duty, perhaps, but not out of respect. He was, he knew, often underestimated.

President Manouche had been in touch with Al-Medawi about an old friend, Major Chaka Kassam. Manouche had asked Al-Medawi to include Kassam in the Cyrenian celebrations. He had refused. He was wary of 'old friends'. Did he think Kassam was allied to the Coming Storm? Not necessarily, but prudence was always better than regret – what the late Professor Fayard used to call 'the precautionary principle'. And he had read the transcripts from the interrogation of Amaury Barra's would-be assassin.

The Coming Storm just means attacks of all kinds. It isn't about the weather or the wind. And it will never end.

Al-Medawi pondered the idea of a storm that would 'never end'. The attempt on his own life in Algiers had been a shock of course, but not a surprise, in the same way that a sudden clap of thunder in the midst of a storm can be expected but still make one jump. The Coming Darkness conspiracy had been fuelled by a thirst for indiscriminate destruction. Was there now a new threat, an intelligence that sought power rather than a calamitous *tabula rasa* or 'clean slate'? If so, that thirst for power was in polar opposition to Prime Minister Mourad's idealism.

A group of three politicians exited the safe room. It would soon be his turn. The issue he wanted to discuss was the upcoming medal ceremony at Aswan, honouring Zeina Yaseen, an Egyptian citizen who had found herself almost crushed by the cruel gears of the Coming Darkness conspiracy. The trip seemed to him fraught with danger.

Prime Minister Mourad's personal assistant – a uniformed staff officer – emerged from the panelled door and looked round for him, unable to pick him out. Al-Medawi smiled to himself. It was a kind of superpower to seem so insignificant.

He made himself known and was invited inside the cedar-panelled safe room. He made his case and eventually prevailed. He would go to Aswan himself, in Mourad's stead.

The Egyptian delegate to the North African Defence League – the man with the scars of childhood chicken pox on his brow, Naguib Al-

Baghdadi – was in a truck on a desert road from the Cyrenian border towards Aswan, accompanied by Major Chaka Kassam of the Malian engineering corps. Having made much of his delight at welcoming his visitor, he was now sitting quietly, making his own political calculations.

Ever since Egypt had withdrawn from all international treaties and decided to plot its own course through the era of environmental degradation and transgenic disease – isolated diplomatically as well as physically, with closed borders and no international data connections – his ambitions had been stymied. That didn't mean that he wanted Egypt to revert to its previous destructive path. Wasn't that how the current degraded state of the world had been created?

There was a lot of talk of 'beacons' in modern politics, but it usually came back to a pair of central ideas, dancing hand in hand: that every single human life must be safeguarded, whatever its actual value as a productive member of society; and that the best way of achieving this was to prioritise economic growth above everything else.

Naguib Al-Baghdadi wasn't convinced by the idea that every human life was valuable or that more humans per square kilometre was always better than fewer. He was of the opinion that Egypt had it right, that the level of engineering sophistication attained at the end of the twentieth century – an analogue world enhanced by carefully chosen elements of clearly circumscribed digital technology – was ideal, but no more. Certainly, no machine intelligences with their dangerous and misleading certainties.

But he also wanted wealth and influence for himself.

It was only a small step, but ingratiating himself with President Manouche by inviting his old friend Major Chaka Kassam to the medal ceremony at Aswan would, he believed, put him in a good position to broker a deal for Malian lithium, a substance in desperately short supply in isolationist Egypt.

Major Chaka Kassam knew the value of lithium, of 'white oil'. At the

Al-Jaghar military and scientific base – where repairs and rebuilding were still in train – he had disembarked his heavy copter flight from Bamako with three cumbersome cases of samples. Ground crew had loaded them onto a truck for the short journey by desert road to the Egyptian border. Naguib Al-Baghdadi had met him at the dusty frontier post and they had driven on together.

Sitting alongside Al-Baghdadi, Kassam knew why the man with the scars of childhood chicken pox on his brow had invited him to the medal ceremony at Aswan, several days in advance. It was in order to try and bring him – and therefore the Republic of Mali – onside as a supplier of the miracle metal with its myriad medical, technological and military uses.

Naguib Al-Baghdadi, however, was unaware that the use Kassam intended to make of his samples was quite different.

27

The Saint-Médard valley had been cut, over millennia, by a stream that grew into a river, known locally as a '*gave*', lined with stones to which aquatic plants clung, the cold water dragging out their fronds in long green strands, as if the current was forever trying to scour the rocks clean.

In the farmhouse, Mariam was sitting at the kitchen table, watching the flame of the citronella candle. It burned non-stop to discourage insects, flies in the daytime and mosquitos at night. Her aunt came in from the front room where she had been laying a table for the wake. She looked older than her fifty-five years, drawn and weather-beaten from a life spent outside in sun and wind, a scar and a significant dent above her left eye from the aggressive surgical removal of a malignant melanoma.

'This day had to come,' she said, then added 'as God willed it', employing the local patois, a dialect of French embellished with Spanish and Basque. 'And it is better it is done.'

'Who's to say?' said Mariam. 'They might have preferred life to death.'

'That was no life. Once Ablah died, Janaan had no more reason to survive. It was meant.'

'By whom?' asked Mariam quietly. 'By what?'

'Just meant,' said her aunt.

Mariam could understand how Sara might think that a life of infirmity might not have been worth living. Sara had spent her entire life in this Pyrenean valley, tending crops and sheep and goats, with no television or computer, just a radio that she used solely for weather reports and farming programs. When they had briefly discussed the Coming Darkness conspiracy, Sara had merely shrugged and commented: 'Perhaps there are arguments on both sides.'

'All's ready,' the older woman said. 'I expect most of them will come. You will speak to them, thank them for their time and trouble?'

'I know my duty,' Mariam agreed.

She went outside, standing on the doormat in her socks. She had to acknowledge how at home she felt here, despite the clash of cultures, in this rustic farmhouse almost six hundred metres above sea level. A couple of days before, though, when she and Benjamin had visited the café in the closest town, at the bottom of the valley, to invite some of the more distant neighbours, Mariam had discovered that Benjamin felt the opposite – that he was restless, driven by the need to find a romantic partner. He had wanted to know about Paris and whether people there were as 'free and easy' as the radio said.

'Some,' she had told him.

'If I come, will you show me?' Benjamin had asked, as if she had a magic key that would open a secret door.

'Sure,' she had told him. 'Of course.'

It had rained heavily overnight. Mariam pushed her feet into a pair of Wellington boots, folding the hems of her suit-trousers tight to her shins. Aunt Sara came to join her.

'You could stay here,' she said. 'You could live here, away from all that.'

'I could,' said Mariam.

The extensive vegetable garden covered about half a hectare, carefully tended with several dozen varieties of edible plants in different stages of growth, maturity and decay, depending on the rhythm of their lives. At the end of every other row was a beehive and, in one corner, a pile of stones, stacked against a bank of rising ground.

It had always been there, Mariam remembered, always renewed, the place where anyone tending to the *potager* – planting, mulching, digging – would toss any stones they found in the soil. Now and then, they might be used as a building material, but the ground constantly provided more, as if there was a never-ending conveyor belt of rock fragments being pushed up from beneath their feet through the soft earth. She could see a stone herself, right now, at the foot of a green-bean plant, up against the hazel pole that supported it. She picked it up, weighed it in her hand, then tossed it away onto the pile, causing a tiny cascade of smaller stones to run down the side.

'Every field has its pile of stones,' said her aunt from the doorway.

'I know,' said Mariam.

Loading the plane didn't take anywhere as long as Amaury expected. He had only just finished his plant-meat steak – surprisingly good, as it happened – when the driver came to find him and tell him that departure was imminent.

Back at the hangar, he took a vision-call from Damien Gerest. He was in his office where Amaury had seen Alex flip the desk. The broken executive toys were lined up at the front edge, the neck of the dipping bird mended with adhesive tape, the steel balls on the Newton's cradle tangled on their fishing-line threads. Gerest reminded Amaury of his role.

'You'll give a speech for the reopening of the Cyrenian parliament building. You'll admire their idealism and sense of purpose. Then you'll get a good night's sleep before travelling on to Egypt.'

'Understood. I assume there will be no international press at Aswan?'

'None whatsoever.'

'And this woman, Zeina Yaseen?'

'She's nobody. Her involvement was a complete accident.'

208

'But she deserves recognition?'

'I suppose she does.'

'Anything I should be wary of?'

'No, it's all just protocol. Get back here safely. I have half a dozen more in-person interviews lined up in Paris.'

On the island of Haré, news from across the globe was constantly being sifted and synthesised by machine learning, providing Alex's unseen enemy – the wheelchair-bound, prematurely-aged owner of the castle-like residence – with up to date information at all hours of the day and night.

What were day and night, in any case? An arbitrary rhythm determined by the position of the Earth relative to the sun, conditioning human beings to a cycle of wakefulness and sleep that wasn't necessarily the most efficient way of spending the brief span allotted to each individual by fate. So he slept when he felt like it and woke when his body required him to do so, within the limits imposed by his linked medical conditions – none of which, happily, had impaired him mentally. In fact, the loss of physical independence had sharpened, he thought, his mental processes.

The events to which he was currently paying attention were evolving thousands of kilometres away. He was able to remain aware of them because he was at the centre of a web of undersea connector cables that criss-crossed the globe, providing physical communications links between continents. He was a major investor in such infrastructure. Part of the Coming Darkness conspiracy had been to selectively destroy his competitors' cables, providing himself with a near monopoly of certain comms pathways, once they had also taken down the satellites. Some of that had worked, but not all and not for long.

There were gaps in what he wanted to know. His man – the Malian military engineer, Major Chaka Kassam – was now in Egypt, and he had received no further communication from him once he had left the range of Cyrenian ground relays.

He abandoned his holos and drove his wheelchair outside onto the terrace that surrounded his mansion. Looking to the north, he could see the runway.

It had been difficult to level an appropriate strip of land on the awkward slopes of the island of Haré. Then it had been hard work reinforcing the honeycombed ground beneath the tarmac. It would have been trickier still had he needed four kilometres of runway or more, as was normal for heavy intercontinental passenger or transport aircraft. The needle-like Ae4, however, despite its ultra-long range, could manage take-off and landing on a strip of only 2000 metres.

Mariam's aunt's electric vehicles were trickle-charged from a solar array on a south-facing slope on a rota – a quadbike, a mid-sized van, three small agricultural robots. In addition, her aunt shared two diesel-driven heavy-duty vehicles with three neighbouring farms under licence from the Ministry of Food. But the funeral wasn't using powered vehicles. They were making their way down, alongside the cold-running *gave*, in a cart drawn by a bull, sedate and slow-paced.

All three of them were on board – Mariam, her aunt and her cousin Benjamin. Mariam was wearing a sober suit of charcoal-grey cotton, brought with her from Paris, her cousin a dark suit, home-made to a utilitarian pattern from recycled fabric – not because the farm was failing, but because thrift and frugality were a way of life. Sara wore her 'best' navy-blue dress, her hair covered by a headscarf with a pattern of bright flowers.

The two small coffins, woven from local hazel and wicker, were on a separate cart, attached behind with timber shafts. As they progressed downhill, neighbours came out of their houses and joined the procession. Others were already there, making nearly fifty people at the fence that surrounded the graveyard, where Mariam, Sara and Benjamin disembarked. Mariam and her aunt carried the smaller coffin, containing the mortal remains of Ablah. Benjamin and a neighbour carried Janaan. They went very carefully, the woven coffins awkwardly bendy, and put each one down on two pairs of ropes that had been laid ready to receive them. The grave was open, a headstone already positioned:

Ablah et Janaan
2025-2037

This new stone was alongside their mother's, carved from the same material but smaller, because at the time Mariam hadn't been able to afford anything grander.

Aliyah Jordane
1990-2025

The graveyard was full of drought-resistant plants. They were knee-deep in lavender, rosemary, yarrow, Californian poppies, sedums, society garlic, trumpet lilies and bulbines. The patch of ground around the new grave had been trodden flat, but not cleared, giving nature the best possible chance of bouncing back. Flying insects were everywhere and many of the mourners wore face-nets attached to the brims of their hats, long sleeves and trousers. Some even had gloves. Mariam wondered whether they were worried about human contact as well as insect-borne diseases.

Sara began reminiscing about her sister's childhood in the Saint-Médard valley, then spoke of her wish for Aliyah to be 'reunited in peace with her younger daughters'. A few others expressed similar sentiments before it was Mariam's turn.

At first, she found she had nothing to say. Then, something deep inside her, some folk memory of how things ought to be, loosened her tongue and she told everyone that she had loved her sisters and that they had lived and perhaps dreamed and it was, she thought, enough that they should be celebrated here, in this cleft of mountainside where their mother had grown up, happy within the jagged walls of limestone.

When she stopped speaking, nobody moved. They were waiting for her to prompt the next action – lowering the woven coffins into the ground.

Mariam bent and took hold of one of the ropes. Sara, Benjamin and the neighbour did the same. Once the woven coffins were side by side at the foot of the hole, Mariam took a shovel to begin covering them with dirt. Then she handed the shovel on to Sara with the ritual phrase: 'From my hand to yours.' Her aunt followed her lead, then passed the shovel on to Benjamin.

Mariam turned away, wandering alone through the knee-high meadow, past the bull standing placidly by the fence, up the lane, past the neighbours' houses. At her aunt's gate, she washed her boots in the disinfectant trough and wandered up and down the rows of the vegetable garden, looking for stones to throw onto the ever-growing pile.

Inside the impressive white-limestone pilgrimage cathedral in Bilbao, there was a stair that led high up into the gothic spire. Towards the top, as the roof panels narrowed to a vertiginous point, it was possible to gain access to the outside air. This was where Jaime Moreno went, well within the five-hundred metre perimeter allowed by his house-arrest ankle tags, clinging precariously to the weather-worn stone.

He had an uninterrupted view across the skyline of the city. He no longer believed in a just God, or even a vengeful one. His mind had been broken by the machine interrogation, meaning he lived in a permanent state of waking nightmare, as if still strapped to the chair, the sickening images assaulting every second of his pointless days.

He looked down, seeing the tiny shapes of people who knew nothing of his torment, and sobbed. The stonework was gritty beneath his fingers. The breeze whipped at the open neck of his shirt. He touched the tattoo on his collarbone with the tips of his fingers: UDSMC, an abbreviation of a phrase that meant acceptance of mortality: *Un día será más corto*.

It was true. For every living person, one day would inevitably be shorter than all the rest – the day of their death.

He summoned up a cocktail of courage and despair, finding the will to leap out into nothingness and fall to an abrupt and concussive death on the flagstones of the plaza far below.

28

It was Alex who found Konaré's body, folded like a baby on the floor of his office, surrounded by a pool of sticky blood, already a feast for blow-flies.

He went looking for help and, in Konaré's absence, it seemed there was a void of authority until a politician could be despatched from the town hall to take command. Alex ordered Konaré's assistant – who had just driven him from the Hôtel Étoile – to 'show him the surveillance footage'.

'You mean the files?'

'Yes, the files.'

They shut the door on Konaré's office so as not to hear the buzzing of the blow-flies and sat down at the desk in the lobby, untidy discarded paperwork on the floor around their feet. The assistant activated his LED screen, logging in with an alphanumeric password, like in the old days.

The surveillance files were accessible from a shared drive on servers hidden somewhere in the basement of the building, where it was easier to keep them cool. The assistant told him that he sometimes went down there 'to refresh himself'.

'Okay,' said Alex. 'Can we hurry?'

'We can go as fast as the servers respond,' said the assistant in his strong Malian accent.

Finally, they were able to select the appropriate location and time. And yes, there was Aminata Sidibé sitting politely on the bench in the lobby. Then there was Konaré in the doorway, sending his assistant away to get lunch and fetch Alex from the Hôtel Étoile, inviting the young woman into his plush office. Then the two of them disappeared from the screen.

'Okay, now switch,' said Alex.

'Switch where?'

'Inside his office.'

'No cameras inside, sir,' the assistant replied.

'What?'

The assistant shrugged.

'Privacy.'

Of course, thought Alex.

'Wind it on.'

'Wind what?' asked the assistant.

Alex realised he was using his mother's phrases, talking about digital recordings as if they were video tape or microfiches. That was why the man hadn't understood 'footage' earlier on.

'I mean fast-forward. I want to see her leave.'

'Yes, sir.'

At quadruple pace, each minute of real time took fifteen seconds of accelerated viewing to elapse. Finally, after three minutes of watching, Aminata Sidibé emerged, wearing different clothes – a very loose-fitting beige jellabiya cinched round the hips with a woven belt. She went to the desk, looking for something on the surface, then opening the drawers.

'What do you think she's doing?' asked the assistant.

The jerky, accelerated figure emptied the drawers on the floor, took a few sheets of paper from the printer, rummaged through the in-tray on the desk and found something else she wanted, partly sheltered from the camera by her body.

'Normal speed,' Alex instructed.

The assistant made a mess of the command, reducing speed to one-half normal. Alex took over, rocking the action back and forth to be sure.

'What did she do?' asked the assistant.

'She found some official notepaper and wrote a note. Then she found a letter with Konaré's signature on it and copied it by writing over it with her own note underneath, so it made an impression on the second piece of paper. Then she inked it in.'

'What did she write?'

'I have a good guess,' said Alex. 'Take me to the vehicle compound.'

The assistant did as he was told, leading Alex outside to a dusty patch of unkempt ground. In one corner was an electric charging station with four connectors. The only vehicle was the police pick-up they had been using.

'Why isn't it plugged in?' Alex asked.

'Overnight is cheaper,' explained the assistant.

In another corner, a man in oil-stained overalls was sitting in a deck chair under a faded canvas pergola, smoking a shisha. Alex strode over.

'Was there another vehicle charging?' he asked.

The man's eyes widened, then he awkwardly sat forward in his deckchair and pulled earbuds out of his ears, answering confusedly in Bambara. Alex repeated the question.

'Yes, sir,' said the mechanic. He twitched his head to one side, indicating the gate. 'Another vehicle for the chief's girlfriend.'

'She wasn't his girlfriend,' said Alex. 'She's gone?'

'Yes, sir.'

Alex turned to the assistant.

'When did he ask the woman to come to his office?'

'One-thirty.'

'But he told me to come at two.'

The assistant shrugged.

Alex thought back to watching the surveillance footage with Konaré's assistant. How much time had passed? They'd watched the empty antechamber for three minutes at quad-speed, meaning twelve minutes in real life. Then they'd seen Aminata slip out in different clothes and complete her subterfuge with the fake note. How far away might she be now?

'The other EV,' he asked the mechanic. 'Was it fully charged?'

'Yes, fully charged.'

'What range?'

'Two-fifty at a steady speed.'

'Do you have any other vehicles?'

The man waved a hand to indicate the empty car park.

'All out,' he confirmed.

Alex pondered.

'The one she took: it has a transponder?' He looked from one to the other. Their faces were blank. This wasn't their area of expertise. 'Can you take me to your despatcher?' More blankness. He put a hand on Konaré's assistant's shoulder. 'The comms link to patrols. Who runs that? Take me there.'

The despatchers' office was on an upper floor with lovely French windows that opened onto Juliet balconies, overlooking the Niger. There were three male operatives, wearing police uniforms of pale blue trousers and shirts. Two of them were talking down the line, using headsets so Alex couldn't hear what calls they were responding to, only the instructions they were giving. He paused, listening to both at once.

A traffic violation and a hit and run.

That made sense. Even in a modern city with a majority of electric vehicles, a high proportion of police work was traffic management.

The third despatcher was filing his nails – long and curved over the ends of his fingers.

'There was a police EV in the yard on charge. It was taken out about twenty, twenty-five minutes ago. Do you know where it is?'

'Who are you?'

Konaré's assistant initiated a quick back-and-forth in Bambara, then the despatcher stood up, his mouth wide with shock.

'The chief is dead?'

'We don't have time for this,' said Alex. 'Show me where the vehicle is.'

The despatcher used a large touch-pad to scroll across a schematic map of the city, displayed on a large LED screen – Bamako laid out in fine detail with two dozen green circles with ID numbers, indicating police vehicle locations. About half were in motion.

'She won't have stayed in the city.' Alex heard his voice becoming edgy. 'Ask the system to find her.'

The despatcher opened a dialogue and inputted the appropriate ID. The system zoomed out then back in. The vehicle was on a road south of Bamako, near a place called Dialakoroba.

'RN7,' said the despatcher.

'How far to the border?' said Alex.

'Two hundred and eighty kilometres to Côte d'Ivoire.'

'So she would have to stop and charge?'

'Or turn off at Keleva. The road is not so good but she will reach the frontier with Guinea in only two-fifty.' The despatcher nodded. 'Through Yanfolila.'

'The location of the new mine?' said Alex. The two men looked blank. 'Never mind.'

Alex used the device-search facility on his comm-watch to find and take control of the despatcher's terminal, trying to piggyback as far as the police vehicle Aminata Sidibé had stolen, hoping to be able to shut it down. It wasn't possible, however. Police Central didn't have operating system control over its fleet.

'Set me up,' he told the despatcher, 'with a feed from your system to my comm-watch via satlink.'

The despatcher did as he was asked, pairing with Alex's device.

'What next?' asked Konaré's assistant. 'Should I order her to be intercepted?'

'Not yet. Make a report to the appropriate chain of command, but let's find out where she's headed. And where can I find a car?'

It turned out there was a rental office right opposite Police Central, but that didn't immediately solve the problem.

'You have to be joking.'

'No, sir, not joking,' said the owner. 'We have six cars available with ranges up to three hundred and fifty kilometres, but there is an automatic software upgrade in progress.'

'Don't they roll those out one vehicle at a time?' said Alex, realising he had said the same words before – not long ago, in fact.

'That is normally the schedule, but in this case, the fleet has been bricked.'

Alex shook his head.

'Where else is there? Can you call one of your competitors?'

The owner nodded. 'I have done so. This is city-wide. Who knows, worldwide?'

The man laughed, as if the idea of that sort of co-ordination was absurd.

'Every hire car in the city is bricked?'

'Temporarily, sir.' He consulted a screen recessed in his desk. 'We are at eighty-eight percent. Then reboot. Maybe another ten minutes?'

Alex nodded.

'I'll wait.'

He moved away from the desk and went to stand at the window beneath an air-con unit set in the wall above, and looked out into the street, thinking about how Amaury had told him the exact same story – of a hire fleet getting bricked by simultaneous upgrades to all vehicles.

Was it likely that would happen twice in quick succession? No, but unlikely things happened all the time. Was it the sort of thing that someone with skill and know-how could infiltrate into a system as a deliberate bug? Might there be a timeline on it, an acceleration, with the supposed 'upgrades' happening more and more frequently, in more and more places, as a kind of gratuitous disruption?

No, not gratuitous. It was meant – and if it was meant, it was purposeful.

Poiret had told him: *I want you to look into the use of time-lapse trojans disrupting travel infrastructure. It is an increasing problem.*

But for what purpose?

The same purpose as the destruction of state databases – the desire to unmesh the hyperconnected world.

Alex popped out a holo map from his comm-watch, still paired with Police Central, and looked at the slow-moving dot on the road south. It would be at least an hour ahead of him, maybe halfway to its destination, but his car would be quicker and more powerful. As he watched, the dot reached the junction at Keleva and branched off onto the Yanfolila road, the one that was 'not so good'.

Alex thought about Davide Castile's private jet. Had that still been at Bamako airport, he would have been tempted to commandeer it and fly south to Bougouni, the regional capital. But Bougouni was more than an hour by road from the smaller town of Yanfolila and …

Alex checked his messages. Nothing from Mariam. Chambon had written to tell him that Castile would soon be *en route*. Amaury would soon be in the air too, on his way to Cyrene City for the reopening of the parliament building. A transcript of the results of the interrogation of Amaury's would-be assassin demanded his attention with a red flag – indicating it was urgent – and a pull-quote:

The Coming Storm just means attacks of all kinds. It isn't about the weather or the wind. And it will never end.

That just confirmed Fayard's warning – that a storm of more minor disruptions might prove harder to combat than a single massive attack.

He scanned the transcript for ninety seconds, then shut it down.

I don't have time for this.

He felt a familiar unease, concern that his focus was constantly being drawn to the wrong things – the past, not the future, what was over and done with, rather than what was to come.

29

Kadidia Sidibé had abandoned the stolen police pick-up on the outskirts of Yanfolila. Perched on the back of a mobike taxi, she had made her way to an unfinished neighbourhood, alongside a construction site for the anticipated influx of mine-workers. Disembarking a couple of blocks away, she had walked to the house she shared with Hamady Dara – but she would not find him there, because he had not survived the second ambush. In the house, with access to her encrypted comms, she had received a message from her sister Aminata.

I don't know what you've done but Drissa is dead and I'm coming.

She took a few deep, calming breaths, a nascent headache behind her eyes. She wondered how their brother had died. Hamady had told her that he and Drissa might have been observed at the café where Drissa's favourite *bouille* dessert was served. She and Drissa had agreed that they should keep Aminata out of the conspiracy. Clearly, that had now failed.

Kadidia felt poorly but, strangely, quite safe – perhaps a result of the adrenaline still coursing through her body. She knew the feeling would soon fade, just as she knew that next year's drought would always and forever be longer and harsher than the one before. She wiped her brow with her forearm, finding it sweaty and feverish. Had she been free to do so, she would have checked herself into a medical clinic for tests. She went and looked in the rudimentary bathroom, finding a few everyday meds in the cabinet above the washbasin, but no antivirals. Seeing her own face in the mirror, Kadidia realised she had a clammy, unhealthy appearance.

Was that fear or the aftermath of violence? Or was it from the stranger's blood that had splattered her face, contaminating the mucus membranes in her nose and mouth?

No, it was all going to be fine. Aminata would come, then they would head for the border with Guinea. There were roads without surveillance where one could cross and leave all this behind.

Perhaps it was best that Drissa had died. He would have insisted they fight on. His hatred of all authority burnt with a fierce flame, fuelled by Narissa's murder at the data centre in Marseille. Of course, they said she shot herself, but …

Kadidia felt a waft of nausea.

Maybe she would go out and find a pharmacy. Antivirals only worked if you took them early.

Aminata Sidibé's electric police vehicle was low on charge, the indicator orange. The sun was sinking but still hot. She had the windows open to try and keep cool, spoiling the aerodynamics, running down the power. But the air-con would deplete it even more quickly. It didn't matter. Yanfolila was not so far away now.

She felt a heaviness in her heart. So much death. Not just Drissa, but also their sister Narissa, back in the summer in Marseille, for reasons Drissa and Kadidia had refused to explain.

Looking in her rear-view mirror, she saw an unmarked car that she had noticed before, hanging back but on her tail. Were they tracking her? Would she have to abandon her vehicle and make her way across Yanfolila some hidden way?

She wasn't entirely ignorant of her siblings' motivations. If she made it that far, Kadidia might tell her off, telling her that she should have stayed in Bamako, innocent as she was, that she could have taken advantage of Chief of Police Konaré, learning how the machinery of coercion and control functioned from the inside, how state violence became indiscriminate, simply an expression of power.

The dashboard blinked red and told her to find somewhere to charge, the range below thirty kilometres. She passed a road sign informing her that she was entering the city, the unmarked car a few spaces distant.

Aminata wondered why she had not been intercepted. There could only be one answer – because they hoped she would lead them somewhere important: to someone more important. But she knew nothing, except the fact of her siblings' desire to destroy because they saw the world in black and white, future and past, true and false, deserving and undeserving, purposeful and pointless, good and bad.

Maybe I can take Kadidia away from all that?

Alex was following much more quickly in a superb saloon vehicle with a very low centre of gravity from its heavy battery array, packed into the floor. He had details of a service station in Yanfolila where he could get the tired batteries swapped out on arrival. From his link to Bamako Police Central, he knew the destination Aminata had programmed into the stolen police car's satnav. He had also received a notification from Chambon that Castile was inbound, requesting Alex's presence in the capital for a meeting the following morning with President Manouche himself.

I'll do my best.

In a modest forensics lab, attached to a private medical clinic and pharmacy in Yanfolila, a set of samples retrieved from the attack on the supernat tank at the mine site had just been put through analysis by a junior med-tech, rendering a positive ID of the attacker from the slow-to-answer Malian population database.

The results were conclusive. The woman was twenty-six years old. Her family name was Sidibé, first name Kadidia. Her parents were dead from natural causes, both within the last five years. Kadidia had three siblings – a younger sister called Aminata, an older brother called Drissa and an older sister called Narissa, a student in telecommunications, delegated to attend a university exchange program in Marseille in the south of France, beginning the previous September.

Deceased.

The med-tech leaned in to scan a very brief summary of the circumstances – shot beneath the chin, up into her brain and out through the top of her skull, death instantaneous, no discussion of motives or repercussions. At least, nothing that he could access.

But why would there be? He was merely a functional cog in any investigation. If he hadn't seen the news report of the mine attack on his screen, he wouldn't even have known the reason he was looking into this cursed family.

He followed another link to the ID record of Kadidia Sidibé's younger sister, Aminata, a resident of the capital, Bamako, employed in the post office – a blameless life. He followed the link to data on the brother, Drissa, who …

The file was unretrievable, in the process of being updated.

He waited, fetched a glass of water from the cooler by the door, then refreshed the connection.

There it was, the update complete. A cursed family, indeed.

Drissa was also dead – a drug dealer, shot by a rival gang just days before, at the Independence Day celebrations on Place de la Liberté.

Kadidia felt worse but she wasn't concerned – at least, not overly. Even if the viral load from the blood she had swallowed or inhaled was heavy, she had probably encountered it before. As everyone knew, it was travel that was most dangerous, running the risk of meeting a pathogen your immune system wasn't accustomed to, which you had no resistance against. And Yanfolila had been her home for three years.

She couldn't be sure, though. Hamady's burst of gunfire that had sent a spray of blood spattering across her face – whose blood was it? One of the two security men, surely, one on each minibus, armed with lightweight weapons. Could he have been a mercenary brought in from far away, maybe picked up by one of the drivers on the north-south route through Côte d'Ivoire? Who knew what strange bugs such a person might transport?

Kadidia stood up, leaning on the back of a chair for support, her dress clinging to her skin with sweat.

There was a medical clinic not far from the safe house, on the edge of the new development. Couldn't she step out for a few minutes and buy some everyday drugs – antivirals, anti-inflammatories, something to bring down her fever?

Aminata was twenty minutes away from her destination, according to the map function on the dashboard. But the destination she had programmed into the nav system was a deceit, somewhere she wanted the Bamako police to surround with a tight perimeter, deploying all available officers.

Luckily, the vehicle that had been following her was held at a previous light, maybe two hundred metres back. She stopped and got out, leaving the engine running, ran to the side of the road and jumped onto an anonymous scooter-taxi driven by a kid who appeared barely of age for his meagre job.

She gave an address and they pulled away.

Yes, the despatchers in Bamako would know from the transponder in the police vehicle that she was stationary. Once that had lasted too long, they might assume that she had run out of charge. They would check with the on-board computer, discover it wasn't true, then tell the follower to investigate, not expecting to find her there, anticipating that she might have fled, but perhaps still focused on the location she had programmed in the nav.

She would not be there either.

It was quite late in the day and the med-tech had allowed his colleague at the pharma counter to go home, telling her that he would deal with any customers and lock up when the time came. Ten minutes later, the bell rang and he didn't even check the video relay, just pressed the button to release the lock and allowed whoever it was to enter. The woman who stepped into the antiseptic pharmacy looked weary, dusty and … well, frankly ill.

She approached the counter and requested antivirals, anti-inflammatories and analgesics. He served her at arm's length, glad of the perspex screen. When she paid, it was with paper currency. He told her he couldn't accept it. She left the notes on the counter and walked away, her face clammy, breathing heavily.

Once she had gone, the med-tech put on eye protection and activated the ultraviolet sterilisation units, then chose a heavy tester bottle from the toiletry shelves, an aftershave branded 'Timbuktu number 17', its antiseptic astringency derived from the Malian shrub *Tribulus terrestris*, known as 'Devil's thorn'.

He rubbed it on his hands. People said it was capable of warding off disease. Perhaps they were right.

He made a phone call to the Notifiable Diseases hotline, describing the symptoms he had observed.

'No, I didn't get a name or traceable payment details, but she can't be far away,' he confirmed. 'I'm going to follow her.'

Having stumbled from the med-centre, unaware it also housed a forensics lab, Kadidia Sidibé approached a street café and store. Two workmen in blue overalls were sitting outside in the sun. They had just been served two bowls of a milky pudding garnished with honey and mango. Not knowing quite what she was doing, she snatched up one of the bowls and carried it away.

'Hey,' said one of the workmen, half-rising from his plastic chair.

Then he saw her sweat-stained dress and clammy face and thought better of it. 'Never mind. Good luck,' he said kindly.

Kadidia stagged off the high street into a shaded corner. She tipped the bowl of pudding into her mouth, relishing its cool sweetness. In three mouthfuls, it was gone. She dropped the plant fibre bowl on the ground, tearing at the packaging of her medication, swallowing two antivirals without reading the instructions. Then she lurched away from the shaded corner and stumbled on.

Where was Aminata? Would she soon be here? Should she warn her sister that she was sick?

The milky pudding lay heavy on her belly, but she felt she had more energy. She crossed the road, emerging from the shadows into a low sun, shining like a fierce orange searchlight from the end of the street. She had no choice but to walk towards it, her eyes almost closed, back to the stark house where, she was beginning to realise, she would find no safety.

The med-tech picked up the plant-fibre bowl with his nitrile-gloved hand, watching the woman hobbling towards the sun. She was a hundred metres away at the far end of the street, her hand on a gatepost. He watched her walk uncertainly towards an unfinished house of bare concrete blocks. He followed her just far enough to make a note of the number, seeing a child of eight or nine years old kicking a football against the garden wall opposite. He hoped the little girl would keep her distance.

The child was called Sweetie, a difficult name to use in anger. All the same, her mother tried, shouting from the kitchen for her to stop her noise and come inside to eat. Sweetie picked up her ball and disappeared through the garden gate.

The sky had changed colour. Alex glanced at the nav panel. Twenty minutes to the centre of Yanfolila. Then what? Aminata Sidibé had abandoned her EV and must be continuing on foot or in a taxi or …

Maybe someone had met her already? Maybe one of the perpetrators of the mine attack?

Alex wanted to look her in the eye as he questioned her. Would he get to her before she again slipped away? Maybe yes, maybe no.

He knew from the wary look he had seen in her eyes in the car park at the morgue that Aminata Sidibé wasn't a fool. The one place Alex would not look for her was the destination she had programmed into her nav.

Back at the pharmacy, the med-tech's equipment wasn't the most modern available, but it was capable of running a DNA check from the saliva on the plant-fibre bowl. Sluggishly, the rudimentary police AI began correlating it with its established database, within a few minutes establishing a connection with a sample collected from a trace of blood on the IED used in the mine attack.

Kadidia walked wearily up the path and into the unfinished three-room dwelling – a living room with a kitchen area in one corner, a single bedroom, a rudimentary bathroom. She made for the toilet, knelt down at the bowl and was sick.

Perhaps I'll just lie down, she thought, when she was done.

Instead of going to the bedroom, she made for the front step instead, hoping to find the relative cool of early evening. She slumped down on the bare concrete, leaning against the rough breeze-block façade, unfocused eyes contemplating the dusky sky.

Yes, this is a good idea, she thought. *I will rest here for a little while. Then, later, when my strength returns and Aminata arrives, we will …*

She shifted position, unable to get comfortable.

The med-tech watched the confirmation of the DNA result pop up on his screen: a match with a confidence level of 95%.

For a second, he hesitated. Did he want to be a part of this? Then he recognised that he had no choice. He was already involved.

He placed a call to the police, telling them precisely where the terrorist could be found.

30

Aminata climbed off her scooter-taxi about a kilometre from Kadidia's address. She had taken a roundabout journey and given the kid a generous tip. Now, she was approaching her destination through a residential building site where only foundations and basic services had been poured and installed. Through habit, she kept to the shade of the corrugated fencing, though the sun was almost gone, just a sliver still visible above the horizon.

Would Kadidia be ready? They would have to steal another vehicle, but surely that would be easy in the suburbs?

Alex knew now where he should go. There was a basic interconnectivity in Malian security services, despite Konaré's protestations that they would only function *à la malienne*. The information he received was a product of algorithmic cross-matching of data in real time – what people liked to call artificial intelligence. But it wasn't actually intelligence. There was no independent thought. There was just a pre-programmed system capable of pointing out connections: in this case between the storm of violence unleashed on the mine and its workers; DNA traces on the IED; a likeness captured by a camera at the mine entrance; and a woman who refused to allow herself to be identified in a med-centre equipped with facial recognition. And then those connections confirmed by a DNA match.

All kinds of red flags for the satlink connection to Alex's comm-watch.

Sweetie, the child with the football, had gobbled up her tea and gone back outside, looking for other children to play with. The nearby construction site provided all kinds of interesting improvised toys: loose bricks; lengths of timber; PVC and metal tubing; a huge plastic cistern for water-harvesting if ever the houses were finished and there were roofs to channel the rain.

Should it ever rain.

But no other children were playing out and she drifted towards the gate of the house opposite where she had noticed that someone was home, a woman lying slumped against the wall, her breaths irregular, ragged and uneven.

Sweetie went closer, but not too close. The child knew what serious illness looked like. The woman was clammy, her eyes half-closed, her position awkward, like a doll dropped on the concrete step.

Sweetie ran home and told her parents what she had seen. Her father immediately phoned the infection hotline while her mother took the girl upstairs into the shower and scrubbed her skin and hair.

Alex depressed the brake and brought his powerful EV saloon to an almost silent halt. He got out and stood quite still, looking around, listening. He heard the sounds of ordinary life: faint voices, entertainment screens, barely perceptible traffic. From an upstairs window opposite, he could make out water running and a crying child being scolded.

Then he saw the woman slumped on the front step of the unfinished suburban house, her cheek awkwardly squished against the bare concrete. He took a step closer, thinking he saw a family likeness on the handsome but drawn features, sheened with fever-sweat, but was distracted by movement in his peripheral vision.

He turned towards it – a slim figure he recognised, someone with the same bone structure as the woman on the ground, Aminata Sidibé, emerging from behind a corrugated metal fence on the edge of a building site a hundred metres away. Her eyes locked with his and he saw rather than heard her gasp.

She turned and ran.

Alex sent a message requesting medical assistance, then moved quickly but warily along the new-laid pavement. Aminata Sidibé had killed Konaré with a knife, but she might now be more dangerously armed.

Just past sunset, the sky was still light. He came to the truncated fence at the edge of the site and scanned the loose bricks and blocks, the lengths of timber, PVC and metal tubing. He saw a huge plastic cistern that hadn't yet been buried in the foundations of the unbuilt homes.

Alex paused to listen. Were Aminata still running, he would be able to hear her. As he couldn't, the only place she might have concealed herself was behind the huge water collection tank. It was the only substantial cover.

Once she was clean and dry, Sweetie was sent to her room. She didn't think about the woman on the ground outside. It was only death, and death was never very far away. She put her headphones over her ears to watch and listen to the latest funny videos from anywhere across the whole hyperconnected world.

Alex approached, unable completely to silence his footsteps on the rough ground, drawing his non-lethal son-imm, edging round the tank.

There she was, on the ground, sitting against the plastic wall of the cistern, her knees drawn up, her arms wrapped around them. She glanced up at him.

'My sister is dead, isn't she?'

'No, I don't think so.'

'But you won't let me help her?'

233

'I've summoned first aid. Tell me what you hoped to achieve.'

The half-formed plan of escape spilled out of the young woman, the words tripping over one another. Alex marvelled at the coincidence that he had been present when the oldest sister, Narissa, had died. But, of course, as Professor Fayard had been fond of saying, there was no such thing as coincidence, just unexplained patterns of cause and effect. And he was here in Yanfolila because this was a story that involved him, one that he knew well – a tale of resentment and despair, death and violence imagined like a cleansing stream.

'I watched Narissa kill herself,' Alex insisted. 'I know you probably believe that she was shot by the security services, but she wasn't. Her attack failed and she committed suicide.' Aminata's wide eyes met his. 'And your other sister's IED failed to blow the supernat tank at the mine,' he told her.

'I didn't know anything about that, but that man, Konaré, he killed Drissa.'

'Yes, he did, but Konaré was one man. He wasn't part of a system.'

'Drissa would say that he didn't know he was part of a system, that he was ...'

Her voice tailed off, not knowing what else to add. It was clear to Alex that her older siblings had kept her at arm's length from their actions. But she was guilty, all the same.

'Yes, he gave the order,' Alex agreed.

Aminata pulled her arms tighter around her knees.

'I'm glad I killed him. I thought if I got here soon enough, we could drive across the border into Guinea and Kadidia and I could start again.'

Alex heard police cars approaching, their unnecessary sirens less than a minute away.

'There is no "start again".'

Aminata sighed and asked him: 'What next?'

'Police will come. They will arrest you and question you. Then, I imagine, you will spend the rest of your life in prison. Your sister, too,

234

if she gets better.'

'I will kill myself too,' she said, as if it was the most natural thing in the world.

Alex took a moment, surprised by the speed at which the desire for action could transform into a wish for death, as if that too could be a victory, a kind of adolescent fantasy of revenge through self-harm. He felt deep sadness for the young woman and her siblings.

Of course, he ought to feel sad for Chief Konaré too. That would be an appropriate reaction, based in humanity and duty. But he didn't. He felt deeper sympathy for the misguided losers, crushed by the monumental machine of modern life.

The beams of the headlights of two police cars swept across the building site. Aminata looked up at him. Was there anything else to learn from this deluded young woman? Almost certainly not. The last Sidibé sibling had nothing more to share. Drissa's and Kadidia's digital traces would be studied, but with end-to-end encryption, self-eliminating comms and parallel networks, it was extraordinary how the digital world could escape the security services' grasp, slippery like mercury.

'If I run, you'll let me go, won't you?' she asked.

Alex didn't answer. Would it be right to let her seek death, when he – with his superior strength – could easily prevent it? He wasn't sure, but he knew that, with the murder of the chief of police, she had crossed a threshold.

'Yes,' he told her. 'If you run, I won't stop you.'

She sprang to her feet, lithe and beautiful, full of purpose.

'Which way should I go if I want to die?' she asked. 'Away from them or towards them?'

'Towards them,' said Alex.

'Thank you.'

She took a deep breath and ran, round the huge plastic cistern, shouting something he couldn't understand in one of the Malian

235

languages.

Alex lay down flat, finding cover, hearing the police officers calling out in reply, giving their official warning that they were about to fire, to use lethal force, unaware that was what the young woman wanted, running at their guns.

31

In the farmhouse halfway up the Saint-Médard valley, the wake was ending. The congregation of neighbours and friends had almost all left, each one sent on their way by Mariam's aunt with a small clay pot of home-made honey – because honey was eternal. Hadn't honey – still fit to eat – been found in the tombs of the pharaohs?

Mariam went to the end of the drive to look at the dark bulk of the mountain against the blue-grey sky, just beginning to reveal its stars. The breeze off the peaks was fresh, meaning no biting insects to worry about. For the time being, no one could peer into her eyes, questioning with a glance how she felt, what she would do next, without her sisters to care for. Or, worse, how it had felt to know the world as we knew it might be ending if Alex wasn't able to …

No, to be fair, no one had asked her about that.

A man with long hair tied back in a ponytail approached. She could see from the angle of his arm that he held something in his hand and assumed it was his gift of honey, but he offered it to her.

'Can I give you this?'

She noticed a tiny pinprick of red against his dark palm – some kind of electronic device.

'What is it?'

'A viewer. I know you don't have access to the streams at your aunt's farm and … Well, this is something you should know about.'

'Who are you?'

'My name is Pudu. I'm friends with Benjamin. You don't know me.'

'Pudu?'

'It was my mother's idea,' he said, nodding.

Mariam could hear the smile, but he was little more than a silhouette – around her height, his face an indistinct oval, his ponytail a slightly different density of dark from the mountains behind.

'I don't know what Pudu means,' she told him.

'It's a rainforest deer, tiny, about fifty centimetres tall when fully grown. I've thought about changing it.'

'But your mother would be displeased?'

'My mother is dead.'

'I'm sorry.'

There was a pause, then he spoke more decisively.

'She was the leader of Lenca. We are a campaigning organisation.'

'I know who Lenca are.'

'We want to preserve the sacred valley – this sacred valley. She was killed by Davide Castile, the head of the corporation that owns the dam, just a couple of weeks ago. He hit her with his helicopter. I know that probably sounds completely crazy.'

'I know something about it,' Mariam told him, wondering where this was going.

'Okay, good. Well, we, that is Lenca, we have a demo camp outside the perimeter, next to the access airfield. They want to extend the dam, build it higher, drowning more of the mountain upstream. Look …' He held out the viewer with its tiny red tell-tale. 'Please watch this. Please tell the people you work with about what's happening. I know you have influence. I know you can contact people who don't know we exist or, if they are aware of us, we don't know who they are. Castile is too powerful for us to reach.'

Mariam took the object, not because she was convinced by Pudu, but because she knew that Alex was involved with the same man –

238

Davide Castile.

'Come and visit our camp,' said Pudu, waving a hand towards the top of the mountain. 'I'm so very sorry for your loss.'

'And I am sorry for yours,' she replied.

He turned away and headed in the direction of a cart with a small horse in harness, his boots squelching in the wet dirt from the previous night's rain. Mariam looked at the device in her hand. She supposed she could activate her comm-watch and scan it for dangerous malware, but her aunt had no networked devices to protect.

Is this a lead? At the very least, it's a connection. But could it be a connection with consequences?

'How about I come with you now?' she called in a loud voice.

'Landing in Cyrene City in fifteen,' said one of the flight engineers.

Amaury grunted in reply.

He was strapped to a flip-down bucket seat attached to the side of the fuselage and had already changed into his dress uniform, surrounded by the military equipment he had seen being loaded back in Toulouse, sent by France to support the new republic. He was keen to be off the noisy plane, but not looking forward to the ceremony.

Using the in-flight satlink, he found the weather on the ground was 'unusually mild', meaning not excessively hot. This tended to happen when the jet stream brought colder air from the North Atlantic. Now and then, it would bring rain, even in summer.

He read a draft of one of the speeches he would have to listen to later. It wasn't all good news. Since Cyrenia had seceded from Libya, every year had seen temperatures in the highest top-thirty summers of recorded history. The role of the enlightened state was to moderate the inevitable excesses of the unquenchable thirst for gain that was the fuel in the engine of a profit-based economy. Despite the global move away from hydrocarbons – limitations on air travel, renewable energy, the whole shebang – it might yet take multiple generations to reverse two hundred years of accelerating damage, and that was a challenge for the new democracy. In order for Cyrenia to persist as a beacon of hope, of tolerance – rule for the benefit of the many rather than the few – the people's sufferings needed not to exceed their patience, their endurance.

In the end, Amaury reflected, it was a question of choice, of the allocation of resources. Of course, there could be structural shortages at certain times. But, in a well-managed economy, subsistence ought always to be assured. Amaury knew the myth of scarce resources was just that – a lie promoted to explain why a few must enjoy plenty while the majority suffer want.

The transport dipped and banked and soon touched down. Amaury was escorted by a modest motorcade of three official vehicles to the parliament compound, its well-watered gardens decorated by its famous rose borders. They drove past the dormitory building where he had hidden mere months before, awaiting the drama of extraction under fire, then up to the main entrance, a ceremonial staircase leading to a pair of massive carved wooden doors.

The doors stood wide open, and in the stark light from hi-intensity lighting panels provided for live relay by the news streams, he could see a kind of guard-of-honour, a Cyrenian military band holding traditional and classical instruments, playing a version of the French national anthem, the *Marseillaise*. It sounded squeaky and – to his ear – discordant, giving him an uncomfortable urge to laugh.

He climbed the stairs, feeling awkward in his brand-new dress uniform. Of course, it was technically a good fit, but that was not the same as really fitting, just as a synthetic perfume can never quite imitate the olfactory and tactile sensation of smelling a rose.

At the top of the steps, he had to wait for the anthem to be completed, then a small man in a sober suit stepped forward to greet him, announcing himself as 'Faroukh Al-Medawi, Mayor of Tobruk and member of the Presidential Council'. Amaury knew who he was – how important he was – despite his unimposing demeanour.

240

They went inside. As a representative of France, Amaury was ostensibly the centre of attention, but in reality, the purpose was a captive audience for a succession of protocol-led events for which he was merely the pretext, punctuated by a moderate dinner. There were speeches, a traditional dance troupe, a selection of poems read by schoolchildren. Between the dessert and the cheese course, the principal guests got up for the official reopening of the damaged parliament building.

Amaury wasn't prone to flashbacks, but when he and Al-Medawi climbed the stairs to the viewing gallery high in the atrium, touching his fingertips to the bullet impacts still visible in the plaster of the walls, he felt a searing phantom pain beneath the velcro straps of his prosthetic hand.

'These scars will be preserved in the redecoration,' said the Mayor of Tobruk, 'as a reminder.'

'I understand,' said Amaury shortly.

'You carry your own reminder,' the little man insisted, perceptively.

Amaury realised he was cradling his prosthetic in his weaker left hand, as if it was real injured flesh-and-blood, rather than a collection of servomotors and metal digits and gears, wrapped in flexible synthetics.

'I do,' he replied.

'Please forgive us our interminable ceremony. We, too, lost something – perhaps our innocence – but our determination has been strengthened.' Amaury took a step to the parapet, looking for where the shots had come from. 'You were fighting with us, not against us,' insisted the small grey man. 'You were unlucky.'

No, thought Amaury. *We were all lucky, in the end.*

The evening concluded in the rebuilt parliament chamber itself with a kind of news report-cum-documentary, projected onto a giant screen, at the end of which the delegates stood and applauded and he was obliged to respond with the speech André Chambon had sent him, countersigned by Damien Gerest, with an instruction not to deviate 'by so much as a comma'. Once that was done, he was shown to the visitor accommodation at the rear of the parliament building where, before he was able to take off his stiff new uniform, he received a 3D holo call from Paris, Gerest himself, requesting 'reassurance that all went off as planned'.

'It did.'

'And they are happy?'

'Delirious,' said Amaury.

A frown crossed Gerest's features, then he appeared to decide to take Amaury's comment at face value: 'Excellent. Well done. Good night.'

The 3D holo disappeared in characteristic fashion, as if sucked back inside his comm-watch.

Amaury removed his dress jacket and threw it on a chair. Then he slipped the braces from his shoulders and allowed himself to flop backwards onto the wide double bed. He felt tired but oddly peaceful. It wasn't so hard to nod and smile and read from a teleprompt.

Yes, he thought. *Why shouldn't I just let the flow take me?*

For Major Chaka Kassam, everything had fallen very easily into place. To start with, he had been suspected and then absolved – by President Manouche himself – of being a traitor, not because the accusation had been proved false, but because his old friend had assumed his loose tongue had been the fault of stupidity, not treachery. Then he had been given a diplomatic role in the medal ceremony at Aswan.

He had been in the country for three days, arriving overland from Al-Jaghar, at the invitation of Naguib Al-Baghdadi, the Egyptian observer delegate to the North African Defence League. At Aswan, he had visited the archives. The weary staff were as proud of the vast dam as they were of the pyramids built by their distant ancestors, allowing him free access to the facilities and the archive.

Seen in profile, in cross-section, the structure of the dam was a hill of natural stone and mud, with a column of non-porous material at its heart. Its location had been chosen for stability from tectonic or volcanic activity because, however strong a dam, if the land moves below or either side of it, failure becomes inevitable. Kassam was, to his regret, unable to bring about an earthquake or an eruption, so his goals had to be – as a PhD paper in the archive defined them – 'overtopping' or 'piping'.

Overtopping meant water cascading through a breach in the upper lip, a flow of multiple millions of tonnes quickly deepening and widening the gap. The paper estimated a catastrophic peak outflow of three hundred and eighty cubic metres of water per second.

Piping was a different kind of failure, within the body of the dam, with the water tunnelling through a breach below the lake surface. A 'natural' failure might begin with an underwater landslide, maybe halfway up the slope on the upstream side. Massive water pressure from Lake Nasser would force a passage that would, by erosion, catastrophically widen. When the piping breach was large enough, the layers above would cave in as well, converting the disaster into a massive overtopping event.

Kassam had chosen to create a piping breach. Given VIP access to the dam facility, inadequately staffed by the penniless Egyptian state, he had managed to introduce his lithium-based explosives into four different locations in tunnels designed to ensure drainage of any river water that managed to infiltrate the structure. If he was successful – and there was no reason why he shouldn't be, surely, now everything was in place? – the devastating outflow would drown cities all the way to the Mediterranean coast – Asyut, Luxor, Cairo and Alexandria – hundreds of tonnes of water crashing through for each and every one of its likely victims.

32

Alex gave a full verbal report to the police, including a formal identification of Aminata Sidibé's body, riddled with gunshots. Then he drove away to find the service centre he had researched earlier, where his powerful electric saloon car was cleaned by the valeting service while its tired batteries were swapped out for new ones with a full charge.

He pulled away, heading north, back to the capital. He was unlikely to arrive in time to speak to Davide Castile that evening, but he would get up bright and early the next day to accompany him to the office of the president.

The road was disconcertingly dark, the contrast between the beams of his headlights and the mostly featureless landscape hard to adjust to. Once he was beyond all conurbations, he turned them off, relying on bright moon and starlight.

After a mile or two, he realised he was worried – not by anything he had seen, but by a sense of dislocation. One of the reasons for the security services' late response to the Coming Darkness conspiracy had been separation, a lack of co-ordination. He, Mariam, Amaury and others had found themselves each working alone, unaware that the information they were collecting was connected. Now, Alex felt, the same thing was happening again.

What use was he, wasting his time and energy on a bland tract of Malian landscape? What was the point of sending Amaury to the ceremonial reopening in Cyrene City? What dangers might Mariam be facing in the data shadow of her aunt's farm, a deliberate gap in the global network of connectivity?

He checked his own service. The satlink provided by the Malian police was still strong. He placed a call to Amaury, casting the 3D holo from his comm-watch to the heads-up 2D display on the windscreen. Amaury was already in bed.

'What can I tell you?' he said. 'They wish it was you but they're making do with me.'

'Will you return to Paris?' Alex asked.

'I'm not supposed to tell you.'

They carried on talking. Amaury had a lot to say, reminiscing about their time spent in training together at the École Militaire. Alex mostly listened. Eventually, Amaury told him: 'They don't want to end up a mafia state with all the wealth concentrated in the hands of a small number of the cleverest international gangsters. That would be an elephantine error.'

They broke the connection, Alex leaving his friend to sleep, but with an irritating idea that Amaury had been trying to tell him something. His friend wasn't the sort of person to indulge in idle reminiscence.

Alex put his lights back on as he began to encounter traffic. Soon after, he received details from Chambon of when and how, tomorrow morning, he would be taken to meet Castile. Then he was surprised by a pre-recorded voice note from Mariam, telling him she had been contacted by the protesters up at the dam and was using their satlink. It wasn't strong enough for a live sight-and-sound connection, but she wanted to know if they could speak in the morning. He dictated his reply.

Yes, either before nine my time or maybe after eleven.

No answer came and he wasn't sure if the connection had failed or if Mariam had felt no need to elaborate.

He drove on, the lights of Bamako an orange glow on the horizon, still wondering about what Amaury had hidden in his apparently-innocent words. Was it the talk of a 'gangster elite'? What did that suggest? The mess of competing Russian factions?

Alex entered the outskirts of Bamako, driving along a four-lane expressway along the Niger, heading for the Hôtel Étoile. Perhaps, while he slept, the unseen connections might become apparent in his dreams.

The lightweight buildings of the protest site were hard up against a four-metre fence topped with razor wire, separating it from the airstrip. Beyond that was the ageing concrete wall of the dam, wedged into a cleft in the valley.

How long was the lake, stretching back between the steep slopes? Mariam didn't know for sure, but at least five kilometres, maybe even ten or twenty.

On arrival in Pudu's two-person cart, drawn by a rugged pony, it had crossed her mind that there must have been a pass through the peaks until the dam came and drowned it. Perhaps a route through which herds of sheep or goats or cattle might be driven either side of the Pyrenees according to the seasons: winter and spring on the sunny Spanish side, until drought parched the ground and suppressed the grazing; summer and autumn on the shaded French side, until the cold became too much for the livestock to bear.

If the pass had provided a path for herds of animals, it had probably served as an escape route for people too, fleeing whatever regime was persecuting them, from south to north or from north to south, depending on the prevailing winds of oppression.

Pudu left her to gather his community together, giving her time to finish watching the pre-recorded 3D projection from the handheld viewer, holding it close to her face to catch the audio over the noise of the tumbling water: excerpts from a mock trial; the history of the hydro installation; weaknesses in construction; Castile Energie's plans for 'unreasonable expansion'. It didn't go into engineering detail but it set Mariam thinking. The plan was to raise the height of the dam by three metres. What did that actually mean?

She did some quick mental maths, working from the assumption that her middle estimate of the length of the lake was right, ten kilometres, with an average of one kilometre wide, broader in the middle, narrowing to a few hundred metres at either end. Each cubic metre of water added would weigh a metric tonne. Ten thousand metres in length times a thousand metres in width times an added three metres in depth made thirty million tonnes of water.

Thirty million additional tonnes.

She happened to know that the rebuilt Notre Dame Cathedral weighed the same because it was a popular factoid that in the old days, the population of Paris used to produce the same mass of waste, until habits of frugality and recycling became enforceable by law.

But those thirty million tonnes were just the additional top slice. What vast mass was already retained by what Pudu's video claimed was an elderly and potentially failing dam?

She copied a sat-connection from the viewer to her comm-watch and used it to send a brief message to Alex, asking if they might speak in the morning. He replied almost straight away, but one of the members of the protest camp – an older woman with a friendly face – came to hang a nosebag from the pony's bridle, gesturing to Mariam to follow.

'We are ready.'

The camp was made up of eight or ten low tents plus two larger prefabricated buildings, reminding Mariam of flat-pack emergency housing of the kind sent to disaster zones. The buildings were modular and had been linked together to form a larger space, six or seven metres across and very crowded. Mariam supposed she was looking at the entire population of the camp – nearly thirty people, including four or five children and one baby, being held by Pudu himself. Everyone was seated in a rough circle on rugs that covered the uneven floor. Here and there, Mariam could see the grass of the hillside poking through.

All at once, she felt unsure. What was she doing here? Why had she called after Pudu and invited herself to go with him, not telling her aunt where she was going, not knowing who these people really were? Why were they all so quiet? What were they waiting for?

'This is my brother,' said Pudu, indicating the child he held in his arms. 'When Castile's helicopter struck my mother, he survived. But when she died, something in all of us died.'

A faint murmur went round the makeshift building – not speech so much as sounds of approval. The breeze from the peaks of the mountains was making the thin walls flex and bow.

'Is he all right?' she asked.

'He is undamaged in his body but weakened in his soul. And, of course, without his mother, he has no anchor.'

A small man with a grey-flecked goatee beard reached out for the child and took him from Pudu's arms.

'My son,' he said to Mariam. 'Berta and I were together.'

Mariam realised everyone was looking now at the small man, as if the baby were a token that, when held, made it appropriate to speak.

'What did you want to show me?' she asked.

Pudu gestured, lifting his hands and opening them, palms upwards, as if to say: *This, just this.*

The small man adjusted the position of the baby in his lap and told her: 'We speak with one voice.' Again, the murmur of approval went round the whole community. 'You must stay with us. Your presence will validate our protest. We will make you welcome.'

He spoke with a smile but the words sounded sinister to Mariam's ears. And they were all looking at her with a kind of insistence, both adults and children, as if trying to impose their will upon her.

'I should have told my aunt where I was going. She will be worried.'

'We will send a message,' the small man told her and there was

248

another murmur of agreement.

Mariam stood up.

'It's very stuffy in here. I've had a long day.'

She moved quickly to the doorway, pulling aside a heavy cloth hanging, fumbling the catch on the fragile door, then almost tripping on the threshold as she stepped gratefully outside. She took a few steps away, holding out a hand and resting it on the withers of the pony, its head bent, cropping the grass. The sensation grounded her.

She heard footsteps and turned. It was Pudu.

'You find us strange. We don't mind that,' he said.

'Why are you here?'

'I told you – to make people aware.'

'Of what, exactly?'

'That there are special places and this is one of them.'

Mariam raised her head to take in the dark and jagged mountain skyline against the slightly paler sky. She breathed the damp fresh air. The pony shifted and she dropped her hand, feeling conflicted, connected to the landscape but dislocated, too. She wanted to believe in the protestors, but she knew from her own experience that power was something it took time and trouble and political skill to obtain and wield. These people were deluding themselves, weren't they, if they thought their insignificant actions could change the world?

And yet, they were here because they believed this place special – and perhaps it was.

The protesters began filing quietly out of the makeshift community building, most moving directly to their individual tents, others wandering away, perhaps going to use an outdoor latrine or simply taking the air after the stuffy enclosed space. She gave back the viewer.

'You watched everything?' Pudu asked.

'I did.'

'You understand our purpose, then.'

'You want to return the valley to nature. You believe the dam is already unsafe, that increasing its height will make it more so. You want justice for your mother's death.'

'That's right.'

Mariam turned fully to face him.

'How did you know who I was?'

Pudu smiled.

'You've been on the streams. We aren't cut off, here. We're aware of what's happening in the world.'

'No, I mean how did you know that I was connected to this place?'

'Oh,' he said. 'Your cousin Benjamin. He sometimes comes up to the dam to talk to us and use our satlink.'

'I see.'

'And he's lonely with just his mother for company,' said Pudu. 'Your aunt has a severe personality.'

Mariam thought about Benjamin's desire for female company. Might there be someone among the community of protestors that he was interested in? She wished Alex were with her. Together, they might laugh at the simplicity of the connection.

'I must go,' she told him. 'There's cloud coming in. The path will be dark soon, without moonlight.'

'I will come with you, just as far as the turn where you can see your aunt's house.'

'There's no need, unless you have something else to say to me?'

'I've already said it.'

He gave her a brief smile and turned away. She descended the valley, now and then slipping on the damp rock, shifting her weight back onto her heels against the slope, jarring her knees each time her boots struck the ground. Alongside were the rush and roar of the *gave*, the torrent stream allowed through by the dam turbines, tamed but still powerful. Between the grass and mud, the pale limestone shone almost like silver. About halfway home, she paused, looking for a dark entrance to one side of the rocky cleft, activating the home screen on her comm-watch

250

for illumination.

No one, she thought, *has come this way for a long time.*

The grass and flowers were untrodden by human feet, though she noticed animal spoor on the ground. She kept to one side, not wanting to disturb the pioneering growth. Then the ground hardened, rising slightly to a bank of broom, its spring-yellow flowers browned by the dry season, its branches bushing out in grey-green waves. She pushed between them, finding a place of secret childhood memory.

Not really secret, of course. Just a place she used to go when visiting her grandmother – the woman from whom Aunt Sara had inherited the farm. A dark passage into the mountain, giving access to an underground river, wide enough and deep enough to navigate on a small raft made with her child's hands from a fork-lift truck pallet with a few oil cans strapped to its underside.

'Limestone is special,' her grandmother had told her, more than twenty years before. 'Almost human.'

'*Pourquoi, grand-mère*?'

'Why? Because it dissolves in water.'

'So the water can escape?'

'Water always finds a way.'

Alex parked his rented EV in the subterranean garage beneath the Hôtel Étoile and got out, his back and shoulders stiff from that morning's punishing workout in the hotel gym and more than five hours at the wheel. All the same, he took the stairs to his room on the fourth floor, letting himself in with a four-digit code of his own choosing.

The room was stuffy, so he opened the windows overlooking the bronze statue. The air outside was warmer than inside – probably still close to thirty degrees – and it was only ten o'clock so he wasn't quite ready for sleep. Neither was the city. Cars and scooters and minibuses circled the Heroes of the Black Army, while pedestrians hurried by on their way here or there, past café terraces on the far side with barely a table free.

Alex went to the bathroom, took off his clothes and folded them carefully over the towel rail, then took a tepid shower, just cool enough to tighten his skin and banish the vibration of the saloon car's wheels on the tarmac.

Once he had finished, he turned off the lights and stood in the centre of the room, allowing himself time to dry, watching the lights and the people, like distant actors in a film whose plot he didn't yet fully understand.

33

In the western suburbs of Paris, Emmeline Cantor had been working late at the headquarters of the Directorate General for Internal Security, until being relieved by the dark shift, agents paid an additional bonus for agreeing to reverse their circadian rhythm and work all night and sleep all day. That had been shown to have much worse health outcomes than staying up very late or waking very early. On her way out, she encountered Sébastien Ménard. He was carrying an overnight bag.

'Beautiful sky,' he told her. 'So many stars.'

For a few minutes, they talked about the weather forecast, the likelihood of storms, the persistence of drought. Sébastien told her he was taking an overnight train and Emmeline assumed he was heading south to join Mariam Jordane's security detail. They bid one another 'safe travels' and Emmeline left the climate-controlled DGSI headquarters, glad to be breathing free air in the almost-silent streets.

Is it still yesterday or already tomorrow?

Of course, officially it was tomorrow because it was after midnight, but it was also still yesterday because she hadn't yet been to bed.

Emmeline took a service autodrive into Paris proper, allowing the on-board AI to choose its own route to a small ground-floor apartment just off Place Joséphine Baker, between Montparnasse Tower and the cemetery of the same name. Tired from her long day at work, she briefly stumbled, steadying herself with her palm on the timber of her front door.

Once inside, she drank a glass of fresh water at the sink, then lifted a rug to reveal a trapdoor. She pulled it open, releasing a tiny gasp of trapped air, then hesitated, listening for a sound, a vibration she had noticed that morning before she left, maybe a Métro train going past underground.

But there was nothing.

Far beneath the mighty Aswan Dam, there were always vibrations – from the pumps, for example, that worked constantly, removing the water that seeped through into inspection galleries, deep inside. Alongside the pumps, in four different locations, were Major Chaka Kassam's lithium-based explosives – inert for the time being, almost innocent.

Kassam was awake, despite the lateness of the hour, lying on a hard mattress in the cell-like bedroom he had been allotted – windowless, airless, not far from the dam's control room – his mind flip-flopping between a desire for action and the knowledge that he could have a greater impact if he waited.

He was alone, of course, with no way of contacting anyone beyond the Egyptian border, unanchored. Trained in military discipline but drawn to the philosophy of chaos, everything he had ever done was narrowing down to a single sharp point, an act of grotesque but cleansing destruction.

He adjusted his meagre pillows against the rough concrete-block wall and sat up, thinking about what he had witnessed at the Al-Jaghar airbase in southern Cyrenia, after the flight from Bamako, before the overland journey into the Kingdom of the Pharaohs, with his 'gift' of lithium ingots in three secure cases. He had felt personally wounded to see the destruction wrought by the failure of the Coming Darkness conspiracy: the wreckage of the control tower, half covered by drifting sand; the scar from the impact of the aborted rocket in the myriad panels of the photovoltaic solar array.

That was what failure looked like. He, on the other hand …

There was a timeline, of course. If he waited for just a little longer, it could happen in the midst of the ceremony to honour the Egyptian refugee, Zeina Yaseen, who had stumbled into the midst of the Coming Darkness conspiracy and, without knowing how, derailed it. The story had been spread throughout the impenetrably encrypted network of messaging that emanated – though Kassam did not know this – from an island citadel on the Caribbean island of Haré.

What did that messaging assert?

That Zeina Yaseen had no idea what she had done. That her involvement had been an accident. That no one could have predicted the calamitous consequences of her interference – calamitous for the conspiracy, not for the world.

Kassam reached beneath his thin pillows for his belt and holster. It was the perfect hiding place. No one could reasonably ask what was inside. It was too obvious. But concealed within was the transmitter – an inanimate assemblage of steel and plastic and silicone-chip, powered by a tiny lithium battery – that he would use, when the time came, to detonate all four parcels of explosive.

For the time being, the transmitter remained inanimate. Only when the time was ripe would Kassam's malign intent bring it, catastrophically, to life.

Damien Gerest woke abruptly in an antechamber to his office at the headquarters of External Security. He had been sleeping on a soft memory-foam couch in an indentation that mirrored the shape of his body after an over-copious dinner. He rolled over, his eyes vague and his brow creased, feeling uncertain.

Why?

Because he feared he was failing.

Not failing in his role as overall head of the French security services

– at least, not in a way that would bring notice from Claudine Poiret in the office of the French president. But failing to impose his new pattern, his new culture, one based in procedures and protocols, with a clear reporting hierarchy.

Why was that important? Because the treachery at the heart of the last conspiracy would surely have been uncovered sooner if a man like him – methodical, trained in systems – had been in charge, instead of Professor Fayard with his vague meandering mind and his convictions that 'there is no such thing as coincidence' and that there would always be 'time enough'.

Well, there almost hadn't been.

Gerest hauled himself off his couch and reached for his short dressing gown.

'Lights, twenty per cent.'

The voice-activated system brought the constellation of tiny ceiling LEDs to the required level. As he walked through to his office, the system followed him, anticipating that he would want the same low level of illumination in there as well.

That, he thought, *is effective resource management, based on patterns and prior knowledge. Is that so hard to understand?*

He knew, though, that people like to be free to act as if they possess a unique and private understanding of the world, even though logic and reason are common to all.

Gerest sat heavily in his office chair, his dressing gown rucked up beneath him, feeling a little chilly from the overnight climate control, set quite low because he sweated in his sleep. Of course, it knew he was now awake but there would be a lag before the system caught up.

He reached out a hand for one of the damaged executive toys on his desk, the long-necked bird that used to dip its beak to a comforting rhythm. Not any more. The subtle equilibrium between mass and gravity had been undermined by the mend to the broken glass.

Gerest's frown grew deeper. Lamarque was a problem. His celebrity was a problem. The authority of his triumph as 'the man who saved the world' was a problem.

He touched one of the shiny silver balls on the Newton's cradle. He had untangled its fine strings but it, too, no longer functioned quite as it should. The pattern of cause and effect – the conservation and transfer of momentum – had been compromised when Lamarque flipped the desk.

What was wrong with him, for God's sake?

In the midst of the previous crisis, Claudine Poiret had used Gloria Lamarque's illness to keep her son onside. Gerest had decided to use a similar ploy – had gone so far, in fact, as to instruct André Chambon to introduce a mild poison into her food, one that ought not to do her any real harm. Unless, of course, it had unexpected repercussions. Could it, for example, make the original virus mutate, as Doctor Labeur said Fayard's had, combining somehow with a remnant of the previous pathogen? He had been quite pleased with himself, telling Lamarque that there would be 'no need for an alpha-fold study'.

Gerest yawned, realising he could easily go back to sleep. The disturbance had been momentary, just a brief indigestion.

He lurched upright, his hands on the edge of the desk, unpeeling his thighs from the leather of his seat, then shuffled back to the memory-foam couch in his antechamber and lay down in the same warm dent, pulling the covers up to his ears.

34

Just before sunrise the following morning, in the delta of the Nile in Northern Egypt, Zeina Yaseen was sitting on a dusty veranda, beneath a collapsing timber roof, undermined by salt, blistered by sun and gnawed by termites. She was chewing a betel leaf, one of her two useful crops, watching the aquatic birds wake from their low nests.

Zeina was feeling nostalgic for her childhood, when her family's fields flourished with sorghum, cassava, sweet potato and yams, and they all lived together in the pleasant house, designed like a Roman dwelling, a square of rooms surrounding a central courtyard. Whatever the time of day, whatever the season, there was somewhere to sit that was either warmed by the sun or cooled by the shade.

But rising sea levels in the delta had leached into the arable soil, making it less productive year-on-year. And the heat forced them eventually to work the crops at night, relying on the moon and touch. Then, incredibly, the waters of the mighty Nile began to fail – obstructed, withheld and harvested by nations upstream of Egypt.

After her grandmother died, Zeina had left, drawn by the promise of new beginnings, and became a refugee, then an applicant for citizenship of the new republic of Cyrenia, then a grain of sand in the gears of the Coming Darkness conspiracy – lucky to escape with her life. Lucky, also, to make it back home, finding the place crumbling, deserted.

But she arrived with the germ of an idea. An Indian colleague from the solar array at Al-Jaghar had told her about the many beneficial properties of the betel leaf, a kind of miracle crop that could fight diabetes, depression, halitosis, cancer … The list went on.

Zeina had set about obtaining some established specimens by post, using the last of her savings from her robotic job cleaning the photovoltaic panels of Saharan dust. The betel plants arrived, needing a hot and humid environment and regular watering, but not direct sun. She decided to cultivate them indoors.

Zeina broke up a decrepit outbuilding and used the timber to make planters. She collected brackish water from what had been, in her youth, a sparkling irrigation stream. She poured the water into low basins covered with plastic sheets, weighted in the centre with a stone, positioned directly over a jug or a basin. The hot sun evaporated the trapped water. The steam condensed on the plastic sheet, then ran down to the centre and dripped into the receptacle. With seven of these homemade desalination units, powered by the sun, she had enough fresh water to nurture several dozen thriving betel plants, fertilised with her own well-rotted nutrient-rich dung.

Her plants were, in a sense, her only family now, and had reached almost two metres tall, the size she would keep them, plucking and discarding the tougher leaves, retaining only those that remained tender, offering them for sale in the market.

She needed more. The income from her betel leaves wasn't quite enough for subsistence. Hungry and isolated, she had even taken to eating her crop – not for the nutritional value, which was negligible for a human digestive system, but in order to keep her jaw occupied, fooling her stomach into believing that proper meals weren't just a memory from an increasingly distant past.

As life became more difficult, she thought about getting in touch with the authorities in Cyrenia or even France in order to beg for some assistance. But she had no way of reaching a foreign government using the ring-fenced comms of isolationist Egypt.

Then, out of the blue, she had received a message. A motorbike would soon be sent to take her from the farm to Alexandria, whence she would travel by train to Cairo, the capital, then onward south to Aswan where she was to receive a medal, commemorating her accidental heroism. The motorbike taxi had arrived the previous evening and stayed the night, so as to be ready for the early start. Just then, the driver emerged blinking into the low light of dawn.

'We should go,' he told her. 'Do you have any coffee?'

Zeina grew, dried and roasted her own beans, her second useful crop.

'Yes, I do.'

She took him indoors to a cold shelf in the kitchen and passed him a cup made the previous day.

'What water is this?' he asked. 'I've heard about microbes and parasites in the delta.'

If it's good enough for my betel plants, it's good enough for you, she thought.

'It was distilled by the sun,' Zeina told him.

While he drank the cold brew, she put together a few belongings in her backpack. The messenger finished his coffee, put on his helmet and kick-started his motorbike. Zeina climbed on behind, feeling like she was living in the past, in some vintage black-and-white movie.

And, of course she was, compared to the high-tech military-industrial campus at Al-Jaghar.

She wrapped her arms round the man for safety. They pulled away, along the narrow track between the despoiled irrigation channels, frightening the aquatic birds, sending them squawking up into the air out of their fragile nests.

Mariam's presence in the Saint-Médard valley had been concealed by travelling under a false identity. Since then, she had only made one visit away from the farm to the café at the foot of the valley – to make sure that all the neighbours were aware of her sisters' burial ceremony. All the same, her presence had become known.

It happened because two days earlier, one of the members of Pudu's Lenca group – the small, bearded man, the father of Berta's baby – had posted Pudu's intention to bring 'the celebrated Mademoiselle Jordane' to visit the protestors, inviting people to think that she approved of their message and purpose. Trapped in the data shadow of her aunt's farm, Mariam had no idea this had happened. Someone else, however, had taken an immediate interest.

That someone was the journalist that Mariam had almost thrown into the tributary of the Garonne, in the tourist enclave just outside Bordeaux, where she and Alex had stayed the night before their expected return to the capital.

The journalist – Emilie Olsen – was unbowed by their confrontation. The altercation, half-caught on camera, had granted Olsen a kind of secondary celebrity in her own right. It sounded unlikely but, if she could now find a way to bring Mariam onside, it would bolster her profile further.

Olsen could do without any more aggro, however. There was no point allowing herself to be portrayed as an enemy of the woman who had played such an important role alongside 'the man who saved the world'.

That morning, Olsen woke early after catching a good night's sleep in a comfortable room above the café from which – though she did not know this – Mariam's Aunt Sara had called her niece to receive news of Ablah's death. Over a copious breakfast of eggs and greens – during which she watched some distressing news footage of more devastating storms in the Caribbean – she debated with herself whether to get her drone in the air, or to approach the farm in person and run the risk of getting herself thrown down a well or off a mountain ridge.

In the visitor accommodation within the parliamentary compound in

Cyrene City, Amaury showered, washing his hair and thickening beard. Breakfast was delivered to his room – flatbread with labneh, plus some strips of a plant-based bacon substitute. He felt quite full still from the previous evening's reception, but he forced himself to eat it. He was uncertain how long he would be travelling today.

Leaving his room, he was escorted politely to the same formal dining room as the previous evening, where a breakfast table had been set up for another photo and video opportunity, with a few soft-ball questions from carefully chosen journalists. Amongst other things, they wanted to know about Alex.

'What's he really like?' one of them asked, eagerly.

Once Amaury had given an acceptable answer – that Alex was strong and intelligent and caring and kind – he was escorted by car to the airport, his bag carried by an attendant, feeling more and more like a fraud.

Because Alex and Mariam had had enough of speaking to the media, Director Gerest had ordered Amaury to take their places.

'Why me?' Amaury had asked.

'It isn't ideal for me either,' Gerest had told him, 'but it will play to your advantage. As will that,' he had pointed out, indicating Amaury's stump with distaste. 'A serious injury gives traction in public opinion …' Gerest had droned on, making sure that Amaury knew he was dispensable, unlike Alex, the true hero, and Mariam, who had saved Fayard, though he had not then lived for very long. 'But no one must know how you lost your hand or it will change the pattern of sympathy – and sympathy is currency.'

Amaury reviewed the timetable of his journey to Egypt. It would be accomplished in two stages with, first, a flight south to Al-Jaghar, providing another media op at the desert launch site that had been at the heart of the Coming Darkness. Then about five hours by road to Aswan, arriving at the dam in the early afternoon.

As he got out of the car, ready to board the fast X^3 helicopter, he wondered if Alex had understood his message. He thought he'd been quite clever. No one could accuse him of sharing secret information over an unencrypted link and Alex was more than capable of joining the dots, wasn't he?

It had only been a game, though, a kind of riddle between friends. Amaury had no reason to suspect anything bad was going to happen – at least, no more reason than on any other day.

'You went to see those people,' said Aunt Sara.

'I did,' Mariam replied.

Sara was sitting at the kitchen table, in front of an old, rucked-up towel, on which a handful of tools lay in a pattern determined by the sequence in which she had used them. Her hands were busy with a piece of misty-white sandstone, carving, repeatedly pulling the corner of the blade of an old chisel towards the centre where the thickness was greatest, so as not to cause chips at the edge. She was making a rough likeness of a human form for a traditional funerary shrine beneath the west-facing kitchen window. To her right, also on the rucked-up towel, was another effigy, one she had already completed.

'Will you make them different?' asked Mariam.

'I will make them as similar as the stone allows,' said Sara.

Mariam watched her aunt work. She had intended to call Alex that morning, but grief was clouding her intentions.

'What did they say to you?' asked Sara.

'They told me about the sacredness of the Saint-Médard valley and the shared goals of their community. You know the woman who died? They wanted to show me her baby and tell me ...' What had they said, Pudu and the small man, Berta's partner? 'They wanted me to know that they all speak with one voice.'

'That's all?' asked Sara.

'Then I left. I didn't like it there. There is a hint of the same madness as in the people we defeated ...'

263

Mariam stopped. She thought her aunt wasn't really listening. She went to look at the shrine, a nest of fragrant branches in a large iron tray on the deep windowsill, in which a few lumps of charcoal were smouldering, perfuming the room with the smoke of rosemary, sage and cedar, the scents of remembrance and death.

'It's done,' came Sara's voice from behind her. Her aunt was running her rough fingers over the stone. She held it out. 'You should place it.'

Mariam took the organic shape and weighed it in her hand. Her aunt had given the sandstone effigy approximate human form. The indentations from her chisel all ran in one direction, from the vaguely defined head, across the widening shoulders, to the legs. If anything, it evoked a scaly mermaid.

Mariam placed it in the nest of fragrant smouldering branches then came back for the second effigy, handling it for the first time, realising it was a little bigger, that her aunt had made her symbolic representations of Janaan and Ablah different sizes.

'Thank you for doing this,' she told her.

'It's our way. You would know if you had lived here.'

Sara put her tools away in a drawer under the heavy rustic table, folded the towel over and went outside to shake the dust and shards of stone onto the path. Mariam followed her.

'I do understand this place,' said Mariam.

'Do you?' asked Sara.

'I was here every holiday as a child.'

'That's exactly what I mean,' said Sara. 'You have no idea.'

Mariam glanced at her aunt's face. It was tilted upwards, looking in the direction of the dam, high in the valley, but out of sight, beyond the turn in the rock cut by the torrent of the *gave*.

'Don't trust those people,' Sara commanded.

'I won't,' Mariam reassured her. 'I don't trust anyone anymore.'

As if to give the lie to her words, she heard footsteps on the wet path, and all at once saw someone she did trust – a tall man with wide shoulders and long black hair; her colleague from internal security, Sébastien Ménard, striding towards them, carrying a small bag, past the flourishing vegetable garden, a determined expression on his face.

'Why are you here?' she asked.

'Captain Lamarque asked me to protect you. He told me nothing is more important.'

35

Alex was under escort, on his way to the presidential palace in Bamako, a low-rise building in white stone on a rise in the landscape, with a view across the city. Unlike the Malian police officers, experts in doing the bare minimum, the military guarding access to President Manouche were models of professionalism.

Alex was in a diesel or veg-oil minibus, seated in the front for the view. It slid out through the crowded city centre, using the priority lanes, into a neighbourhood of office blocks and light-industrial units. Then they crossed a surprising frontier between the city and the palace grounds – a shanty town enclosed by high metal fences with entrance and exit points patrolled by severe-looking armed soldiers.

Who were the inhabitants of the shanty town? Refugees from fighting in Burkina Faso, perhaps? Indigenous Blanks? Almost certainly a mixture of the two, plus other drifting populations, always moving on, hoping for better, often finding worse, purposeless jetsam, tossed up on foreign sand by the receding tide of history.

Beyond the shanty town, the minibus went through two checkpoints, one at the main gate and another where the sloping grounds became more manicured. Alex's arrival at the official entrance, accompanied by a diplomatic escort, was documented by a videographer who asked him three questions whose answers he had been primed to prepare.

'How do you feel to be meeting President Manouche?'

'Very much honoured, of course. France is cognisant of his remarkable achievements in service of the Malian people.'

'How have you been enjoying your time in our country?'

'Enormously. I am grateful for my warm welcome and have been impressed by the vigour and intelligence of the people.'

'What message do you have for the Malian people, given the awful calamity the world might have faced, were it not for your own actions?'

'We must all stay vigilant and strong and work together for a brighter future. The Republic of Mali can be a beacon for us all.'

Inside the palace, Alex was led through a wide lobby with tall chairs and what he thought were merely decorative columns with no real purpose holding up the concrete span of the roof. Like so many governmental and royal residences, the architecture was a riff on Ancient Greece – but without the charm of antiquity or the gravitas of cultural authenticity. At the far end of the lobby, his escort showed him through an open-plan office where at least a dozen people were working on the day-to-day business of the state. He asked for a log-in, explaining he was expecting an urgent call, not telling them it was from the woman he loved, rather than a general or a diplomat.

'The "Visitor" network is free access and ring-fenced, but beware of journalists trying to see what you are doing while connected. They use it, too.'

'There's no chance of that,' Alex told her, making his connection and finding that Mariam had not yet called.

At the far end of the open-plan office, wide-open doors gave access onto an enclosed courtyard and water garden, beyond which he could see a terrace with a fabric roof, pulled taut on roundwood poles, reminiscent of a Saharan nomad's tent. Alex's escort murmured something discreet that he didn't quite catch, so he hesitated on the threshold. Beyond the water garden, beneath the fabric roof, President Manouche was seated behind a large desk. Opposite him was a tall man with wide shoulders, wearing a silver-grey suit, perched uncomfortably on a hard carved chair.

Davide Castile.

The only path through the water garden, with its well-tended aquatic plants, was a sequence of stepping stones, spaced quite close together, forcing Alex to shorten his stride. Was it deliberate, a way of making the path through the lilies and nenuphars an easy one, whatever one's stature? Or was it deliberate in another way, obliging the visitor to move slowly, tentatively, approaching the presence of the 'supreme commander'?

'Here he is,' called President Manouche. 'Good morning, captain.'

Alex stopped a respectful distance away, taking in the large iroko-wood desk, two chairs for guests, all intricately carved, no visible screens or devices, not even a fixed-line phone.

'Good morning, sir. Good morning, Monsieur Castile.'

'Come and join us,' said Manouche, lounging back in his generous swivel chair, not giving Castile a chance to speak. 'We are discussing the End Times. You know all about that, don't you?'

'I will be delighted to hear what you have to say,' Alex replied respectfully.

He sat down, taking the seat to the left. Castile was on his right, twisting a gold *chevalière* ring on his middle finger.

'So, your presence is entirely opportune, perhaps in more ways than one,' laughed Manouche. He stabbed a finger at his desk, as if he was repeatedly squashing a bug. 'But you are "the man who saved the world".'

Castile frowned and spoke as if there had been no interruption, his focus on the president.

'This reality is with us now. We might have acted sooner in mitigation and adaptation, but we didn't. Now, we have no choice.' He had a pleasant voice, Alex thought, but he was having to make an effort not to become hectoring. 'Mitigation and adaptation cannot turn back the clock,' Castile went on. 'Things are getting worse and there is no

268

reason to expect anything else.'

'We are managing,' said the president.

'But I can make you rich, as well,' said Castile, unexpectedly.

'When you say "you",' said the president, with a smile, 'you refer to the Republic of Mali?'

'Of course,' said Castile. 'Your people.'

'I have read about your carbon scrubbers,' said the president. 'Your devices perform at an unprecedented level of efficiency. Bravo. You suck carbon out of enclosed atmospheres, but you want to put this dangerous gas underground in cavities in the rock of my country.'

'Yes,' said Castile.

'And monitor it, I suppose, unfailingly, eternally?'

'Not quite eternally,' said Castile, his face serious. 'But yes, of course.'

The president drank from a tall glass of iced water. Alex noticed that neither he nor Castile had been offered refreshment.

'I was born in 1970,' said Manouche. 'I am sixty-seven today. When I was sixteen, I was taking my exams and when we emerged from the gym where we had sat scribbling our answers, we all went to the pool hall to celebrate and the news was on the television and what did we see? You must have heard of it.'

'In 1986?' said Castile.

'It was August. I was a naughty boy. My friend Chaka and I were in a catch-up summer school.' The president laughed. 'But I have achieved things, all the same. Now, Monsieur Castile, what do these dates mean to you – and the connection with your carbon dioxide plan?'

Castile looked uncomfortable.

As Manouche intended he should, Alex thought.

'I don't know,' said Castile shortly.

'And you, Captain Lamarque?' said the president. 'I have heard only good of your intelligence and acuity. Who hasn't? The whole world is grateful. What does this mean to you?'

Alex let 'August 1986' settle in his imagination. A map drifted into focus. Was it Mali? No. A neighbouring country? No, not that either. Further afield. A border region between Nigeria and Cameroon, a volcanic landscape ...

The memory crystallised.

'Lake Nyos,' he said.

'Very good,' said Manouche. He lounged back in his chair once more. 'Monsieur Castile, are you aware of what Captain Lamarque and I are discussing?'

'No,' said Castile. Alex thought he was suppressing anger at how the president was playing him. 'You both have me at a disadvantage.'

'It was,' said Manouche, enjoying himself, 'a limnic eruption. At the time, all kinds of stories circulated. After all, there was no violence – just village after village of dead Africans and dead African livestock. Do you remember how many, Captain Lamarque?'

'Not precisely. Fewer than two thousand people, I think?'

'Very good. Monsieur Castile, is this ringing any bells? How old are you? Approaching fifty? I forget the notes I had my assistant prepare for me.'

Alex thought the president was lying. He was sure Manouche remembered every detail of his brief.

'I am forty-seven,' said Castile with an attempt at affability, 'but most people tell me I look younger, not older.'

The president ignored the transparent invitation to reply with a compliment.

'The Lake Nyos disaster was triggered by tectonic movements that released hundreds of thousands of tonnes of carbon dioxide in a huge belch, you understand me? It rose and then, CO_2 being much heavier than air, it fell and suffocated the lowlands all around.' He smiled. 'As I said, we naughty summer-school boys talked about aliens with a terrible death ray or some mysterious new weapon wielded by the Americans or the Soviets. This was the time of the Cold War, fought by proxy in

Africa, you remember. Even today, there are people who do not believe in the story of the "belch". What do you believe, Monsieur Castile?'

'I could research it and feed back to you.'

'And you would like to scrub CO_2 from the air,' said Manouche, again squashing the imaginary bug, 'and sequester it in the rocks of southern Mali because our landscape is, you assert, propitious. You wish to save the world from the foolishness of the past, from Western greed. You wish to hide the evidence of overpopulation and overconsumption and overindustrialisation here, in Africa, just as you used to ship us your recycling and your obsolete cars and your rusting propane bottles.'

'Has the disaster at Lake Nyos happened again?' asked Castile.

'No,' said the president.

'Then science has successfully monitored and controlled the circumstances.'

'Perhaps the "belch" needs many more years to prepare itself,' said the president. 'Perhaps the non-repetition is luck, nothing more.'

'I will look into it, I promise you,' said Castile, 'but the processes that my organisation proposes are not comparable. We will turn the carbon scrubbed from the atmosphere into a stable solid, via a patent process.'

'Yes,' said the president. 'The oh-so-secret patent process. I have looked into this and I have learnt that it is common to bind the CO_2 to a liquid solvent such as aqueous ammonia. But that is a temporary and reversible process, is it not – the CO_2 can escape the solution?'

'Yes,' said Castile. 'Our process begins there but that is not all. We will also build a chain of new solar power stations and integrate them with desalination plants. Our goal is to re-green Mali. This is geoengineering as well, planting trees, creating swamps and wetlands, pushing back desertification. We are involved in the Sinai project as partners, returning the landscape to what it once was, five or even eight thousand years ago, rivers flowing from the mountains in the south, northwards towards the Mediterranean. You are aware of it, I am sure.'

'Tell me your involvement.'

'It is a holistic project, led by a Dutch team. We are technological sub-contractors.'

'How did they get the Egyptian government to agree?'

'The project was initiated before Egyptian isolation. Our strategy is a partnership aimed at nothing less than the complete greening of the landscape. The success of Sinai, though it might take two more human generations, will change the regional climate. It is already drawing in immigration. Lake Bardawil is no longer a dying lagoon, but a healthy ecosystem connected to the sea.'

'If I give you permission to sequester your scrubbed carbon in the rocks of Mali, you will reverse desertification and create a "green and pleasant land", as the English say?'

'We will – not tomorrow, but soon.'

The president swung his leather office chair.

'What do you think of all this, Captain Lamarque?' he asked.

'I have no opinion, sir. I am not briefed.'

'Then why are you here?'

'I believe,' said Alex, 'that Monsieur Castile believes that my celebrity will enhance his marketing, making you more likely to entertain his coordinated project.'

The president laughed.

'You are brutally honest. Yes, that is the second way in which your presence is "opportune". Monsieur Castile asked your government to delegate the "man who saved the world" for the gloss it would add to his negotiations because you bring with you an odour of triumph and optimism.'

Castile looked as though he was recalculating, wondering how to turn all this to his advantage.

'It is also evidence of the strength of French government support,' he said, quickly. 'And our geological science has been established through analysis of fracking – a dangerous last-gasp hydrocarbon folly whose scars have, however, brought us huge learnings that we can now turn to our advantage.' He sat up straighter on his hard wooden chair. 'This is carbon removal through restitution of a green landscape and through scrubbing the CO_2 out of industrial processes. The former will not be enough without the latter. The latter will not restore the landscape without the former.'

'Why the Republic of Mali?' asked the president.

'Because, through our partnership with MaliLith, our organisation is already present in your country. Otherwise, how would I have managed to obtain this meeting?'

'Yes, good; you have an answer to everything. I congratulate you.' Manouche pursed his lips. 'What of the alternative?'

'The alternative?' asked Castile.

'Solar geoengineering.'

Alex felt a chill. Solar geoengineering was, he instinctively thought, a deadly and uncertain wager. He was relieved to discover that Castile agreed – or, at least, pretended to agree.

'You are talking about blocking incoming sunlight and sending it back out into space, creating a cooling effect?' said Castile. 'And you would do that by diffusing reflective gases or particles into the stratosphere?' He shook his head. 'Fraught with danger. What if it destroyed plant adaptations evolved over millions of years? What if …?' He waved a hand to indicate that he was about to offer a fanciful idea. 'What if it changed the colour of the sky and caused mass human depression or hysteria? No,' he stated, categorically, 'it is too risky.'

'There are treaties against it, in any case,' said Manouche languidly. 'But tell me, why is your company, your private enterprise, mobilising to do all this?'

'For my family's portfolio, it is essential to stay ahead of changing circumstances. My father's vision has always been – if we are profitable, we can do good.'

'Mali would become a beacon?' mused the president. 'We saw and heard what you said about beacons, Captain Lamarque.' He gestured to the fabric ceiling and Alex saw, from a faint luminescent outline, that there was some kind of screen sewn into an angled panel. 'But we are poor, so we have little choice.' He drank again. 'Captain Lamarque, I ask again, what do you think?'

'I think there are risks as well as advantages in being a beacon.'

'You are thinking of Cyrenia. Perhaps I should discuss this with Prime Minister Mourad.' The president stood up. Castile and Alex did too. 'I have another appointment.'

'Thank you, sir,' said Castile. 'I am grateful for your time.'

A Malian diplomat emerged from the private space beyond the outdoor office, perhaps summoned by a discreet button on the president's desk, and they were ushered away. On the way out through the open-plan office, Castile used the bathroom and Alex surreptitiously asked his comm-watch to penetrate the diplomatic network, confident his cutting-edge tech would remain undetected by the second-rate Malian equipment.

It took only a moment. He was able to discover that President Manouche was reading – on the screen in the fabric roof of his outdoor room – the same background briefing on Davide Castile that he had perused on his boat. Meanwhile, one of the operatives in the outside office was synthesising a summary from a set of reports into the terrorist attacks in the south.

Castile returned, a fixed expression on his face. When they reached the minibus at the main door, Alex got in the back alongside him and he finally spoke, an edge of anger to his voice.

'You were very frank. There was probably no need to undermine my position, don't you think?'

'Did you kill the protester on purpose?' Alex asked, then waited so long for an answer that he began to think Castile would refuse to comment. 'At the dam in the Pyrenees, did you kill the protester on purpose?'

274

'We can speak of this later.'

'Later where?'

'Once we are in the air with no risk of being overheard.' He shook his head. 'Anyway, we're in charge here. This is all a game. President Manouche will bite and we will reel him in because he has no alternative – if there's time.'

Alex didn't like the expression, as if the man and his country were a fish to be caught and eaten.

'You haven't answered my question.'

'No, I did not kill her,' said Castille. 'What would have been the point?'

'Vindictiveness? Anger?'

'Don't be ridiculous. Look at the hassle it's brought. Time is short.'

'In what sense?'

'Each of us has two lives. You know that? One lived in ignorance, up until the point you realise you will only live once. Then everything changes and your second life begins – with no time to waste.'

Alex thought there was an element of truth to that.

'So how did it happen?'

Castile's glance went to the driver of the minibus.

'On the plane I'll tell you – and I have some questions for you, too.'

Alex looked at Castile. Although there was an edge to his mood, he radiated a controlled sense of purpose. The moments of impatience or irritation as President Manouche had goaded him had been nowhere near the volcanic scale Alex had anticipated.

'We will go via the Hôtel Étoile for your luggage,' said Castile.

'You didn't need me here, then?' Alex asked. 'Not really.'

'Oh, but I do,' Castile replied, twisting his ring. 'I want to offer you a job.'

'I have a job.'

'An escape route, then.'

'From what to where?'

'From the present into the future,' said Castile.

36

Using the dedicated traffic lanes, the minibus was soon parked in front of the hotel on Place de la Liberté. Alex fetched his things, including his gym kit from laundry services, and came back out into the harsh light. Castile was leaning against the side of the vehicle, his eyes closed, his face turned towards the sun. Alex was struck by the idea that he looked like someone saying goodbye, reluctant to leave, knowing he had no choice.

On the way to the airport, Alex sat in the back for privacy and quietly used the twenty-minute journey to dictate two thousand words on all he had seen and done since arriving in the country, the text popping out from his comm-watch as a 2D holo to mimic the physical process of composition. As he did so, he was revisited by the idea that he was in the wrong place, that he ought to be with Mariam or Amaury, that they shouldn't have allowed themselves to separate. But Mariam had wanted to be alone with her family and her grief, and Amaury had taken on the burden of representing their triumph to a watching world.

Then what? What had Mariam wanted to say to him? Why hadn't she called? And where was Amaury now? What had he been hinting at? Alex realised there was just one phrase Amaury had used that stood out.

That would be an elephantine error.

Arriving at the airport, the minibus passed through a military checkpoint, avoiding civilian security, and drove directly across the tarmac to a chic low-rise departure building, where they got out of the minibus beside a private jet that looked sharp, like a needle.

'The last time you flew in something like this, you failed to bring it home in one piece,' Castile reminded him. 'This is a different beast from the Falcon. It was inspired by NASA's X-plane programme and has ultra-long range.'

'You mean Castile Corporation poached two NASA engineers and appropriated the technology.'

'Sure, yes. Public money made it possible. Private money made it useful. That's how innovation works. You recognise it?'

'It's an Ae4, twelve seats—'

'Mine is fitted out for six,' Castile interrupted. 'Lighter means further.'

'Capable of supersonic speeds.'

'Mach 1.6,' said Castile with a smile, like a parent talking about their child's exam successes. 'Nearly two thousand kilometres per hour, capable of reducing the Atlantic to an afternoon's flight. But slower speeds mean we can stay in the air for longer. Fuel efficiency is maxed at around 550 knots. In any case, my favourite part is the redesign.'

'No windows,' said Alex, looking at the completely streamlined fuselage.

'For greater aerodynamic efficiency. But you won't miss them.'

Alex didn't argue but he thought he probably would.

'What fuel?'

'We have an interest in solar flight but what's the point?' said Castile. 'Yes, one or two passengers can glide through the sky in a vehicle with the wingspan of an airliner whose skin is almost entirely made up of solar cells. Yes, you can stay in the air for a week at a time. But it has to be no heavier than a car and needs to be towed by a hydrocarbon engine to get it off the ground.' He gestured to the Ae4. 'This uses SAF, sustainable aircraft fuel. We are global producers with seventeen percent of the market. We offset at 200%.'

'Impressive if true.'

'You're goading me,' said Castile, 'like President Manouche. You've looked into my background and you're wondering if I'm unstable, like the rumours say.'

'We all have different reactions to stress.'

'You need to understand that I'm a different man today, different from the one in the files. I told you earlier that a person lives two lives. Maybe you thought it was just a clever phrase. In my case, you should believe it.'

'I spoke to Arnaud Sy. That's what he told me, too,' Alex acknowledged. 'Even when you were under most pressure in the artificial stress-test of the biosphere, he thought you did what was best and right.'

'Look, Captain Lamarque, your job is to identify hidden enemies. I promise you – I am not one.'

'That's exactly what a hidden enemy would say.'

Alex caught the same expression on Castile's face that he had seen outside the hotel, something like regret, before he turned away and took the steps two at a time. Alex thought it cost him considerable effort, making this display of energy and strength. Was he limping, in fact?

Alex followed him on board and saw what Castile meant about the absence of windows. The fuselage was lined with eight screens, four each side, relaying images from outside. They were beautifully designed, running into one another in a strip that ran the entire length of the port and starboard walls, as if there truly was a window on each side that reached from front to back of the cabin. Two large reclining seats at the rear were laid out flat as beds. Further forward was a nest of four more, grouped around a circular table. Everything was muted cream and beige, the screens and illumination adjusted so as not to use too much harsh blue light.

'Restful, isn't it?' said Castile, taking off his jacket and hanging it in a slim wardrobe at the front of the cabin. He gave Alex his own explanation for the 'freak accident' – the protestor running forward as a cold down-gust came rolling off the mountainside, the controls on the X^3 slow to respond, a calamitous coincidence, nothing more. 'Believe me or don't believe me, it doesn't matter.'

He shuffled out of his sandals and took off his shirt and trousers, taking a set of in-flight pyjamas from a shelf above the short hanging rail. With a jolt, Alex noticed a medical port in Castile's stomach and a pouch containing some mechanism for delivering drugs strapped to his abdomen. Castile wore a brace on his left ankle as well. It made Alex think about his own injuries. The ache was gone, except when he woke. The immobility of sleep made his knee seize up a little overnight.

'Would you like to change?' Castile asked.

'No, I'm fine. Will we fly supersonic?'

'Of course.'

'Where will we break the sound barrier?' Alex asked. 'People on the ground get frightened of the sonic boom.'

'We've mitigated it with micro-array flow control so it's barely noticeable,' said Castile. 'I don't really care. There's a limit to how many things a person can care about.'

True, Alex thought. And there's a limit to what can be achieved with a single lifetime, a single understanding, a single reserve of energy and determination. The question was, how did Castile intend trying to make Alex's energy align with his own? Castile noticed him contemplating the med-port.

'I expected to outlive my father, but that is perhaps now in doubt.'

'You took over from him at Castile Energie?'

'A common misconception. Someone put it on the web and the idea proliferated. My father remains chief executive of our family corporation but his own physical frailties prevent him from joining public life.'

'Are you terminal?' Alex asked.

Castile paused, thrown off balance for the first time since President

Manouche's outdoor office.

'We're all terminal, captain. You know that.'

'But some sooner than others.'

Castile seemed to repress a sigh.

'I'm going to talk to my pilot.' He opened the armoured door to the cockpit with his thumbprint. 'Please take a seat at the table so we can talk. I have a story to tell you. There's stowage alongside for your bag.'

Castile closed the cockpit door behind him. Left alone, Alex soon felt the thrust of acceleration and take-off, the world flashing past on the eight screens. Once they had levelled out, Castile re-emerged and stood by a serving unit on the opposite side of the cockpit door from his slim wardrobe.

'The calamity you prevented, what if it had happened?' said Castile. 'What if you – or someone like you – had been too late?'

'Then everything would have changed. Humanity would have had to find a new way to exist.'

'What would have been the struggles?'

'Food security, first. Safety from people who have nothing, who want what you have. Maintaining purpose within your community. Working together.'

'I agree with all of that.' Castile had prepared vodka and cranberry for Alex. Somehow his preference had become public knowledge. 'I added zests of lime instead of lime juice,' Castile told him. 'I think it's better, but I can change it.'

'It'll be fine.'

Castile sat down with his own glass of what looked like plain water. He put the two glasses down on a cloth napkin to stop them sliding around in flight. Was he unable to drink alcohol because of his drug regime? What was his drug regime, Alex wondered?

'What's the next big thing, captain?'

'You mean the next global calamity? Nuclear war, obviously.'

'That doesn't help. A global nuclear war … Would you want to survive it?'

'I'm not sure I would, no.'

'So, at a lesser scale.'

'A pandemic that kills more than fifty percent of people? An asteroid impact? I suppose our imaginations are hyped up by movies and TV shows—'

'Never mind where the ideas are from,' Castile interrupted. 'If we go with the second, the asteroid, the devastation is the same as nuclear, but without the radioactive nightmare to follow?'

'And it's possible to rebuild,' Alex agreed.

'And the first one, the fifty percent pandemic … Ebola kills about half of its victims, by the way.'

'Or it could be a result of biological warfare or a biosecurity failure.'

'What are the issues afterwards?'

'Lack of labour, loss of expertise. Resource management completely falling apart. Our supply chains are stretched too far, too thin. Redundancy is no longer built in.'

'Why is that?'

'For reasons of economy. You know that.'

'And how is it dressed up?' Castile insisted.

Alex smiled, interested to be led down a pathway that his thoughts often took of their own accord.

'It's dressed up as efficiency, but actually it's skating on the edge, hoping not to fall.' He sipped his drink. 'And don't forget, every population centre will be choked with decaying bodies.'

Castile shook his head. Alex thought he wasn't interested in visions of horror. He wanted to focus on different pragmatic details.

'What then?'

Alex half-closed his eyes, visualising a changed world.

'People have been prepping for this for a generation. New Zealand and Alaska are favourites, but there are other places that seem isolated enough but still feel like civilisation.'

281

'And both New Zealand and Alaska are, as it happens, on the chilly side,' Castile agreed. 'Temperate, with hills and mountains, so maybe resistant to global heating and sea level rise.'

'But fracking in Alaska has contaminated the groundwater. Your companies are involved in that.'

'I told Manouche, only in order to learn to do it better.'

'That's often a pretext for destructive industrial practices. "How can we improve if we don't make a mess first?" True?'

Castile again refused to become diverted.

'If you start in a shelter,' he asked, 'does it need its own air supply?'

'A shelter like a bunker?'

'Yes.'

'If it needs its own air supply, it's because the atmosphere outside has become unbreathable, so what's the point? The air supply eventually runs out and you die in a hole in the ground.'

'You might have lithium scrubbers or you might only need to shelter for a short while. Maybe a matter of months. How do you maintain authority?'

Alex considered Castile, sipping his water, his face drawn, but in this moment, quite relaxed. He thought about being super wealthy, insulated from the world and its mistakes. Here, in the cabin of this exceptional supersonic jet, might be the place where Castile felt most untouchable. Was he contemplating these scenarios because he thought them inevitable, or because he would strive to bring one of them about?

'You're ex-military,' Alex replied. 'You know how.'

Castile nodded. 'A combination of routine, habit, fear and logic. In the end, it's the authority of the chain of command – the trust that the best decisions are being made – that makes people accept and obey.'

'Leadership has to be perceived as benevolent and wise.'

'And that's where you come in, captain.'

Alex watched Castile scanning the screens that imitated a long strip of windows. They were flying above a bank of thin cloud, the ground invisible, the sky above stark blue, almost artificial – or perhaps that was an effect of the external camera technology.

'I'll be there, will I?' he asked.

He was beginning to see what Castile had meant with his 'escape route from the present into the future'.

'The survivors,' Castile suggested, 'will accept hard decisions because they perceive themselves as protected from external threats.'

'Yes, that's often a way to keep people in line. But you're talking about bunker complexes with, what, stores of dried and vac-packed goods, a circular water supply, hydroponics for agriculture, waiting out the period of floods and scouring winds and dust-choked skies after the asteroid hits and …' Alex deliberately left the idea hanging. He knew from the news streams that you could buy a pointless shelter complex under the southwest US deserts – many of them equipped with a swimming pool and a bowling lane – for ten million dollars. 'You'll have your own private army, I suppose?'

'Don't talk about me. This isn't about me necessarily.'

'There'll be private armies in these bunker complexes. By the way, they'll need to be built on uplands if there are threats of flooding, which isn't always easy when you're digging hundreds of metres underground. You don't want to find your air and food running out, decide it's time to emerge and your sealed environment is at the bottom of a new salt-water lake.'

'Can we focus on maintaining authority, captain?'

'Whoever you exclude will want in and you'll have to use force to keep them out. Your survivors will be busy tending the hydroponics, filtering the water, finding ways to dispose of growing heaps of human waste, keeping things clean, eradicating lice and fleas – your closed post-calamity world won't be immune to insects and microbes, rodent vermin.' Alex shook his head. 'It's easy to imagine everything clean and new, but how about six weeks on or six months on?'

'And maintaining authority?'

'Say you have a trained force that believes in you and your leadership.'

'Like people all over the world believe in you, captain.'

Alex shook his head.

'Like I said, your military have to be prepared to kill outsiders, and perhaps, if things get bad and there's not enough to go round, insiders too. That means you need two food supplies – one for the hierarchy and the defence force, another for the expendable population. But the population isn't expendable, because you've chosen them to do specific and important jobs without which your closed system breaks down.'

'Yes,' said Castile, his brow furrowed.

Alex wondered which part of what he was saying was causing Castile most concern.

'It's back to redundancy,' Alex explained. 'In the global chains of exploitation all around us today, there's a surfeit of people. They're everywhere, infesting the planet, each one with a hungry mouth and a desire to live and love and make more humans, year on year. That's very handy when you want to move your mining operation or your furniture factory to a new location with lower costs and better access to primary resources or whatever, but there's no redundancy in your closed system. Have you considered how you might pay them?'

'Apart from with safety, with survival?'

'After the event, if they've survived, that's a reward they've already received. Going forward? I suppose your money's useless now. You may have gold coins or whatever, but—'

'Crypto?'

'It's the same problem. Things – including virtual things – are only worth what someone wants to give you in return. We're discussing, say, the member of your community who decides that they just don't want to tend to the plant-protein racks any longer.'

'How do you make them see sense?'

'Everyone will be traumatised. How do you manage their PTSD, their alienation and ennui? Drugs, maybe, in the water supply, a kind of synthetic prophylactic medication against depression?' Alex drank. 'And have you considered mutiny in your private army? What if you last a few years and you start to look tired and old and they, I imagine, are still young?'

'I could control food access with biometric locks.'

'So, they cut off your thumb and keep it in a Ziplock bag to use it as a key.'

'I could live alone, served by robots.'

'Maybe, but – outside of repetitive, pre-programmed actions – robot technology continues to fail.' Alex finished his drink. It was quite strong. He guessed Castile had done this deliberately to loosen his tongue, but he felt no inhibition in any case. 'In my opinion, there's no alternative to co-operation. Lack of co-operation is the thing that will bring on the calamity, the event, whatever it might be. The only sane response has to be working together. That's how we've degraded the environment, but it's also how we survive it when it turns against us. Your greatest investment will always be people, not numbers in books or in digital records, cataloguing your imaginary money. All money is imaginary once everyone decides they don't want paper wealth anymore because, as conventional wisdom has it, you can't eat it or take it with you.'

Castile finished his water, using the last few centimetres to help swallow a pill.

'If you know Arnaud Sy, then you know about the biosphere experiment.'

'Yes,' said Alex. He thought there was actually a look of pain in Castile's eyes at the memory. 'There was talk about it preparing for Mars or some exoplanet.'

'Fantasies,' said Castile contemptuously. 'There is no planet B.'

'No,' Alex agreed.

'Just as there's no uploading the brain,' Castile went on, as if it was something he had discussed many times. 'I know people who think that can make them live forever – three who died in the last couple of years whose remains have been cryogenically frozen in the expectation that one day they will be revived. They ignore that fact that consciousness exists within the body and brain together.'

'Say it were possible,' Alex asked. 'Why, in the future, would anyone else want these frozen people revived?'

'Each of them believed themselves valuable and loved,' said Castile, quietly. 'Perhaps, if that affection endured …'

Alex hadn't expected to be discussing love.

'Was it the biosphere experience that changed you?' he asked. 'Your military career came to an end soon after and you began reshaping the activities of your family's conglomerate. Is that when you realised there's no escape hatch?'

'It made me think about safeguarding a future. Isn't that what motivates you, Captain Lamarque?'

'Safeguarding the present, so that there might be a future – that's more my domain.'

Castile activated the motors in his wide leather seat, leaning it back, an extension sliding out for his bare feet, his eyes closed. Was it a momentary impact of his medicine, making him weary or nauseated? Then he spoke very quietly.

'There are dozens of strongholds, dozens of strategies for preparing for some kind of catastrophic event,' he said. 'It's a way of thinking that makes the catastrophe more likely. If you think you can survive …'

His voice drifted off and Alex wondered if the drug was actually a tranquilliser of some kind – a strong analgesic for chronic pain with a side effect of drowsiness.

'I agree,' Alex told him, pitching his voice a little louder. 'The "bunker mentality" or the "planet B mentality" are excuses not to care about now.'

'I have a plan,' said Castile quietly, his eyes still closed. 'Several strongholds, with people committed to the idea.'

'What idea?'

'An agrarian economy, bolstered by long-lasting supplies stored in perfect conditions, plus resilient legacy tech from our current civilisation, including hydro-power. Fewer people, obviously. What did you call us humans? An "infestation"?'

'I did, yes,' said Alex. 'But every one of us has value.'

'Not in all circumstances,' said Castile, in a murmur. He shifted in his seat. 'You could be there with me – my second-in-command. The authority of your success, your celebrity, would keep the survivors' focus.'

'On what?'

'On survival.' His voice faded. 'I'm sorry. My medication ...' Castile pulled himself up a little, becoming marginally more alert. 'What do you say?'

'I'm not interested.'

'That's a shame – for you and for me.'

Alex watched Castile tip his seat further back, nestling his head into the side of the headrest to support his neck. He thought about what the most important skills in a post-calamity order would be – shooting, physical strength, animal husbandry, green fingers. Not new skills, just a selection of old skills. His mind went back to an earlier question. How long would the survivors have to 'shelter in place'? Maybe a year might finally be enough, depending on the horror outside?

Alex saw Castile's drawn face slacken as sleep came surprisingly quickly. Would Castile have thought to include a dentist amongst his chosen few? And a back-up dentist? And a back-up to the back-up? Then Alex imagined the moment of moral crisis when a desperate stranger from outside the community – perhaps a child – came asking for help. Would there be a cost-benefit analysis before deciding whether to let them in or drive them away? If Castile was serious – that Alex might be first minister to Castile's king in a devastated, post-apocalyptic world – was that a decision he would want to have to make?

287

Alex tipped his own seat back. They had been talking for some time and were travelling at supersonic speed. He wouldn't be surprised to soon feel the needle-shaped Ae4 begin its descent into Paris. Maybe another twenty minutes?

He reflected on the potential disasters they had not yet discussed, like a solar storm that took out most of the tech but left the population of the planet untouched: nine billion hungry mouths; six hundred million diabetics desperate for insulin; a billion elderly craving whatever exhausted palliatives made their reduced existences tolerable. Who would be the fittest to survive?

Alex realised they hadn't mentioned private islands. Yes, New Zealand was made up of islands, but not the kind he was now contemplating. What the billionaire preppers wanted were 'goldilocks' islands, not too big, not too small, but just right. They had to be large enough to support an agrarian lifestyle, reinforced by stores salvaged from the pre-calamity economy, with a 'ring of fire', a circle of gun emplacements capable of driving away raiders. Otherwise, the whole bunker idea was absurd, useful only in the narrowest range of circumstances – where the period of hiding was short and the world remained a welcoming place once you emerged.

Thinking about it all made him feel weary. Sleep wasn't far off – perhaps influenced by Castile's slack expression just two metres away. Before allowing his eyes to close, he reminded himself that the question of survival always came back to that one eternal truth – the fact that other humans, those without foresight or without the resources to make proper preparations, would come and try and take what you had by force.

37

Zeina Yaseen was on a train whose tracks ran parallel to the mighty River Nile, Egypt's fundamental artery. She was about halfway through her journey – motorbike to Alexandria, a first train to Cairo then a fifteen-minute change onto a remnant of pre-isolationist infrastructure, a heavy diesel locomotive with a dozen rattling carriages that would take her all the way to Aswan.

She was in First Class, for what it was worth, the springs in the upholstery pressing hard against the worn carriage-cloth. A waiter brought her snacks. Hungry as she was, the bland flatbread and flavourless white cheese were disappointing.

Zeina had been given a dog-eared pamphlet describing her journey, with instructions to return it when she got off. In a while, they would briefly stop in Luxor. Would she get a glimpse of the temples and monuments of the nation's pharaonic past? The Valley of the Kings would be to her right, lost in the dunes, as the original builders of those extraordinary celebrations of life and death had intended.

For the time being, the train was travelling along an embankment. Out of the left-hand window, she saw dusty and rusting cars driving around the ring road of the city of Asyut. Two bridges crossed the vast Nile, linking the islands. She got a brief glimpse of Paradise Park, a place she had heard of but never visited, where Egyptian holidaymakers could sit beneath mature trees just a few kilometres from endless desert sands.

The waiter came to enquire if she needed anything else. She thought he was angling for a tip at the end of the journey. He was going to be disappointed. She couldn't afford to give him one, however sympathetic she felt to people whose wages didn't cover their bills.

She asked for tea and sweet biscuits and he mooched away to prepare it. Meanwhile, she pondered different ways of translating her accidental celebrity into practical advantage. If she was to be awarded a medal, might there be some government job that would save her from the remorseless downward spiral of failing subsistence farming?

She felt a pang of pre-emptive nostalgia. If she did find a way to give it all up, it would still be a wrench to leave the farm for a second time. How many generations of her family had worked the rich land in the mighty Nile's fan-like delta, rendered fertile by organic sediments transported in the annual floods? At least a dozen, beyond the reach of paper records.

Her tea came, sweet and bitter, both at once.

She traced a finger on the map in the pamphlet, seeing that Aswan was as far south in Egypt as Al-Jaghar had been in Cyrenia. How far away, exactly? Maybe five hundred kilometres across the Great Sand Sea.

She finished her tea. The moment she put it down the waiter came to remove the empty glass. It left a small ring on the dusty table. That was a fact of life in the desert. There was always dust.

She looked out of the window again. They had left the city of Asyut well behind.

Not long now.

Deceit was a way of life for Emmeline Cantor, not just for the profession she had chosen – an operative in the Directorate General for Internal Security – but also because of a decision she had taken to be the keeper of a great and dangerous secret.

Today, she would remain at home because, under Damien Gerest's new regime, 'excessive hours' were frowned upon. Attendance in the building in Levallois-Perret was monitored – obviously – and curtailed. 'Relief days' were mandatory. Cantor had reached her ceiling of attendance.

She wondered if there might soon be a pushback of some kind. The old chief, Professor Fayard, had been in the habit of referring to the organisation as a 'family' and Cantor thought he had been right. There had been a kind of unanimous acceptance that everyone had a role, whatever their training or rank; that different ways of thinking or being were accepted and valued. That had fostered a culture of intense focus but also of openness. After just a couple of months though, it no longer seemed possible that a lowly trainee might be taken seriously – as Alexandre Lamarque had respected her. Director Gerest had imported a rigid hierarchical system of reporting with opaque layers of management.

Cantor felt a vibration from her comm-watch. Overnight, she had been slow-cooking an extravagant *boeuf bourguignon*, her apartment full of the rich odour of lab-grown beef and bacon, onions and red wine sauce.

She decanted half the *bourguignon* into a metal tin with an airtight lid and put it in a string bag, hooked over her wrist. She raised the trap-door beneath the rug, revealing a steep metal staircase that descended a couple of metres into artificial light. She climbed down, feeling her way, as she had done many times since the fake burial in Montparnasse cemetery, just a couple of streets away from her carefully chosen and recently acquired home.

Amaury was in a viewing room, his eye compelled by the mighty expanse of water outside, harshly bright in the sunshine and stretching as far as he could see. It was the vast and placid surface of Lake Nasser, held back by one of the world's mightiest artificial structures – the massive Aswan High Dam.

He didn't know it, but his mind travelled a similar pathway to Mariam's when she contemplated the Pyrenean dam in the Saint-Médard valley. What length and width of lake? What weight of water?

The answers were all laid out for him in the centre of the viewing room, on a bronze model of the landscape, about the size of a table-tennis table. The reservoir was called Lake Nasser in memory of the ultimate hero of Egyptian independence. It stretched more than 450 kilometres south into the territory of North Sudan, but was seldom more than 16 kilometres wide, except here and there where narrow inlets infiltrated the valleys on its banks. It stored a quantity of water beyond imagination. The dam's turbines generated tens of billions of kilowatt-hours of hydroelectric power each year.

Amaury moved to a wall display relating an alternative tale: how the Nile grew from 'the tears of the goddess Isis', grieving the death of her brother Osiris at the hands of their brother, Set. Her weeping followed a seasonal pattern – actually the cycle of monsoon and drought in the Ethiopian highlands – leading to an ancient pattern of flood, growth and harvest, linked to the movement of the moon and stars, dragging fertile sediment from the uplands into the desert valleys.

Back in the days when the annual flood was a natural phenomenon, untrammelled by engineering, the first indication of the post-monsoon inundations would come in June, with a rise in the river at the long-drowned Aswan cataracts, followed two days later with floods at Luxor and five days after that at Cairo. The river might rise seven or eight metres, before rushing on and spilling out, a day later, through the delta into the Mediterranean Sea.

But no more. Immense and mighty as it was, the monsoon-fed river seemed to have accepted its imprisonment.

Was it useful?

Of course.

Was it wise? Wasn't it like balancing a bomb with a hair trigger on a high shelf, knowing the danger but simply hoping for the best?

Time would tell.

Amaury went back to the window and lowered the blackout-cloth blinds against the bright sun.

Deep beneath Amaury's feet, the charges that Major Chaka Kassam had placed in positions of inherent weakness in the structure of the dam – positions that were, ironically, accessible because they were so closely monitored – were ready. There was a kind of irony, wasn't there, that he had been able so easily to smuggle them into the closed nation by the old ruse of a gift, like the wooden horse with which the Greeks tricked the Trojans? He had been helped by the fact that his cases of valuable 'white oil', lithium, came direct from President Manouche. He wished he had a remote control that would permit him to flee east or west to higher ground, away from the river valley, and detonate the charges from there. But that wasn't possible. He had to be close at hand or the cellular signal would not reach within the mass of concrete and stone.

He had thought about setting a timer, but what if the dinner with its accompanying medal ceremony dragged on? He couldn't know for sure when he and the other guests would be escorted back down to the railhead for the train downstream to Cairo.

It was not his intention to board that train. He would find a vehicle and flee the valley, because – unlike some of his more ecstatic fellow-believers – it was Kassam's intention to survive.

At the end of the long day of travelling – up before the dawn, hours and hours of rattling train tracks under the steel wheels – Zeina fell into a doze and missed the moment of arrival. The waiter roused her, let her use the bathroom then helped her down onto the platform. She was about to tell him she had no money to tip him with when a young man in a crisp white military uniform came to greet her.

'Welcome to Aswan, Zeina Yaseen. Please follow me.'

He led her from the station to an open-sided electric buggy. They got in and drove away, through busy city streets, slowly climbing, then out onto a narrow road in a deep cutting, travelling steeply uphill, until finally they arrived at a tall concrete building whose windows were protected from the sun by a deep veranda.

They went inside. Zeina was requested to present her plasti-card ID whose details were laboriously transcribed onto an official form by a sad-faced woman in a drab abaya with dirt under her fingernails. The young soldier in the white uniform indicated a passageway leading to a stairwell.

'Six floors, madame. Will you manage? The lower lift is momentarily out of service.'

'I will manage.'

They climbed in silence. On each half landing, a small window looked out on a vast wall of dirt and concrete that Zeina knew must be the dam. Between the fourth and fifth floors, she caught a glimpse of the top with the sky behind. Between the fifth and sixth, there was no small window. Then they came to a much plusher lobby and the entrance to the viewing room. The soldier gestured to her to go ahead.

The room was dark. From the slits of light at their edges, she realised that blinds had been drawn. As her eyes adjusted, she made out a large bronze relief map of the terrain. She moved closer, touching her fingertips against the peaks of hills, running them down onto the smooth surface of the metal water.

'Impressive, isn't it?' came a voice, speaking Arabic.

Startled, Zeina snatched back her hand. The voice came from a stockily-built man in dress uniform, with long dark hair and a ragged beard. She felt underdressed in her everyday robes.

'Who are you?' she asked.

'My name is Amaury Barra. Would you like to see it?'

'Yes,' said Zeina, surprised, thinking how different he looked in real life.

He pulled a cord and raised one of the blinds. She moved towards the glass, drawn by the extraordinary view.

'The sun was very bright so I closed them,' he told her. 'Here it is.'

Zeina didn't reply. She was transfixed by the vastness of what she saw, the incredible feat of engineering – something to rival the pyramids, surely? She could almost feel the weight of the water held back by human ingenuity, tamed to create power and light.

'I am glad to meet you,' said Barra. 'I know who you are.'

'I know who you are, too,' she told him, her eyes returning to the distant southern horizon where the lake blurred into the hills, beyond her eyes' capacity to focus.

'Welcome to the sacrifice.'

Zeina started.

'I don't understand –'

'I'm sorry,' he interrupted. 'I don't mean that literally – the sacrifice to celebrity.'

The young soldier came to tell them that, in an adjacent room, a table had been laid for a banquet to accompany the medal ceremony.

'Can we take a look?' asked Barra.

They went through the plush lobby and in through double doors to a longish table with a white cloth and a foolish overabundance of glasses and cutlery. There were four chairs down either side and one at each end. The soldier showed them their places either side of the head, separated by an empty chair that would be occupied by Naguib Al-Baghdadi, an Egyptian diplomat. On Barra's other side would be Faroukh Al-Medawi, the Cyrenian politician whose quick thinking had helped Alex in his final desperate mission. Opposite him would be Major Chaka Kassam of the Malian military. Beyond them were the Moroccan and Algerian members of the North African Defence League. The three seats at the other end were allotted to diplomats from the office of the Egyptian president.

'They will expect you to speak,' said Barra. 'Have you prepared something?'

'No one has told me anything,' said Zeina hesitantly.

'You should simply tell your story. You needn't go into detail. Make it short, just a couple of minutes. You have time to prepare.'

Zeina nodded gratefully.

'Thank you for your good advice,' she told him.

'All will be well,' he replied.

38

Mariam told Sébastien all that had been happening, over a pleasant lunch that stretched into the afternoon. Then he had a rest from his broken night of travel and she sat quietly reading. Soon after, he woke and came to find her, hearing the angry sound of a diesel motor being gunned up the slippery track outside the farm gate. Mariam, Sébastien and Aunt Sara all went outside to see who and what it was – a black 4x4 with tinted windows, the design choices of a villain in a movie.

The driver was neither of these. It was Davide Castile's marketing director, whom Mariam knew about from Alex. With a bright smile, Léa Dujardin told them that she was on her way to talk to the Lenca protestors to try and put forward the point of view of the company regarding all the benefits that would accrue from the expansion of the Saint-Médard reservoir: economic growth, jobs, water security, power security. She added that she was empowered to make concessions.

'The X^3 was faulty. There is no doubt of that. Perhaps a manufacturing fault? But the X^3 was our responsibility, too – I mean, remains our responsibility, always was. The faults could – maybe should – have been picked up by routine maintenance. There is already an inquiry. If there were faults, making the controls unresponsive to an experienced pilot, we cannot be sure at this point whether they ought to have been apparent. But I can show you the exhaustive, professional inspection record for the aircraft if you wish. I have brought paper printouts in case there's a problem with connectivity.'

'The protestors have a satlink at the top of the valley,' said Mariam, swayed by the woman's enthusiasm and openness.

'Good. That's good. Anyway, please wish me luck. I know Monsieur Castile wishes he could turn back time but …' She gave them a rueful smile, taking in all three of them in turn. 'In the absence of miracles, he wants to do the best he possibly can for the unfortunate victim of this terrible accident.'

'Victims, plural,' said Mariam. 'There's also a child left without a mother, a bereaved son, a partner.'

'I know. Isn't it awful? Monsieur Castile has spent his whole life working to mitigate the impact of poor climate decisions. It's ironic, isn't it, that the X^3 should have been a victim of a freak air current, driven by our less and less predictable weather?'

'I thought Davide Castile spent the first half of his adult life in the army?'

'Not Monsieur Davide – his father.'

'Oh.'

Léa Dujardin bid them a cheery goodbye, climbed back into her 4x4 and went zig-zagging up the wet track, churning through the potholes and puddles, deepening them.

'That will all need repairing when we get some dry weather,' said Sara with disgust and stomped away to the barn.

Mariam thought about what Alex had told her – the involved story of ladybirds and aphids, about predators and prey, and how later he had thought it made her sound sinister.

'What's your impression of that woman?' she asked.

'She seemed honest,' said Sébastien.

'Yes,' said Mariam. 'But why did she go to such efforts to "seem honest" if she's got nothing to hide?'

Sébastien frowned. Speculation was not his area of expertise.

'To put us off taking too much interest in what she's doing?' he asked, hesitantly.

'That's what I was thinking.'

Mariam looked up the slope. The 4x4 was finding it difficult to get good traction. Dujardin moderated her speed, just now making the turn where – for her – the dam would come into view, past the cave entrance to the underground river.

'Go after her,' Mariam told Sébastien. 'Find out what she says to Pudu and the rest. Take the quadbike. It's on charge.'

'*Oui, mademoiselle*, but I've come all this way to resume my protection duty. It would be frustrating to find that—'

'Don't worry. I'll be quite safe.'

While Sébastien went to disconnect the quadbike from the solar array, Mariam slipped indoors, determined to contact Alex and find out what he was doing, where he might be, if he had discovered anything new. But neither vision-calls nor audio-calls received any reply. She sent him a text nudge to be in touch as soon as possible.

Sébastien came to tell her that the quadbike had a flat. They went to find Sara, who showed them a spare wheel in the barn.

'Should I follow on foot?' asked Sébastien.

'How long will it take to change it?'

'Half an hour, maybe?'

'Do that,' said Mariam. 'I don't want you to be trapped up there without a vehicle.'

Sébastien nodded and followed Sara to find some tools.

Mariam wondered: *Why did I say that? 'Trapped' by what?*

Léa Dujardin was no fool. Her mask of affability and charm was a way of concealing her true thoughts. But because her chosen mask required her to talk a lot, she knew that sometimes she provided clues for the most alert and perceptive observers. Alexandre Lamarque, for example, or Mariam Jordane. On balance, though, she thought Mariam had taken her words at face value.

Struggling with the 4x4 up the valley track wasn't natural for her. She would have liked to delegate the job to a driver, but that would have spoiled her spin as an innocent emissary of the apologetic corporation, Castile Energie.

She rounded the bend in the track and the dam came into view. She had studied the terrain and was heading for an area of flat ground away to the right – well out of sight of the Jordane farm – where she could park and set up her deadly equipment. Seeing her destination, she felt the faintest shiver of doubt.

Is this what I want?

From the protest camp next to the small landing strip below the dam, Pudu looked down the valley. His attention had been drawn by a black 4x4 with tinted windows that was creeping along, swinging away from the most direct approach to a small area of flat ground over to one side. It stopped and he saw a woman in a smart suit get out on the driver's side. She looked up the hill towards him, noticed him watching and waved cheerily. Taken by surprise, he waved back.

Léa Dujardin dropped her hand and turned away. How far away was he? A couple of hundred metres. Close enough for him to perhaps see what she intended and run down and prevent her.

Is that what I want?

She contemplated the conifer forest and the high limestone peaks beyond the treeline, the sky like a bruise promising more welcome rain, the circling raptors – the glory of the natural world exploited almost to death by humankind.

She went to the trunk. The equipment inside needed some assembly. It wouldn't take long but, aided by the slope, the man could easily be on her in no more than twenty-five seconds. And if she was stopped, then the lover of 'the man who saved the world' would survive to encourage and inspire.

To allay any suspicion, she decided to follow through on her cover story and go and talk to the protesters, offering them the fictitious compensation and public apology. She opened the trunk to find the boots she kept in there for visits to construction sites. They were wedged under the missile apparatus and she had to tug them free. Then she shut the trunk and sat on the bumper to pull them on, giving the man at the protest site another cheery wave and miming her intention to come up and speak to him.

The time has come, she thought. *Hope must be destroyed. This, too, is the Storm.*

39

In Paris, in the neighbourhood of Montparnasse, Emmeline Cantor was in the secret basement of her ground floor apartment, seated in a bentwood chair with her feet up on a footstool. She was reading a book by her companion's favourite author.

'The thing she does,' her companion said abruptly, 'is to show you how ordinary people become extraordinary.'

He, too, was reading – re-reading, in fact – one of a set of twelve or thirteen novels, all of them set in powerful hinge-moments of human history, when huge forces exerted exceptional pressures on populations and individuals – wars, pogroms, persecutions, occupations, droughts, floods.

'I agree,' said Emmeline. 'This is brilliant.'

'Which one is that?' he asked. She showed him the cover. 'Ah,' he told her. 'The Second World War. The sweep of emotion through the final hundred pages is almost unbearable.'

'Don't tell me.'

'No, I won't.' He stood up. 'Will you excuse me?'

Professor Fayard left the cramped room for the bathroom. She knew he drank several litres of water each day as part of his convalescent regime. Emmeline stayed where she was, looking around: the painted brickwork of the basement walls; the dehumidifier that operated 24/7 and that Fayard emptied twice each day into the toilet bowl;

the battered desk and the wires trailing up through the ceiling to data and power points concealed beneath her bed in the room above. She wondered about what they had done – finding and quickly refurbishing the apartment, finding a way of bringing him here from the tomb in Montparnasse cemetery without being seen.

Of course, it had been Fayard's idea. She would never have thought of it alone – never dared suggest it. He had invited her to the secure Faraday cage of his private rooms on the sixth floor of the headquarters of the Directorate General for Internal Security and outlined his plan. Doctor Labeur was in on it of course, providing the drug that had given the impression of death and spinning his convincing story of the mutation in the malicious pathogen. Otherwise, the fiction would have been impossible to maintain.

'I must seem to have died,' Fayard had told her, 'in order that I should be discounted. Meanwhile, I hope to be of some use. I will be able to monitor what is happening through our comprehensive databases.'

That had turned out not to be the case. Professor Fayard had lived like a blind mole, the traitor's posthumous destruction of the security services' digitised records making his plan of intelligent, covert surveillance moot, his fake death no more than a piece of pointless, secret theatre.

One street over from Emmeline Cantor's apartment, a team of three construction workers was studying a ground plan on a large-format tablet, taking instructions from a red-haired man with all the appropriate digital certification as a representative of the city council. But he seemed a very different kind of manager from the jobsworths the ground-workers were used to meeting.

The plan on the touchscreen was for remedial work designed to give strength to the terraced townhouses that the job site backed onto. Apparently, there was a problem with subsidence, though it wasn't apparent from the outside – no significant external cracks radiating from door lintels or window openings. All the same, it was a common issue throughout the bowl of land in which Paris sat. The city's foundations absorbed water in the wet season, expanding into every crevice. Then, in each dry season, the layers contracted, sinking and shifting, putting a huge strain on the superstructure of buildings above.

The most common remedy for such a problem was underpinning – digging out a big hole under a corner and filling it with concrete – but that was often very disruptive, creating large work-sites blocking entire streets. An alternative was to sink a vertical shaft, and from it drill narrow horizontal boreholes, many metres long but no more than three or four centimetres in diameter. Into these boreholes could be pumped a quick-drying, expanding construction foam. Because it was under pressure, the foam would find its way into every gap and void, swiftly hardening into a kind of lattice, forming a new and surprisingly strong artificial bedrock.

The red-haired man left.

'Shall we get on with it?' said the team leader.

'Is it urgent?' asked one of his two colleagues, thinking of food and an early finish.

'He said there'd be a bonus if we got it done right away,' said his second colleague, the man responsible for the reel of pipe on the back of the truck. 'Can you get down far enough in that drain shaft?'

There was a sewer intersection at the corner of the street, so there was no need to dig their own shaft to get down to the level of the foundations. There was even a stair of metal hoops in the brick, down which they could climb to stand in their waders in the flow of effluent.

'Yes,' said the leader. 'The horizontal route for the boreholes is eight-and-a-bit metres. It's taken three days to go seven, but we can finish this today.'

'All right, if we have to,' said the second man, with resignation in his voice. 'How big are the voids?'

'The size of a couple of rooms,' said the leader, scrolling the notes on his tablet. 'Will we have enough?'

The man in charge of the truck slapped the side of a massive steel drum. 'Topped up this morning. We won't run out, not unless we're trying to fill the nave of a church.'

'All right, then,' said the leader. 'Let's do it.'

In his office in the Rothschild Institute, Doctor Labeur had finally got to the bottom of Gloria Lamarque's relapse. It had only been a matter of days, but he had felt a sense of urgency throughout – though it was difficult to decide precisely what to do with the information.

His technicians had discovered no new infection nor any mutation of a prior infection, but they had isolated a drug commonly used recreationally by people with whom Labeur would not have expected Gloria to have any contact, one designed to induce sedation and amnesia, pushing consciousness into a trance-like state of 'absence'. For the recreational user – for whom these were the desired outcomes – such symptoms would be expected and welcomed. For the accidental user – in this case Gloria – they would be disturbing, inexplicable.

The drug was ketamine.

Labeur had called Alexandre Lamarque but got no reply. He had briefly considered Professor Fayard, but Labeur was under strict instructions not to get in touch. In any case, trapped in Emmeline Cantor's basement, living the life of a spider cut off from its web, what could he do if he knew?

Director Gerest? Labeur didn't trust him. He had no material reasons for this, except for a lifetime of learning to read people, developed and honed in the taking of medical histories. The man, he had decided, was weak and self-centred.

Who, then?

Labeur had met Claudine Poiret, the high official responsible for the security services within the French government. He knew that she was now working exclusively in the office of the president. He also knew that Alexandre Lamarque had confidence in her judgement.

How, though, would he reach her, without compromising his hard-won knowledge?

He would go, he decided, in person to the Elysée Palace, that very moment, and have himself announced. In that way, his message couldn't be intercepted or eavesdropped.

What message?

Gloria Lamarque was poisoned.

Fayard came back from the bathroom.

'You know, my dear, that I no longer notice the constant hum of the dehumidifier, but it is odd, is it not, that I am disturbed by the less insistent noise of the Métro? It seems more prevalent today than ever before.'

Emmeline put down her book and listened.

Yes, she thought. *That's true. I was listening for it earlier, wasn't I?*

She felt a chill, an unnerving intimation that they had missed something important.

'Could you power up your holo and access a Métro map?' she asked.

Having left the team of three construction workers with their orders, André Chambon had walked round the block to sit on a low garden wall opposite the front door of a townhouse. On the ground floor was a pleasant apartment, recently acquired by Emmeline Cantor, an agent of the most junior rank at the Directorate General for Internal Security.

How had she afforded it?

She hadn't.

Since the death of the man that they all referred to as 'the traitor' – as if they were scared of pronouncing his name – Chambon had conducted his work alone. On reflection, there had been a moment when he might have given himself away, just before Alexandre Lamarque's mission to extract the Cyrenian prime minister under fire. It was Chambon who had notified 'the traitor'. But since the meltdown, the log of that interaction had been wiped from the records. The only person likely to recover it, because he had been given responsibility for rebuilding the security services' databases, was Chambon himself.

Using that responsibility as cover, he had quickly been able to cross-reference financial records with land-registry information to discover that Cantor had received sudden and massive financial assistance. He had also been able to establish that this money did not come from her parents – one a poorly-paid teacher, the other a labourer in the building trade. The transaction references asserted that it was a lottery win, but the account number from which the money came did not tally with any of those used by state or private gambling sources.

That being the case, Chambon had taken it upon himself to look more closely into the life and habits of Emmeline Cantor, discovering that she bought more food than might be judged appropriate for a single woman living alone, and that her life seemed to comprise no third factor – just work and home, home then work.

Using the city plumbing system as a kind of back-door into her flat, he had introduced a powerful microphone into the u-bend of her kitchen sink and used it to monitor what went on behind her double-locked front door. He employed an AI to examine and define all the sounds and quickly discovered that there was one that was flagged by machine intelligence for his human attention – a rattle, a creak and a gasp of air. It didn't take him long to reach the conclusion that it must be a trapdoor. Later on, the microphone had picked up the voice of a man and identified it. Chambon hadn't been shocked. He realised he had almost expected Fayard's death not to be the end.

This was the moment when he had decided to contrive a fake identity as a manager in the city planning department, making himself copies of Emmeline Cantor's keys, briefly purloined from her locker at Internal Security.

It was better this way. Secrecy was his weapon. Deceit was his method.

He knew that the plan he had put in place was cruel and grotesque, but his skills and experience precluded a more direct physical confrontation. He'd had fifteen years of sedentary experience as an analyst, whereas Cantor's three years' training as a field agent would inevitably make her his superior in hand-to-hand combat.

The builders had told him their timeframe. He would slip inside just a little before they began to pump their product and push some heavy piece of furniture over the trapdoor, sealing in the occupants of the basement to be suffocated and crushed by the expanding industrial foam. His listening device told him that both Cantor and the Professor were currently down there, unaware that they were soon to die an appalling and claustrophobic death.

40

At Aswan, the medal ceremony was concluding. Amaury and Al-Medawi, as representatives of the French president and the Cyrenian prime minister, had presented Zeina Yaseen with twin medals of honour. The Cyrenian one had a simple design, like an oversized gold coin, embossed with an outline map of Cyrenia on one face and a dedication in Arabic, Berber and French on the other: 'For courage in service of the nation.' The French medal was much showier – star-shaped with inlaid enamel in blue, white and red, mimicking a *tricolore* ribbon.

The ten guests moved on to the meal of celebration – Amaury would not have called it a banquet. Zeina fell upon it, devouring first her mixed salad with hard white cheese, then her shredded plant meat with beans and rice. Then she had been called upon to make her speech.

She did well at first, thanking Cyrenia and France, saying very little about the actual events at Al-Jaghar. Then, as her tongue loosened, she began describing her pitiful subsistence on the crumbling family farm in the delta of the Nile. Naguib Al-Baghdadi got up – his chicken pox scars very prominent under the white downlights – and cut her off, praising her as 'a hero of the Egyptian republic'. Al-Medawi, invited to respond, praised her in similar terms as 'a hero in the defeat of Darkness'.

The Moroccan and Algerian delegates to the North African Defence League each proposed a toast in the tamarind juice they were all drinking. Finally, it was Amaury's turn. He delivered his carefully-chosen words above all for the attention of the three Egyptian diplomats at the far end of the table. They listened to him in silence, looking very non-committal. When he had finished, the Malian guest – a late addition, apparently – excused himself to go to the bathroom. He was not required for the formal photographs in front of a viewing window onto the lake, using superannuated equipment from the early years of the century.

Once the official images had been captured, they all went and stood behind their seats as the Egyptian national anthem was played, during which Amaury thought he felt a kind of shudder beneath his feet. The Malian returned and dessert was served – a delicious Um Ali. With the formal part of the event complete, the atmosphere seemed to become more relaxed.

From the Rothschild Institute to the Elysée Palace was not very far, but it was an awkward journey, through several checkpoints where Doctor Labeur was required to confirm his right to exist in certain circumscribed physical locations: the controlled heart of the city; the neighbourhood of the presidential residence; the courtyard where visitors were screened for admittance.

He had expected to find that his most difficult moment would be there, at the outer gateway of the Elysée Palace, where a minor official would reject out of hand his application to be put in touch with Madame Poiret, but that was not the case. He realised that he was underestimating the power of the name of 'the man who saved the world'. He had only to say: *Gloria Lamarque has been poisoned.* From that point on, all doors were open.

All but one, however. The door to Claudine Poiret's office remained resolutely closed.

Why?

Because she was out of the country – in Haiti, in fact, supervising the relief effort.

Doctor Labeur wasn't given to flights of fancy. He didn't catastrophise. He understood that one person could not be in two places at once. Wasn't it the same in his profession? Often, he would have liked to give his undivided attention to a single patient, to the exclusion of all others, believing that his unique combination of intuition and experience was the sick individual's best hope. Claudine Poiret was his best hope but Claudine Poiret was away, doing good and important work.

Wasn't his message, though, an even more important focus for her attention? He thought it might be.

He wrote a note on a sheet of official palace notepaper, signed it and put it in in the hands of a smooth-looking civil servant.

'Make sure this is read by someone in authority,' he insisted, hoping for the best, fearing the worst. 'Someone who can reach Madame Poiret before it is too late.'

At Aswan, Amaury had finished his Um Ali and could hear that, somewhere, an alarm was sounding, like a doorbell being rhythmically pressed. The three Egyptian diplomats at the end of the table were paying no attention. Then a white-uniformed soldier whispered in Al-Baghdadi's ear, who nodded impatiently, stood and wearily asked if all nine other guests would 'kindly accompany him to a meeting point on the ground floor', explaining that false alarms such as this one were common, that the dam infrastructure was under constant surveillance and it was always better 'to err on the side of caution'.

The lift was back in service and the ten diners took it in two pods of five. By the time they had reassembled in the lower lobby, the noise of the alarms had grown from a single insistent ringing to a kind of multidirectional argument, like the doorbells of many houses, each at a different pitch and intensity, being rung on every side, each demanding exclusive attention.

In a strained voice, Al-Baghdadi explained that the 'cycle of drills' was not under his command, that they were randomly generated by safety protocols that he 'could only admire for their insistence on maintaining the highest levels of security'.

Amaury heard his words and understood that they were meant to be reassuring, but he felt obliged to compare them to the expressions on the faces of the three Egyptian diplomats – those with knowledge and expertise in relation to the dam.

Their eyes revealed worry and confusion.

41

Because the wheel nuts on the quadbike were rusted and seized, it took Sébastien nearly an hour to install the spare. Finally, he set off up the track, the breeze whipping his long black hair across his face, the thick tyres bouncing through the rain-carved furrows.

Mariam went back indoors, feeling uneasy. With Alex and Amaury in different corners of Africa and Fayard dead, she felt as though an alarm that she had long ignored was ringing somewhere, demanding her attention.

She went to the deep window and contemplated the shrine. The stone effigies were black with soot, as was intended, indicating the twins' passage into death. Mariam was struck for the first time by how macabre the ritual would seem to an outsider.

She heard the distinctive whine of the farm van. A few moments later, her cousin Benjamin came strolling in, followed by a face she recognised – Emilie Olsen, wearing a black peaked cap, carrying a large black rucksack and another case on her hip, the strap diagonally across her body.

'I was in the café,' said Benjamin with a foolish grin. 'This lovely lady wants to speak to you, Mariam. She rode up with me.'

He stopped, clearly unable to compute the angry expression on Mariam's face. Mariam took a step forward and grasped Olsen's jacket in her fists.

'What are you doing here?'

'Nothing bad,' said the woman, quickly. 'Let me just tell you that there's a camera built into my cap, recording everything happening here.' Mariam snatched the hat off her head and tossed it into the cold ashes in the kitchen fireplace. 'And the camera is broadcasting to headquarters, like the one you broke on the bridge,' said Olsen.

'Not from here,' Mariam assured her. 'No connectivity in the valley.'

'*Merde*,' said the journalist. 'Look, I'm sorry, but I didn't want to cause any more upset and your cousin here was kind enough …' She stopped and tried to melt the icy atmosphere with a sympathetic smile. 'And the funeral, of course. That's a really sad story. Why don't you tell it? I mean, I could help you get your side across.'

'I have no side to get across,' said Mariam, releasing her. She turned to Benjamin. 'How did she trick you? Did she pretend she was interested in you?'

'I don't understand,' said Benjamin, looking foolish and hurt.

'This is the journalist who tracked Alex and me to Bordeaux. I almost threw her in the river. I should have done.'

'But why?' asked Olsen. 'I'm on your side. I want to help you share your truth.'

'What if I just want to be left alone?'

Olsen smiled.

'That isn't possible. From the moment you and Captain Lamarque became heroes, you became public property. I can make that easier for you, smoother, less intrusive. Give me a fragment of access and we can satisfy people's curiosity and manage how and when the streams take an interest in you.'

Before Mariam could answer, they heard an explosion from the top of the valley. Surprised and worried, Mariam rushed outside, followed by her cousin and the journalist. They stood at the edge of the porch, looking up over the spacious vegetable plot towards the peak of the mountain. Sara came out of the barn, her gaze also on the peaks.

'Did you bring a drone?' barked Mariam.

'Er, yes, of course,' said Olsen.

'Get it in the air.'

The alarms were ringing at Aswan because a 'piping' breach had been identified by sensors deep underground. At that moment, in the control room, no one knew the cause. Was it due to tectonic movement, or was it possible that someone with malign intent had found a way to infiltrate the structure and penetrate the vulnerable substrates – vulnerable because, to a certain extent, they were out of sight and out of mind?

The monitoring team comprised three operatives: two men and one woman. The woman was seated at a bank of lights and dials. The men were standing behind her, looking over her shoulder. The senior of the two – who had a wife and two children, plus his own parents, living in a modest house downstream in Asyut – told them to stay where they were. He was 'going to speak to someone in authority'.

The senior operative left the control room. There was a pause during which several more sensors began blinking their messages of imminent catastrophic failure. The woman looked over her shoulder at her junior male colleague.

'He's not coming back,' she said.

In Paris, not far from Montparnasse cemetery, Emmeline Cantor and the supposedly-deceased boss of the Directorate General for Internal Security, Professor Fayard, were looking at a map of the Paris Métro. It was, of course, a schematic map, designed to make the city easier to navigate. The distances between stations were not precise or realistic. The geographical relationships between Paris landmarks weren't to be relied on.

Fayard picked up his glass of water and drained it.

'This doesn't help,' he said.

315

42

Emilie Olsen had her drone in the air and was flying it about thirty metres above the ground, following the torrent of the *gave*. Mariam was watching the images it captured on a tiny screen about five centimetres square on the control console.

'Can I cast this to another device?' Olsen asked.

'There are no other devices,' Mariam told her.

'What about your comm-watch? I could pair it as a local network, then you could pop it out as a holo?'

'Good idea.'

'I'll have to land the drone to get at the system controls.'

'Do it.'

Olsen fiddled with the joystick, bringing the drone down, then tapped and swiped at the tiny touchscreen. Mariam accepted the pairing request and popped out the image, turning away under the porch to get out of the light. It showed an area of flattish ground – some muddy grass and a few stones and pebbles.

'Get it back in the air,' she said, thinking that this was wrong, that she should have gone with Sébastien, that the key for those fighting for right was always to stick together, not allow themselves to be separated. She and Amaury and Alex, too, ought to be standing side by side. 'Quickly.'

Olsen did as she was told. The image from the drone expanded as the craft rose into the air once more. The vista – the torrent and the fields either side, a wall of limestone beyond – swung as it flew. She actioned the joystick and, by mistake, sent it chasing downstream towards them because she had become disorientated when they had turned round to see the holo more clearly.

'Oops, sorry; hang on.'

The image banked and dipped as the drone turned and flew swiftly over the muddy ground, following the path and the torrent up to the bend in the valley. Then it swung right, giving Mariam a lurch of motion sickness, so thoroughly was she focused on the progress of the camera through the air.

Then she saw the quadbike, upside-down, its thick, knobbly tyres hard up against a wall of stone, and Sébastien pinned beneath its weight, his head and shoulders visible. The drone homed in. His eyes were open but without life. Beyond him, the black 4x4 was parked, its nose pointing back down the hill, the rear door open and facing the dam.

At Aswan, the ceremonial party had been escorted from the lower lobby to street level. It was clear to Amaury that a full-scale evacuation was under way. Uniformed and civilian staff were streaming away from the offices and technical installations, some leaving on foot, others in rusting, dusty vehicles, others on bicycles, all in an atmosphere of controlled anxiety.

Amaury and the other guests were going to be driven to the railway terminal where, apparently, they would board the next service heading north. Meanwhile, the 'temporary problems' would be resolved by 'dedicated professionals'.

Amaury didn't like this idea. If there was a breach of the dam – and what else could it be that everyone seemed to fear? – even a minor event would be sure to swamp the railway line that ran alongside the river. There might even be enough water to lift the train from its tracks and cause a derailment, leaving its passengers marooned, some of them badly injured. Or the carriages could be buoyant enough to be carried by the flood into the mighty Nile itself, leaving the occupants trapped and drowning…

Yes, all of that is very possible.

What was the alternative?

A vehicle of his own. Independence.

Two standard saloon cars had been pressed into service to take the dignitaries to the railhead, all ten dinner guests, plus two uniformed drivers, crammed into not quite enough seats. Amaury was sitting in the front of the second one, alongside a young soldier in a crisp white uniform, his boyish features tense and set, his brow damp with sweat. Zeina was on the rear bench seat, squeezed between Al-Medawi, Al-Baghdadi and the Malian military engineer.

The journey to the train station took only a few minutes. When they got there, the occupants of the first car were already climbing out, several of them breaking into a shambling jog, heading for the waiting locomotive, but not wanting to betray their mounting panic.

Amaury evaluated the terrain – a valley that would channel the dam burst squarely down the train tracks – and put a hand on the driver's arm.

'Give me your keys,' he said.

In Paris, in an ante-chamber to the office of the president, the highest office of the French state, the handwritten message delivered in person by Doctor Labeur had reached Claudine Poiret's deputy, a woman of unimpeachable integrity. She immediately took the only appropriate first step, commanding a security detail to Gloria Lamarque's room at the Rothschild Institute with instructions that no one should be allowed to enter without Labeur's direct say-so.

'And in person,' she told the officers. 'No remote orders, no messages sent by a third party.'

'Understood, madame.'

They left, looking briskly efficient.

Professor Fayard was still seated at the desktop holo, an old-fashioned version, salvaged, as it happened, from Alexandre Lamarque's boat when the grateful nation had upgraded all his kit. Emmeline had appropriated it from stores at DGSI headquarters.

It wasn't bad quality, but Fayard was old-fashioned enough himself to prefer an opaque physical screen.

A soft chime on his comm-watch warned him that it was time to take the prophylactic medicines of which he had built up a considerable store before his so-called death, so that he shouldn't run out during his secret afterlife. He picked up his empty glass and took it through to the basement bathroom to fill it up.

Sitting on the low wall opposite Emmeline Cantor's building, André Chambon was glad that he had powered down all his personal and professional comms, instead relying solely on those he had spoofed in order to pass himself off as a member of the city planning department. The three groundworkers had taken much longer than he had expected, setting up their underpinning operation. His absence from duty would have been noted, he was sure, because it was so out of character. No one, so far, had come looking for him, however.

He shifted position on the warm stone, and at that very moment received a message from the construction crew to his fake identity.

Preparing to break through.

He stood up and crossed the road, taking out his copies of Emmeline Cantor's keys. He began opening the triple-locked door, uncertain which key was which, making several abortive rattling attempts to disengage the wrong lock. Perhaps because of his clumsiness, he was assailed by a moment of doubt.

Isn't this way too easy?

Emmeline heard the unaccustomed sound of her front door being unlocked by someone else. It was a sound with no previous record in her memory because it had never happened before. There was no one to whom she had given her keys, no one who could have a legitimate reason for possessing them.

She scampered quickly up out of the basement and was in her bedroom, looking for her weapon, when she heard the faint creak of the hinges.

43

Mariam was running up the valley path, her wellingtons slipping in the mud, her calves complaining, her breath coming in ragged gasps. It felt so much further uphill than it was down. The other evening, it had seemed to take no time at all to wander back from the camp, hesitating by the entrance to the underground river, before returning to her loneliness and grief.

Why hadn't she asked Alex to come with her for the funeral? Amaury, too. Why hadn't she persuaded Alex that they should all go to Egypt? The medal ceremony could have been postponed until they were all free.

What if we die, each of us, so far apart?

She pounded on. The drone was up ahead, thirty metres up in the sky. She heard a shot and the flying camera canted over, spinning on itself, one of its four helico-blades smashed by the unseen projectile. Then it careered out of sight behind the rock wall.

Back at the farmhouse, Emilie Olsen was swearing to herself, screwing up her eyes to view the tiny screen on the drone's control console. She no longer had the larger holo from Mariam's comm-watch, but the on-board camera was still working, beaming its images to where the journalist stood, on the porch beside the well-stocked vegetable garden. Benjamin was leaning over her shoulder.

'What's happening?'

She angled the device so he could make out a narrow view of gravel and grass, out of focus because it was too close to the lens.

'It's crashed,' she told him. 'It's on the ground.'

'Did you hit something?'

'No, of course I didn't hit anything. Someone shot it down.'

Breathless, Mariam rounded the turn in the valley and was astonished to see the inhabitants of the protest camp running down towards her in a stampede, thundering into the bottleneck, clumsily following the contours of the land, staggering right and left on the uneven rock and slippery mud.

Mariam clambered to one side, into the broom bushes on the left-hand slope, seeing the panic on their faces and the fear in their eyes. The small man – Berta's lover – was carrying their tiny child in his arms, clinging tight to it as if it were a precious package, but he was stumbling and struggling as his momentum carried him forward, almost faster than his feet could keep up. The same was true of the others – all ages, dressed in their oddly assorted clothes, many of them holding scraps of belongings that, as they clattered past her, some dropped on the ground, abandoning them without a backward glance.

Last came the older woman – the one who had come to find her with the nose bag for the pony. She seemed already to have fallen at least once as she was slick with mud all up her left side.

'Don't just stand there,' she bellowed as she limped past. 'Run for your life.'

Mariam paid no attention. Instead, she climbed another twenty metres further on, still clinging to the left-hand side. The land opened out to an uninterrupted view of the dam, about fifteen hundred metres away, high and proud. In the same instant, her attention was snagged by the black 4x4 as it lurched backwards, reminding her of the recoil of a gun. Then she saw an explosion at the rim of the dam wall, blasting out a tumble of rock and concrete, and realised there must be some kind of rocket launcher in the trunk.

Paralysed by the folly of what was happening, she saw Pudu running across the flat area beside the camp, heading for the 4x4, brandishing a length of timber or maybe one of the struts of a tent. Dujardin stepped out from behind the black car, holding out her arm to aim, too far away for Mariam to see exactly what weapon she carried, and shot him, two sharp cracks that were carried down the valley on the downdraft of cool breeze from the peaks. Pudu fell, a dainty, remote puppet whose strings had suddenly been cut.

Mariam didn't know what to do. She was far too far away to reach the woman and prevent her from firing again at the weakened dam wall. A trickle of water was already running down the concrete face. No, not a trickle – a cascade, made to look smaller by the distance.

Dujardin moved out of sight and moments later the black 4x4 lurched once more. Another projectile struck just below the point of impact of the first, blasting out an inverted triangle of rock and concrete, through which a huge cataract of pent-up water instantly crashed.

All this took only a few seconds, allowing Mariam just enough time for a momentary flashback to the dangerous surfing wave she had ridden in the big seas off Biarritz – how worried Alex had been, how exhilarated she had felt.

Dujardin ran to a position in the very middle of the valley, opening her arms to welcome the flood. The crushing tide of destruction picked up the fuel bowser from the end of the runway, using it to demolish the tented village, whipping the pre-fabricated buildings up into the air and churning them downwards on a terrible swirl of white foam, tearing them to pieces, ripping their frames into weapons.

The fuel bowser slammed into Léa Dujardin, her arms still held wide in some kind of insane ecstatic delight, and the cataract came barrelling down to where Mariam stood, defenceless and alone.

44

Sara had come to join her son Benjamin and the new intruder. Not the big man with the excellent manners and the long black hair who had asked politely to borrow the quadbike. The other one, the nosy journalist with her sharp inquisitive eyes, her panoply of annoying modern equipment and her unbecoming black clothes, more like an undertaker than a presentable young woman. From the farmhouse porch, the sound of the two explosions had been oddly muted. No, not muted. Dispersed.

'What was that?' Sara asked.

The others made no reply. Their eyes were fixed on the bend in the valley, the place where Mariam had stopped and then suddenly disappeared. Then the ground began to tremble beneath their feet.

All at once, a confused gaggle of people came running and staggering into view. Then a vast crashing wave hurtled after them, picking the fleeing protesters up and tossing them like detritus in its foam.

Fayard took his tablets in front of the bathroom mirror, then drained his glass. He wondered – as he had many times before during his voluntary confinement – if it had all been worth it, the subterfuge of the fake funeral, drawing Emmeline Cantor and Doctor Labeur into the deceit.

He heard a noise from somewhere near floor level – the same insistent vibration but louder and slightly percussive. Then all at once it stopped and there was a new noise and a strange chemical odour that he found impossible to place.

Emmeline had her weapon in her hand – a standard issue son-imm with an effective range of about ten metres. She observed Chambon for a moment through the crack between the door and the frame and was surprised to find that she wasn't surprised. She had never liked his cold, calculating gaze, his slavish devotion to whoever was currently in charge.

She stepped into the room, just as Chambon was moving one of her two armchairs on top of the closed trapdoor. She saw him look up, clock her weapon, then meet her eye. In his expression she saw cunning and guilt.

Amaury was in no mood for argument.

'Give me the keys, *merde*,' he insisted.

The young officer in the crisp white uniform had a final moment of indecision, then another louder siren began wailing its distress and he dropped them on the ground and ran, his gangly limbs every which way, heading for the railhead, followed by the Egyptian diplomat, Al-Baghdadi.

Amaury bent to pick up the keys, noticing in his peripheral vision that the man he didn't really know, to whom he had only briefly been introduced – the Malian engineer, Major Kassam – had drawn some kind of electrical weapon from the pocket of his lightweight jacket. To ward off the inevitable blow, Amaury straightened and brought his prosthetic hand up in front of his heart, the obvious target for a disabling strike from a taser.

Kassam's face contorted into a grimace of confusion as the sharp terminals of his weapon penetrated the synthetic skin in a glancing blow, revealing the metal beneath. In the same second, Amaury saw Zeina draw her own weapon – a short, sharp paring knife that he knew she had used before in self-defence, and thrust it into the side of the

325

Malian's neck, releasing a gout of hot blood up her arm.

The Malian staggered away. Amaury understood that these were the last images he himself would ever see, the last sensations he would ever feel. His body was shutting down. He had only moments of consciousness left.

There was, he knew, a weakness in every human system. In the case of his immensely strong prosthetic hand, it was the fact that it connected directly into his nervous system via the probe implants in his forearm. The shock of the electrical weapon had travelled deep into his viscera and stopped his heart.

He fell to his knees, the world becoming black and white and grey through lack of oxygen. He wondered how many seconds had passed and how many he had left. Quite quickly the answer came.

Not even one.

The storm of life was over. Now, there would be only darkness.

45

In the valley of Saint-Médard, there was no one left to see what had happened. The dam was fully broken, the inverted triangular cleft having widened to become a vertical breach almost the entire height of the wall. The immense cataract was still funnelling out, dragging with it huge quantities of silt from the bottom of the reservoir, as well as scouring out the fertile loam from the rich fields of the valley, undoing thousands of years of evolution of the landscape.

It had already slammed through the walls of the Jordane family farmhouse, piling up its violently dismantled bricks, slates, timbers and stones in a ragged heap against a granite extrusion on the east side of the valley, beneath which lay three bodies, ragged and crushed and torn – Sara and Benjamin Jordane, Emilie Olsen.

Further down its route, the flood had picked up the newly-laid gravestone dedicated to Mariam's twelve-year-old twin sisters and carried it, bouncing and tumbling, end over end, all the way to the town at the foot of the valley, where it crashed through the window of the café at around thirty kilometres per hour, destroying the pool table and the pinball machine before coming to rest behind the bar. There, for the foreseeable future, it was destined to remain, at the bottom of a brand-new swirling lake of turbid water, through which the contents of the high dam would continue to flow for several hours, as if they had their own suicidal intent, making their way determinedly downhill, finally to lose themselves in the infinite anonymity of the ocean.

Zeina's right arm hung loosely by her side, the paring knife still in her fist, the blood – not her own – dribbling down onto her jellabiya. The Malian was choking, writhing on the dusty ground. Sirens were blaring from the high dam. She used her free hand to loosen her headscarf and wipe away the gore.

Al-Medawi said something that Zeina didn't hear because the train whistle was also sounding and the locomotive was – slowly, slowly – beginning to drag its carriages out of the station.

'There's nothing more we can do here,' insisted the Cyrenian. 'Quickly.'

Zeina saw Al-Medawi pick up the car keys from the dirt and climb in on the driver's side. Her mind was slow to react, her eyes on the lifeless face of Amaury Barra, half-hidden by his long hair and ragged beard, but indubitably dead.

'I don't ...' she began.

'Come,' Al-Medawi shouted over the noise of the veg-oil engine.

She felt water running over her sandalled feet and realised it must be coming from the dam. She looked up to see three places where rivulets of water were running through and down the wall – no, not rivulets, streams, growing streams.

She climbed inside the lightweight vehicle. The Cyrenian gunned the engine and pulled away, following the only available road, running parallel with the track of the train and the mighty – soon to be untamed – Nile, driving at dangerous speed until he was obliged to brake hard behind a traffic jam, pulling up so close that they were almost touching the bumper of the van in front. Zeina put her hands over her ears to cover the cacophony of honking horns and hoarse sirens.

Suddenly, the vehicle they had almost hit – a pick-up with decals advertising a building company – reversed into them, shunting their car backwards, before swinging off-road, up the dusty bank, its rear wheels spinning in the sand.

'Follow them. Go that way,' said Zeina, at last finding her voice. 'We must get to higher ground.'

In his office at the Piscine, the headquarters of External Security, Damien Gerest felt out of sync. His most important collaborator, André Chambon, a man in whom he had placed more or less limitless trust, had gone offline. He was neither returning Gerest's calls nor could any of External Security's systems tell the director where he was.

Gerest was contemplating this conundrum while trying – and failing – to rebalance the motion of the Newton's cradle Lamarque had damaged when he flipped the desk. It was beginning to dawn on the director that this pointless labour might be seen as a metaphor for his administration: a terrible event had come to destabilise the apparatus of the French security services and he, Damien Gerest, was doing his best to re-establish smooth co-operation and seamless intelligence.

Of course, the data he had instructed Chambon to collect and synthesise went beyond the legal remit agreed by parliament.

Oh, and he had illegally manufactured Gloria Lamarque's medical crisis to continue to exert influence on her son.

His hands became still. Was there something else, some other duty he had failed to perform?

On his desk, the screen on his comms console began to flash. Before he could press the touch-sensitive button to pop out the holo and find out what the North Africa desk wanted to tell him, another alert was signalled, this one from the military intel group based at Bordeaux-Mérignac airport.

Not knowing which to answer first, he hesitated and – to his horror – saw a third dialogue box open, demanding his attention, a communication at the highest level of urgency from the office of the president.

Zeina was surprised to discover that the prim Cyrenian official was a good driver, once he had got over his first panic and struggle to familiarise himself with the vehicle's controls. Because their service vehicle was extremely light and equipped with wide tyres to enable it to cope with tarmac that was often inundated by sand, it made short work of the incline, whereas the heavy pick-up simply beached itself halfway up and its driver got out and ran.

At the crest of the rise, they found an agricultural track on firmer ground that led away from the deepest part of the river valley, climbing to a cluster of low beige houses a couple of kilometres away.

'If we can make it there, do you think we will be all right?' asked Zeina.

'Do you know how much water there is trapped behind that dam?' said the Cyrenian.

Zeina was good at arithmetic and remembered the approximate dimensions of the lake from the bronze relief map in the observation room – sixteen kilometres wide and more than four hundred kilometres long. She multiplied out a single slice, one metre deep, and told him the result of her calculation.

'I was being rhetorical,' he replied, with a hint of dry humour. 'I didn't need to know that.'

46

Because André Chambon wasn't an active field operative, he didn't immediately recognise the weapon in Emmeline Cantor's hand as he launched himself at her. The shock of the son-imm knocked him backwards, winded and disabled. She said something he didn't hear, so loud was the blood in his ears, driven by adrenaline and desperation.

Is it over, then?

Emmeline contemplated Chambon, on his back on the rucked-up rug, his head rocking from side to side. Then he seemed to come back to himself, inserting his right thumbnail under the crown of the *chevalière* ring he wore on his left middle finger, revealing a dose of white powder that he brought quickly to his mouth and deposited on his tongue. Appalled, she watched as the neurotoxin tensed all his muscles so brutally that several of his bones snapped under the pressure of competing contractions. Mere seconds later, she realised that he was no longer breathing, that the light had gone out in his emotionless eyes.

Then, at last, she smelt a strange chemical odour that, because of her father's trade, she found quite easy to place.

Foolishly opening the bathroom door, Fayard had seen the builders' nozzle poking through the wall, spewing out its deadly product, an orange industrial foam that expanded on contact with the air,

331

multiplying in size – five times, twenty times, fifty times – creating a growing mass that, even at a distance of a couple of paces, he could see was also thickening, hardening. The grotesque creature – for it seemed like a creature with deadly intent – was swelling across the room in his direction, knocking over his table with its second-hand comms, pushing the rug ahead of it.

Fayard tried to slam shut the flimsy bathroom door, but he was too late. The rug was in the way, preventing it from closing, pinched against the jamb. And that meant that the foam would soon be able to push through the doorway, despite him using all of his strength to resist it. And still he could hear the hiss of the pipework, pumping in more and more of the awful suffocating substance.

Then, by some freak interplay of the expanding foam with the space it was trying to invade, the rug was dragged aside and Fayard was able to slam the door shut with just a few shreds of the orange filler on the inside, still glistening and damp but rapidly hardening.

For mere seconds, he felt able to think. He was trapped and sealed underground – entombed, in fact. He would eventually suffocate unless Emmeline could do something to help him.

Then he noticed that the cheap panels of the bathroom door were bowing inwards, the latch and the hinges creaking, and an obscene tongue of the orange foam began forcing its way through, beneath the bottom edge.

At the headquarters of External Security, Director Damien Gerest had been brought up to date with the bare bones of what was happening in the Saint-Médard valley, which, because of the presence of Mariam Jordane, was an operational and – more importantly for his career – reputational calamity. He also knew, from the North Africa desk, about the crisis unfolding at Aswan – an event that might, if the dam failure became complete, bring about the deaths of several million people whose homes crowded the fertile farmland and the built-up regions along the banks of the Nile. Finally, he had taken the call from Claudine Poiret's office, informing him that Gloria Lamarque was now under round-the-clock protection from the office of the president – that the matter had been taken out of his hands.

He slumped back in his chair. For Damien Gerest, this was the real disaster, not the innumerable innocent deaths. On further investigation, André Chambon would be found and would inevitably reveal that he had personally introduced the ketamine into Gloria Lamarque's diet. And he would also be bound to share that he had done it on Gerest's direct order.

The director made himself sit up, looking at the broken neck of the glass dipping-bird.

Where is Chambon, though?

Then another question occurred to him, one that he had been so pleased with himself and his promotion that he had failed to allow himself to answer.

Why had Chambon needed no great persuasion to poison the mother of 'the man who saved the world'?

The answer, surely, was that it fitted with Chambon's own objectives – which meant …

Gerest sent an urgent order to Camera Control.

'Priority one alpha. Locate André Chambon – DGSE analyst.'

Chambon was dead. Emmeline had checked his pulse, taking the precaution of donning a mask and pulling on a pair of nitrile gloves from the dispenser on her kitchen counter in case his poison was contagious. Then she had opened the trapdoor to discover a solid wall of orange foam, hardening to a dense and impenetrable carapace.

'*Mon Dieu,*' she said aloud, recognising the substance for what it was. 'How did he do that?'

Because Gerest's location request had been labelled 'priority one alpha' and came from the office of the director, Camera Control replied within ninety seconds, cross-matching its employee records, with their multiple images of 'André Chambon – DGSE analyst', against the network of surveillance cameras that formed an almost complete record of the comings and goings of every single inhabitant of the city. Chambon had been located and identified, sitting on a low wall not far from Montparnasse cemetery, then had been recorded entering a house that another fragment of the security services' employee database revealed as belonging to Emmeline Cantor.

His mind reeling with incomprehension from desperate competing priorities, Gerest immediately despatched an intervention team from the gendarmerie of the 14th arrondissement.

Fayard didn't know it, but it was Emmeline opening the trapdoor that released a little of the pressure and prevented the bathroom door from immediately collapsing under the strain. But that didn't solve the problem of disappearing oxygen.

Emmeline was quick witted and perceptive. It only took her a few seconds to work out that somewhere in the nearby streets there must be a construction team, possibly one that was unaware of the deadly result of what they were doing.

Leaving the trapdoor open to relieve the pressure, she ran outside, looked left and right, then ran round the back of the terrace, finding a team of three labourers. Two of them were working in a sewer shaft, one of them on the back of a truck with a compressor running, making it hard to get him to understand what she was saying. She jumped up onto the flat bed and hit the big red emergency cut-out button.

At just that moment, two junior officers with excited eyes from the local gendarmerie came stomping up the street, having jogged over on foot. Emmeline shared her DGSI credentials then led the two gendarmes and the three builders back round to her apartment, all of them crowding into the small living room as she showed them what she had discovered.

'And there's someone down there?' one of the officers said, appalled. He saw Chambon on the rug, his face contorted and grey beneath his ginger hair. 'Who's that?'

'That's the council planner,' said the lead labourer. He turned to his mates. 'Go and fetch the shovels and the pick. If we're quick, we might be able to dig it out and cut an escape route before it completely goes off and hardens – or at least give access to fresh air.'

Yes, thought Emmeline, as the other two jogged away for their tools, *as long as he isn't already dead.*

Then she almost laughed, feeling the need for a release of tension while she waited, impotently, for others to take the next purposeful steps.

As long as he isn't dead for a second time.

47

When Alex woke, he realised straight away that his sleep had not been entirely natural, that he had been drugged with some mild but insistent sedative. How much time had passed, he wasn't sure, but from the heaviness of his muscles, he estimated several hours.

He was still sitting reasonably comfortably in the nest of four leather seats on board the Ae4. Davide Castille appeared not to have moved, but was he watching him? No, his breathing was shallow and regular, a flicker of movement behind his eyelids indicating rapid eye movement and dreams. He was one of those people who sleep with their eyes not quite closed.

Alex stayed quite still. He had been woken by an idea, cutting through the grogginess of whatever it was that Castile had put in his drink, its flavour disguised by the bitterness of the lime zest – zolpidem, perhaps, or rohypnol, both date-rape drugs.

He glanced at his comm-watch, searching for a satlink or a ground relay. Nothing. Satlinks were perhaps jammed to protect the aircraft controls. The absence of ground relays meant they were probably over open water. But he was able to see the time and work out how long they had been in the air.

He glanced at the eight screens that replaced proper windows, showing blue sky above and cloud below.

Is this just a kind of movie, he wondered, *or is this the actual view outside?*

Because of the lack of real windows, Alex had no idea of direction and could only estimate distance since their time of departure. Assuming a speed somewhere around the Ae4's impressive cruising velocity, maybe six thousand kilometres from Bamako, a little less if the winds were against them? Long enough to be over the Indian or the Atlantic Oceans.

His mind returned to the idea that had woken him – the meaning of Amaury's cryptic phrase. He had an image in his mind of a map showing a vast lake, incredibly long and narrow, with crinkly edges creeping up into narrow lateral valleys. And the lake was held back by a dam, beneath which was an island, the largest among many that studded the mighty river that human hubris had tamed.

The dam had been built at the site of the giant cataracts that formed part of the ancient border between Egypt and Nubia. The largest island was, historically speaking, the oldest part of the city of Aswan, a superb defensive location dating back four thousand years. In its earliest days, the island was known in demotic Egyptian as Elephant and, in modern French, as L'île Éléphantine.

What had Amaury said?

That would be an elephantine error.

He remembered Poiret's pre-recorded message about the resumption of diplomatic relations with Egypt.

I hope Monsieur Barra is an effective presence. You and I need to discuss how best to exploit your celebrity for our desired outcomes of peace and prosperity.

Thinking about the dam, Alex remembered the flight on the hydrogen BWB from Bordeaux, coming in to land at Paris-Orly, seeing the vast reservoir created by damming the Seine south of the airport, drowning the suburbs of Vigneux and Draveil, displacing 200,000 people. He remembered thinking about how, according to official documentation, the project was deemed a huge success, counterbalanced by his own impression that it looked like a threat.

And hadn't he perceived the same thing, contemplating Mariam's home valley?

And now Amaury was at Aswan?

Alex frowned. It had been a mistake for the three of them to go their separate ways. Of that he was certain. But he wasn't quite sure how it was that he had known to fear the weight of water.

There must be a rational explanation.

He thought back to a moment that should have worried him, but he'd been in too much of a rush – from Gerest to Chambon and then onto the jet from BA 117. On board, he'd asked Léa Dujardin about the secure transport of lithium ore south through Côte d'Ivoire and she had replied: *Who's going to steal a forty-tonne truck and what would the robbers do with a mountain of part-processed lithium ore?*

Of course, at that moment, the hijack had already happened. She had been pretending not to know about it from a habit of secrecy and guilt. And he had perhaps made her evasive by questioning her about water security and the Sélingué dam and so on.

His train of thought was interrupted as Davide Castile moved in his sleep – as if he, too, was on the verge of waking. Had he taken a sleeping pill of some kind in his glass of what Alex had assumed was water?

Water again.

Alex thought about the name-search he had conducted, prompted by the sat-images of Mariam's aunt's farm, discovering the name of the valley and then following through to find out who Saint-Médard was and of what calamity he was reputed to be the patron.

Of storms.

He thought about the people close to him. They would all, by now, be in great danger, though he did not know where that danger came from. He would soon find out though, because it was – inevitably – wherever the pilot was under instructions to land the Ae4.

Something Castile had said came back into his mind.

You only have two lives. You know that? One lived in ignorance, up until the point you realise you will only live once. Then everything changes and your second life begins – with no time to waste.

And here Alex was, on the needle-shaped Ae4, alone with his enemy – or, at least, one of his enemies – on his way to who-knew-where. This was, perhaps, the last moment of quiet at the eye of the Coming Storm.

He saw Castile stir, so he got up and moved quietly to the wardrobe, finding a satin robe from which he removed the belt. When he got back to the nest of chairs, Castile was fully awake, about to spring up. Alex slammed a knee into his abdomen, leaning in with his whole weight, targeting the area of the deliberate wound of the med-port beneath his lightweight in-flight clothes.

Castile gasped and snatched at Alex's knee, trying to relieve the pressure, shouting obscenities. Alex grabbed the napkin from under the two glasses, sending them spinning across the floor, and forced it in between Castile's teeth, then lifted him bodily off the leather chair, slamming him face down on the floor, knocking all the breath out of him, finding him surprisingly light, illness having wasted the muscle from his broad frame.

With his knee now hard on the back of Castile's neck, Alex dragged the man's hands together and lashed them tightly with the satin belt, then carried him to the rear of the cabin like a roll of carpet, dropping him heavily on one of the flat beds, face down. Then he strapped Castile down with the safety belt. As he cinched it as tight as it would go over his wrists, Castile managed to spit out the napkin.

'There's nothing you can do. You can kill me, but I'm dying anyway.'

'We're all dying,' said Alex. 'Tell the pilot to turn the plane around.'

Castile laughed.

'There is no pilot.'

'What are you talking about?'

'I only went into the cabin to program the flight control module. It

339

needs no human intervention.'

Alex didn't doubt what Castile had said. All the same, he went and tried the armoured door to the flight deck, finding it impenetrable, banging foolishly with his angry fists.

48

In the bathroom in the basement of Emmeline Cantor's apartment, Professor Fayard was crouched on the floor when the foam broke in the flimsy door and began expanding inexorably into the room, the only space it had yet to fill. He was worried about oxygen, trapped as he was in a small space without windows or access to the air.

Except …

He was struggling to unscrew the U-bend beneath the washbasin. If he managed to get the white PVC elements apart, he could remove the airlock of trapped water designed to prevent bad smells rising up out of the drains beneath the building.

He didn't have enough grip. His elderly hands couldn't grasp the knurled connectors sufficiently tightly. He reached out for a towel, drying his sweaty fingers, and used it to give himself more purchase, at last managing to just get the connector to move anticlockwise. He undid the nut, pulling the U-bend free, immediately catching the rank odour of the underground sewers, wondering if it was 'good air' and if he might be poisoning himself by breathing from the PCV tube.

Meanwhile, the bulge of expanding foam was halfway across the small space, leaning into the shower cubicle. Pushing forward with irresistible slow force, the foam cracked and then splintered the tiled partition. A triangular shard of ceramic broke away and fell directly onto Fayard's leg, penetrating his trousers and digging into his calf. He gasped and shrank back beneath the washbasin, hoping the movement of the foam was slowing, but not believing it. The product was designed after all to keep swelling until every void was filled.

His calf wet with blood from the accidental wound, he felt the foam begin pressing against his foot, creeping slowly but discernibly across the pattern on the vinyl flooring. He felt a kind of panic at the appalling claustrophobia of being squeezed into a smaller and smaller shape, almost foetal, pressed up against the bathroom wall beneath the washbasin, beyond which was Parisian bedrock. Between the aggressive synthetic odour of the foam and the pungency of the sewer – and perhaps from oxygen deprivation – his head began to spin.

Wearily, he felt himself begin to accept his fate. Later on, he supposed, Emmeline Cantor would ensure that he was dug out of his awful prison, like an archaeologist liberating a victim of the Vesuvian eruption at Pompeii from their tomb of pyroclastic rock and ash.

So this is real death, he thought. *I didn't expect it to feel so much like failure.*

Claudine Poiret was on board a French frigate standing off the coast of Haiti, whence she had been co-ordinating the relief effort. She was in the communications centre inside the ship – a windowless room staffed by two relatively junior sailors, a male IT expert with a 'full set' of moustache and beard, plus a female comms operative with sleek brown hair tied in a tight bun. The man gestured to an old-fashioned LCD monitor with a schematic map of the local geography and a moving trace, travelling east to west across it.

'You don't know who or what that is?' Poiret asked.

'No call sign, *madame*. I've made the gunners aware.'

'How far have you been tracking it?'

'The flight path originated over the Atlantic.'

'You don't know any more than that?'

'I keep having to reboot the systems when everything hangs up.

We're still under cyber-attack.'

'I'm aware,' said Poiret. Even her priority channels had become unreliable. She leaned in. 'The aircraft is within a hundred kilometres.'

The woman with the tight bun asked: 'Madame Poiret, are all these comms failures related to the corruption of the state databases?'

Poiret didn't answer. Rather than speculate on the increasingly widespread disruption, she wanted to know if the incoming, unidentified aircraft was a threat.

'What size is it?' she asked.

'Not that big,' said the man, judiciously.

'Be more precise,' barked Poiret.

'*Je m'excuse*. Bigger than a missile, smaller than a commercial plane.'

'Something like a private jet – a Falcon or an Ae4?'

'*Oui, madame.*'

In the control room beneath the Aswan Dam, the alarms were still ringing. The two junior members of the monitoring team were still there, deserted by their senior colleague. From seismology data, they could see that the 'piping incident' wasn't due to an earthquake. Other than that insight, they were entirely impotent.

'Should we go?' the woman asked.

'Go where?' said the man. 'The valley will be drowned for hundreds of kilometres downstream.'

The woman frowned.

'Maybe up?'

Al-Medawi brought the lightweight service vehicle to a halt. He and Zeina Yaseen had made it up the slope, level with a point about two-thirds as high as the dam, fifteen hundred metres to the west. They both got out, raising their hands to shade their eyes as they looked back at the mighty structure.

As they watched, the piping breach widened with a cascade of concrete and rock as well as water, several smaller streams combining into one mighty outflow. They saw it sweep aside the few remaining parked vehicles and, perhaps twenty seconds later, engulf the railhead. Neither said so, but they were both aware that, at that moment, the bodies of Amaury Barra and Chaka Kassam were being rolled and dismembered by the chaotic forces of the flood.

Then they heard threatening noises of creaking and grinding, caused by the fault lines beginning to zigzag across the dam wall, as if the entire mighty structure was disaggregating from within, losing its integrity, preparing utterly to fail.

Without a word, Al-Medawi and Zeina got back into their vehicle. Al-Medawi put it in gear and drove on, up the slope towards the cluster of low beige houses, intending to put as much distance between them and the calamitous flood as their vehicle's fuel supplies would allow.

In a cavern of the underground river, high up on the left-hand flank of the Saint-Médard valley, the body of a woman lay inert on a damp limestone shelf. As the dam wall had split from lip to foot, the cataract of water had rushed past the entrance to the caves where Mariam had taken refuge, the speed and volume causing a pressure drop that sucked air out of the subterranean channel, leaving her choked and gasping.

Disoriented and oxygen-deprived, Mariam had stumbled, falling forwards into the stream, at risk of drowning. Then, another unanticipated interplay of hydrological forces had caused the water level abruptly to drop.

A few minutes passed, then the river began slowly to rise. By then, though, the air pressure had equalised and Mariam could breathe normally.

She dragged herself up out of the flow, beginning to shiver because the water was cold, about twelve degrees. She managed to reach the smooth shelf of limestone, worn by water and time into a kind of platform.

For a little while, Mariam simply lay there, inert, unaware of how much time was passing, knowing from cold hard logic that her aunt and her cousin must be dead, as well as her friend and colleague Sébastien. Then, feeling herself drifting off into unhealthy sleep, she told herself to move to ward off the deadly risk of hypothermia.

It would be so much nicer though, she thought, *simply to let go*.

49

Alex left off his futile struggles with the armoured door to the flight deck and turned back to Castile. He was straining against his bonds, trying to remove his large *chevalière* ring behind his own back. Alex strode over and pulled the ring from Castile's sweaty finger, holding it up close to the recessed cabin lights. Castile shouted in frustration. Alex could see a groove below the crown and a tiny indentation, like the location of a catch.

'What is this?' he asked. 'Some kind of weapon?'

'It's a gift,' said Castile, bitterly. 'Take it. Enjoy it.'

Alex took the ring to the serving counter. As a precaution, he pulled a pair of nitrile gloves out of a dispenser and put them on. Then he used the edge of a teaspoon to carefully prize open the crown, revealing a small compartment packed with a dense clump of yellowish powder.

'Is this your last resort?' Alex asked, keeping it a safe distance away from his mouth and nose. 'A suicide potion? Or did you think you might get the chance to blow it in my face?'

Castile twisted his head round, still face down on the flat bed.

'Taste it, why don't you?' he spat. 'You might like it.'

Alex carefully closed the ring, dropping it into a glass on the counter for safe keeping, and removed the gloves.

'We're going to see your father, aren't we?' said Alex. 'That's the great mystery.'

'Yes, and there's nothing you can do about it.'

'I might be able to find a way of crashing the plane,' Alex mused. 'Or maybe I can land it. Where are we?'

Castile turned his face away. Alex remembered not being able fully to believe in Arnaud Sy's evaluation of his officer.

Davide Castile was fine – a normal officer, right? The sort you feel you can trust to make a decision, whether or not that decision turns out to be the right one.

But later, Sy's own doubt had become apparent, planting a barb in Alex's unconscious, making him wonder if it might just be a coincidence of words.

It was a thing he used to say – that there would be darkness, that a storm was coming. I don't know – some kind of prepper crap.

No, as Professor Fayard had always maintained, there was no such thing as coincidence.

Alex tapped the screen of his comm-watch, activating a device search. Very quickly, he found the on-board flight computer. It had two layers of software security to protect itself from remote control, but his state-of-the-art device soon penetrated these. Then he instructed the comms to send his own secure call-sign instead of the one embedded in the aircraft's operating system by Castile Energie.

'What are you doing?' Castile demanded. 'Look, this is all a misunderstanding. There's so little between us – how we both see the world.'

Alex ignored him and said: 'When we were at President Manouche's palace, I was able to penetrate his systems. When the assassins tried to take me out on my boat – I assume they were yours?'

'That was a mistake.'

'Why did it happen?'

'Members of a Paris cell, freelancing, thinking they were doing the right thing. I've always thought we should be on the same side, you and I.'

347

Again, Alex followed his own train of thought.

'Anyway, I was able to do the same, taking control of the disinfectant truck – the one with the jammer on board to prevent me calling for help.' Alex popped out a holo. It emerged as a vee of light, thickening and darkening to reveal a set of holographic controls that he could operate by the movement of his hands in space. 'I think I can manage this. Look, there's the flight-path and the destination. The island of Haré in the Caribbean Sea. Meaning we will soon be over land.'

'Damn it,' bellowed Castile. 'Do you want to die? The storm has come. I was offering you a way out.'

'Why did you try to sell President Manouche a pathway to a brighter future? What was the point of that, if you believe that everything must burn?'

'Because maybe it doesn't have to. It isn't written. Why couldn't you join me? I offered you the future. You could have been my right hand, but you were too short-sighted, too stupid. When we land, my father will—'

'We're not going to your father,' said Alex.

Alex picked up the napkin. Castile turned his head away and clamped his mouth shut. Alex reached over and pinched his nose to force him to open it and stuffed the pad of cloth back inside. Then Alex took off his own belt and strapped it round Castile's head, holding the gag in place.

50

In the bathroom in the basement of Emmeline Cantor's flat, it was over at last. Professor Fayard was dead, asphyxiated, despite his access to foul air from the drains, the breath squeezed out of his lungs by the pressure of the foam on his brittle elderly bones, many of which had snapped under the strain.

As things turned out, his corpse would be significantly more damaged than those retrieved from beneath the soft ash of the Vesuvian eruption at Pompeii.

On board the French frigate standing off the coast of Haiti, Claudine Poiret had managed to establish contact with the office of the French president in Paris. Made aware of Doctor Labeur's information, she quickly reached the obvious conclusion and ordered a security team to detain Damien Gerest.

'There's a coded signal we can read, *madame*,' said the bearded IT expert, 'from on board the Ae4.'

'Who is it?'

'I don't know. It's a secure call sign. Should I tell the gunner to prepare to fire?'

'Show me.'

The bearded sailor pointed to a small dialogue box open in the bottom right corner of the screen.

'It says "*constant-certain-connu*".'

'No,' said Poiret. 'Stand down the guns.'

'Do you know who it is?' asked the woman with the sleek bun.

'That's Alexandre Lamarque.'

'Oh my God, what should I do?' she asked.

'Send an acknowledgement.'

From the control room beneath the Aswan Dam to the lip of the vast structure – a kind of artificial mountain blocking the progress of the Nile northwards to the Mediterranean – was a slog up a dozen flights of stairs. The two control-room operatives didn't speak as they emerged into the fresh air, breathless and exhausted. As they did so, the concrete and stone beneath their feet began to become unstable, as if the roadway itself was turning to shifting sand. Then they fell with the rock into the maelstrom.

Al-Medawi found the road blocked by a crowd of people at the entrance to the cluster of low beige houses. He and Zeina got out and spoke to the villagers, all of whom had collected at the head of the rise, trying to see what was happening two kilometres away at Aswan. In a few brief words, Al-Medawi and Zeina told them what they had seen. The villagers looked uneasily at one another. Although this was higher ground, was it high enough?

In her safe space in the cavern of the underground river, Mariam was wading upstream, looking for an exit that wouldn't lead her out into the violent cataract of water that she could still hear cascading down the valley. She saw light ahead, descending in a vertical shaft from a sinkhole in the rock above, once a narrow fault in the limestone but widened over millennia by snowmelt running down from the peak of the mountain.

It would be a tight climb, but she thought she could make it.

51

Alex's comm-watch received a signal from a ground relay – or, rather, a seaborne relay on board a French frigate moored off the coast of Haiti. Just for a moment he couldn't remember why Haiti had recently been in his thoughts, then it came back to him – the sudden flood that had forced all the snakes and spiders and other creepy-crawlies out of their hiding places to invade the human world.

Alex instructed his comm-watch to permit the channel of communication and was immediately appalled to discover that doing so interrupted his on-board control of the flight deck. He had put the Ae4 into a holding pattern of wide circles but he could feel the aircraft banking to revert to Castile's earlier instruction to fly direct to Haré.

With regret, he shut off the connection to the French frigate and re-established the holding pattern. He needed an airport with a runway of at least two thousand metres. That shouldn't be a problem, even at smaller internal hubs, but without direct communications with a control tower he couldn't be sure the landing strip would be clear.

He had a sudden idea. Maybe he could cast a camera view from the cockpit to the screens down each side of the plane.

He swiped the holographic controls, burrowing into the settings. He found a category labelled 'external cameras' and discovered that the Ae4 was equipped with a set of eight exterior lenses, capable of sharing with the eight fake windows. He confirmed his choice and immediately felt reassured as a recognisable coastline came into view along the interior of the fuselage. He requested a front camera feed behind the holographic controls and took the Ae4 down just above approach altitude.

Alex recognised the terrain. Haiti formed the western end of the island of Hispaniola and was shaped like an enormous open claw. He made for the northern peninsula where he would find a major airport he had used before: Cap-Haïtien International.

It took a little more than ten minutes to overfly the area. Several times he felt the aircraft resist his instructions. When, finally, he came close, he was disappointed to discover that the airport infrastructure had been swamped by storms, with rubble and uprooted trees across the runways.

Then the Ae4's software security systems began fully fighting his commands, attempting to wrest back control.

52

It had taken three complete reboots of the ship's mainframe, but the bearded sailor with excellent IT skills thought he had finally managed to purge the ship of the disabling trojans. Poiret knew, therefore, about the destruction of the dam in the Saint-Médard Valley and, with it, the probable death of Mariam Jordane.

She also knew about the emergency unfolding at Agent Cantor's house in Montparnasse and was furious that Fayard should have deceived her, faking his death and going into hiding. Efforts to reach him were ongoing but hope had faded.

She knew, too, about the unimaginable catastrophe unfolding in the Nile Valley and the probable deaths of Amaury Barra, her Cyrenian ally Faroukh Al-Medawi and the innocent hero Zeina Yaseen.

What she didn't know was the whereabouts of the Ae4, last identified heading east towards the Dominican frontier, too low for the frigate's tracking capabilities.

Poiret and the comms officers were joined by the *capitaine de vaisseau*, the ship's commander.

'Have the winds eased sufficiently to send out choppers?'

'Not yet, *madame*,' he told her. 'But the forecast says soon.'

'The moment it's safe, I want your team out there searching,' she told him.

'You think it's worth it?' asked the captain. 'Do you think he's likely to have survived? The Ae4 seemed out of control. It's a lot of effort, just to bring back a body.'

'What did you say?' Poiret demanded, then controlled her anger by balling up her fists. 'Get the choppers ready,' she told him, her voice tight. 'Dead or alive, I want Alexandre Lamarque on board this ship.'

'*Oui, madame.*'

The commander saluted and left. Poiret went to the porthole, looking out across the choppy waters towards the coast. Was it possible Lamarque had managed to land safely? If not, with Jordane, Barra and Fayard also dead, it all came back to her. She would be alone.

Claudine Poiret took a moment to promise herself and her fallen colleagues that, whoever had done all this, she would find them and she would bring down fire.

EPILOGUE

Seen from the ground, the progress of the Ae4 was erratic. A bunch of schoolchildren holed up in a gymnasium, a hundred kilometres beyond Cap-Haïtien International, saw the plane fly over, veering drunkenly away to the north then banking back to the east, heading towards the uplands and the border with the Dominican Republic.

The Ae4 was observed by a small convoy of French relief drivers, picking their way with difficulty through the storm-lashed interior with their humanitarian supplies. They were travelling one of the most important arterial highways, that wound its way uphill on a sequence of switchbacks. Over their citizen's band radio sets, they told one another that the aircraft was flying dangerously close to the ground and seemed unable to maintain its course.

Further up-country, the Ae4 was noticed by a church congregation as they from a corrugated-iron house of worship on a hillside covered with the stumps of felled trees. The plane was doing its best to follow the line of a road that was little more than a wide track linking their village to the next, too narrow, surely, for the pilot to put down.

Two minutes later, a couple of sheep-farmers on a high pasture watched the aircraft flying a little below them on the hillside, skimming close to the grass, as if the pilot was so desperate to put down that they would try anywhere at all, regardless of prudence or safety. Then the aircraft swung away north towards the sea, as if tugged by an invisible hand, before circling round and flying on.

Finally, the Ae4 was seen following one of only a few tarmac roads connecting Haiti to its eastern neighbour. In the aftermath of the storms in the Caribbean, there was little traffic, just the drivers of a pair of fuel tankers with an armed police escort, who saw the needle-shaped jet scorch overhead, overtaking them. They saw the undercarriage lowered, then the nose dipped and the aircraft bounced on the tarmac, as if the controls were out of sync or the pilot was struggling to keep command.

Because the road was ramrod straight, the tanker drivers were able to hit their own brakes and watch the Ae4, a kilometre ahead, apply reverse thrust and begin to slow. All might have been well had the right wheel-cluster not hit a rip in the surface where a gnarled tree had been toppled by high winds, tearing out its roots and, with them, a chunk of tarmac.

The Ae4 skewed round, extraordinary shearing forces bending and then splitting the aircraft into two pieces. The nose and flight deck spun away off the road into a gulley where it wedged between rocks. The remainder of the fuselage bounced several times, but the wings prevented it rolling over.

Unsure if it was safe to approach, the tanker drivers and their police escort hung back. After a minute or so, a figure emerged from the wreckage, clambering out of the torn end and staggering into the centre of the road, a dark shape against the jagged white body of the devastated jet.

Before they could go to his aid, he stumbled away and disappeared into a gully between the stumps of trees.

ACKNOWLEDGEMENTS

Thanks are due to the generous support of many writing colleagues – authors, festival directors, bookshop owners, bloggers and more – in particular my (alphabetical) early professional readers Lee Child, Anthony Horowitz and Lesley Thomson.

But there would be no books in this series were it not for the encouragement, business acumen and editorial expertise of Jason Bartholomew and Joanna Kaliszewska of BKS Agency.

Moonflower Books prove over and over that they are a gem of a publisher – thank you Christi Daugherty, Jack Jewers, Emma Waring and Jasmine Aurora – and Gareth Armstrong is a superb audiobook reader.

I'm not sure how many authors have cause to be grateful for the brilliant 'additional writing brain' that Flora Rees provides, but I am one.

Finally, it only remains to acknowledge the professionalism, creativity, love and support of the best and only Kate Mosse.

Piece Of My Heart by Penelope Tree

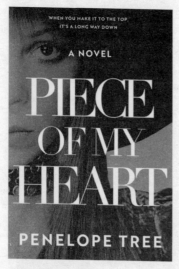

OUT 23 MAY 2024

SCAN ME TO FIND OUT MORE

Fame. Money. Beauty. Sex. Love. Ari wants them all. And when she becomes the face of the 1960s, it seems like they're hers for the taking. Overnight, her life is transformed into a dizzying whirlwind of drugs, photoshoots, and parties, all with notorious bad boy photographer Bill Ramsey by her side.

But in the fickle world of fashion, nothing lasts forever – and addiction, Ari's eating disorder and her increasingly dysfunctional relationship with Ramsey send her life spinning out of control.

How much more of herself must Ari lose to keep the things she always thought she wanted?

Based on a true story, *Piece of My Heart* is a stunning piece of autofiction in the vein of Esther Freud's *Hideous Kinky* and Chris Kraus's *I Love Dick*.

About the author

Model, writer and activist, Penelope Tree was the ultimate Sixties It girl. Born to a Conservative MP and an American socialite, she was discovered at the age of 13 by the photographer Diane Arbus and became an overnight sensation after an appearance at Truman Capote's Black and White Ball. A career in modelling followed – as David Bailey's muse, Penelope appeared on the cover of *Vogue* and travelled around the world. Now a practicing Buddhist and charitable ambassador, Penelope has two adult children and splits her time between Sussex and London.

MOONFLOWER

www.moonflowerbooks.co.uk

Pagans by James Alistair Henry

OUT 20 FEBRUARY 2025

SCAN ME TO FIND OUT MORE

Britain, 2023... only in this Britain, the Norman Conquest of 1066 never happened. An uneasy alliance of ancient tribes – the Celtic West, Saxon East and an independent Nordic Scotland – has formed, but the fragile peace is threatened by a series of brutal murders.

As the threat rises, Detectives Aedith and Drustan must put aside their personal differences to follow the trail, even when they uncover forces behind the killings that go deeper than they could ever have imagined.

Set in a world that's far from our own and yet captivatingly familiar, Pagans explores contemporary themes of religious conflict, nationalism and prejudice in a smart, witty and refreshingly different police procedural that keeps you guessing until the very end. Perfect for readers of Ben Aaronovitch, Neil Gaiman and Terry Pratchett.

About the author

Screenwriter and editor James Alistair Henry first started writing while working as a bookseller. He joined the writing team for Channel 4's *Smack the Pony* and went on to write the BAFTA award winning *Green Wing*, ITV comedy *Delivery Man* and cult hit *Campus* as well as episodes for smash-hit children's television shows *Bob The Builder* and *Hey Duggee*. James lives in Cornwall with his wife, a writer and medieval historian, and their two children.

MOONFLOWER

www.moonflowerbooks.co.uk

The Fortunes of Olivia Richmond
by Louise Davidson

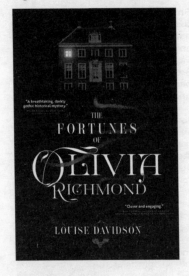

After a terrible tragedy, governess Julia Pearlie finds herself with no job, home, or references. When she's offered a position as companion to Miss Olivia Richmond, she's relieved. But Mistcoate House is full of secrets. And Julia has more than a few of her own.

As the danger grows, and the winter chill wraps around the dark woods surrounding Mistcoate, Julia will have to fight to uncover the truth, escape her past – and save herself.

Original and engrossing, this Victorian Gothic thriller is an outstanding piece of storytelling from an exciting new talent. Perfect for fans of Stacey Halls and Michelle Paver.

About the author

Louise Davidson was born in Belfast and has always worked in the creative arts in some capacity, from working as an assistant to theatre directors, to holding scriptwriting classes in prisons and teaching English and drama to A-Level students. Louise lives in London with her husband and step-son. *The Fortunes of Olivia Richmond* is her debut novel.

SCAN ME TO FIND OUT MORE

MOONFLOWER

www.moonflowerbooks.co.uk

The Coming Darkness by Greg Mosse

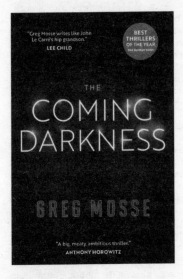

Paris, 2037. With a double threat of rising temperatures and new diseases jeopardising public health, the world has never been more dangerous.

French special agent Alexandre Lamarque notices signs of a new terror group and connects it with an ominous sequence of events: a theft from a Norwegian genetics lab; a string of gory child murders; a chaotic coup in a breakaway North African republic and the extraction under fire of its charismatic leader. And as the one man able to see through the web of lies, Alex may be the world's only hope.

About the author

Greg is a director, writer and writing teacher. He has lived and worked as a translator in Paris, New York, Los Angeles and Madrid. He now lives in Sussex with his wife, the novelist Kate Mosse.

Praise for The Coming Darkness

"Admirable audacity. One of the best thrillers of 2022."
THE SUNDAY TIMES

"A clever, fast-paced thriller."
THE INDEPENDENT

"Superb. Greg Mosse writes like John Le Carré's hip grandson."
LEE CHILD

**SCAN ME TO FIND
OUT MORE**

MOONFLOWER

www.moonflowerbooks.co.uk

The Lost Diary of Samuel Pepys
by Jack Jewers

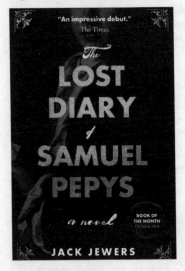

"An impressive debut."
The Times

The
LOST
DIARY
of
SAMUEL
PEPYS

a novel

BOOK OF
THE MONTH
The Independent

JACK JEWERS

**SCAN ME TO FIND
OUT MORE**

MOONFLOWER

www.moonflowerbooks.co.uk

The diaries of Samuel Pepys have enthralled readers for centuries with their audacious wit, gripping detail, and racy assignations. Pepys stopped writing at the age of 36. Or did he?

This action-packed historical thriller picks up where Pepys left off as he is sent from the pleasures of his familiar London to the grimy taverns and shipyards of Portsmouth. An investigator sent by the King to look into corruption in the Royal Navy has been brutally murdered, and it's down to Pepys to find out why. But what awaits him is more dangerous than he could have imagined.

About the author

Jack Jewers is a filmmaker and writer, passionate about history. His films have been shown at dozens of international film festivals including Cannes, New York, Marseille and Dublin, and have received awards from the Royal Television Society and a BAFTA nomination for Best Short Film. The Lost Diary of Samuel Pepys is his first novel.

Praise for The Lost Diary of Samuel Pepys

"Book of the month... A zestful imagining."
THE INDEPENDENT

"One of the best historical fiction books of the year."
THE TIMES

"Swashbuckling action-packed drama."
WOMAN AND HOME

Blue Running by Lori Ann Stephens

In the new Republic of Texas, guns are compulsory and nothing is forgiven.

Fourteen-year-old Bluebonnet Andrews is on the run across the Republic of Texas. An accident with a gun killed her best friend but everyone in the town of Blessing thinks it was murder. Even her father – the town's drunken deputy – believes she did it. Now, she has no choice but to run. Because in Texas, murder is punishable by death.

About the author

Lori Ann Stephens is an award-winning author whose novels for children and adults include Novalee and the Spider Secret, Some Act of Vision, and Song of the Orange Moons. She teaches creative writing and critical reasoning at Southern Methodist University in Dallas, Texas.

Praise for Blue Running

Book of the Month
THE INDEPENDENT & THE FT

"If there's one teen novel this year that readers will never forget, it's this one..."
BOOKS FOR KEEPS

"Brilliant."
HEAT MAGAZINE

"Gripping."
THE GUARDIAN

SCAN ME TO FIND
OUT MORE

MOONFLOWER

www.moonflowerbooks.co.uk

About Moonflower Books

The Independent Publishing Association's Newcomer of the Year 2023, Moonflower is a young, UK-based, independent publisher. Our award-winning books are the kind that make you sit up in your seat. Books that break the mould. That are hard to categorise. In short, the kind of books that deserve your attention.

moonflowerbooks.co.uk

MOONFLOWER